"Be thankful, even astonished that it exists.... Banks has now become...the most important living white male American on the official literary map, a writer we, as readers and writers, can actually learn from, whose books help and urge us to change."
—*Village Voice Literary Supplement*

"With *Affliction*, Mr. Banks has come as close as anybody has any right to expect to following up one masterpiece with another." —*Atlanta Journal and Constitution*

"Russell Banks writes with barely contained heat. It's a style, sometimes plainspoken, sometimes stirring, that, paradoxically seems to issue from some high, cold Olympian perspective while generating enormous emotional power....Part thriller, part psychological study, part indictment of the American way of violence, *Affliction* succeeds on every count. Wade Whitehouse looms large among the creations of recent American fiction." —*Newsday*

"In the fullness and power with which it answers that question ['What happened to his life?'] *Affliction* achieves its brilliance."
—*Wall Street Journal*

"*Affliction*...offers a three-dimensional view of an ancient machismo gone off the deep end. If you're going to write hard-edged realism, it helps to have the heart and nerve to make it human." —*Boston Sunday Globe*

"Banks's idiom is now vigorous and gritty, perfectly suited to the life of his characters and place...with *Affliction* especially he joins that group of small-town realists—writers like William Kennedy, Andre Dubus, Larry Woiwode—who have worked to sustain what may in time be seen as our dominant tradition. Like them, Banks unfolds the sufferings of ordinary life, of those who must worry, who can't be happy."
—*The New Republic*

AFFLICTION

ALSO BY RUSSELL BANKS

Success Stories
Continental Drift
The Relation of My Imprisonment
Trailerpark
The Book of Jamaica
The New World
Hamilton Stark
Family Life
Searching for Survivors

AFFLICTION

RUSSELL BANKS

📘 HarperPerennial
A Division of HarperCollins*Publishers*

Grateful acknowledgment is made for permission to quote from "The Love of God and Affliction," from *Simone Weil: Collected Essays 1934-1943*, translated by Richard Rees and published by the Oxford University Press, 1962.

A hardcover edition of this book was published in 1989 by Harper & Row, Publishers, Inc.

First HarperPerennial edition published 1990.

LIBRARY OF CONGRESS CATALOG CARD NUMBER 89-45075

ISBN 0-06-016142-6
ISBN 0-06-092007-6 (pbk.)

98   RRD   15 16 17 18 19 20

for Earl Banks (1916–1979)

*The great enigma of human life
is not suffering but affliction.*

—SIMONE WEIL
"The Love of God and Affliction"

AFFLICTION

1

THIS IS THE STORY of my older brother's strange criminal behavior and his disappearance. No one urged me to reveal these things; no one asked me not to. We who loved him simply no longer speak of Wade, not among ourselves and not with anyone else, either. It is almost as if he never existed, or as if he were a member of some other family or from some other place and we barely knew him and never had occasion to speak of him. So that by telling his story like this, as his brother, I am separating myself from the family and from all those who ever loved him.

In numerous ways I am separated from them anyhow, for while each of us is ashamed of Wade and burdened with anger—my sister, her husband and kids, Wade's ex-wife and his daughter, his fiancée and a few friends—the others are ashamed and burdened in ways that I am not. They are dismayed by their shame, astonished by it, as they should be (he is one of them, after all, and they are good people, in spite of everything); and they are confused by their anger. Which is perhaps why they have not asked me to keep silent. I myself am neither dismayed nor confused: like Wade, I have been ashamed and angry practically since birth and am accustomed to holding both those skewed relations to the world: it makes me, among those who loved him, uniquely qualified to tell his story.

Even so, I know how the others think. They are secretly hoping that they have got Wade's story wrong and that I can somehow get it right or at least get it said in such a way that we will all be released from our shame and anger and can speak lovingly again of our brother, husband, father, lover, old friend, around the supper table or in the car on a long drive or in bed late at night, wondering where the poor man is now, before we fall asleep.

That will not happen. Nevertheless, I tell it for them, for the others as much as for myself. They want, through the telling, to regain him; I want only to be rid of him. His story is my ghost life, and I want to exorcise it.

As for forgiveness: it must be spoken of, I suppose, but who among us can hope to proffer it? Even I, at this considerable distance from the crimes and the pain, cannot forgive him. It is the nature of forgiveness that when you forgive someone, you no longer have to protect yourself from him, and for the rest of our lives we will have to protect ourselves from Wade. Regardless, it is too late now for forgiveness to do him any good. Wade Whitehouse is gone. And I believe that we will never see him again.

Everything of importance—that is, everything that gives rise to the telling of this story—occurred during a single deer-hunting season in a small town, a village, located in a dark forested valley in upstate New Hampshire, where Wade was born and raised and so was I, and where most of the Whitehouse family has lived for five generations. Think of a village in a medieval German folktale. Think of a cluster of old and new but mostly old houses and shops and a river running through and hillside meadows and tall trees. The town is named Lawford, and it is one hundred fifty miles north of where I live now.

Wade was forty-one that fall and in bad shape—everyone in town knew it but was not particularly upset by it. In a village, you see people's crises come and go, and you learn to wait them out: most people do not change, especially seen

2

from up close; they just grow more elaborate.

Consequently, everyone who knew Wade was waiting out his gloom, his heavy drinking, his dumb belligerence. His crisis was his character in sharp relief. Even I, down south in the suburbs of Boston, was waiting him out. It was easy for me. I am ten years younger than Wade, and I abandoned the family and the town of Lawford when I graduated high school— escaped from them, actually, though it sometimes feels like abandoned. I went to college, the first in the family to do that, and became a high school teacher and a man of meticulous routine. For many years, I regarded Wade as a gloomy, alcoholic and stupidly belligerent man, like our father, but now he had gotten into his forties without killing himself or anyone else, and I expected that he would, like our father, get into his fifties, sixties and maybe seventies the same way, so I did not worry about Wade.

Though he visited me twice that fall and called me on the telephone often and at great length, several times a week and usually late at night, after he had been drinking for hours and had sent everyone near him scurrying for safety, I was not moved much one way or the other. I listened passively to his rambling tirades against his ex-wife, Lillian, and his mournful declarations of love for his daughter, Jill, and his threats to inflict serious bodily harm on many of the people who lived and worked with him, people whom, as the town police officer, he was sworn to protect. Preoccupied with the details of my own life, I listened to him as if he were a boring soap opera on TV and I was too busy or distracted by the details of my own life to get up and change the channel.

It would pass, I felt, with the pain of his divorce from Lillian and of her remarriage and departure from town with Jill in tow. Six more months, I felt, would do it. That would put him three full years beyond the divorce, two years beyond Lillian's move south to Concord, and well into springtime: snowmelt running off the hills, the lakes breaking free of ice, daylight lingering into evening. Maybe he will fall in love with someone else, I thought. There was a woman he said he slept with now and again, a local woman named Margie Fogg, and for the most part he spoke fondly of her. If nothing else, I thought, Jill will eventually grow up. Children often force parents to grow up by first growing up themselves. Though I am childless and unmarried, I know this.

* * *

Then one night something changed, and from then on my relation to Wade's story was different from what it had been before, since childhood. That night willed detachment got replaced by—what?—sympathy? More than sympathy, I think, and less. Empathy. A dangerous feeling, to both parties.

I mark it by the change I heard in Wade's tone of voice during a phone call he made to me a night or two after Halloween. It may have been the first or second of November by then. He was in the middle of one of his garrulous complaints, and I heard something that I had not heard there before, and for an instant I wondered if I had misperceived my brother all along. Perhaps I had misjudged him, and he was not so predictable after all; perhaps his character and this crisis were not one thing, were instead quite distinct from one another, or the nature of the crisis was such that it would soon make them distinct; perhaps my brother was as real as I, a man whose character was as I understood my own: process, flux, change. This was a new thought to me and not an altogether welcome one. And I did not know where it came from, unless it was from the simple accumulated weight of familiarity; for, without my being aware of it, a subtle balance had shifted, as if in my sleep, so that suddenly I was no longer distantly monitoring my brother's confused painful life but was instead practically living it. And I despised Wade's life. Let me say it again. I despised Wade's life. I fled the family and the town of Lawford when I was little more than a boy to avoid having to live that life. That is only one of the differences between Wade and me, but it is a huge difference.

Wade was making the ex-husband's complaint about the ex-wife's infinite capacity for cruelty—the result of some minor humiliation a night or two before. I had not quite got it but had not asked for clarification, either—when suddenly I heard a shift in his tone of voice, a change of register and pitch, little enough to notice ordinarily, but for some reason enough to sit me up straight in my chair to listen to him closely, to gather my wandering attention, and instead of regarding his life as merely a minor part of mine, I saw the man in his own context for a change. It was as if the story he was telling were enlarging and clarifying my story: the chronic toothache he had complained of earlier in the conversation, though worse

4

and significantly different from my periodic headaches, suddenly became a troublesome echo, and his financial difficulties, though described practically in another language than mine, rhymed anxiously with mine, and his ongoing troubles with women, parents, friends and enemies, grotesquely reversed versions of my troubles, gave mine painful articulation.

He had been describing the events of Halloween Eve, and he began to speak of the weather that night, colder even than usual, well below freezing, colder than a witch's tit, he said, that first cold night when you know winter's a-coming in and there is nothing you can do about it and once again it is too goddamned late to head south. You just put your head down, bub, and you accept it.

The change, the shift, may well have been in me, of course, not Wade. He used the same words he always used, the same clichés and oddly reflective expressions; he affected the same weary stoicism he has affected since adolescence; he sounded, to all intents and purposes, the same as always—yet I heard him differently. One minute his story did not matter to me; the next minute it mattered in every way. One minute my mind and eyes were focused on the television screen in front of me, a Boston Celtics game with the sound turned off, and then suddenly I was visualizing Lawford Center on Halloween Eve.

Which is not difficult for me to do: in the fifteen years since I last spent a Halloween there, which is to say, since I was in high school, the place has not changed much. In fifty years it has not changed much. But visualizing the place, going there in memory or imagination, is not something I care to do. I studiously avoid it. I have to be almost tricked into it or conjured. Lawford is one of those towns that people leave, not one that people come back to. And to make matters worse, to make it even more difficult to return to, even if you *wanted* to go back—which of course *no one* who has left the town in this half century wants to do—those who remain behind cling stubbornly as barnacles to the bits and shards of social rites that once invested their lives with meaning: they love bridal showers, weddings, birthdays, funerals, seasonal and national holidays, even election days. Halloween, as well. A ridiculous holiday, and for whom, for what? It has absolutely no connection to modern life.

But Lawford has no connection to modern life, either.

5

There is a kind of willed conservatism that helps a remnant people cope with having been abandoned by several generations of the most talented and attractive of its children. Left behind, the remnant feels inadequate, insufficient, foolish and inept—everyone with brains and ambition, it seems, everyone with the ability to live in the larger world, has gone away. So that with the family, with the community as a whole, no longer able to unify and organize a people and provide them with a worthy identity, the half-forgotten misremembered ceremonies of ancient days become all the more crucial to observe. As in: Halloween. The rites affirm a people's existence, but falsely. And it is this very falsity that most offends those of us who have left. We know better than anyone, precisely because we have fled in such numbers, that those who refused or were unable to leave no longer exist as a family, a tribe, a community. They are no longer a people—if they ever were one. It is why we left in the first place and why we are so reluctant to return, even to visit, and especially on holidays. Oh, how we hate going home for the holidays! It is why we have to be coerced into it by guilt, or tricked, if not by ourselves, then by the wider, sentimental culture. I teach history; I think about these things.

Wade rambled on, half drunk, as usual, calling from his wind-battered trailer by the lake up there in Lawford, and I envisioned the town he was talking about, the people he alluded to, the hills and valleys, the forests and streams he passed in his car on his way home every night and out again in the morning to work, the diner where he stopped for breakfast, the well-drilling company he worked for, the town hall where his part-time police chief's office was located: I visualized the setting for my brother's life as it had been a night or two before, when the events he was describing to me had taken place.

The air was dry, and the sky clear as black glass, with belts and swatches of stars all over and in the southeast a crescent moon grinning. I remember those cold fall nights, with the smell of oncoming snow in the air. On the side of the hill, between the spruce woods climbing the eastern ridge of the valley and the long yellow meadow that slopes toward the river at the bottom, a bony thicket of birches clings like a brief porous interval. The river below is narrow, rock-strewn, noisy, with a forested moraine on the farther bank and a two-lane road running north and south along the near. This is the town I grew up in.

There is a row of large, mostly white houses that face the road from the east. Vehicles following pale wedges of light roamed north and south along the road. Some of them pulled in and parked at the center of town, where there are three steepled churches, a two-story wood-frame town hall and an open square and a ball field; others stopped in front of one or another house in the settlement; while short strings of small dark figures raveled and unraveled along the shoulders of the road and entered and departed from the same houses visited by the cars.

Imagine with me that on this Halloween Eve up along the ridge east of the settlement it was still and silent and very dark. The wind was down, as if gathering for a storm, and from the houses below not even a watchdog's bark floated this far. The moon had just slipped behind the spruce-topped black ridge. Suddenly out of the thicket of birches a small gang of boys, five or six short shadowy figures, emerged running from the woods. Their breath trailed behind them in white streaks, and they darted like a pack of feral dogs downhill over the crumbly ground of the meadow, then sneaked across the scoured back-yard of a neat white Cape Cod house with barn and sheds attached at the far side, where, as if at last sighting their prey, the boys dashed around the corner of the barn toward the front.

They wore knit caps and brightly colored jackets and were ten or twelve years old. Twenty years before, I might have been among them, or ten years before that, Wade himself. Indian file, they slipped along the side of the house that faced Main Street, ducking under windows and around a single Scotch pine. At the edge of the porch, they gathered into a group and ran straight to the front steps and seized two large lighted jack-o'-lanterns that had been posted there.

The boys lifted the tops of the pumpkins with purpose, as if releasing imprisoned spirits, and for a second their small faces were transformed, turning them orange and wild. With a puff, they extinguished the candles and raced with the dead jack-o'-lanterns back into darkness, grinning to one another with fear and pleasure, as if they had stolen a giant's beloved goose.

Silence. A moment later a yellow Ford station wagon, seams and rocker panels rotted by rust, pulled up in front of the same house, and the driver, a thick-bodied young woman wearing a cloth coat and blue ski cap and gloves, got out, opened the back door and helped two tiny costumed children—one a fairy godmother with a wand, the other a vampire wearing huge blood-tipped plastic incisors—exit from the car. Lugging shopping bags, the children followed the mother to the front door of the house, where they climbed the steps and the mother rang the bell.

The door opened, and a woman with crisp features and short white hair stood in the doorway. A person of indeterminate age, somewhere between fifty and seventy, she wore green twill trousers and shirt and men's work shoes, and her pointy face was expressionless for a second. From the bottom of the steps the children held their bags out to be filled and shrieked, "Trick or treat!" and the white-haired woman opened her eyes wide, as if startled. Flopping long hands in front of her chest, the woman, whose name is Alma Pittman, feigned alarm. She is the town clerk and a certified public accountant and notary public and is not skilled at amusing children. I knew her when I was a boy, and she has changed not at all.

"You, now," she said to one child, "you must be an angel. And you," she said to the other, "you're a wolf-man or something, I bet." She stared down at them from her considerable height, and the children withdrew their bags and looked at their feet. "Shy," Alma observed.

The mother smiled apologetically through blotches of freckles. The mother's name is Pearl Diehler. She has been living on welfare and food stamps since her husband left her and moved to Florida two years ago—Alma Pittman knew this, of course, and Pearl knew she did. Everyone knew it. Small towns are like that.

Alma quickly smiled back and swung open the door and waved the children and their mother inside. As the three passed by her into the warmly lit living room, Alma glanced down at her stoop and saw that her jack-o'-lanterns were gone. Both of them.

For a few seconds she stared at where they had been, as if trying to remember placing them on the stoop earlier, trying to recall carving them out herself that afternoon on her kitchen table, trying to remember buying them from Anthony's Farm Market last Friday—a solitary irritable woman more organized and better educated than most of her neighbors, and though somewhat intolerant of them, trying nonetheless to be kind to them, to join them somehow in their holiday.

As if waking from sleep, she blinked, turned quickly around and went inside her house, closing the door firmly behind her.

A fast-flowing river, the Minuit, runs south through the town, and most of the buildings in Lawford—homes, stores, town hall and churches, no more than fifty buildings in the center in all—are situated on the east side of the river along a half-mile stretch of Route 29, the old Littleton-Lebanon road, replaced a generation ago by the interstate ten miles east.

The Minuit was named and then fished for centuries by the Abenaki Indians, until in the early 1800s woodcutters from Massachusetts came north and started using the river to float tree trunks south and west to the Connecticut. By the time the burgeoning muddy lumber camp had evolved into a proper village and shipping point called Lawford, there was a pair of small brick mills on the river manufacturing wood shingles and spools. For a brief period the town prospered, which accounts for the dozen or so impressively large white houses strung along the road at the south end of town, where the valley widens somewhat and the glacial rubble, filtered by a long-gone primeval lake, becomes glacial till and, cleared by those early lumbermen, for a few years offered speculators several thousand acres of good salable farmland.

In the Great Depression, the mills got taken over by the banks, were shut down and written off, the money and machinery invested farther south in the manufacture of shoes. Since then, Lawford has existed mainly as someplace halfway between other places, a town people sometimes admit to having come from but where almost no one ever goes. Half the rooms in the big white colonial houses that face the river and the high dark ridge in the west have been emptied and sealed off against the winter with polyurethane and plywood, imprisoning in the remaining rooms elderly couples and widows and widowers abandoned by their grown children for the smarter

9

life in the towns and cities. There are, of course, grown children who stay on in Lawford, and others who—after serving and being wounded in one of the wars or messing up a marriage elsewhere—come back home to live in the old house and pump gas or style hair in town. Such children are regarded by their parents as failures; and they behave accordingly.

Lots of homes in town double as businesses: insurance; real estate; guns 'n' ammo; haircutting; arts & crafts. Here and there a particularly well maintained and—discounting the greenhouse, the sauna in the barn and the solar heat panels—lovingly restored mid-nineteenth-century farmhouse accommodates the complex social, sexual and domestic needs of a graying long-haired man and woman with an adolescent child or two in boarding school, svelte couples who have come north from Boston or New York City to teach at Dartmouth, twenty miles south, or sometimes just to grow marijuana in their large organic gardens and live off inherited money in the region's dead economy.

Most of the rest of the townspeople live outside the center, nowadays usually in mobile homes or small ranch-style bungalows built by the owners with borrowed money on rocky three-acre lots of hilly scrub. Their children attend the cinder-block elementary school on the outskirts north of town and the regional high school in Barrington, where the Lawford boys even today have enviable reputations as athletes, especially in the more violent sports, and the girls still have reputations for providing sexual favors at an early age and for going to their senior proms pregnant.

These are not the only people who reside in Lawford. There are a small number of part-time residents, summer people with houses built on the gravelly shores of the lakes in the area, sprawling wood-frame structures they call "camps," built back in the 1920s by large wealthy families from southern New England and New York forcing themselves to spend time together. A few of these family compounds came later, in the 1940s and '50s, but by then it was difficult to buy attractive lakeshore property from the early comers, and they often got built on marshy land with no easy access to the road.

Beyond this, there are only the deer hunters to speak of, and one must speak of them, for they will play an important role in Wade's story. Almost all of the deer hunters are men from lower New Hampshire and eastern Massachusetts, who every November come north brandishing high-powered rifles with scopes and normally spend no longer than a weekend in the area. They drink all night in motels and roadhouses on Route 29 and tramp from sunup to sundown through the woods, firing at anything that moves, sometimes even killing it and hauling it back to Haverhill or Revere on the fender of a car. More often than not, they return home empty-handed, hung over and frustrated—but nonetheless sated from having participated, even if only marginally and ineptly, in an ancient male rite.

Near the center of Lawford, three houses north of the town hall and situated on a large flat lot, are a pair of incongruous buildings—a huge slate-blue hundred-year-old renovated barn and next to it a matching blue sixty-foot cathedral-ceiling mobile home—the pair of them surrounded by an acre of asphalt paving, as if the blue buildings were dropped by helicopter squarely into the middle of a shopping center parking lot. This is the business place and home of Gordon LaRiviere, well driller, who, unless you count those who went away, is Lawford's only success story—despite his motto, painted on every vehicle and building he owns: LARIVIERE CO.—OUR BUSINESS IS GOING IN THE HOLE!

LaRiviere's story, too, will get told in due time, but at this particular moment, still early on Halloween Eve, let us picture six teenagers, four boys and two girls, out in the field behind LaRiviere's blue barn—his combination office, workshop, garage and warehouse—working in darkness in LaRiviere's garden, a meticulously laid out and maintained plot of earth half covered with black plastic and mulch for the winter, the other half, with rattling dry cornstalks and dead tomato plants and sprawling pumpkin vines, not yet turned over. The teenagers guzzle king-sized beers and laugh through harsh whispers as they strip the few remaining vines of the few remaining pumpkins. I know this because I myself did it, not to Gordon LaRiviere's pumpkin patch but to someone else's. And I did it because my older brother Wade did it, and he, too, had merely followed the example of an older brother, two of them.

Soon the teenagers are up and running, awkwardly, clutching beer cans and pumpkins, around the far side of LaRiviere's house—impossible to call it a trailer or mobile home, for it is set on a permanent foundation and has shutters, porch, breezeway, chimney attached—racing toward the road out front, then down the road a ways to where a boy waits in a ten-year-old Chevy with dual exhausts gurgling.

The thieves pile into the car with their pumpkins, hard goofy laughter now drifting back toward LaRiviere's on the cold night air, and the kid driving pops the clutch and spins off the gravel shoulder onto the road, his tires burning rubber as they hit the pavement, the car fishtailing down the road toward the town hall, hurtling past it, the kids cackling out the windows and giving the finger to a large group of adults with children in costumes gathering outside the town hall.

Most of the adults have stopped moving and talking and stare bitterly at the old Chevrolet sedan as it blasts past. In seconds, the car has rounded the slow turn on the far side of town and is out of sight. The people clustering outside the town hall hesitate a second, as if waiting to hear a crash, then resume what they were doing.

A short ways north of the town hall and the Common and the three churches facing it—First Congregational, First Baptist and Methodist—and out along Route 29 beyond Alma Pittman's house, from whose darkened door Pearl Diehler and her children had long since departed, there were a few straggling houses with porch lights still on for the last of the trick-or-treaters, kids whose parents had sat around the kitchen table drinking and arguing too long to drive them into town in time to join the others. This late they joined only a battalion of older greedier kids who would not stop until no one any longer answered the door, when they would commence their more serious work of the evening, what they had come out to accomplish in the first place: the gleeful destruction of private property. They intended to cut clotheslines, break windows, slash tires, open outdoor spigots so the wells would run dry and the pumps burn out.

A short ways beyond the settlement one comes to Merritt's Shell Station—a cinder-block bunker, closed, dark, with car parts scattered around the building like rubble after a terrorist's attack. On this night, a dim light from a rear window indicated that someone was still in the office—not Merritt, of course, who, as always, had gone home promptly at six and tonight was down at the town hall, attending the annual Halloween party in his official capacity as one of the selectmen. More likely it was Merritt's mechanic, Chick Ward, leafing slowly, like a monk studying scripture, through a pornographic magazine from Sweden that normally he keeps hidden under the carpeting of the trunk of his car, a purple Trans Am that Merritt lets him work on in the garage after hours. Tonight he furrowed his narrow brow in concentration, smoked his cigarette, took a pull on his beer and turned the page on one type of pink contortion and began to examine another. He put his beer can on the floor and rubbed his hand across his crotch, back and forth, as if stroking the head of a sleeping dog.

Beyond Merritt's Shell Station, the residents of the few remaining houses in town had finally shut their porch lights off, a signal to the trick-or-treaters that the night was nearly over. On the road there was only a scraggly group of small children in homemade costumes, brothers and sisters and cousins from the Hoyt place, a shack settlement on the river set in among the wreckage of an abandoned mill there. They traveled along the side of the road, gobbling their loot as they walked, now and then grabbing an apple or a piece of candy from one another's sack—a hit and a kick and a cry; then a laugh—as they continued down the road toward town and the party.

A mile past the Hoyt kids on the right, where Route 29 bends sharply east, one passes Wickham's Restaurant, still open but in the process of being closed for the night by Nick Wickham and his waitress, Margie Fogg. Back in the kitchen, Wickham, a lean dark man with a long wet mustache, poured three fingers of Old Mr. Boston vodka into a juice glass and knocked it back in two swallows, then stared intently at Margie Fogg's wide rounded backside as she filled the napkin holders at the counter.

From Wickham's all the way north practically as far as Littleton there are deep woods on both sides of the road, with the Minuit River still rushing through the darkness west of the road. The sky was a narrow black velvet band overhead, and there were no buildings visible from the road in those woods or overlooking the river, except for Toby's Inn, three miles from town on the river side of Route 29. Toby's is a battered two-story farmhouse converted into an inn when the Littleton-Concord Stage Line opened back in the 1880s, and it operated now as a roadhouse, with rooms for rent. Tonight the parking

13

lot outside Toby's had fewer than the usual ten or twelve local cars and pickups pulled up against the building and a surprisingly large number of out-of-state cars—surprising, until you remembered that tomorrow, the first day of November, was also the first day of deer-hunting season.

$$\underline{\text{ＶＡ}}$$

2

LET US IMAGINE that around eight o'clock on this Hallow-een Eve, speeding west past Toby's and headed toward town on Route 29 from the interstate turnoff, there comes a pale-green eight-year-old Ford Fairlane with a blue police bubble on top. Let us imagine a dark square-faced man wearing a trooper's cap driving the vehicle. He is a conventionally hand-some man, but nothing spectacular: if he were an actor, he would be cast as the decent but headstrong leader of the sheepherders in range-war westerns of the '50s. He has deep-set brown eyes with crinkled corners, the eyes of a man who works outdoors; his nose is short and hooked, narrow at the bridge, with large flared nostrils. He looks his age, forty-one, and though his mouth is small, his lips thin and tight and his chin boyishly delicate, his lower face, tinged gray by a five o'clock shadow, has the slight fleshiness of a healthy hardwork-ing athletic man who drinks too much beer.

Seated next to him is a child, a little girl with hair like flax and a plastic tiger mask covering her face. The man is driving fast, clearly in a hurry, talking and gesturing intently to the child as he drives. The child appears to be about ten years old.

15

For anyone who lived in Lawford, the car would be instantly recognizable—it belonged to the town police officer, my brother, Wade Whitehouse. The child beside him was his daughter, Jill, and anyone would know that he was bringing her up from Concord, where she lived with her mother and stepfather, for the three-day weekend and the Halloween party.

And Wade was running late, as usual. He had not been able to start the hour-long drive south on the interstate to Concord until finishing work for LaRiviere (besides being Lawford's entire police force, Wade was also a well driller, Gordon LaRiviere's foreman). Then down in Concord, after stopping at the shopping mall north of the city for a Halloween costume that he had promised but forgotten to purchase and bring with him, he had been compelled—again, as usual—to negotiate certain complex custodial arrangements with his ex-wife, Lillian, after which he had to pick up a Big Mac, strawberry shake, fries and cherry pie to go for Jill's supper, all before even starting the drive back to Lawford.

Now he was late, late for everything he had planned and fantasized about for a month: late for trick-or-treating with his daughter at the homes of everyone in town he liked or wanted to impress with his fatherhood; late for showing up at the party at the town hall, where, like all the other parents for a change, he could see his kid win a prize in the costume contest, best this or that, scariest or funniest or some damned thing; late for the sleepy drive back to the trailer afterwards, Jill laying her head on his shoulder and falling peacefully asleep while he drove slowly, carefully home.

He tried to explain their lateness to her without blaming himself for it. "I'm sorry for the screw-up," Wade said. "But I couldn't help it that it's too late to go trick-or-treating now. I couldn't help it I had to stop at Penney's for the costume," he said, stirring the air with his right hand as he talked. "And you were hungry, remember."

Jill spoke through her tiger's mask. "Whose fault is it, then, if it's not yours? You're the one in charge, Daddy." She wore a flimsy-looking black-and-yellow tiger suit that Wade thought looked less like a costume than a pair of striped pajamas with paws and a scrawny black-tipped tail, which she held with one paw and slapped idly into the palm of the other. The bulbous grinning mask looked more hysterical than fierce but was perhaps all the more frightening for it.

"Yeah," he said, "but not really. I'm not really in charge."
Wade worked a cigarette free of his pack with one hand, stuck
it between his lips and punched in the dashboard lighter. They
were coming into town now, and he slowed down slightly as
they began to pass darkened houses. "There's damned little
I'm in charge of, believe it or not. It is my fault I had to stop
for the costume, though, and we got slowed up some there."
He reached for the lighter and got his cigarette going. With the
lighted cigarette bobbing up and down, he said, "I did screw
that up, I admit it. Stopping for the costume. Forgetting it, I
mean. I'm sorry for that, honey."

She said nothing, turned and looked out the window and
saw the Hoyt kids in a loose group on the shoulder of the road,
making their disorganized way toward the center of town.
"Look," Jill said. "Those kids are still trick-or-treating. They're
still out."

"Those're the Hoyts," he said.

"I don't care; they're out."

"I care," Wade said. "Those're the Hoyts." What he
wanted to say was *Shut up.* He wanted credit, for God's sake,
not criticism. He wanted her cheerful, not whining. "Can't you
see . . . look out there," he said. "Can't you see that nobody's
got their porch lights on anymore? It's late; it's too late now.
Those Hoyt kids, they're just out to get in trouble. See," he
said, pointing past her mask to the right. "They put shaving
cream all over that mailbox there. And they chopped down all
of Herb Crane's new bushes. Damn." He slowed the car almost
to a stop, and behind him the Hoyt kids scattered into the
darkness. "Those damned kids tipped over Harrison's
toolshed. Jesus Christ."

Wade drove slowly now, peering into yards and calling
out the damage as he saw it. "Look, they cut the Annises'
clotheslines, and I bet there's a hell of a lot more they done out
back where you can't see it," he said, rolling his hand again, a
habitual gesture. "And there, see all those smashed flowerpots?
Little bastards. Jesus H. Christ."

In front of the elementary school was a flashing yellow
caution light. Wade had to steer carefully around the fleshy
remains of three or four smashed pumpkins, hurled, surely,
from a speeding Chevy sedan with dual exhausts.

"See, honey, that's all that's going on out there now," he

said. "You don't want to deal with that kind of stuff, do you? Trick-or-treating's over, I'm sorry to say."

"Why do they do that?"

"Do what?"

"You know."

"Break stuff? Cause all that damage and trouble to people?"

"Yeah. It's stupid," she said flatly.

"I guess they're stupid. It's stupid."

"Did you use to do that, when you were a kid?"

Wade inhaled deeply and flicked his cigarette out the open vent window. "Well, yeah," he said. "Sort of. Nothing really mean, you understand. But yeah, we did a few things like that, I guess. Me and my pals, me and my brothers. It was kind of funny then, or anyhow we thought it was. Stealing pumpkins and smashing them on the road, soaping windows. Stuff like that."

"*Was* it funny?"

"*Was* it funny. Yeah. To us it was. You know."

"But it's not funny now."

"No, it's not funny now," he said. "Now I'm a cop, so now I have to listen to all the complaints people make. I'm a police officer," he announced. "I'm not a kid anymore. You change, and things look different as a result. You understand that, don't you?"

His daughter nodded. "You did lots of bad things," she declared.

"What? I did what?"

"I bet you did lots of bad things."

"Well, no, not really," he said. He paused. "What? What're you talking about?"

She turned and looked through the eye holes of her mask, revealing her blue irises and nothing else. "I just think you used to be bad. That's all."

"No," he said flatly. "I didn't use to be bad. No, sir. I did not. I did not use to be bad." They were pulling into the parking lot behind the town hall, and Wade nodded to several people who had recognized and waved at him. "Where do you get this stuff anyhow? From your mother?"

"No. She never talks about you anymore. I just know," she said. "I can tell."

"You mean *bad* kind of bad? You mean like a bad man,

I used to be? Like that?" He wanted to reach over and remove her mask, find out what she really meant, but he did not dare, somehow. He was frightened of her, suddenly aware of it. He had never been frightened of her before, or at least it had not seemed so to him. How could this be true now? Nothing had changed. She had only uttered a few ridiculous things, a child talking mean to her father because he would not let her do what she wanted to do, that was all. No big deal. Nothing to be scared of there. Kids do it all the time.

"Let's go inside," she said. "I'm cold." She swung open the car door and got out and slammed it behind her, hard.

The town hall is a large squarish two-story building on the north side of the small field called the Common, where, even in the dark, one can make out the Civil War cannon aimed south and the block of red granite that the townspeople, after the Spanish-American War, set up as a war memorial. Then and after each later war they inscribed on the block the names of the town's fallen soldiers. In the four wars in this century so far, fifty-four young men from the valley—all but seven of them enlisted men—have been killed. No women. The names are for the most part familiar ones, familiar at least to me— Pittman, Emerson, Hoyt, Merritt, and so on—many the same names one sees today on Alma Pittman's tax rolls.

Wade's name, my name, Whitehouse, is there—twice. Our two brothers, Elbourne and Charlie, were killed together in the same hooch by mortar fire near Hue during the Tet offensive. Charlie was on his way to Saigon and had stopped to visit. He wasn't supposed to be there. Wade heard about it weeks after it happened, weeks after we heard about it at home. I was in grade school, the youngest of the five children; Wade was in Korea, an MP stopping fights between drunks in bars. He did not really believe that his two older brothers were dead, he told me, until sixteen months later, when he got home and saw their names on the war memorial by the town hall.

Wade had grown up looking at the names of dead men carved into red granite, seen them every Fourth of July, Memorial Day, Veterans Day. Even playing softball on the Common in the summer league, if you played left field, as Wade usually did, you got to read the names carved into the stone. For him, when your name got listed there, you were truly, undeniably, hopelessly dead. Those were men who had no faces, who were gone beyond memory, forever, to absolute elsewhere. Even Elbourne and Charlie.

Outside the entrance to the town hall, a small group of people had gathered, mostly men smoking cigarettes and talking in low voices that went silent as Wade and his daughter walked from his car across the lot and up the path. The men faced him in a friendly way, and one said, "Howdy, Wade. Got you some company tonight, eh?"

Wade nodded and, opening the door for his daughter, passed into the large, brightly lit hall. It takes up the entire first floor of the building, with a staircase in the far left corner, a small stage at the rear and rest rooms on the other side. The unpainted walls and ceiling are made of narrow tongue-in-groove spruce boards, and the place smells of the forest and of the fire in the big Ranger wood stove that heats it. The wooden chairs that usually fill the room had been folded and stacked to the right by the door. Half a hundred adults were gathered around the room in bunches close to the walls, and the children, all in costumes and makeup, were in the middle, as if penned.

Picture, if you will, clowns, tramps and robots of various types and sizes, at least two pirates, an angel and a devil, half a dozen vampires and as many witches. There were astronauts and a scarecrow and the hunchback of Notre Dame, and among the younger children, the toddlers, there were several species of animals represented, rabbits, lions, a horse, a lamb. Most of the costumes were homemade and depended for their effect on the viewer's willed suspension of disbelief—willed only for the viewer, however, not for the wearer of the costume, whose disbelief got suspended regardless of will, for all the children, clearly, were eager to be out of their child's body, if only temporarily, and into a more powerful one. They smiled, sometimes laughed outright, looked through their masks and makeup straight into the eyes of adults as they never would otherwise and seemed strangely independent and sure of themselves and a little dangerous.

Standing among them, like a nervous ringmaster surrounded by small but unpredictable and possibly hostile animals, was Gordon LaRiviere, clipboard in hand, in a loud voice urging the throng of children to start moving clockwise in a circle around the room. A large beefy red-faced man in his mid-fifties with a silver flat-top haircut and tiny bright-blue eyes, LaRiviere, as chairman of the Board of Selectmen this year, was the costume contest judge, a responsibility he seemed determined to exercise with great seriousness and attention to detail, for he repeatedly called out the various categories, alerting the audience and engaging its sympathies, as the children began to march in a slow swirl around the room. "We're looking for the Funniest Costume!" LaRiviere shouted. "And the Scariest! And the Most Imaginative! And the Best Costume of All!"

Standing near the door, Wade put his hand on Jill's shoulder and nudged his daughter forward. "Got here just in time for the judging," he said. "Go ahead in. Just jump into line. Maybe you'll win a prize."

The girl took a single step forward and stopped. Wade nudged her a second time. "Go on, Jill. Some of those kids you know." He looked down at the tiger's tail drooping to the floor and the child's blue sneakers peeking out from under the cuffs of the pathetic costume. Then he looked at the back of her head, her flax-colored hair creased by the string from the mask, and he suddenly wanted to weep.

He decided it was because he loved her so, and then the impulse passed. His stomach fell, and his chest heaved, and he took a deep breath and said to her, "Go ahead. You'll have fun if you just go on and join the other kids out there. See how happy they seem," he said, and he looked out at the children moving in a thick slow circle around the room with Gordon LaRiviere at the hub, and they did indeed seem happy to him, a parade of monsters and freaks delighted to find themselves admired for once.

Jill took another step away from Wade and the adults nearby, several of whom were staring at her now, aware, of course, that she was Wade's daughter visiting him for the weekend, an event that for the last year and a half had occurred on a more or less monthly basis. Lately, it seemed, folks had not seen the girl much, possibly not since the Labor Day picnic, when Wade and Jill had played together in the father-daughter softball game and Wade had to leave in the seventh inning to get her back to Concord by dark because she had school the next day—though no one quite believed that, since the Lawford and Barrington schools never started the school year till the Wednesday after Labor Day, and Concord was unlikely to be on a different schedule. That ex-wife of his, Lillian, was a hard case. Everyone in town thought so. She had always been kind of a hard case—uptight and fussy, one of your more demanding women. Snooty was how some people described her, even though she was a Pittman and had been born and raised right here in Lawford and from the beginning and up to today was clearly no damn better than anyone else in town. Worse than some, if you wanted to know the truth.

Of course, Wade was a sonofabitch. That was truth too. Pure fact: the man got really mean when he wanted to. Still and all, he loved his daughter and she loved him, and there was no reason why the mother had to keep coming between them like she did. Whatever it was Wade did to Lillian back when they were married, it couldn't have been so bad, since she married him twice. So it was hard to say why the man deserved such shabby treatment, now that they were divorced again. He was a hard worker, a fair-minded cop who liked to drink with the boys down at Toby's Inn, and a slick left fielder for the local softball team who could probably still play Legion ball if he wanted to. That's what most people in town thought.

"I don't want to," Jill said. She continued to stare at the other children, ignored by them but rapidly becoming of greater interest than they to the adults who were gathered near the entrance.

"Why? Why not?" Wade asked. "Go on, it's fun. You know lots of those kids, you know them from when you were in school here," he said. "It hasn't been that long, for God's sake." He threw out his arms, hands open, feigning exasperation, and laughed.

She backed up to him, as if into his arms, and in a low voice that only he could hear, she said, "It's not that."

"What, then?"

"Nothing," she said. "I just don't want to. It's stupid."

"What's stupid? Sure it's stupid. But it's fun," he said. "Jesus." He looked around him as if for advice. There was Pearl Diehler and three or four others he knew well and a couple more he knew only slightly. There was probably no one in town that he did not know in some way or another—757 year-round residents and another 300 or so in the summer. Wade carried all their faces and almost all their names in his head, and he did it with a certain pride, making sure that whenever he saw new folks in town, at Golden's store, say, or Merritt's, he got into a chat with them, asked their names, found out where they lived and where they used to live, learned what they did for their money. He would forget some of that, naturally, but seldom the name and rarely where they used to live and never where they lived now and what they did for their money. Wade was smart.

Suddenly Jill was squirming next to him, trying to get between him and the door and out. "Hey, what's going on? Where're you going, huh?" He reached out and grabbed her arm, and the child looked up at him, facing him with her bulbous plastic tiger mask, looking frightened even through the mask, her blue eyes wide and filling with tears.

Wade let go of her arm, and she pulled it to her, as if he had hurt it. "I want to go home," she said quietly.

He leaned down to hear her better. "What?"

"I want to go home," she said. "I don't like it here."

"Oh, Jesus, come on, will you? Don't mess this up any more than it's already been messed up, for Christ's sake. Now get in there," he said, "and join the other kids. Do that, and before you know it you'll be happy as a goddamned clam." He turned her with the flat of his hand and pushed her slowly forward into the open area, toward the circle of children. Gordon LaRiviere had spotted her and was waving her on with his clipboard, drawing attention to her from all over the room.

Now, Wade thought, her friends will see her and will come over to her. Then she will have to join in, and she will have a good time and be glad that she is here again. Maybe she will even want to go to school tomorrow with the Lawford kids, instead of hanging around with him at work all day.

He had not figured that one out yet—how he was going to amuse her during the day while he ran the rig down in Catamount. Two weeks before, during one of his regular twice-a-week phone conversations with Jill, Wade had learned that, because of a local teachers' convention, the Concord children had the Friday after Halloween off. Immediately, he had insisted that she come up to Lawford for the Halloween party and spend all three days of the weekend with him. But when Lillian had discovered that the Lawford children would be in school all day Friday, she quickly telephoned Wade and demanded to know just what he thought Jill would be doing by herself while he was at work. "You amaze me," she said. "You keep on amazing me, year after year, the same old ways."

Her demand had angered him, and he had responded by saying that he had it all figured out, damn it, so leave him alone, he was not required by law to account to her for how he spent every single hour of his weekends with his daughter. Consequently, it was only now, with his anger abated, that he was able to admit to himself that indeed he did not know what he was going to do with his daughter tomorrow. When she made herself happy with her Lawford friends tonight, she would want to go to school with them in the morning, he assured himself. Especially when she saw what the alternative was—sitting in the cab of the truck all day while he finished drilling a well in Catamount.

Relieved, he turned away, smiled down at Pearl Diehler and stepped out the door for a quick cigarette and a chat with the boys. From somewhere way back inside his jawbone, his toothache was giving him distant early warnings, and it had occurred to him that a cigarette might help postpone the onslaught of pain that he knew was coming.

There were five or six of them out there, a couple of women too, smoking and probably drinking: Jimmy Dame and Hector Eastman, brothers-in-law whose wives and children were inside. Also Frankie LaCoy, a skinny kid from Littleton whom Wade suspected of selling grass to the local high school kids but who otherwise seemed to cause little harm, so Wade was content to let it ride. Standing next to him was LaCoy's girlfriend, Didi Forque, still in high school, but she had moved out of her parents' house last summer, taken a job waitressing at Toby's Inn, and now shared an apartment in town with the other girl here, Hettie Rodgers. Wade liked looking at Hettie, even though she was only about eighteen and was very much the girlfriend of Jack Hewitt, who worked for LaRiviere with Wade and was a damned good kid. Hettie had her own car and after graduation last June had gone to work as a hairstylist at Ken's Kutters in Littleton, but she had continued to live here in Lawford because of Jack.

Jack Hewitt himself was coming slowly up the walk from his pickup, which he had double-parked directly in front of the building. He was a tall man in his early twenties, rangy, sharp-featured, some would say clean-cut, and intelligent and good-humored looking, with a reddish complexion and rust-colored hair. He walked with a slight hitch, almost a skip-step, which probably had started out as an adolescent affectation and had become a habit and made him look as if he had just played a practical joke on someone and was dancing sneakily away before the firecracker went off. In one hand he held what appeared to be a pint of whiskey in a brown paper bag. In the other he carried a rifle.

"What you boys up to?" Wade said, cupping his hands to light a cigarette.

"Same old shit," one of the men said. Hector Eastman.

"You see some of that shit them kids got into tonight?" Frankie LaCoy asked Wade. "Little sonsofbitches been causing some wicked damage this year, I'll tell ya. Jesus," he said. "Little sonsofbitches."

Wade ignored him. He did not really like LaCoy, but he enjoyed tolerating him. He believed that LaCoy's talky servility was practically endless, and although Wade knew that eventually it could make the man dangerous, he enjoyed feeling as superior to another human being, especially another man, as he felt toward Frankie LaCoy, so he usually appeared to listen to him and then refused to acknowledge that Frankie had said anything. It was a pleasing form of dominance.

"You're going to have to move that truck, Jack," Wade said to Hewitt.

"I know it." He showed the older man his sideways smile and held out the whiskey. "Take a bite?"

"Don't mind if I do," Wade said. He reached for the bottle, put it to his lips and took a good-sized swallow. I need a drink, he thought. He had not believed he would tonight, but Jesus H. Christ, did he need a drink. That kid had made him all jumpy tonight. He did not know what the hell had gotten into Jill, but whatever it was, he had let it get into him too. It was only more of the same old stuff her mother had been putting out for years, he thought, and no matter where it came from, Jill or Lillian herself, it always had the same effect on Wade: it made him want to hang his head in shame and run. He said to Jack, "That the gun you were bragging on today?"

"No brag. Just fact." Jack tossed the rifle to Wade, who caught it expertly, snapped it into his shoulder and sighted down the barrel for a few seconds. Then he examined the gun more carefully, turning it in his hands as if it were the corpse of a small unfamiliar animal. It was a Browning BAR .30/06 with a scope.

"What'd it set you back?" Wade asked. "Four fifty, five hundred bucks?" Jack just smiled, so Wade turned and handed the gun on to Hector, a towering grim man in overalls and solid-red wool shirt and plaid cap with the earflaps down.

Hector weighed the gun in his thick hands and aimed it at his huge distant feet. "Nice."

Jack had taken up a position next to Hettie Rodgers, the girl in jeans and blue down vest who had been Jack's girlfriend since the spring of her sophomore year in high school, the spring Jack got cut by the Red Sox organization and came back to Lawford and went to work drilling wells for LaRiviere with Wade. Jack slung his arm around Hettie's shoulders and watched proudly as the men passed his rifle back and forth and examined it.

Wade studied Hettie, who seemed distracted, lost in thought, her long dark hair half covering her heart-shaped face. He might have been thinking that Lillian used to look like that, when she was a kid and she was fresh-faced and happy just from being present and accounted for when Wade was around. Lillian would stand next to him thinking God knows what, off on her own, while Wade and his friends drank and laughed the night away, and there never seemed to be anything wrong with it, so long as he pulled away from his friends when she wanted to go. Then they would drive home and after they got married make love in that first apartment they rented and later they would do it in the bedroom of the house he built out on Lebanon Road. Just like Jack and Hettie—who will head out of here in a little while in Jack's burgundy truck for his parents' place on Horse Pen Road, or else, if that kid LaCoy keeps hanging around here at the town hall with Hettie's roommate, they will pop over to Hettie's apartment above Golden's store and make love there.

There was nothing wrong back then, nothing, or so it seemed then. And for Wade, looking back from a point twenty years later and then studying this young couple in front of him, it still seemed that nothing had been wrong. Those were wonderful times, he thought, truly wonderful times. After that, things all of a sudden started going wrong. They were only kids, he and Lillian, and they did not know how to repair anything, so when something in the marriage broke, they just went out and got divorced, and then came the army and his getting sent to Korea instead of Vietnam like he wanted, and all the rest followed—their getting married again, Jill, more troubles, getting divorced a second time: the long tangled painful sequence that had brought him, at last, aged forty-one, to where he was now. He was a man alone, hands jammed in pockets against the cold, while his only child, against her mother's wishes, grumpily spent one weekend every month or two with him. The rest of the time his thoughts were mostly locked on his work, day in and out, drilling wells for Gordon LaRiviere—which he found boring, difficult and, because of the low pay and LaRiviere's peculiar personality, demeaning—and being the part-time police officer for the town as well, which seemed to him almost accidental, an automatic consequence of his solitary condition and of his having been made an MP in the service.

Wade still believed in romance, however. That is, he had somehow managed to sustain into his forties a romantic view of love. Thus he looked back upon those few brief years when he was in his late teens and early twenties, when he and Lillian were happy just from being in the same room with each other, as the model against which the rest of his life had to be measured. And held against that warmly golden glow, his present life looked grim and cold and terribly diminished to him, and increasingly he found himself regarding men like Jack Hewitt—handsome young men in love with handsome young women who loved them back—with something like envy and, to avoid rage, sorrow. He had made the connections himself many times late at night lying in his bed alone—between rage and sorrow, and between sorrow, envy and romance—and he had tried to dispel his painful feelings by changing his view of love. But he could not. There was the love he had known with Lillian when he was very young, and that was perfect love, and there was the rest, which was a diminishment.

But by God none of that sadness kept him from being a good cop. Abruptly, he passed Jack's rifle back to him. "Don't leave your truck there," he said.

Then he turned and went back inside, where he saw right off that LaRiviere had already chosen the winners of the costume contests and was parading them up onto the stage at the far end of the hall. People were clapping their hands, some more enthusiastically than others, for some were the parents of the joyful winners and others the parents of hard losers. Pearl Diehler's daughter, the fairy godmother with the wand, was among the winners, but her son, writhing in agony next to Pearl and directly in front of Wade, was a hard loser. Pearl clapped with energy for a few seconds, then turned her attention to the vampire at her side.

Wade looked for Jill up on the stage with the winners. There was a boy dressed like a hobo up there, and next to him a clown of undetermined gender, and scowling and clawing the air behind the clown came a larger more theatrical version of Pearl Diehler's vampire, and bringing up the rear, no doubt the winner of Best Costume, was a tall kid covered with feathers and wearing a huge yellow cardboard beak, a reasonably successful attempt to look like a popular television-show character.

Jill was not there, Wade observed, and he began to search for her in the crowd of children who had not won a prize. Most of them had remained in the loose circle LaRiviere had herded them into while he made his selections, but a few had wandered toward the additional amusements, the apple-bobbing tank, the long white table where refreshments were being set out, the ring games. But Wade could not find Jill anywhere among them.

Maybe she went to the bathroom, he decided, and he made his way through the crowd in the direction of the rest rooms to the right of the stage, when suddenly there she was, standing alone in the corner next to the pay phone, looking forlorn, tiny, abandoned. She had kept her mask on but had unbuttoned the top half of her costume, exposing the green-and-white ski sweater underneath, and she looked oddly disheveled.

At once Wade realized that he should not have left her alone without first making sure that she had found a friend among the kids, and he said to her in a hearty way, "Hey, sweet stuff! How's it going? What're you doing way over here by yourself?" He put his arm around her and drew her to his side and peered out and scanned the room as if looking for an enemy to protect her from.

"Some party, huh? Sorry I lost sight of you for a few minutes," he said. "I just had to step out for a smoke. You find anybody you know here? There must be some kids here you used to know from school. They got school here tomorrow," he added. "You want to go in with any of them? See your old teachers?" he said. "Want me to take you by? Be more fun than hanging out with me all day."

"No," she said in a low voice.

"No what?"

"No, I didn't see anybody I know here. And no, I don't want to go to school here tomorrow," she said. "I want to go home."

"C'mon, Jill, will you? You *are* home. There's lots of kids you still know. You were playing with a whole bunch of kids Labor Day, don't you remember?"

"They've changed," she said. "They're different."

"Kids don't change that fast. Any more than you do."

"Well, I've changed a lot," she declared.

Wade looked down at her. She was staring at her feet.

"Hey, what's the matter, honey?" he asked quietly. "Tell me."

She said, "I don't want to be here, Daddy. Don't worry, I love you, Daddy, I do. But I want to go home."

Wade sighed heavily. "Jesus. You want to go home." He looked at the ceiling, then at his feet, then at his daughter's feet. "Listen, Jill, tell you what. Tomorrow morning, you still want to go home, I'll drive you down," he said. "Okay? But not tonight, not now. It's too . . . it's too late, for one thing. Tomorrow, we'll see. What the hell," he said, perhaps warming to the idea. "I'll tell LaRiviere I'm sick or something. He owes me one. Maybe we can find something to do in Concord tomorrow afternoon, maybe we can go to the movies or something. And if you really and truly still want to stay down there, then I'll drop you off and come back up here alone," he said somberly. "And we'll just wait till the next time or something. Though by then it'll be Thanksgiving . . ." He trailed off. "Well, anyhow, we'll work that one out when the time comes," he said, chopping the air above her head with his right hand. "Right now, okay. If tomorrow you want to stay down there in Concord, it's okay."

She was silent for a few seconds. Then she said, "I called Mommy."

"What?" Wade stared down at her in disbelief. "You called her? You called Mommy?" He glanced over at the pay phone as if checking the evidence. "Just now you called her?"

"Yes."

"Jesus. Why?"

"I . . . because I want to go home. She said she'd come and get me."

"Come and get you! Shit! It's a damn hour and a half drive up and another hour and a half back," he said. "Why'd you make her do that? Why didn't you talk to me about it first, for God's sake?"

"See, I knew you'd be mad," she said. "That's why I called her to do it, because I knew you'd be mad, and I was right. You are mad."

"Yeah. Yeah, right, I am mad," he declared. "It's . . . it's spoiled," he said. "It's just being spoiled, this kind of stuff. Your ma doesn't want to come all the way up here just to get you when you're supposed to be spending the damn weekend with me. What'd you tell her, for Christ's sake?" He shoved his hands into his pockets and rocked back and forth on his heels. "Jesus."

"I just told her I wanted to come home. Daddy, don't be mad at me." She slowly drew off her mask and turned to him.

He said, "Well, I guess I am. It's hard not to be mad at you, for Christ's sake. I planned this, I planned all this, you know. I mean, I know it isn't much," he said. "It's sort of pathetic, even. But I planned it." He paused. "You shouldn't have called your mother," he announced, and he grabbed her hand and said, "C'mon, we're gonna call her before she leaves."

"No way, José," she said, and she stepped back.

Wade sealed her hand in his huge one and pulled her toward the stairs and up to the long narrow unlit hallway on the second floor. They walked rapidly past the frosted-glass doors that led to the Office of the Selectmen, Office of the Town Clerk and Tax Collector, to the end, where the sign on the door said simply POLICE. Wade pulled out his keys and opened the door and snapped on the light. It was a small efficient cubicle with pegboard walls and a large window, a file cabinet and a gray metal desk and chair, with a straight-backed chair beside it. There was a locked glass-enclosed rifle rack with two shotguns and a rifle on one wall and on the other a geological survey map of the forty-nine square miles of Clinton County that made up the township of Lawford, New Hampshire.

Wade closed the door solidly behind him, flicked on the overhead neon light and sat down in his chair facing the desk;

Jill plunked herself into the chair beside the desk, crossed her legs and rested her chin on one fist, as if lost in deep thought. Quickly he dialed the number, put the receiver tight to his face and waited while it rang. I will just tell her, he thought, that she should forget it, stay home, Jill's only acting up a little because she has not kept up with any of her friends here and she is kind of shy and this is her way of dealing with shyness, that's all. Simple. Nothing to worry about, nothing that was Wade's fault, nothing to be mad at, and certainly no reason to drive all the way up here to Lawford, for Christ's sake. She should stay home in Concord in her fancy new house with her fancy new husband and watch TV or something and forget about him, forget about him and Jill, forget about everything that had happened.

The phone buzzed like an insect, over and over, and no one answered, until finally he concluded that Lillian and her husband had already left for Lawford, and at once he felt flooded by anger, overwhelmed by it.

"She's gone already!" He slammed the receiver into the cradle and stared at it. "Fucking gone already. Couldn't wait."

"Yes."

"That's all you got to say, 'Yes.' "

"Yes."

"She won't be here for at least an hour," he said. "Think you can stand it that long?"

"Yes."

"Well. Where do you expect to wait for her? Obviously downstairs with the other kids isn't good enough for you." Wade was locked into an old familiar sequence: his thoughts and feelings were accelerating at a pace that threw him into a kind of overdrive, a steady high-speed flow that he could not control and that he knew often led to disastrous consequences. But he did not care. Not caring was only additional evidence that he was in this particular sequence again. But there was not a damned thing he could do about it, and not a damned thing he wanted to do about it, either, which was yet a third way that he knew he was in this particular gear again.

"You can sit right here, dammit, sit right here in the office and wait for her all by yourself," he told his daughter. "That's fine with me. Dandy, just dandy. I'm going downstairs," he said, and he stood up.

Jill looked toward the window. "That's fine with me too,"

she said in a low voice. "I can wait up here fine. When Mommy comes, just tell her I'm up here." She uncrossed her legs and stood up too, and putting her mask back on, she grabbed the chair with both hands and dragged it over to the window. "I'll wait here. That way I'll see her when she comes and can come downstairs myself." She lined the chair up against the window and sat down again, and with the mask still covering her face, she peered out the window into the darkness.

"Jesus, Jill, you really are tragic," Wade said. "No kidding, tragic. Sitting there in your tower like some kind of fairy princess or something, waiting to be saved from a fate worse than death."

Jill turned toward him and said calmly, "I'm a tiger, Daddy, not a fairy princess. Remember? You bought the costume." Then she went back to looking out the window.

"Yep, that's my doing, all right," he said, and he wrenched the door open and stormed out. He slammed it behind him, rattling the glass, and stalked down the hallway to the stairs.

Passing through the crowd in the hall, ignoring the noise and the faces, the few waves and nods tossed toward him, Wade made his way across the room to the door. He arrived there just as Margie Fogg entered. She wore a dark-green down jacket over her white waitress's uniform and was probably hoping to see Wade here. Not wanting it to seem so, however, to him or anyone else, she had come with her boss, Nick Wickham, despite his usual designs on her. The same age as Wade, Margie had been one of his girlfriends back in high school, before Lillian—though it was not until years later, when both he and Margie were married to other people, that they had actually ended up in bed with each other. They were old friends by now, however, and possibly too familiar with each other ever to fall in love, but in the absence of particular strangers, there were many cold and lonely nights when they depended on each other's kindness.

She touched Wade's shoulder as he brushed by her, and when he turned, Margie surely saw at once, as we all did with Wade, that he had gone to someplace deep inside himself, a place where he was kept from doing more than merely recognizing her. His deep-set dark-brown eyes had a membrane laid over them, and his thin lips were drawn tightly over his teeth, as if fighting to hold back huge and derisive laughter. Over the years, Margie Fogg, like many of us, had seen that expression enough times to know how to respond intelligently, which was simply to get out of the way and stay out of the way until he came looking for her again.

She pulled her hand back as if she had touched a hot stove and went directly into the hall, with Wickham coming along behind her, toothpick slanting jauntily from under his dark drooping mustache.

She should have known, she later told me. Wade was out of it that night, the way he can get, but with his daughter Jill in town with him, and with him stone sober, it was strange, and she should have known that something important had gone sour for him, one more thing, maybe the one that finally, truly, because of what it added up to, mattered in a way that none of the others had, not the divorce itself and all that ugly business with the lawyers, not losing his house the way he did, and you know how he loved that little house he built, and not Lillian's moving down to Concord. "I just should have known, that night at the town hall. Not that it would've made any difference," she said.

She reached across the table and took my fork from my hand and cut a bite off my slice of raisin pie and popped it into her mouth. "Sorry. I love Nick's raisin pie. Let me get you another fork." She laughed. "I can't help myself." She is a tall large-boned woman with a broad Irish face, downturned green eyes and pale skin. Due to her size, perhaps, and the suddenness of her movements, she looks awkward, but she is in fact uncannily graceful and a pleasure to watch move. Her frizzy hair is the color of cordovan, and she had it tied back in a loose thatch with a piece of black ribbon, showing to advantage her long and handsome white neck.

"No, that's okay, we can share," I said, but she got up from the table anyhow and brought a clean fork from the counter. We were at Wickham's, and Margie had served me coffee and pie. It was a slow Thursday night, and I was at the moment the only customer. Wickham was out back in the kitchen, watching the Bruins game on a portable TV, ignoring my presence, by now used to my showing up alone at odd hours once or twice a week to ask questions of him or Margie or the odd customer, questions about Wade, about Jack and all the others, asking what happened, what was said, what was thought and imagined, asking what was true. Was it true that on Halloween Eve down at the town hall party Wade was acting strange? Or was he the same old Wade, all knotted up, to be sure, but no different than usual? How did he act? What did he say? What do you think he was thinking?

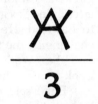

3

OUTSIDE, WADE INHALED DEEPLY, filled his lungs with cold night air and walked rapidly down the path to the narrow lane where Jack Hewitt's high-bodied burgundy pickup was still double-parked. It was a four-wheel-drive Ford with extra-long shackles that kicked the body high off the running gear. It had a roll bar and a rack of running lights, chrome exhaust extensions rising behind the cab, oak paneling on the floor of the bed and elaborate pin-striping all over the body—a work vehicle with too many accessories and too fine a paint job to be of much use for work. Jack sat inside with the motor running and Hettie beside him, and Frankie LaCoy and his girl-friend stood on the driver's side, passing a joint back and forth through the window.

"I thought I told you to move that sonofabitch!" Wade hollered. He stopped a few yards from the truck and placed his hands on his hips.

It was a nice-looking truck, Wade had to admit. Nothing but hair and muscle, that truck. The kid was lucky—he made decent money working for LaRiviere, a hell of a lot more than he had ever made playing double A baseball, and all he had to do with it was spend it on his goddamned truck and new rifles and his girlfriend. The kid is under the impression that he is going to live forever, Wade said to himself. Wade believed that what had happened to him since he was Jack's age was going to happen to Jack someday. It had to, as much because of who the kid was as because of who he was not. And Wade believed this because he had to—as much because of who Wade was as because of who he was not. "You can't escape certain awful things in life," Wade once opined. He was sitting in my kitchen, drinking beer late on a summer Sunday afternoon, after a Red Sox game at Fenway, before heading back up north to Lawford. He looked me in the eye, and I knew he was challenging me to contradict him, to say, as I surely wanted to say, "Yes, Wade, you can escape certain awful things in life. Look at me. I have done it."

But I said nothing. I looked at my watch, and then he looked at his, and he sighed and said, "Well, old buddy, I better hit the road if I want to get back to the land of milk and honey before dark."

LaCoy and his girlfriend stepped quickly away from Jack's truck. Jack leaned out the open window and said to Wade, "Relax, Chief, we're leaving now. You wanna toke?" he offered. He smiled broadly, a handsome young man, still a boy, practically, who was genuinely pleased by his own good looks and the physical and social pleasures they kept on bringing him.

Wade said, "That shit's still illegal, you know. You get too cocky, I'll run you in for it. I'm fucking serious, Jack."

"Run me in? For what? The cockiness or the grass?" Jack grinned. LaCoy laughed. That Jack Hewitt, what a guy.

"Cockiness, you wiseass little bastard. I'll run you in for cockiness," Wade said, and now he, too, was smiling, and he drew closer to the truck. "Listen, you got to be more careful about that shit. LaRiviere or Chub Merritt or one of those guys sees you smoking that wacky tabacky around me, they'll expect me to bust you. I don't, I'll have to start looking for another job. Me personal, I don't give a shit you smoke it, you know that. So long as you keep it among yourselves and don't start peddling it. But you got to be a little cool, goddammit. This ain't goddamn Greenwich Village or Harvard Square or someplace, you know."

"Yeah, yeah, I know," Jack said. "Here, for chrissakes,

have a hit. Relax a little," he said. "Don't be such a hardass, man. I know you got problems, but everybody's got problems. So relax, for chrissakes." He extended the half-smoked joint to Wade.

"Not here," Wade said. His tooth had started to throb painfully again, after having lightened somewhat for almost a week, and he wrapped the right side of his jaw with his right hand, as if to warm it.

"Well, c'mon, then. Get in, and we'll take a little ride, my man."

Wade rocked back on his heels and looked up at the clear cold dark-blue sky. The moon had swung around to the south, and the stars, pinpoints of white light, seemed like secrets whispered to him from a vast distance.

"Can't," Wade said. "I got Jill tonight." I'm lying, he thought. She had only been loaned to him, and the loan had been called in early. Meanwhile, he was standing here, pretending to be a good responsible father whose child needed him to stay close by. Wade remembered Jill's words: "I can wait up here fine. When Mommy comes, just tell her I'm up here."

Abruptly, he ducked his head and walked toward the front of the truck, just as Jack switched on the bank of running lights and the headlights, and then Wade made himself pass slowly, deliberately, through the glare of the lights, pausing for a second there, a man with nothing to hide being screened for contraband. He rounded the front of the truck and opened the door on the passenger's side and climbed up next to Hettie, and when he reached across her and took the joint from Jack's fingers, he smelled her perfume and shampoo. Nice.

Jack dropped the truck into gear and pulled out onto the lane, and as the high powerful vehicle eased down the lane toward Route 29, Wade placed his left arm on the seatback behind Hettie, turned and, peering between the pair of rifles hanging on the rack, looked out the rear window. His glance passed over the red granite war memorial next to the town hall. It stood in the pale moonlight like an ancient dolmen, and he saw above it, in the lighted window of his own office, his daughter, Jill, still wearing the hideous plastic mask, looking back at him.

* * *

They drove north on Route 29 for a few miles, passed Toby's Inn and went all the way out to the interstate, where they luffed along the southbound lane a ways, smoking a second joint and then a third. The land falls away to the west out there, then rises in a long dark forested ridge that hides the Minuit Valley and Lawford. Beyond that is a second, somewhat higher ridge, called Saddleback, that terminates in the spruce-covered knob called Parker Mountain. From the truck Wade could make out several of the half-dozen small lakes in the flats southwest of the valley, shining dully in the moonlight like hardened spatters of melted lead. He had calmed down considerably now—marijuana had a positively soothing effect on him, erasing toothache, anxieties and anger in one swipe, leaving him to drift a short distance outside and behind time without worrying about it, as if being anywhere on time, even at his own death, meant nothing to him.

At the Lebanon cloverleaf they turned around and slowly drove back along the shoulder of the northbound lane. Jack seemed to enjoy holding the speed of his truck way back, keeping it under forty, as if by restraining the truck's immense power he was better able to exhibit it. Hettie was hunched forward over the dash so she could hear a new James Taylor tape, which Jack had turned down so that he could answer Wade's question about his plans for deer hunting this year.

Jack said he had a job starting tomorrow at sunup, guiding some Boston business connection of LaRiviere's, but then he planned to take Saturday and hunt for himself. All the client wanted was to kill something with horns—anything, Jack said, even a cow—but he would take him up to Parker Mountain, where they could use LaRiviere's cabin as a base and where Jack figured he could find the old guy a deer and also track and mark a big buck off to go back and kill later for himself.

Wade knew the client, the way he knew everyone who spent much time in Lawford, even the summer people, which this man was. His name was Evan Twombley, some kind of Massachusetts union official or something, and he owned a fancy house out on Lake Agaway that he used maybe a month at the most in the summer and, since it was winterized, week-ends and holidays over the rest of the year. In recent years the place had been used more by Twombley's daughter and her husband and kids than by Twombley himself, but Wade remembered the man nonetheless and believed he was rich and thought Jack was lucky to have the chance to work as a guide for him.

"Oh, I don't know about lucky," Jack said. "The guy's a full-blown asshole. I'd just as soon be out there for myself tomorrow as work for some clown in a red suit who shoots at shadows with a gun he's never used before. Pay's good, though. Hundred dollars a day. I got to guarantee a kill, of course. Which I can do. There's some monster bucks hiding out up there."

"How'd you get the job?" Wade asked.

"LaRiviere," Jack said. He inhaled, held his breath and passed the joint back and kept talking. "You know Gordon, he's always got some kind of angle working," he said. "Right now looks like he's keeping Twombley happy, and I suppose I'm his boy."

Hettie said, "Do you mind?" and reached forward, flipped the tape over and turned the volume up enough to make the men shout to one another to be heard. They had reached the Route 29 turnoff, and Jack tooled the truck down the ramp onto the narrow road to Lawford.

"You should get close to Twombley!" Wade yelled.

"How come?"

"The fucker's loaded," he said. "That's why. If you want to get ahead, my boy, you got to learn to make a guy like that need you. Get irreplaceable."

Jack laughed, flashing white teeth, and Hettie laughed too, and Wade watched her place her left hand on Jack's thigh.

"Follow your example, eh?" Jack said.

"You bet. Look at LaRiviere," he said. "The sonofabitch couldn't get along without me."

Jack laughed again. "Yeah, he'd go broke tomorrow if you quit him, right? And you, you'd be sitting in the catbird seat, right?"

"Right!" Wade said, and he grinned like a lizard, when he noticed in the side mirror next to him the glare from the high beams of a car coming up behind them fast.

Jack said, "Bastard's got his lights on high."

The driver hit his horn once sharply, and as the car passed them on the left, Wade looked over and recognized it—the silver Audi owned by Lillian's husband.

"Shit," he said.

"What?" Hettie said.

"My ex-wife. Lillian and her new husband," he said. "That was them in the Audi that just passed us."

Jack said, "Audi's a good car."

"Lillian?" Hettie said. "What's she doing up here? Lillian, jeez, I haven't seen her since—what?—years. Since I used to baby-sit Jill for you guys, remember?" she said, and she smiled warmly into Wade's face.

"Yeah."

"What's she up for?" Jack asked.

"Aw, shit, she's here to get Jill. Pain in the ass," Wade said. "Me and Jill had a little argument. Listen, Jack, I got to get back, I got to get back to town. Move this thing, will you? See if you can get back to the town hall before they get there, okay?"

"Piece of fucking cake, man." He hit the accelerator, and the truck leapt ahead, the exhausts suddenly roaring, like a steady high-pitched wind sweeping through pine trees.

Wade was jumpy again; the effect of the marijuana was instantly and wholly gone. He was inside his own time now, and running late, as usual. Staring over the flat hood of the truck at the curving narrow road ahead of it, he asked himself over and over, as if he had the answer lodged someplace in the back of his brain, why the hell the night had to work out like this. It could have been an ordinary and decent evening, just a divorced father spending time with his ten-year-old daughter. Not much to ask for. No big deal. Nothing complicated. Now the whole thing was a humiliating mess, and it was getting worse by the minute.

The silver Audi kept ahead of the truck all the way into town. At the blinking yellow caution light in front of the school, with the truck less than a hundred yards behind it, the car, without slowing down, lurched around the heap of smashed pumpkins. Jack plowed straight through, splashing chunks and halves of pumpkin like orange slush into the air and off to the sides of the road, but he could not catch the car on a straight stretch of road where he could pass, so that he was still trailing the Audi when it slowed suddenly at the Common and pulled in and double-parked in front of the town hall.

Jack braked the truck by dropping into lower gears, turned left off Route 29 and drew slowly, almost delicately, toward the Audi, just as the driver and the woman in the passenger's seat got out. The woman, Lillian, wore a tailored lavender ankle-length down coat with a hood; her narrow angular face seemed aimed out of the hood like a weapon at the door of the town hall, where a large number of people, adults and children, were coming out.

The driver, Lillian's husband, is named Bob Horner. He is a tall thin man with an extremely high forehead and strips of sandy hair that he combs carefully over the top of his head from a part just above his left ear. He wore that night a tan tweed shooting jacket, belted, with suede patches on the elbows and across the right shoulder and breast, and before he closed the car door, he reached inside and grabbed from the back a felt Tyrolean hat and put it on.

By this time Jack had drawn his truck up next to the Audi, hood to hood and towering over it, and Wade swung open the door and stepped down to the ground. "Lillian!" he called, and she wheeled around to face him, while her husband, caught standing next to Wade, stepped quickly back and away.

As if merely curious, Lillian asked, "Where's Jill?" She smiled lightly.

Lillian, as usual, was playing a role in a scene, Wade decided. And its purpose was to manipulate him into playing opposite her. Though he was not fooled by the tactic, it was effective nonetheless. It was an old story: she was too fast for him. At least when it came to setting up their respective roles—controlling what he said to her and how he said it. He always realized a few seconds too late that their encounters were contests, games with high stakes, and that winning them had nothing to do with rightness or wrongness or even with will power—God knows, he had plenty of will power, everyone said so, even Lillian herself. No, it had to do with who could set the rules of the game first, which, as he always found out a little too late, came straight from the nature of the roles they played. If she was yellow, he had to be red; if her die was six, his was forced to be one.

He leaned forward and placed his hands flat on the trunk of the Audi, as if he were being frisked, and spread all ten fingers out and studied them for a second. "Me and Jill, we just had a little spat, Lillian," he said. "That's all. She felt kind of strange, I guess, and shy. From not knowing some of the kids or something. You know, from not knowing them like she used to, feeling like an outsider, I think. So she decided the best thing was to call you to come up here to bring her home. I didn't know she called you. I don't know what she said, but I . . . I tried to call you, to get you to forget it, you know? But you'd already left."

"Well, where is she now?" she asked. "In there, in the truck with your friends?" She leaned forward as if to see inside the truck. Jack and Hettie had the windows closed and were wrapped around one another, necking.

"You know she's not there. No, she's inside the town hall, at the party."

Lillian turned around and faced the crowd of people coming toward her and spreading over the lot, headed toward their cars. "Really? Looks like the party's over," she said. Then she glanced up at the lighted window above and to the left of the door—Wade's office. "Oh, look!" she exclaimed. "Isn't that Jill up there with the mask on? What's she doing up there? Isn't that your office?" Lillian waved her hand, and suddenly Jill's face disappeared from the window. A second later the light went out.

Wade said, "She told me she wanted to wait for you there."

"Oh. While you went off for a few beers with your friends in the truck?"

"No. She wanted to stay up there alone," he said. "Once she got it into her head that she was going back to Concord, I guess she felt a little uneasy around me or something. I mean, I wasn't exactly tickled by the idea," he said. "I looked forward to this weekend a lot, Lillian."

"Yes, I imagine you must have." She looked past him into the cab of the truck. "Is that Hettie Rodgers there, with whatziznamt?"

"Yeah."

"She's grown up some, hasn't she?"

"Oh, Jesus, lay off, will you?" he said. "It looks like you've won this fucking round already, so lay off a little, for Christ's sake." Wade was vaguely aware of Bob Horner off to his left by the car door, and as Jill came out of the town hall, Horner walked quickly around the front of the car and started toward her.

"Horner!" Wade said. "Leave her be. This's got nothing to do with you, so you just act like the chauffeur. Got it?"

"Wade," Horner said, and he stopped and stuffed his hands into his jacket pockets as if suddenly searching for a match. "Nobody wants any trouble," he said in his high reedy voice.

Lillian had already turned and was walking almost regally to greet her daughter, who had removed her mask—at last, Wade thought. That goddamned mask.

In a voice loud enough to stop several people crossing near them, Wade said, "I don't want her to go, Lillian."

"Don't cause a scene." She had her hand on her daughter's shoulder and was escorting her to the rear door opposite Wade. Lillian peered across the top of the car and said to him, "The child is obviously upset enough. No one's trying to win any 'rounds.' We're both, I assume, only interested in Jill's happiness," she announced. "Don't make it any worse, will you?"

"Goddammit," he said. "I'm not making it worse. *You* are. You and this clown here. Me and Jill, we could've worked this thing out okay on our own, for God's sake. It's a normal thing, a spat like this. I mean, it's normal for a kid to feel a little strange coming back here like this. It's even normal for me to get a little touchy about it. Believe it or not. You two, you come butting in here like this, how the hell do you think it makes me feel? Treating her like some kind of tragic victim or something, how do you think it makes me look to her?"

People leaving the town hall for the parking lot were now cutting a wide circle around the Audi and Jack's truck, many of them staring as they passed, for this was another public and potentially exciting chapter in the ongoing twenty-year saga of Wade and Lillian Whitehouse.

Horner had walked back around the front of the car to the driver's side and opened the door. With his back to Wade, he said quietly, "Get in, Lillian."

"You motherfucker!" Wade said, and he grabbed Horner's shoulder hard with his left hand and shoved him down into his seat, knocking his hat to the ground. "Jesus, Horner, you just fucking wait until we're through, goddammit!"

To Lillian, standing at the door on the other side, Wade said, "Don't you say a fucking word. I didn't hit him. I'm not going to hit anybody."

Her face had gone white and rigid. Slowly, she tightened her lips and shook her head from side to side, as if to deny having done anything that might have offended him, and in silence, she drew the car door carefully open and let herself in, then closed it and instantly leaned around and locked both rear doors and her own. Horner swiftly closed his door, and Lillian reached over his shoulder and locked it, then stared straight out the windshield, as Horner started the car and edged it through the crowd of people crossing the lane in front of them. The crowd parted for the silver Audi, and in a second the car was at the end of the dirt lane, turning right onto Route 29, and gone.

Wade looked at the ground and saw Horner's dark-green Tyrolean hat. Leaning down, he picked it up and examined it with care, as if unsure of its function.

Hettie had rolled down the window next to her, and now Jack leaned across the girl's lap and said to him, "Wade? Hey, you okay, man?"

"Yeah, I'm okay. Sonofabitch lost his hat," he said, and he started walking toward the town hall.

"You want to get a beer, man? We're going to Toby's— you want to meet us there?"

Wade didn't answer. He heard Jack's truck start up and lumber off. Then, in front of him, leaving the town hall, came Nick Wickham and, a few steps behind, Margie. Nick nodded agreeably as he passed, but Margie stopped and smiled.

"Hi. Party's over," she said.

"Yeah. I got to do some stuff in my office."

"New hat?" She pointed at the crumpled hat in his hand. He shook his head no.

"Jill's up, I see."

He said, "Yeah, for a while."

"How's she doing?"

"Okay," he said. "She's fine."

"Nice. Well, listen, give her my love, will you?" She took a step away from him.

"Will do."

"You two want to do anything tomorrow you need a third party for, give me a call, okay? I got no plans, and I'm off tomorrow."

"Like hell you are," Wickham interrupted from behind her. "It's the first day of hunting season, and I'll need you at least in the morning," he said. "I thought I told you this morning already."

Margie slowly turned and faced him. "No, Nick, you didn't."

"Yeah, well, so long as you ain't got any plans, whyn't you come in at six and work through lunch. Take Saturday off instead." He started walking away. "See you later, Wade," he called back.

"Yeah."

Margie shrugged helplessly and smiled. "Well, that's that."

"Yeah. You be careful of that little bastard," Wade said in a weary voice. "He's dying to get into your pants, you know."

"No kidding. But don't worry, I can protect my virtue okay. I mean, c'mon, Wade, give me a break." She laughed and showed him her large good-humored face.

He turned away and said, "Listen, I gotta go. See you tomorrow, maybe."

"You okay?"

"Yeah." He grabbed the door and pulled it open.

"Well, give my love to Jill!"

Wade nodded without turning around and went in. There were still a half-dozen people inside the hall, chatting and cleaning up—LaRiviere, Chub Merritt and his round little wife, Lorraine, and the Congregational minister and the priest from Littleton who served the Lawford parish part time and one or two others. Wade slipped by them and got up the stairs without anyone's seeming to notice him and walked slowly down the long hallway to his office and let himself into the darkened room.

Crossing to the window, he sat down in the chair Jill had dragged over from the desk, and he looked out the window at the parking lot below, the few remaining cars there, the one or two stragglers walking down the lane toward the road. He saw a Chevy sedan with raucous exhausts and a load of kids careen past, and he thought about all the damage the kids in town had done in the last few hours—minor damage, most of it, easily repaired, easily forgotten, but more than irritating. Even though they had done nothing to him, had destroyed or vandalized nothing of his, he could not keep himself from taking their acts personally, somehow, and he felt his stomach tighten with resentment. He tried to remember how he had felt when he was a kid doing that kind of damage on Halloween Eve, but he could not remember any of it, at least no more than the fact of it—that he and his friends and his older brothers and later his younger brother, Rolfe, had indeed in an organized way caused a considerable amount of damage around town. Why? he wondered. What were we so pissed at? Why are all these kids so damned mad? It is like the kids want to attack us adults for something that they think we did to them way back or something that we are going to do to them now first chance we get, but they are scared of us, so they wait until Halloween and they do it this way, making it look legitimate and almost legal.

Below him, LaRiviere's silver head exited from the door, with his large body following, and behind him came the Merritts and the others. LaRiviere waited until they had passed and then he locked the door, and together the group strolled down the path, their breath coming from their mouths in small white clouds as they walked. Wade heard the car doors open and thunk shut, saw the headlights come on, watched the cold cars one by one leave the lot and drive away.

Then he was alone in the town hall, sitting in darkness upstairs by his office window. For the first time that day, he felt good, he told himself. All those plans; then the fears and worries and arguments and explanations that follow: it never seemed to change for him. He lit a cigarette and smoked it down and told himself again that he felt good. A few seconds passed, and the back of his bottom jaw began to throb with low-level pain; it was palpable but with very little heat, and it did not bother him much. He knew, though, that as the night wore on, it would get worse and then worse until the toothache would be the only thing he could think of, the only thing that could abide in his mind.

AΛ

4

ONE MIGHT LEGITIMATELY ask how, from my considerable distance in place and time from the events I am describing, I can know all that I am claiming to be a part of my brother's story. How can I know what Wade said to Jill and she to him when they were alone in his office? How can I know what Wade thought about Hettie and Jack out there in the parking lot by the town hall, or who won the costume contest? Who indeed?

And the answer, of course, is that I do not, in the conventional sense, know many of these things. I am not making them up, however. I am imagining them. Memory, intuition, interrogation and reflection have given me a vision, and it is this vision that I am telling here.

I grew up in the same family and town as Wade, side by side with him, practically, until I was eighteen years old, so that when I yanked myself away from both, I took huge chunks of them with me. Over the years, family and town have changed very little, and my memories of them, which are vivid, detailed, obsessive—as befits the mind of one who has extricated himself from his past with the difficulty that I have—are reli-

47

able and richly associative, exfoliating, detail upon detail, like a crystal compulsively elaborating its own structure.

And, too, I have been able to listen to my brother Wade during all the years of my adult life that preceded the events set down here and especially during the weeks when they were actually taking place, when I was able to hear Wade's version of his story as it unfolded. I was able to listen to him, and once I started paying serious attention to him, which, as I said, occurred shortly after Halloween, I asked him questions. Interrogated him. Later, after his disappearance, when I pitched myself wholeheartedly into learning everything I could about the strange complex violent acts that led to his disappearance, I interrogated everyone even slightly involved, all the people mentioned in this account who survived those acts and even a few not mentioned here—police and legal officials, firearms experts, psychiatrists, journalists, teachers. I investigated land records, local histories, family traditions. I accumulated a roomful of documents and tape recordings, upsetting my domestic order, jeopardizing my job, curtailing my social contacts—in short, I allowed myself to become obsessed. Why I did this I cannot say, except to observe that when Wade began in early November to come undone, I understood it too well, too easily, as if I myself were coming undone in exactly the same way. Or, perhaps, as if I myself *could* have come undone, had I not left home when I did and the way I did, abruptly, utterly, blasting the ground with the force of my departure, with no goodbyes and never again returning—until after Wade, too, had left.

The third factor in the making of my vision—intuition— might be better understood as an uncanny ability to know fully how things must have been, how and what people must have said or felt at a moment when neither I nor Wade, my main witness, was present. There are kinds of information, sometimes bare scraps and bits, that instantly arrange themselves into coherent, easily perceived patterns, and one either acknowledges those patterns, or one does not. For most of my adult life, I chose not to recognize those patterns, although they were the patterns of my own life as much as Wade's. Once I chose to acknowledge them, however, they came rushing toward me, one after the other, until at last the story I am telling here presented itself to me in its entirety.

For a time, it lived inside me, displacing all other stories, until finally I could stand the displacement no longer and determined to open my mouth and speak, to let the secrets emerge, regardless of the cost to me or anyone else. I have done this for no particular social good but simply to be free. Perhaps then, I thought, my own story and, at last, not Wade's will start to fill me, and this time it will be different: this time I will truly have left that family and that town. Will I marry then? Will I make a family of my own? Will I become a member of a tribe? Oh, Lord, I pray that I will do those things and that I will be that man.

A half hour before dawn the wind drops, and the temperature rises quickly from fifteen degrees above zero to thirty. It is the first of November; the night is nearly over. Four miles south of Lawford Center, on the eastern shore of a small gravel-and-rock-bottomed lake puddled among a pile of wooded hills, there begins to emerge from the silken darkness the rough cluttered profile of a trailer park—ten or twelve dingy mobile homes set parallel to one another alongside the lake and perpendicular to a paved lane running at a right angle off Route 29.

From a distance, a half mile down the road, the trailer park in the dim new light looks like an abandoned migrant workers' camp or a deserted military post. At half that distance, the trailers resemble metal coffins awaiting shipment. From the side of the road, where the mailboxes are posted, one distinguishes short driveways and squares of lawn bleached yellow by the autumn cold. And as one passes into the park itself, the trailers—pastel-colored iron boxes held above the hard dirt by stacked cinder blocks—seem to bristle in pale skins of frost. Rubbish, toys and old broken tools crowd the steps and driveways; piles of sand, stacks of bricks and blocks and odd-sized boards are left uncovered in the yards; rusting cars and pickups are parked in the driveways, and parts of cars and trucks lie randomly about. In front of many of the trailers there are spindly frost-burnt bushes, and in back, dead gardens looped by half-collapsed wire fences intended to keep the deer out.

In the history, in the development and even in the geology of the place, there is the appearance of disorder, clutter, abandonment. Despite this and despite the ramshackle neglected look of the trailers, the Mountain View Trailer Park and the entire town of Lawford and the valley as well are held in the grip of deep and necessary symmetries that, like death itself, order the casually disordered world that seems to surround it. In an ultimate sense, the place is enclosed by a fierce geometry of need, placement, materials and cold.

The lots and trailers were owned by Gordon LaRiviere and were laid out on a map three years earlier in a calculated and efficient way on a brush-covered rocky spit of land, an ancient meadow sown with glacial rubble that extended tentatively from the road down to the lake. In the gray half light of dawn one can look from the shore across the pale ice and see a black amoeba-shaped body of open water whose form bears no clear relation to the long narrow teardrop of the lake itself or to the north-south axis of the low hogback hills here on the near side and the higher moraine on the far.

That ridge—in profile, a wide black rip in the western half of the overcast sky—is named for its shape, Saddleback, and it terminates in a tree-covered monadnock called Parker Mountain, named after Major Rubin Parker, the man whose eloquence convinced the Abenakis, and whose shrewd lobbying convinced the New Hampshire provincial legislature, that the Indians, not the British monarch, owned the mountain and thus could sell it and the tall trees on it to him. Which they did—for two chests of hatchets, a dozen hand mirrors, fifty wool blankets, one hundred five-dollar gold pieces and a clock.

Parker Mountain, or seven thousand acres of it, which is essentially all of it, is more hill than mountain. But because it is a monadnock, a single lump of dirt and stone disgorged whole by the retreating glacier, it bears no geological or visual relation to the White Mountains farther north and east or to the Green Mountains west and south, and thus—more or less isolated in a lumpy bed of lesser hills and ridges—it stands out and does indeed resemble a mountain.

Parker Mountain, then, and not Parker Hill, seemed to the white people to be an appropriate name, more so at least than the Abenaki name for it, which early maps translate as Place of the Serpents. The land stayed in the sole possession of Major Parker until his death in bed at age ninety-seven in 1842, when it passed into the shared possession of his seven children, who sold the hill and what little uncut timber remained on it to the Great Northern Wood Products Company of Newburyport, Massachusetts. The Parker heirs promptly moved south to Concord and Manchester, where they disappeared into Victorian bourgeois respectability, setting the precedent for a later pattern of migration.

Ninety years and three generations later, in 1932, after a long decline, Great Northern finally declared bankruptcy, and the Shawmut National Bank and First Boston auctioned off the hill in large slabs for one hundred dollars an acre. These parcels of land were purchased for the most part by local people who owned adjacent farmland. By the Great Depression, family farming in northern New England had diminished almost to a vanishing point, however, and the fields grew quickly back in wild berries and scrub, until crumbling stone walls wandered lost and forgotten in the shade of third- and fourth-growth pine and spruce forests. Widows, children and grandchildren, nephews and nieces, first and second cousins, friends and even enemies inherited the land, as one generation passed the physical world on to the next.

By the late 1980s, these seven thousand acres of rocky forested hillside were in the hands of the members of perhaps a hundred different families. Most of the mountain was still owned and sometimes even lived on by local people, but many of the owners now resided elsewhere, often as far away as California and Hawaii, and were barely aware of the existence of their few acres of useless stony northern New Hampshire countryside, except when the tax bill came in. Questioning the wisdom of holding on to the land, they usually made a few halfhearted attempts to find a buyer and, finding none, either paid the modest tax to Alma Pittman or did not, but in any case forgot about the land for another year. By now, deeds, bills of sale, surveyors' reports, maps and tax assessments were so tangled and in such conflict and disagreement with one another that it was difficult if not impossible to ascertain who owned how much of what. Consequently, people who used the land, either to live on or for hunting and fishing or as woodlots or berry fields, avoided selling the part of it that they used, and they could not imagine buying up anyone else's—so that, more than two centuries after Major Parker's purchase of Parker Mountain from the Abenaki Indians, proprietary rights had come full circle. Once again, ownership of the land was determined more by use than by law. With no one complaining, town officials taxed the users accordingly and were grateful for what got collected.

* * *

The lights had not yet come on in any of the trailers when snow started to fall, specks of it like luminous bits of ash against the black ridge and mountain on the far side of the lake and against the dark circle of open water out near the center. In minutes the snow was coming down harder, straight down in the windless air as if on threads—the first snow of the year, and early, even for this far north, where from the tops of the hills you could look away and see Canada, frigid and rigid and dour as schist.

Soon the ground surrounding the trailer park was white, and the roofs and hoods of cars and trucks and of outbuildings, shanties, porches and toolsheds were covered as if with crisp new bedsheets. The snow brought daylight faster than did the whitening sky, and what the sky would have exposed, the snow hid. It blotted out the clutter of the yards and scrub beyond, the sad and disordered look of the place, with the swift efficiency of amnesia.

In the trailer nearest the road, then in another farther in, finally in a half dozen, lights went on, casting small patches and strips of yellow light against the snow-covered ground. One could discern shuffling and bumping noises as the inhabitants rose from their sleep and prepared to begin the day. One heard the muffled sounds of a baby's cry, a radio, the whine of an electric shaver, a woman's cross shout from the kitchen back down the trailer to a child still huddled in bed, eyes closed and feigning sleep under blankets in darkness and warmth against the light and the cold.

The trailer at the very end, a light-blue two-bedroom unit with rust gathering at the seams, was parked on what might have been promoted in the beginning as the most desirable lot in the park. It was next to a short crescent of beach and, on the other side, a sharply narrowing point of land, so there was no room for adjacent trailers. This was the home and lot that Wade Whitehouse had purchased from his boss, Gordon LaRiviere, two years before, shortly after his final departure from the bungalow in the birch grove on Lebanon Road that he had built himself and shared with his wife, Lillian, and daughter, Jill, for close to eight years.

Wade had run the well-drilling crew that put in the well for the park, a deep-water artesian that cranked out fifty gallons a minute at one hundred thirty feet, and the idea of living by the lake had appealed to him, especially since he hated the alternative idea (the only one he could imagine after the divorce) of staying in one of the apartments over Golden's store in town. Wade was broke, but LaRiviere offered to hold a twenty-year mortgage with no down payment, and he gave Wade the first choice of all twelve trailers in the park. It was July, and Wade thought he liked to fish; and the little beach next to the light-blue Bide-a-Wile looked like something he would enjoy, especially in the warm summer evenings after work.

As it turned out, however, he never got around to buying a fishing rod. And he had not used the beach once in two years, partly because he was so busy in the summer months, frequently drilling wells for LaRiviere out of town and not getting home till after dark, but also because, except for maybe six short weeks in July and August, the lake was too cold to swim in comfortably. Then came his first winter at the trailer park, and with that it became obvious that the place at the end of the row of trailers out on the point was in fact the worst location in the park. It was the place most exposed to the cold winds that swept off Parker Mountain and, picking up speed as they crossed the lake, banged like hammers against the tin sides of the unprotected trailer before swooping on toward the White Mountains beyond. It took two winters before Wade decided that LaRiviere probably had known when he sold him the trailer that it was the least desirable of the fourteen trailers in the park and that if Wade had not eagerly, even gratefully, bought it for $22,000, LaRiviere would have been forced to sell it for much less.

Ah, what a terrible year that was—the year of the second divorce, the year of losing the house to Lillian, the months of living in the dingy apartment over Golden's and the day he bought the damned trailer from LaRiviere. Then, six months later, came Lillian's decision to move down to Concord with Jill in tow, and her marriage to Horner. It is a wonder he survived at all.

He rose from his tangled sheets and blankets like a porpoise surfacing, shocked by the fact of wakefulness itself, and then by cold air, by the sight of his cluttered room, by the smell of stale beer and cigarette butts and his own night breath, by the sound of Kenny Rogers croaking from the clock radio on the blue plastic milk carrier next to the bed—so that the dream he had been dreaming disappeared almost instantly, like the memory of an earlier, less evolved and less vivid life spent drifting between wedges of shadow and beams of pale-green light.

He checked the time, ran his tongue across mossy teeth, reached for a cigarette and lit it and lay in bed for a few moments, hands under his head, smoking and running a fragmentary narrative of the end of last night in front of his eyes. Sitting in the dark by the window in his office at the town hall. Driving out to Toby's Inn in his car. Slumping silently in a booth with Jack Hewitt and his girlfriend, Hettie Rodgers, and three or four other men and women, and later, his toothache anesthetized by alcohol, yakking and laughing in a loud hearty voice with one or two kids he knew only vaguely. Then drinking at the bar alone, and at last, just before the sudden blackness at the end of the loop, standing in the parking lot, examining his pale-green car as if it were a stranger's, finding it unaccountably ugly. Then nothing.

But no memories—and no visible signs—of argument, he thought with relief. An advertisement for a Chevrolet dealer in Concord came on, and he snapped off the radio. He touched his face with the fingertips of his right hand, felt no pain and no swelling in his hands or above the eyes or around the mouth, and plucked his cigarette from his lips and tapped the ash into an empty Budweiser bottle next to the radio. Across from the bed was a plastic-and-aluminum picnic chair—with his clothes laid neatly over the back and arms, he noted. No torn or bloody shirt—he could tell that much from bed. He refolded his arms and slid his hands under his head and spread out his legs, and for a moment Wade thoroughly enjoyed his nakedness under the rumpled sheet and blanket. His tooth ached only a little, a hum, and he did not once think of his daughter or of his ex-wife.

It was not until after he had showered and shaved and was standing in his faded blue terry-cloth robe at the kitchen counter, stirring a cup of instant coffee, that the unique and vaguely familiar quality of the silence that surrounded the clink of his spoon against the coffee cup made him realize that it was snowing outside. He glanced at the window behind the sink, where a week's dirty dishes and pans were stacked, and saw the haze of snow, for it was falling heavily now, like a gauze curtain, and he could make out no more than the rough outline of Saddleback Ridge and Parker Mountain.

He looked at his watch—six-forty. "Shit," he said aloud, and he walked quickly to the frayed plaid couch, where he sighed, sat down and picked the telephone off a tipped pile of newspapers on the end table and dialed a number.

After a few seconds, he began to speak into the receiver. "Lugene? This's Wade. How you doing?" he asked, and without waiting for an answer, said, "Hey, Lugene, look, I was wondering, with the snow and all, you got school today?"

He listened, lit a cigarette from a pack on the crowded coffee table and said, "How the hell do I know? You're the principal, damn it. You're the one who's supposed to know how much it's going to snow, not me. All I'm supposed to do is direct traffic from seven-thirty to eight-thirty, for Christ's sake."

He listened again. "Yeah, okay, I'm sorry, Lugene. I'm running late," he said, "and I only just now saw it was snowing, that's all. My whole day is fucked. I was just hoping you'd have called school off. You know? Because I got to plow all day, and if I don't get over to LaRiviere's early enough, I get stuck with the grader. Whyn't you check the weather bureau? Maybe you should cancel school."

Wade paused a second. "Fuck. You check the weather bureau?"

Lugene agreed to call the weather bureau, but no matter what the prediction, he said, there would certainly be school today. He might decide to send the children home at noon, but clearly not enough snow had fallen or would fall in the next hour to keep the buses from getting safely into town. Then he asked Wade if he talked to everyone that way.

"Okay," Wade said, ignoring the question. "I'll be over in a bit."

He hung up the phone and barreled down the narrow hallway to his bedroom. He would not be drilling wells for LaRiviere today; he would be plowing snow for him. He dressed hurriedly in work clothes—long underwear, blue-and-black-plaid flannel shirt, green twill pants, heavy wool socks and insulated rubber boots with tan leather tops.

At the door, Wade grabbed his dark-blue trooper's coat

and cap off the hook, pulled the cap halfway over his ears and shrugged his way into the coat. He glanced at the thermostat on the wall and set it back ten degrees, to fifty-five, then stood briefly at the door and looked across the room with an empty expression on his face, as if running down a daily checklist.

Let us stop for a moment, while he stands by the door, and look at Wade up close. It is time for that. Examined from a certain angle, Wade's face is a classic example of an ancient type of Northern European face. It is the broad high-cheekboned heavy-browed durable face that first appeared in this form twenty to thirty thousand years ago between ice ages in the marshes along the southern shores of the Baltic, among tribes of hunters and gatherers moving toward the western sea, driven from fertile estuarial homelands by a taller fairer fiercer people who possessed agrarian skills and tools, clever weapons and principles of social organization that allowed them to conquer and enslave others.

He would hate to hear me say this, but I am describing my own face as much as his. This is what we Whitehouse men and women (most of us, anyhow) look like. We wear a face shaped by thousands of years of peering into firelight, into cold mists rising off salt marshes, into deep waters where huge sturgeon cruise slowly past; a face tightened, crinkled and lined from having pursed thin lips thoughtfully for millennia over animal tracks and droppings, over individual wild grains counted into a wicker basket one by one, over small stone figures of women with large breasts and wide hips and bellies. And beyond these ancient habits of expression, there is something deeper and more ancient still, at least in Wade's face. There is an intimacy and a tenderness, a melancholic vulnerability about his dark-brown eyes, especially in the way the heavy slightly protruding brow protects the delicacy of the eyes and allows them to stay wide open, alert to danger even in bright sunlight. The narrow mouth, tightened over large yellowed teeth, gives the impression of intelligence and sensitivity. It is not a noble face, not especially refined, either, but a passionate face, and thoughtful.

Wade's body, like my own, is of a similarly ancient type, evolved over tens of thousands of years of holding the reins of another man's horse in the cold rain while the horseman does business inside by the fire, of climbing rickety ladders with a load of bricks in a hod, of yanking back the head of a boar with one stout arm and reaching around with the other and slashing its throat with a single stroke, of drawing sticks on a cart from someone else's woods to someone else's fire. It is a compact hardy body, flat-muscled and round-shouldered, with a long wide back and short limbs, a body not so tall as to draw undue attention to itself, not so short as to be unfit for heavy lifting or long grueling marches carrying weapons and tents. It is, I suppose, the kind of body that made it possible for European princes and popes to wage war against one another for a millennium.

That is the face and body I see when I see Wade flick the switch by the door and turn off the overhead light in the living room and stand for a second more in the gloomy gray light of the trailer and study the room before him, a sad dirty cluttered room filled with the evidence of a sloppy man nearing middle age and living alone—empty beer bottles on the floor and coffee table, work clothes strewn around the room, ashtrays overflowing, newspapers tossed aimlessly about, empty food cartons and dirty dishes and coffee cups abandoned on the end tables and the TV in the corner.

For the first time in what even he knew must have been months, he looked at the room as if there were a stranger living here, a man he had never met, and he felt his stomach tighten with aversion. He would not want to meet such a man. No, sir. And then, suddenly, he saw how the room would have looked to Jill as she came through the door, tired and sleepy but very happy from all the fun trick-or-treating and afterwards going to the Halloween party with her dad. He would have carried her in from the car, worked the door open with his free hand and switched on the overhead light, and Jill would have turned on his shoulder and looked around, and this awful room, this stranger's room, is what she would have seen.

He looked down and off to his right, a boxer dodging a blow, wrenched open the door and stepped quickly outside. There was about an inch of snow on the ground, and it was still coming down in a light dry powder but falling more heavily now than before, accumulating rapidly. Like a man trying to spot a particular friend in a crowd of strangers, he squinted across the lake at Saddleback and Parker Mountain, hazy dark lumps profiled indistinctly against the white sky, more like zones than solid objects, and he heard it, suddenly but without surprise, as if he had been listening for it, the first gunfire of the hunting season—a rapid series of four distinct shots crackling across the lake and echoing back again.

With his gloved hands, he brushed the snow off the windshield and exposed a rough skin of silvery ice underneath, got inside and inserted the key into the ignition, pumped the gas pedal hard twice and turned the key. The starter moaned but did not catch. He tried again, exactly as before, and still got nothing. This was part of the drill. The third time would do it, and indeed it did, turning the cold engine over once, several times slowly, then rapidly, until at last it caught and came coughing to life.

Sitting inside the car was like hunkering down inside a tent in the Arctic or an igloo—that is how Wade imagined it. Light managed to penetrate the ice on the windshield and windows, but it was an eerie white metallic light that did not so much illuminate the interior of the car as fill it with itself, like Wade's breath, which drifted from his mouth and nostrils in wispy clouds. When the engine was running smoothly and would not stall, he reached forward and switched on the defroster fan. At first it chattered and whined, but in a few seconds it was humming from somewhere behind the dash, shoving air up against the windshield glass.

Wade waited, and before long the air coming from the defroster had melted a dime-sized circle on each side. Slowly the circles expanded, becoming quarters, then saucers, until Wade could look through the glass and see the snow coming down, could see the trailer, could even see the lake beyond.

The melting of his icy sanctuary made him feel oddly disappointed, a little saddened and, for a few seconds, apprehensive. Out in the middle of the lake, which was now a flattened white teardrop, he could see the black circle of open water. It would probably freeze solid and disappear into whiteness by tonight, even there, where the water was over fifty feet deep. Then there would be two utterly distinct worlds, the world above and the world below, with the ice in between like an impenetrable barrier protecting one from the other. He felt that split, that barrier between two worlds, abandon him now, as the ice on his windshield melted into a pair of rapidly enlarging circles, like eyes that could look out but also—as if that

were the price he had paid for the privilege of looking out—
eyes that allowed him to be seen.

Automatically, Wade flicked on the CB, and with the red
dot of light dancing along the scanner, he backed the car down
the driveway, spun the wheel and eased out of the trailer park,
laying down the winter's first set of tire tracks in the fresh
snow. Turning left at Route 29, he passed the row of snow-
crowned mailboxes lined up side by side on a two-by-four like
miniature prairie schooners and headed toward town.

A quarter of a mile north of the trailer park, the Minuit
River suddenly veers in close to the left side of the road, and
from here all the way into town the road and the riverbed
wind and loop in tandem through the narrow valley. Wade
liked the way the river looked in the new snow and milky early
morning light. That is a tourist's idea of New Hampshire, he
thought, with pine trees drooping over the water and snarls of
icicle-laden birches clumped at the edges of eddies and pools,
with large snow-covered boulders in the middle of the stream
and dark-green water churning, swirling and splashing past
and over them, raising a thick white crust of ice at the crest
marks. At moments like this, Wade felt something like pride
of place, a rare and deeply pleasurable feeling that started with
delight in the sight of the country, passed through a desire to
share that delight with someone else and abruptly ended in a
fantasy in which he stands before the scene and spreads his
arms wide as if to embrace it whole, then steps aside and
reveals it to . . . to whom?

He pulled a cigarette from the pack in his shirt pocket,
put it in his mouth and reached to punch in the dashboard
lighter, when, startled, he saw on the seat next to him a green
Tyrolean hat. It was the hat he had picked off the ground the
night before, after the owner of the hat and Lillian and Jill had
driven away. Wade looked at the thing with dismay, as if it
were a severed body part, a piece of irrefutable evidence link-
ing him to a crime he had no knowledge of.

"Oh, Jesus," he said aloud, and he cranked down the window next to him. He let the freezing air blow in and grabbed
the hat and shoved it out. All the way into town he left the
window open, as if pummeling himself with the cold wind to
keep himself from falling asleep at the wheel and swerving and
skidding off the narrow dangerously curving road into the icy
river.

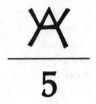

5

WINTER APPROACHES THIS HALF of New England from the northwest. It blows down from Ontario and Quebec, arriving with such ferocity and stunning relentlessness of purpose that you give yourself over to it completely and at once. There are no temporary adjustments, no mere holding actions or delays, no negotiated settlements.

For the tens of thousands of years that these narrow valleys and abrupt hillsides have been populated by human beings, life has been characterized by winter, not summer. Warm weather, high blue skies and sunshine, flowers and showers—these are the aberrations. What is normal is snow from early November well into May; normal is week after week of low zinc-gray overcast skies; is ice that cracks and booms as, closer every night to the bottom of the lake, a new layer of water cools, contracts and freezes beneath the layer of old ice above it.

There are, as it happens, two crucially different climate zones that are divided by an invisible line running across New Hampshire, drawn from Vermont in the southwest corner of the state near Keene, through Concord in the center of the state to the lakes north of Rochester in the east and on into Maine. When, south of that line, in November and December and again in March and April, it rains, north of that line the lakes are still frozen over and it snows. The land is tilted higher in the north, is rockier, less arable, with glacial corrugations like heavy-knuckled fingers reaching down toward the broad alluvial valleys and low rolling hills of Massachusetts and Connecticut and the coastal plain of eastern New Hampshire and Maine. South of that unmapped line, the climate is characterized by weather typical of most of the northeastern industrial United States; north of it, the weather is typical of eastern Canada.

This has been the case since the autumn of the year of the first appearance of human beings in the region—late-arriving bands of Pleistocene hunters drifting south and east all the way from Asia behind the herds of elk and woolly mammoths—and it remains true today, so that, not surprisingly, the lives of the people residing south of that line from the beginning seem to have reflected the generosity and temperance of the climate there, while those who have lived north of it have reflected in their daily lives the astringency, the sheer malignity and the dull extreme of the climate there. It is the difference, let us say, between China and Mongolia, or between England and Scotland, Michigan and Manitoba: people adapt, or they quickly die. Or they move.

Thus, when in autumn in the town of Lawford the first ice and snow of winter arrive—usually in early November, sometimes even earlier—the natives, whether Pleistocene or modern, do not look up in surprise and dismay and hurry to prepare their houses for the coming season. No, they barely notice winter's arrival. They barely noticed its absence in the first place. The ice in the deeper lakes did not break up until late April, and there were gray patches of old snow in the deep woods and on the north slopes well into May. The nights were not reliably free of frost until June, and then it returned by late August, when leaves of maple trees and sumacs near water turned red and birches turned gold. Every day long black V's of Canada geese flew over, and soon the leaves of the oaks and hemlocks, elm, hawthorn and birch, were turned out in brilliant colors—deep red, flame yellow, pink, purple and scarlet. By the first week of October, whole long gray days passed without the temperature's rising above freezing, while the leaves, their colors dulled by the cold, tumbled from the trees and swirled in the autumn winds, and stalks and reeds clattered in the icy clasp of the marshes and ponds, and animals drew into their caves for a six months' sleep.

When the snows do come, it is as natural and as inescapable and in some sense as welcome as gravity. Starting long after midnight, a clear starry sky with a sickle of moon in the southeast fills slowly with low dark gray clouds, until the sky is covered from horizon to horizon and all the light seems to have been wiped from the valley, every dot of it, every pale reflection, every memory. The first scattered flakes drift almost accidentally down, as if spilled while carted by a high wind to somewhere east of here, to the Maritimes or New Brunswick: a single hard dry flake, then several more, then a hundred, a thousand, too many to be seen as separate from one another anymore: until at last the snow is falling over the valley and the hills and lakes like a lacy soft eiderdown billowing out and settling over the entire region, covering the trees, the rocks and ridges, the old stone walls, the fields and meadows behind the houses in town and out along Route 29, the roofs of the houses, barns and trailers, the tops of cars and trucks, the roads, lanes, driveways and parking lots: covering and transforming everything in the last few moments of the night, so that when at dawn the day and the month truly begin, winter too will have arrived, returned, seeming never to have left.

The burgundy 4×4 pickup driven by Jack Hewitt left Route 29 at Parker Mountain Road and lunged down to the narrow wooden bridge, where it crossed the Minuit River and headed uphill, through the woods and past occasional trailers, half-finished ranch houses and now and then, set in among the trees, a tar-paper-covered shack with a rusty tin stovepipe sticking out of the roof, a gray string of wood smoke disappearing quickly into the falling snow. The truck headed toward Saddleback, moving fast along the rough unpaved road, blowing high fantails of snow behind and kicking up loose stones and dirt with its huge knobby tires.

It rumbled past the Whitehouse place, the house where Wade and I grew up and where our parents still lived, crossed Saddleback and continued on to Parker Mountain. Seated next to Jack was a man named Evan Twombley. He was a large burly man dressed in brand-new scarlet wool pants, jacket and cap. He smoked a cigarette that he kept jammed into the right side of his mouth while he talked out of the left. It was a very busy man's way of talking and smoking at the same time, and it had the desired effect: even when he spoke idly, he was listened to.

Although one could not be sure Jack was listening. His head was canted slightly to the side, a characteristic pose, and his lips were pursed, as if he were silently whistling and was listening to the tune in his head instead of to Twombley, who, after all, was only expressing slight anxiety about the weather and its effect on the deer hunting, and this after Jack had already assured him that it would have no effect whatsoever, except to make it easier for the hunters.

Twombley seemed unable to accept Jack's reassurances. "I mean, it's not enough snow, and won't be for a while. Not for tracking the bastards," Twombley said. "There's no advantage there, kid. And it'll be hard, you know, to see very well in the damned stuff."

Three rifles, two with scopes, hung in the rack against the rear window of the cab, and all three swung and clunked against the rack in tandem as the truck dipped into a gully and out. The incline got steeper, and Jack double-clutched and shifted down, and the truck leapt ahead.

Jack said, "Don't worry, Mr. Twombley, I know where those suckers are. Rain or shine, snow or no snow, I know where they hide. I know deer, Mr. Twombley, and this particular piece of land. We'll kill us a buck today. Guaranteed. Before ten." He laughed lightly.

"Guaranteed, eh?"

"Yep," he said. "Guaranteed. And it's *because* of the snow. We'll be still-hunting, see, instead of stand-hunting. This here is your best snow for tracking, actually, real powdery and dry, couple inches deep. You don't want no foot-deep wet stuff. Right about now the does are holing up for the day in brush piles, and the bucks're right behind them. And here we come right behind the bucks. I guarantee," he said, "this gun gets fired before ten o'clock."

Jack crooked his thumb at the rifle hung from the bottom hook of the rack behind him. "Whether it kills a deer or not is more or less up to you, of course. I can't guarantee that much. But I'll put you inside thirty, thirty-five yards of a buck the first four hours of the season. That's what you're paying me for, ain't it?"

"Damn straight," Twombley said. He yanked the cigarette from his mouth and rubbed it out in the ashtray. The windshield wipers clacked back and forth, and large beads of melted snow skittered like water bugs across the wide flat hood of the truck.

At first glance and often for a long time after you got to know him, Evan Twombley gave the impression of being a physically and personally powerful man, and most people tried to give him whatever he seemed to want from them. Often, later on, they realized that they had been foolishly intimidated, but by then it was too late and they would have other reasons for continuing to give him what he wanted. He was one of those American Irishmen who find themselves in their mid-fifties with a body that, in its bloat and thickened coarsened face, looks large, bulky, formidable, when in fact it is a small body, even delicate, with fine hands, narrow shoulders and hips, small precise ears, eyes, mouth. Forty years of heavy consumption of whiskey and beefsteak can turn a dancer's body and a musician's face into those of a venal politician. That other, much younger man, the dancer, the musician, was nonetheless still there and was wide awake somewhere inside and making trouble for Twombley now by questioning the venal politician's right to bully people with his loud voice, by mocking his swagger and brag, his claims of physical fearlessness, and finally making the loud burly red-faced man often come off as hesitant, conflicted, vulnerable, even guilty. In the end, although one neared Twombley feeling intimidated by him and wary of and possibly hostile toward him, up close one quickly discovered a fellow feeling for him and a genuine sympathy, sometimes a protectiveness.

Twombley himself, of course, knew nothing of this transition; he only perceived its effects, the most useful being that it gave him power over people: at first, people were afraid of him; then they warmed to him. In human relations, this is a sequence that invites dominance and creates loyalty. And in Twombley's particular line of work—which, after a long careful climb from the local organizing level, had come to be that of the president of the New England Plumbers and Pipefitters Union, AFL-CIO—dominance and loyalty were extremely useful, not to say essential, for without them he would have been forced back long ago to working with the wrenches in the trenches.

The truck entered a flat S curve in the road, and the rear wheels broke loose, and the vehicle fishtailed from one side of the road to the other; Jack hit the accelerator and nonchalantly flipped the front wheels in the direction of the slide and anchored the truck to the road again.

"You done much shooting with that rifle of yours yet?" Jack reached behind him with his right hand and patted the stock of Twombley's gun.

"Some," Twombley said, and lit another cigarette and looked out the window at the spruce trees and thatches of cedar flashing past.

Jack smiled. He knew that Twombley had not fired the rifle at all. It was a lovely thing, not a scratch or blemish on it, a Winchester M-94 pump-action, a .30/30 with a custom-carved stock. It must have set Twombley back two thousand bucks. Ah, sweet Jesus, these rich old guys and their toys! Jack seemed almost to sigh, but he ended by pursing his lips again as if to whistle. Men like Twombley, over-the-hill fat cats, cannot ever truly appreciate the beauty of things that they can afford to buy. And the men who can appreciate a gun like Twombley's, guys like Jack Hewitt, say, who can remember the feel of a particular gun in their hands for years afterwards, as if it were a marvelous woman they slept with once, will never be able to own it.

Next to Twombley's gun, Jack's new Browning looked utilitarian, ordinary, merely adequate. Yet to buy it he had been obliged to borrow money from the bank, had lied and said that the money was for his mother's medical bills, which was true, in a sense, because he was still paying for her stay in the hospital last summer and the old man was still out of work, and if Jack did not take care of his parents, who would? He had bought the gun, and now he had yet another monthly payment to make. In addition to the $48 a month for the gun, he sent out $420 a month for his truck, $52 a month for insurance on the truck, $35 a month for the engagement ring he bought last May for Hettie, $50 a month to Concord Hospital for his mother, and $200 a month to his father directly, for household expenses and food, which was, after all, the least he could do, since, as his father had explained one drunken night—shortly after Jack went and ruined his arm and quit playing professional ball for the Red Sox farm team in New Britain, Connecticut, and came home to Lawford and parked his ass back in his room the same week the old man got laid off at the mill—there was just no way the old man was going to be able to support him. In fact, if Jack wanted to live with his parents, then he would have to support *them.* So that now, only a few years out of high school, where, because of baseball and his intelligent good looks, he had been one of the most promising Lawford kids ever to graduate from Barrington Regional, Jack was already mired in debt, a man who worked overtime to make enough money to pay interest on borrowed money, and he knew it, and that made a gun like Twombley's fancy Winchester all the more attractive to him. He practically *deserved* Twombley's gun. As a *reward,* for Christ's sake!

Twombley shifted in his seat and rubbed his red nose with a knuckle. "You get me close to a big buck by ten o'clock, kid, there's another hundred bucks in it."

Jack nodded and offered a faint smile. A few seconds later he said, "You might not kill it."

"You think so."

"And I expect you'll have to kill it, for me to get my extra hundred bucks, right?"

"Right."

"Can't guarantee that, you know."

"What?"

"That you won't gut-shoot the deer, say, or cripple him up for somebody else to find and tag a mile downriver from where you shot him. Or maybe you'll miss him altogether. Or just spook him before you even get a shot off. It happens. Happens all the time. Happens especially with a new gun. You want a dead deer, not a live one."

Twombley crossed his arms over his chest. "You take care of your end, kid, I'll take care of mine."

"Yep."

"You understand what I'm saying? Like you say, I want a dead deer, not a live one."

"Yeah. I get it." Jack was not stupid. He knew what Twombley was asking him to do. Shoot the deer for him, if necessary. Discreetly. "Okay," he said in a voice just above a whisper. "No sweat. You'll get yourself a deer, and you'll get him dead. One way or the other. And you'll have him by coffee time."

"And you'll get your extra hundred bucks."

"Wonderful," Jack said. "Wonderful."

The truck crested the hill, where the trees had thinned and diminished in size, scrawny balsams, mostly, and low reddish furze scattered around boulders. Beyond the boulders was a shallow high-country swamp, a muskeg, covered with ice. Barely visible through the falling snow, at the high end of a short rise, was a log cabin with a low overhanging shake roof set in under a stand of drooping snow-covered blue spruce and red pine.

Jack slowed the truck and drew it over to the side of the road. "That there's LaRiviere's cabin he told you about," he said, pointing with his chin toward the small one-room structure. "We can start a fire in the wood stove now, if you want, so's it'll be nice and warm when we come in. Or we can head out for that monster buck of yours right now. Up to you."

"You're a cocky sonofabitch," Twombley said.

"Yeah?"

"Yeah. You only got two and a half hours till ten, and you're willing to waste time building a fire."

"Just trying to please," Jack said.

"Let's get going, then. Forget the fire. I want to kill a 'monster buck' first," Twombley said with a derisive laugh. "Then I'll worry about getting warm."

He swung open the door and stepped down to the ground and slammed the door behind him, while Jack stepped out on the driver's side and started taking out the guns and gear.

"C'mon, kid, let's haul ass," Twombley said, and he walked off the road a short ways and stood, hands on hips, facing downhill along an old lumber trail that ran past the frozen muskeg several hundred yards to where it intercepted a rocky dry riverbed pitching through brush off to the right.

For a second Jack stopped gathering up the guns and his daypack and several pieces of loose equipment, and he glared at Evan Twombley's broad back as if the man were his mortal enemy. Then his gaze dropped, and he went quickly back to the task at hand.

* * *

At dawn, just before the pale smear of first light, the deer had already begun to move, and they moved generally away from the roads and fields along narrow twisting game trails into the deeper woods. In twos and threes and even fours—a buck and one or two does and their fawns, though just as often a buck traveling alone—the deer fled rapidly away from the sound and sight of dark prowling cars and trucks that ground up hills and down, that bumped and lurched as far into the woods as vehicles could go, where, with headlights slashing the pre-dawn darkness, the cars and trucks stopped and let the hunters out, went back and on to another place and parked and let more hunters out, until soon the woods all over this part of the state were swarming with men carrying guns.

As the snow fell, the men talked and sometimes called to one another across brooks and among the oak trees and brush. They laughed and smoked cigarettes and pipes while they walked in pairs along old railroad beds or, alone, set up hidden stands in fallen brush along ridges that gave a long clear view of a meadow and a copse of birch beyond or, ten feet up in an oak tree, perched in a Y in the branches, rubbed hands against the cold, poured coffee and brandy from a thermos into a plastic cup. It was as if, behind every tree, along every ridge, beside every stream, there was a man looking down the blue barrel of his gun, a chilled impatient man waiting for a deer to move into his sight. He saw it walk delicately, warily, through the curtain of falling snow. He saw it step from behind a fallen tree. He saw it emerge from a pile of dead brush into full view, where it posed for one second in the crosshairs, a full-grown massive male deer holding itself absolutely still, ears like dark velvety leaves, white flag of a tail switching, large liquid eyes brushed by long lashes and soaking in as much visual detail as can register in the animal's brain, wet nose searching the breeze for scent that is not tree bark, pine needle, resin, leaf, water, snow, hoof, urine, fur or rut. Then, all across the hills and valleys, up and down the gullies and over the boulder-strewn ridges and cliffs, from up in trees, hillsides, overlooks, bridges, even from the backs of pickup trucks, out of brush piles, over stone walls, behind ancient elms—throughout the hundreds of square miles of New Hampshire hill-country woods—trigger fingers contract one eighth of an inch and squeeze. There is a roar of gunfire, a second, a third, then wave after wave of killing noise, over and over, sweeping across the valleys and up the hills. Slugs, pellets, balls made of aluminum, lead, steel, rip into the body of the deer, crash through bone, penetrate and smash organs, rend muscle and sinew. Blood splashes into the air, across tree bark, stone, onto smooth white blankets of snow, where scarlet fades swiftly to pink. Black tongue lolls over blooded teeth, as if the mouth were a carnivore's; huge brown eyes roll back, glassed over, opaque and dry; blood trickles from carbon-black nostrils, shit spits steaming into the snow; urine, entrails, blood, mucus spill from the animal's body: as heavy-booted hunters rush across the frozen snow-covered ground to claim the kill.

From all the corners and back roads of the district, huge lumbering pumpkin-orange school buses passed north and south through the town, then slowed at the town center, as if by prearrangement, blinked red warning lights and waited for Wade Whitehouse, standing in the middle of the road, to wave them one by one into the schoolyard.

Wade did not enjoy this part of his job—for one hour a day five days a week he was the crossing guard at the school—but it was required. Wade's annual police pay, $1,500, one tenth of his total income, was a line item in the school budget that got authorized every March at town meeting. LaRiviere, who had been a selectman for over a decade, allowed Wade to come into work at eight-thirty, a half hour later than anyone else who worked for him, so that he could claim that he personally saved the school board the extra fifteen hundred dollars a year they would have to pay someone else to do the job if Wade had to be at work at eight o'clock. That way, the town was able to pay for its police officer from the moneys allotted to the school budget, and half those moneys came from the state and federal governments. Gordon LaRiviere was not selectman for nothing.

In the years when his daughter Jill was one of the children riding the bus to school, Wade had loved being the crossing guard. Especially after he and Lillian had got divorced and he moved out and he no longer saw Jill at the breakfast table. Every morning he waited out there in the middle of the road for her bus to round the downhill curve on Route 29, and when the bus finally reached him, he held the driver up for a long time and let all the buses coming the other way turn in first, giving Jill time to get to the window, so that she could see him and wave as, at last, he permitted her bus to pass into the schoolyard. Then he waved back and smiled and watched until the bus stopped by the main entrance and let the kids tumble out, kids alone, kids in pairs, little knots of friends, when a second time he got to see his daughter, with lunch box and book bag, silvery-blond hair freshly braided, clean clothes and shoes, red scarf swinging in the crisp morning air.

She always looked for him then too, and they smiled and waved their hands like banners at one another, and she ran with her friends around to the playground in back, happier with her day, he was sure, than if he had not been there to greet her. Just as, for Wade, those few golden moments every morning were the zenith of his day and colored his attitude toward everything that followed, all the way to the end of the night, and even his sleep was more peaceful because he and his daughter for a few seconds had seen each other's faces and had smiled and waved at one another. Then something completely unexpected had happened: Lillian had sold the little yellow house in the birch grove and had moved down to Concord. And now the school buses only reminded Wade of his loss.

This morning, because of the snow, which had accumulated rapidly and was several inches deep and drifting already, the buses and the rest of the early morning traffic were moving with special care. Wade held them at the crossing longer than usual before letting them turn off the road into the schoolyard, giving the drivers extra time to see through the windblown snow and ease their precious cargoes, the children of the town, around each other and the occasional batches of kids who walked to school and crossed the road from the far side when Wade directed them to cross. Lined up behind the buses were cars and pickups with people hurrying to work and late-rising deer hunters. Their motors idled, windshield wipers clattered, and now and then, when a car passed him, the driver glowered at Wade, as if he had delayed them for no good reason.

He did not care. He was pissed this morning anyhow, and it almost improved his mood that people were mad at him. The faces of the children peering out the windows of the buses seemed to mock him, as if they were still wearing their Halloween masks—little demons, witches and ghosts. None of them was his child; none of them was Jill, eager to wave at him.

He made everyone wait, held long lines of buses, cars and trucks back, letting one child at a time cross the road as he or she arrived, instead of making a group of them gather there first. And he did not permit a single bus to enter the schoolyard until the bus ahead of it had unloaded all its passengers and had pulled out at the far end and was back on the road again, heading north to Littleton.

Now even the bus drivers, who normally acknowledged Wade not at all, as if the discipline it took to keep them from being rattled by the noise and play of their passengers kept them from perceiving Wade as anything but a traffic signal, were staring sullenly at him as they passed, a few shaking their heads with disgust. He did not care. I don't give a rat's ass you're pissed, he thought. One driver, a flat-faced woman with red hair, slid her window open and hollered, "For Christ's sake, Whitehouse, we ain't got all day!" and the kids in the seats behind her laughed to hear it.

He heard the school bell ring and saw the kids come racing around from the schoolyard behind the low light-green cinder-block building to line up in messy formation, girls separated from boys, at the main entrance. The principal, Lugene Brooks, his buttoned sports jacket barely able to contain his round belly, his collar turned up, his thin gray hair fluttering in the wind, had come outside and was mouthing commands at the children, marching them inside like a drill sergeant. He glanced toward Wade, saw that there was still one more bus to turn off the road and unload, and he shouted, "Wade! Hurry up! They'll be late!"

Wade kept his arms straight out, one aimed north and one south, with both hands up. Motionless, expressionless, he held his post in the middle of the road. The yellow caution light directly over his head blinked and bobbed on its wire, and the remnants of last night's smashed pumpkins, half covered by snow and slush, lay scattered at his feet. He looked like a demented scarecrow.

He felt like a statue, however: a man made of stone, unable to bring his arms down or force his legs to walk, unable to release the one remaining school bus and the dozens of vehicles lined up behind it and the dozen more facing it. Someone way in the back hit his horn, and at once most of the others joined in, and even the bus driver was blowing his horn. But still Wade held his arms out and did not let anyone pass.

He wanted his daughter to be on that last bus. Simple. It was his only thought. Oh, how he wanted to see his daughter's face. He longed to look over as the vehicle passed and see Jill's pale face peer out the window at him, the palms of her hands pressed against the glass, ready to wave to him. *Daddy! Daddy, here I am!*

He knew, of course, that she would not be there, knew that he would see instead some other man's child staring at him. And so he refused to allow the bus to move at all. To release that one remaining bus and all the cars and trucks lined up behind and in front of it, horns blaring, windows rolled down and drivers hollering and gesturing angrily at him, to let them pass, would instantly transform his desire to see his daughter into simple loss of his daughter. Somehow he understood that the pain of enduring a frustrated desire was easier to bear than the pain of facing one more time this ultimate loss. He wanted his daughter to be on that last bus; it was his only thought.

Then suddenly, from near the end of the long line behind the bus, a glossy black BMW sedan nosed into the second lane and started coming forward, passing the other cars and trucks and gaining speed as it approached Wade. There was a man driving and beside him a woman in a fur coat and in back a pair of small children, boys, staring over their parents' shoulders at Wade, who behaved as if he did not see them at all or as if he fully expected the BMW to come to an abrupt stop when it drew abreast of the bus.

But it did not. The BMW accelerated, changing gears as it flew past Wade and on down the road and disappeared around the bend beyond the Common. Wade still did not move. As if the flight of the black BMW had been a countermanding signal to the signal Wade's position and posture gave, the last yellow schoolbus drew quickly off the road and entered the schoolyard, and at once the rest of the cars began to move again, north and south, passing Wade on both sides.

Slowly his arms dropped to his sides, and he stood there starkly alone in the exact center of the road. It was only after all the vehicles had passed him by and the road was once again empty and the bus had unloaded the thirty or forty children it carried and had pulled out of the schoolyard and headed back toward Littleton that Wade himself departed from the road. He walked slowly in the blowing snow toward his own car, which was parked just beyond the main entrance to the school.

Standing at the door to the schoolhouse was Lugene Brooks, his arms folded over his chest more as protection against the cold and snow than as a gesture of disapproval, his round face, as usual, puzzled and anxious. Wade walked heavily past the man without acknowledging him and yanked open the car door.

"Are you okay, Wade?" Brooks called to him. "What was the matter out there? Why were you holding everyone up?"

Wade got in and slammed the car door and started the motor. Then he backed up a few feet and rolled the window down and shouted, "That sonofabitch in the BMW, he could've killed somebody."

"Yes. Yes, he could have." The principal paused. "Did you get his number?" he asked.

"I know who it is."

"Good!" the principal exclaimed. Then he said, "I still don't understand—"

"I'm going to nail that bastard," Wade muttered.

"Who . . . who was it?"

"It was Mel Gordon. From Boston. Evan Twombley's fucking son-in-law—he was the one driving. I know where they're headed, too. Up the lake, Agaway. Up here for the weekend, probably. The old man's out deer hunting with Jack Hewitt, so they probably got a big weekend party planned," he said. "Oh, I'm gonna nail the bastard, though. Spoil his fucking weekend for him."

"Good. Good for you, Wade. Well . . . ," Brooks said, stepping halfway inside the school. "I'm the guy who's got to make things run around here, so I better hop to it." He smiled apologetically.

Wade stared at him, remaining silent, so the principal said, "I was just wondering . . . you know, about why the big holdup out there, why you were keeping everybody stopped like that. You know?" He smiled feebly.

"You probably think I got an answer for that question," Wade growled. "You ask more dumb questions than anybody in town."

"Well, yes. No, I mean. It just . . . seemed odd, you know.

I figured, holding the bus like that and all the cars, you'd had a reason for it. You know."

"Yeah," Wade said. "It's logical for me to have a logical reason for things. Everybody else I know does. You, for instance. You got a logical reason for everything *you* do?" he suddenly asked the principal. "Do you?"

"Well, no . . . not really. Not everything, I mean."

"There you go," Wade said, and he quickly closed the car window and started moving away.

He left the schoolyard and turned right onto the road, flipped on the CB and started listening to the squawks coming in from all over—truckers out on I-95, hunters up in the hills plotting their coordinates, a wife in Easton telling her husband he forgot his lunch bag. The snow was coming down with fury, in white fists, and as he drove slowly through the stuff, Wade thought, I can't stand it anymore. I can't stand it, I can't stand it.

In the lot outside Wickham's Restaurant, a half-dozen pickup trucks and as many cars were parked side by side. The corpses of large male deer were lashed to front fenders, slung onto roof racks, stretched out in the corrugated beds, carcasses gutted and stiffening in the cold, tongues flopping from bloody mouths, fur riffling in the light breeze, snowflakes catching in eyelashes. It gave the impression not of the aftermath of a successful hunt but of a brief morning respite in an ongoing war, as if the bodies of the deer were not chunks of meat but trophies, were proof of individual acts of bravery, dramatic evidence of the tribe's rage, courage and righteousness and a cruel warning to those of the enemy who still lived. Counting coup. One half expected to see the antlered heads of the slain deer severed roughly from the bodies and stuck onto poles tied to the rear bumpers of the vehicles. One expected crow feathers tipped in blood.

Out on the highway, cars with out-of-state plates hurried south with the trophies on the roof and lashed to the front fender freezing solid in the wind, the drivers and passengers passing a bottle back and forth while they whooped and detailed in compulsive repetition the story of the kill. And in Lawford, in backyards, deer hung from makeshift gallows, in dark barns on meat hooks, in garages from winch chains or rope tied to I beams; and behind fogged-over kitchen windows, hunters shucked their coats and boots and sat down to tables and ate hearty breakfasts, eggs and bacon, pancakes smeared with butter and covered with maple syrup, huge steaming mugs of coffee: men and women, their blood running, excited in ancient ways, proud and relieved and suddenly ravenous for food.

Jack led the way from the truck onto the flat beside the road, circled the frozen patch of high-country marsh, then angled left on the sloping lumber trail, over rocks and low brush. Immediately, Jack started playing his gaze back and forth across the rough snow-covered ground in front of him, searching for tracks and sign. Whenever Twombley, wrapped like a huge infant in red bunting, trundled close and attempted to come up alongside him, Jack seemed to walk a little faster and put the man behind him again.

He moved smoothly, a natural athlete, long-legged, broad-shouldered, lean and loose—a ballplayer. "I'm a ballplayer," he always said, "no matter what else I ever do." He never said "baseball player" or even "pitcher," and in fact he had been slightly disappointed when the Red Sox turned out to be the only team that wanted to sign him, despite the fact that since early childhood the Sox had been his favorite team, because that meant the American League and the designated-hitter rule: as a pitcher, if he ever made the majors, he would not be allowed to hit. And back in those days he fully expected to make the majors. Everybody in town and even across the state and into Massachusetts expected the kid Jack Hewitt from a hill-country village in New Hampshire to make the majors. "No way that kid won't be pitching in Fenway a couple years from now," people said when Jack with his big-league fastball was drafted in his senior year of high school. "No fucking way. The best ballplayer to come out of New Hampshire since Carlton Fisk." People thought he even looked a little like Fisk, square-jawed and nobly constructed in all the ways an unformed boy of eighteen can be said to be constructed—the kind of boy a town is proud to send out into the world.

The world in this case turned out to be New Britain, Connecticut, but after a season and a half playing double A ball, Jack was back in Lawford, unable to lift his right hand above his right shoulder, where he wore two long white scars that Hettie Rodgers loved to touch with her tongue. Beneath the scars he wore a ruined rotator cuff, ruined, he liked to say, by trying to do what man was not meant to do, throw a slider, and by surgical attempts to repair the damage.

He did not complain, though. At least he had a shot at the big time, right? Most guys never even got that far. He knew lots of pitchers in the minors who had ruined their arms the first year or two, so he did not feel especially unlucky. His story was not all that unusual. Not for someone who had got as close to the big time as he did. That was the unusual story, he felt, getting as close as he did in the first place. More worldly than his neighbors, he took the statistical view and gained comfort from it.

Or so it seemed. Every once in a while, his disappointment and frustration would break through with the force of grief and rage, and he'd find himself beer drunk and weeping in Hettie Rodgers's arms, crying into her soft white neck ridiculous things, like, "Why did *my* fucking arm have to be the one to go? Why couldn't *I* be like those other guys who're pitching in Fenway, for Christ's sake? I was as good as those fucking guys! I *was!*"

Then the next day, after digging wells with Wade all day for Gordon LaRiviere, he would land back at his stand at Toby's Inn, watching the game on the TV above the bar with the regulars and explaining the finer points of the game, dropping bits of gossip and rumor about Oil Can Boyd, Roger Clemens and Bruce Hurst, guys he'd known and pitched against in the minors, diagramming on a napkin the difference between hit and run and run and hit, anticipating managerial moves with an accuracy and alacrity that pleased everyone who heard him, made them proud to know him. "That Jack Hewitt, he's fucking amazing. Only difference between him and that guy Clemens up there on the TV is luck. That's all, shit luck."

Slipping and sliding downhill behind Jack came Evan Twombley, carrying his rifle, lugging it first with his right hand, then with his left, sticking one hand and then the other out for balance as he tried to follow Jack's footsteps in the snow and tripped on a rock or a slick piece of trash wood. Finally, he slung the rifle over his shoulder, like an infantryman, and used both arms for balance. Overweight, out of shape, he was soon puffing and red-faced from the effort of keeping up with the younger man; he began to curse. "Sonofabitch, where the fuck's he think he's going, a goddamn party?"

When Jack had eased twenty yards ahead of Twombley and had actually disappeared from view around a stand of low spruce trees, Twombley hollered at him, "Hey, Hewitt! Slow the fuck down!"

Jack stopped and turned and waited for the man. A look of disgust crept across his face, but when Twombley came lurching awkwardly around the spruce trees, Jack smiled easily and in a soft voice said, "Deer's got ears too, you know." The falling snow spread like a veil between them, billowing from the wind, and Twombley might have looked like a fat red ghost approaching. As if suddenly frightened by him, Jack turned and moved on, a little slower now than earlier, but keeping the distance between them constant.

They were switchbacking down the north slope of Parker Mountain, walking in the direction of Lake Minuit through woods that were lumbered out five or six years before, past stumps and piles of old brush among young pine and spruce trees. The sky seemed huge and low, smoky gray and spewing white ash over the valley. Now and then the sound of gunfire from below drifted all the way up the long tangled side of the mountain, as if skirmishes were being fought down there, isolated mopping-up actions and occasional sniper fire. Out in the open now, they could see in the distance the oval shape of the frozen lake, a white disk with a crystallized roughening at the farther edge that was LaRiviere's trailer park, as Jack thought of it, where Wade Whitehouse lived.

Jack liked Wade. Most everybody liked Wade. Not the way everybody liked Jack, of course, but Wade was twenty years older than Jack, and he had a reputation around town as a man who was dangerous when he was drunk, a reputation Jack knew the man deserved. He had seen Wade clock a few guys himself, and he had heard stories about him that went all the way back to when Wade was in high school, before he tried to go to Vietnam like his brothers but got sent to Korea instead, which people said really pissed him off. People liked to say, "If you rub his hair the wrong way, Wade Whitehouse can turn into a sonofabitch," which is probably why he got made an MP after the army gave him their aptitude tests. Wade had an aptitude for being polecat mean.

Even so, Jack liked Wade—or, more accurately, he was

drawn to him. He watched him closely, knew at all times where in the room he was standing, who in the crowd he was talking to, almost as if Wade were someone's wife Jack was attracted to. He liked the slight feeling of danger he got when he was around Wade, even though the idea of ending up in your forties living a life like Wade's made him shudder and avert his gaze and go quickly back to talking about baseball. Jesus! A smart good-looking guy like that, living all alone out there by the lake in a rusted-out trailer, busting his butt digging wells for Gordon LaRiviere and working as a part-time cop for the town, drinking beer and brawling with the boys on Saturday nights and copping a quick Sunday fuck off some sad lonely lady like Margie Fogg—that was not the life Jack Hewitt planned to live. No way!

He came to a halt at the edge of a steep incline that fell away to a branch of the old lumber trail and a half-overgrown field of scree, the remnants of a spring mud slide. Beyond the lumpy swatch of boulders the forest resumed. The wind that had blown steadily in his face all the way downhill from the truck shifted slightly and cast the sheet of snow briefly aside, and from where Jack stood, up there on the lip of the incline, he could see across the tops of the trees, mostly hardwoods now, oak and maple, down the side of the mountain and through the dip in Saddleback all the way to Lawford, identifiable among the distant trees by the spire of the Congregational church and the roof of the town hall. Jack stared at the town, at the place in the landscape where he knew the town lay, as if searching for his own house, then inhaled and exhaled deeply, and when the wind resumed blowing in his face and the curtain closed, he turned and faced Twombley, who had finally caught up with him.

Scowling and out of breath, the man was about to speak, when Jack raised a finger and silenced him. He whispered, "Stay here, stand where I am," and stepped away from the edge of the incline.

Twombley nodded and moved into place and peered carefully down at the narrow trail and field of glacial till twenty feet below.

"I'm going to move back up a ways, then come in from the west along the trail there," he whispered in the man's ear. "You just stand here and wait." He pointed at the rifle still slung over Twombley's beefy shoulder. "You'll need that," he said. "Be sure the safety's off."

Twombley wrestled his rifle off his shoulder and into his hands. He checked the chamber, then flicked off the safety and cradled the gun under his right arm. He was breathing rapidly now, not from exertion but from excitement. In a tight dry whisper, he asked Jack, "What'd you see?"

"Tracks. It's your monster buck, all right. So you keep your eyes on that break in the trail down there," he said, pointing down a ways to his left, where the trail disappeared around a bend in the cut slope. "And in a while, Mr. Twombley, you'll see what you want to see."

"Where'll you be?"

"Where I can get him if you don't," Jack said. "There's only one direction he can go when you shoot at him from up here. If you miss him, he'll run downhill and back. Which is where I'll be."

"Right, right."

Jack placed his hand on Twombley's back and nudged him a step closer to the edge. "Be ready. You'll only have time to get off a single shot. He'll come facing you, so shoot him right where you'd shoot a man if you only had one shot," he said, and pointed at Twombley's heart and smiled.

Twombley smiled back.

"Good hunting, Mr. Twombley," Jack said. He slung the daypack onto his back and started walking along the lip of the incline toward the line of small pines that grew uphill on the left. Then he turned and came back toward Twombley, who was already staring down at where he expected the deer to appear, and when Jack was about four feet from the older man, he stopped.

Twombley looked up at him, puzzled. "You better get going, kid. You only got till ten o'clock to collect that extra hundred," he said.

Jack said, "Let me check your gun."

Twombley handed it to him. Jack looked it over. He lifted his head, and for a few seconds he stared at Twombley's chest, and then he raised the gun and aimed it and fired.

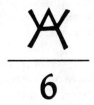

6

MEANWHILE, AT THAT VERY MOMENT in the valley below, Wade drove slowly from the schoolhouse south along Route 29 into the center of town. Occasionally, a vehicle emerged from the falling snow and sloshed past Wade's green sedan—Hank Lank delivering oil, Bud Swette in his jeep starting on his mail route, Pearl Diehler taking her children to school, late again.

Then Wade saw the plow approaching, LaRiviere's bright-blue dump truck with the big double-V plow, driven by Jimmy Dame, who was normally one of Wade's helpers on the drilling rig. The sonofabitch had got to the garage before him, and now Wade was stuck driving the grader again. They should've called school off, he thought. God damn it all to hell.

The vehicle loomed out of the snow like the huge silver-and-blue-helmeted face of a medieval knight, and Wade veered slightly to the right to give the truck plenty of room as it passed. LaRiviere had obtained the contract to plow the town roads nine years earlier, before he ran for selectman and right after the Board of Selectmen introduced at town meeting a rule requiring all bidders on the plowing to be local residents.

Appealing to local pride and suspicion of outsiders, Chub Merritt, then the chairman of the Board, had got it passed, in spite of heavy opposition led by Alma Pittman, the town clerk, who had pointed out that Gordon LaRiviere, with his grader and truck, was now likely to be the only bidder, which was, of course, no surprise to Chub Merritt.

Though he worked for LaRiviere and would probably end up driving one of the plows himself and garnering lots of overtime to help pay for his new house and child, Wade had been against the proposal, telling no one but Lillian: he knew what LaRiviere and Chub Merritt were up to, and unlike most people in town, he did not admire them for it. Wade never understood why folks seemed to confuse envy with admiration when it came to wheeler-dealers like Gordon LaRiviere. A small town is a kind of ghetto, and hustlers look like heroes. But Wade kept his own counsel and never indicated aloud whether he was for or against Chub's new plowing proposal, so everyone assumed he was for it. What the hell, Wade himself would benefit from it: winter work, in a town where unemployment from December till March was close to forty percent.

Chub called it Home Rule and for months before town meeting buttonholed everyone who came into his garage, asking as he pumped gas into their car, "How you stand on Home Rule, bub?" He never bothered to ask Wade. At the meeting, Alma angrily called for a secret ballot and got it. Wade voted Yea. Afterwards, he often wished that he had been more forthright, that he had come right out and said to Chub Merritt, "I'm against Home Rule. All it means is an inside track and inflated charges for Gordon LaRiviere, and we taxpayers end up paying for it." Then he could have voted Nay. It was another of those small compromises that made Wade feel trapped, not so much by public opinion, or even by his cowardice, as by his desire to behave like a responsible husband and father. He believed that, and ate his anger.

The windshield wipers flopped back and forth, and the CB grumbled as state troopers out on the interstate between Littleton and Lebanon bounced calls back and forth. A speeder had been stopped on the northbound lane, and a truck was off the road at Chester. A car had been abandoned at the side of the road a half mile south of Littleton. Wade listened to these calls from habit, not curiosity or need. Though he had called the state police many times on his CB, in four years they had not once called him for help or even for information—not since the forest fire in Franconia. He was like a private security guard hired by the town, a human alarm system whose main functions were to call for the emergency vehicle at the fire station or the ambulance service in Littleton if someone died at home, to break up domestic arguments that got out of hand, to keep the bored and reckless teenagers sufficiently alert so that they did not do irreversible damage to themselves, to ease the children safely into the schoolyard in the mornings, and if anything really serious happened, to call in the real cops.

Sometimes Wade hated being the town cop. At least once a year, and usually in early March, just before the selectmen were due to reappoint him, he actually considered quitting the job. But then, when he was compelled to imagine his life in town without the job, he hated that even more. For Wade, so long as he stayed in Lawford, there were no acceptable alternatives to his present life, not here, and not anywhere in this valley. No alternatives, and so far as he could see, no prospects. Somehow, until now, being the town cop, which once in a while gave him something unpredictable to deal with, had made that almost acceptable.

He could go elsewhere, of course; most of the smart people in town already had. They usually fled south: to Concord, the state capital, like Lillian, who Wade had to admit was bright, or to Massachusetts, like me, whom Wade also regarded as bright and who had gone off first to the University of New Hampshire in Durham and then disappeared into the Boston suburbs, and even like our sister, Lena, younger than Wade and older than I, a woman who was thin when she was young, and pretty, and married a truckdriver for Wonder Bread from Somerville, Massachusetts, and left town with him. He had the northern delivery route the summer Lena was seventeen and met him at the Tunbridge Fair, where he was delivering hot dog rolls. She rode off in his truck with him, got quickly pregnant, and now they are born-again Christians and have five kids and live on the third floor of a triple-decker tenement in Revere. There were others from Lawford who were regarded by Wade as intelligent, mostly older people, and they had sold their land and houses in Lawford—sold them increasingly in recent years to Gordon LaRiviere—and owning for the first time in their lives a few thousand dollars more than they needed to live on, had gone to Florida, Arizona and California, bought a trailer or a condo, turned their skin to leather playing shuffleboard all day and waited to die.

But Wade was different; he had never imagined his life outside the town. Like almost everyone in northern New England, he talked now and then about getting the hell out of this godforsaken place, usually talked about it with Jack Hewitt, who, from the day he returned from playing ball in Connecticut, spoke of "lighting out for the fucking Sunbelt." But their conversations always ended with Wade slapping Jack on the back and saying, "You're a dreamer, kid. You're going to die here in Lawford, and so'm I."

Once Wade had gone so far as to answer a postcard from his friend Bob Grant, the plumber, who had sold his place and moved up to Alaska a few years before, with a letter asking Grant about the job possibilities for a skilled well driller up there. Wade had thought Grant's moving to Alaska was crazy, but on the back of a postcard picture of a moose at dawn, Grant had written Wade that he had just bought a big new house and a new twenty-nine-foot-long RV, and he and the wife were taking a two-week vacation driving down to Oregon. Grant was Wade's age, a tough smart fellow, a hard worker. He seemed to have benefited from moving north in ways that no one who had moved south or west had been able to do.

Wade had pulled out his yellow tablet and had written back: *Well, it looks like you're doing real good now. I guess folks in Alaska need plumbers more than they need them around here. Most everybody here can fix their own toilets and thaw out their own pipes, so we don't even notice you're gone. (Just kidding.) Seriously, how do you think a guy like me could do up there? I'm sick of working for LaRiviere, who is nuts, as you know. And I'm sick of this town too. It's only my kid who keeps me here nowadays.*

But this was not true, and Wade knew it. No, at bottom Wade believed that he was staying on in Lawford year after year, grinding his way through the long winters, in his forties now and drifting into depression—he did not call it depression, but he remembered when he felt another way, not happy, exactly, but better—drinking too much and with increasing frequency enduring spasms of random violence, because at bottom he was shrewd and honest enough to know that he would be in his forties and lonely, poor, depressed, alcoholic and violent anywhere. Below that, however, was yet another truth that he was now and then aware of but surely could not speak of to Bob Grant, although he had said it to me and probably to Margie Fogg; he said it with a wince, a slight ironic twist on his face: he loved the town, and he could not imagine loving any other.

Alma Pittman was out shoveling her front path, a tall woman in a red plaid mackinaw and a man's cap with the earflaps tied under her chin, pitching the snow with large easy swings of her long arms, and as he passed she looked up, acknowledged him with a nod and went grimly back to work. There were a few familiar cars parked outside Golden's store, and farther down on the same side of the road was Wickham's Restaurant, where the parking lot was filled, and for a second Wade thought of going in for something to eat. He was stuck with using the grader anyhow; no point now in rushing over to the garage to get it.

He slowed and peered out his window, but the windows of the restaurant were clouded over, and he could not see anyone inside. He imagined the smell of cigarette smoke and fresh coffee and bacon and toasted bread, and he lit a cigarette and braked the car slightly, and then he realized that Margie would immediately ask him about Jill. Where was she this morning? Had she gone to school for the day? What were his plans for this snowy weekend with his daughter? Maybe the three of them could take Margie's snowmobile out. Maybe they could head up to Littleton for a movie.

He checked his watch, saw he was running real late and, almost relieved, drew back off the shoulder onto the road and drove past the restaurant and made straight for LaRiviere's, a quarter mile beyond and on the left. The heavily falling snow had eased somewhat, and the sky was satiny and pale gray, as Wade pulled into LaRiviere's wide neatly plowed asphalt driveway, rolled quickly by the mobile home in front and parked his car off to the side of the building behind it. The parking lot, the size of a small airport, surrounds both the blue ranch-style mobile home and the matching blue barn in back, which is where Gordon LaRiviere runs his several businesses.

The trucks were all out, Wade observed, except for LaRiviere's 4 × 4 pickup and, of course, the grader, that damned grader. It was parked beside the barn like a blue dinosaur, arched and lean and, like all LaRiviere's vehicles, spotlessly clean. The company motto, LaRiviere's notion of wit, was painted in white on the side of the pickup and the grader as well—OUR BUSINESS IS GOING IN THE HOLE!—just as it appeared on everything owned by Gordon LaRiviere, on business cards, stationery, bank checks, tools large enough to carry it, drilling rigs, rain gear and every one of his numerous meticulously maintained matching blue vehicles. It was as if LaRiviere were a small republic. Even the plots of land he bought were planted as soon as the deed was signed with a small blue sign with white lettering: PROPERTY OF LARIVIERE ENTERPRISES. OUR BUSINESS IS GOING IN THE HOLE! NO SNOW-MOBILES, HUNTING, OR FISHING. NO TRESPASSING. THIS MEANS YOU!

Wade eased himself slowly out of his car as if he had all morning to waste and walked across the lot to the small door next to the large truck-bay doors of the barn and went into the office. Elaine Bernier was at her desk on the other side of the green-speckled Formica counter. The office was as neat and orderly as a showroom for office furniture. There was none of the sloppy evidence of work being done—no stacks of papers, loose files, overflowing ashtrays, drawers left half open, paper food containers—none of it. There were not even any calendars or photographs, although a large red NO SMOKING sign glared from each of the four walls. Elaine was busy typing when Wade strolled through the door, but her desk, too, was clean and, to all intents and purposes, empty. Beyond her desk was the entrance to the inner office and next to it a large plate-glass window behind which sat Gordon LaRiviere, hard at work on the phone, hunkered down close to the receiver, as if proximity to the instrument increased his effectiveness on it.

Elaine looked up, zippered her mouth in a tight smile that was more a grimace and went quickly back to typing. She was a middle-aged woman with a bush of red-dyed hair, a long bony face, plucked eyebrows, green eye makeup and a thin mouth, who overdressed for the job in flouncy full-sleeved blouses and long pleated skirts and high heels that rarely emerged from under her desk. It was Wade's opinion that Elaine Bernier was in love with Gordon LaRiviere, and that Gordon sometimes had his way with her.

Wade unzipped his jacket and took off his cap and slapped

it against his thigh, spraying drops of melted snow over Elaine's desk, and she glared at him. He waved at his reflection in the glass behind her, and LaRiviere hollered from the other side, "Wade! C'mere a second!"

Wade nodded, and stepping toward the door, said with his lips, One, two, three, and in unison with LaRiviere said aloud, *"I want you to take the grader!"* Wade stopped just short of the entrance to the inner office—he could see the silvery crew-cut top of LaRiviere's head while the man stared straight down at the telephone, his face a few inches from the surface of his immaculate desk, as if examining it for dust—and counted to three once more and said, again in unison with LaRiviere, *"Follow Jimmy up Twenty-nine to Toby's and back!"* Then he heard LaRiviere return to his telephone conversation, a rapid-fire whisper, his usual telephone voice, like the hissing of a tape rewinding on its spool.

Wade took two more steps forward and leaned into the brightly lit office. LaRiviere looked up and wrinkled his broad pink brow in puzzlement, and as he started to open his mouth, Wade snapped his middle finger at him and said, "Fuck you, Gordon." LaRiviere's expression did not change; it was as if Wade and he were in different time zones. Wade pushed his cap onto his head, turned and left the office.

Five minutes later, he was up inside the flapping canvas cab of the grader, driving it across the parking lot and down the driveway to the road, the long narrow plow blade bouncing along under the high belly of the machine like a gigantic straight razor.

Jack Hewitt stood at the lip of the incline and peered across the tops of the trees through the dip in Saddleback all the way to Lawford Center. The wind had shifted slightly, or perhaps the falling snow had eased somewhat, for he could see the spire of the Congregational church and the roof of the town hall in the valley below. He might have been trying to figure out where among the distant trees his father's house was located, when Twombley come puffing up behind him.

Red-faced and out of breath from the effort of trying to keep up with the younger man, Twombley was about to speak, no doubt with irritation, but Jack lifted one finger to his mouth and silenced him. Then, stepping off the edge of the low ledge, he leaned into Twombley's ear and said, "Stay here, stand where I am."

Twombley took two steps forward, peered over the edge at the lumber trail twenty feet below and the field of strewn boulders beyond it.

Jack came up alongside him and whispered that he was going to circle back around the ledge on the west. He would cut down to the trail through a stand of pines there and drive the deer back along the trail to where the animal would come into clear view just below Twombley and fifty yards to his left. He told him to make sure he was ready to shoot, because he would only have one shot.

Twombley unslung his rifle, checked the chamber and flicked off the safety. "What'd you see?" he asked.

Jack told him about the tracks and the moist dark-brown pellets of deer shit.

"Fresh?" Twombley said.

"Yup. And wicked big, too. This here's your buck, Mr. Twombley. The one you been thinking about all fall, right?"

Twombley nodded and edged closer to the drop-off. "Get going," he said to Jack. "You only got a little while if you want that extra hundred."

Jack looked at the man for a second, and his mouth curled into a slight sneer. Then he turned abruptly away, as if to hide the sneer, and started walking toward the stand of pines that ran in a ragged line uphill from the ledge. On the farther side of the pines the ground sloped more softly, and the trail nearly flattened out for a ways, and there were several head-high heaps of dead branches and brush that had been stacked alongside the trail some years back by the lumbermen. Jack knew that the big buck was hiding in one of those brush piles, that he was lying down, listening to gunfire in the distance and the snap of a twig fifty feet away, sniffing for the sour smoky odor of humans, large brown eyes wide open and searching for any movement in his field of vision that did not fall into the familiar rhythm of a world without humans. Jack was adjusting, narrowing, his own field of vision, bringing his gaze to a sharp focus on the tangled heaps of brush so that he could determine which of the three hid the big deer, when he heard Twombley cry out, and he started to turn. At the same instant, he heard the gun go off, and he knew that the stupid sonofabitch had slipped and had shot himself.

He thought about it that way and that way only, and he walked slowly, angrily, back to the edge of the incline where Evan Twombley had stood, and he looked down at the man's body splayed in the snow below him. He shouted at the body, "You're an asshole! A fucking asshole!"

Twombley lay face down, with his arms and legs spread as if he were free-falling through space. His new rifle lay beside him, a few feet to his right, half buried in the snow.

Jack pulled out a cigarette and lit it and stuffed the crumpled pack back into his pocket. He dearly hoped the man was dead, stone cold dead, because if he was still alive, Jack would have to lug the stupid sonofabitch all the way back up to the truck and probably haul him all the way to Littleton. "Stupid, arrogant sonofabitch," he said in a low voice, and he started down, slowly, carefully, to find out if indeed, and as he hoped, Evan Twombley had killed himself.

Not until he reached Toby's Inn did Wade—hunched over the large steel steering wheel in the painfully cold windblown cab of LaRiviere's blue grader—finally catch up to Jimmy Dame in the dump truck. This was as far as the town plows went; they and the state DPW plows met and turned around at Toby's and went back to their respective territories. Jimmy had zipped a few complimentary passes over Toby's lot and was sitting in the truck in the far corner of the lot, enjoying coffee and Danish from Toby's kitchen and watching Wade as—compulsively and with great difficulty, because of the size and awkwardness of the grader—he finished scutting Jimmy's residue off to the side of the rutted parking lot.

Jimmy liked watching Wade try to use the grader as if it were a pickup with a flat plow on the front, driving the enormous and grotesquely shaped vehicle forward ten feet, then backward ten feet, short half turn to the right, short half turn to the left, wrenching that huge steering wheel like the captain of a ship trying to avoid an oncoming iceberg. It was crazy, Jimmy thought, and Wade was crazy. He did it every winter: got to LaRiviere's shop late the first day of a snowstorm because of directing traffic at the school, then got stuck with the grader, which naturally pissed him off, since it was like being in an icehouse up there, except that then he'd drive the damned thing like he was glad to have it, really pleased to have the chance to show folks what this here grader could do when it came to plowing snow. After knowing him all his life, Jimmy still did not know if he liked Wade or not.

Jimmy Dame, like Jack Hewitt, was one of Wade's helpers on the well-drilling crew. Wade was the foreman and had been for a decade. But when they were not drilling wells, they all three tumbled to the same level and were paid accordingly. When the ground froze solid and well drilling was no longer feasible, LaRiviere put them to work first on snowplowing, and when that was done, on maintaining equipment, vehicles, tools and matériel, and when everything LaRiviere owned had been brought up to his fastidious snuff, which is to say, in as-new condition, and the garage and toolboxes and storage bins had been swept and squared as smartly as a marine barracks, LaRiviere promptly laid off Jimmy. A few weeks later, he laid off Jack, and last of all, Wade. This usually occurred late in February, which meant that Wade was out of work no more than six weeks.

It was hard to know what factors determined LaRiviere's policy of laying off first Jimmy, then Jack, then Wade. Both Jimmy and Wade had worked for LaRiviere since getting out of the service, and Jack had come on only three years ago, so it was not seniority. And it was not age, either, as Jimmy was two years older than Wade, twenty-two years older than Jack. And it was not on the basis of who had the widest range of skills, because Jack could type and Wade could not, and when given the opportunity to do it, Jack liked office work, whereas Wade felt worse than peculiar, he felt downright terrified, when, as inevitably happened on a cold dark snowy day in February, LaRiviere asked him to come into the office, get out the calculator and an architect's scale and take measurements off a blueprint stretched across the drafting table and help prepare a bid on some spring work for the state. Wade pulled off his jacket and cap and sat on the stool and went to work, listing sizes and lengths of pipe and fitting required, converting those figures into man-hours, calling Capitol Supply in Concord for prices, clicking away on the calculator and every time, without fail, coming up with totals that were so much over or under what simple horse sense told him the job should cost that he felt compelled to start the process all over again. The second time through, his totals once again were so far off, and in the opposite direction of the first set, that Wade could trust nothing—not the drawings and not the architect and engineer who made them, not the calculator, not the supplier and, most of all, not himself. He knew the work, the figures for the materials were all fixed in black and white, and he could read blueprints with ease; but somehow, every time he added up his figures he fumbled, skipping a whole column of figures one time, doubling sums the next. Was he brain-damaged, missing a few crucial cells someplace? Was there something wrong with his eyes, some mysterious affliction? Or was he just made so nervous by LaRiviere sitting a few feet away from him that he could not concentrate on the rows of numbers in front of him? Usually, after a dozen failed attempts to come up with an estimate that approximated his commonsense knowledge of the cost of a job, Wade would start to growl audibly from his stool at the drafting table, a low rumbling canine growl, and LaRiviere would look up from his desk, blink his tiny pale-blue eyes three or four times and tell Wade to go on home for the rest of the winter.

When, at last, Wade had finished plowing the parking lot of Toby's Inn, he drew the grader alongside the dump truck, cut the engine back and flopped open the canvas door. He was a few feet higher than Jimmy in the truck and swung around in his narrow seat and kicked down at the closed window of the truck several times.

Jimmy rolled the window down and hollered, "What the fuck you want, Wade? What you want?"

Wade felt a wave of petulance roll over him, a warm self-satisfied pout, and he kicked his booted feet, right, then left, into the space of the open window below him.

Jimmy dodged Wade's feet and yelled, "What the fuck? Knock that shit off, will you?" He started rolling the window up, but Wade stuck one boot into the window far enough to stop it a few inches from the top. Jimmy peered up at Wade, puzzled, angry, a little scared. "Hey, c'mon, will you?"

Wade said nothing. His face was expressionless, but he was suddenly happy, feeling playful almost, unexpectedly released from the anger and grief that had weighed on him all morning. Even his toothache had eased back. Wade somehow knew that this nearly miraculous and strangely innocent feeling of release would last only as long as he could strike dumbly out, refusing to explain his blows, refusing to rationalize them, refusing even to connect them to anger, to particular offense given or taken: so he pulled his foot free of the nearly closed window and swung both of them hard against the glass.

Jimmy said, "Jesus Christ, Wade! You bust this glass, Gordon'll kick my ass too!" He rapidly rolled the window down again and slid away from the opening and Wade's swinging feet. From his position halfway across the passenger's seat, Jimmy reached over to the steering wheel and stretched to place his feet against the clutch and gas pedal, and he managed to shove the truck into low gear and got it to lurch unsteadily away from the grader. But as the truck moved away, Wade simply stepped up onto the roof of the cab, and now he stood atop the vehicle, legs spread, fists at his hips, banging his feet against the roof in a wild awkward dance.

Below him, Jimmy slid into proper place behind the wheel, and shifting it into second gear, got the truck quickly up to about twenty-five miles an hour and headed straight for the snowbank at the far end of the lot. Then he hit the brakes hard and had the pleasure of watching Wade, like some gigantic dark-blue bird of prey, sail past, over the hood of the truck, over the top of the plow and straight into the high pile of hard-packed snow.

As soon as Wade had landed, Jimmy cut the wheel hard to the left, dropped the truck back into first and pulled quickly out of the parking lot onto Route 29 toward town and commenced plowing the right lane in that direction, as nonchalantly and purposefully as he had plowed the other lane coming out.

After half a minute, Wade managed to extricate himself from the snowbank and stood covered with snow and hunched over in the middle of the lot, freezing, with chunks of snow inside his clothes, down his neck and back, up his sleeves and pants legs and inside his boots, gloves and hat.

Jimmy and the truck were out of sight now; the great unwieldy blue grader chortled at the other side of the lot. Wade reached down and picked up a hard-packed chunk of snow the size of his fist, and just as he was about to throw it—at the windshield of the grader, he supposed, although he hadn't actually decided on a target yet—he heard the sirens.

A few seconds later, two state police cruisers and a long white ambulance came speeding along Route 29 from the interstate, and as they passed Toby's Inn, Wade whirled with them, and he hurled the snowball, splattering it against the passenger-side window of the cruiser in front. The pair of cruisers and the ambulance kept going, however, as if Wade were not there.

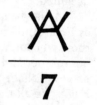

7

FOR YEARS IT WAS A FAMILIAR winter morning sight: people glanced out their living room windows or paused a second with an armload of firewood halfway from the wood-shed to the back porch and watched the big ugly machine chug slowly toward them. It tickled and mildly reassured folks to see Wade Whitehouse out plowing the town roads with LaRi-viere's blue grader.

You usually heard it before you saw it—a low grinding sound slapped rapidly by a hammer—and then you saw through the falling snow the dull waxy glow of the headlights like a hungry insect's eyes, and gradually the beast itself emerged from behind shuddering white waves, a tangle of thighbones and plates of steel with six huge black corrugated tires munching implacably along the road.

Stuck up inside the canvas cab like a telephone repairman perched on a pole, Wade hunkered over the steel steering wheel and shoved the gears and the blade-control levers back and forth, fitting the rigid unwieldy machine to the dips and bends and bone-rattling frost heaves in the old badly maintained roads that ran along the river and crisscrossed the valley and the surrounding hills.

The chilled meat of his body had quickly thickened with numbness; his feet against the metal pedals were soon as cold as ingots; his gloved hands were stiff as monkey wrenches. He knew nothing of what had happened up on Parker Mountain this morning, nothing of anything beyond the immediate range of his body's diminishing senses, and he stared out the plexiglass square at the white road before him, and he dreamed.

As far back as he could remember, certainly as far back as I can remember, Wade was called a dreamer, but only by those who knew him well and had known him for a long time—our mother and father, our sister and us three brothers, and his ex-wife Lillian too, and lately Margie Fogg, good old Margie Fogg. We all thought of Wade as a dreamer. Most people saw him as tense, quick, unpredictable and hot-tempered, and indeed he was all those things too. But since childhood, he seemed, when he was alone or imagined that he was alone, sometimes almost to let go of consciousness and float on waves of thought and feeling of his own making. They were not fantasies, exactly, for they had no narrative and little structure, and not memories or wishes, but warm streams of dumb contentment that flowed steadily through his mind and remained nonetheless safely outside of time, as if they had no source and no end.

A country boy and the third child in a taciturn family that left children early to their own devices, as if there were nothing coming in adult life worth preparing them for, Wade from infancy had found himself, often and for long periods of time, essentially alone. Whether in our mother's company in the warm food-smelling kitchen or at night in his crib with his older brothers in the unheated upstairs bedroom where all three boys slept, he was generally ignored, treated like a piece of inherited furniture that had no particular use or value but might turn out someday to be worth something. Before long, he began to be discovered suddenly underfoot, noticed one morning or early afternoon when his older brothers were in school by our mother on her way out of the kitchen—a small boy seated silently in a corner facing the wall open-eyed as if studying the pattern in the wallpaper, until she scooped him up and held him tightly and, smiling down into his small dark somber face, said, "Wade, honey, you are my dreamer."

He squirmed and hardened his body until it became difficult to hold, and when she put him down again, he ran out of the room ahead of her, letting the screened door slam behind him, and went in search of his brothers, standing by the side of the dirt road and waiting for the school bus to ease up to the house and let the two older boys out.

Behind him, our mother brushed aside the curtain and peered out the kitchen window at him and saw that once again the boy had the dreaming look on his face—impassive, enduring, unworried and unfocused. Our mother's name was Sally, and she was pregnant then with Lena, her fourth child, and I was not born yet. Sally was barely thirty years old, and her husband, Glenn, our father, was a turbulent man who drank heavily, and though Glenn loved Sally, he beat her from time to time and had beaten the boys—not Wade, of course, he was still too young, but the older boys, Elbourne and Charlie, who could be provoking at times, even she had to admit it, especially when Glenn came home late on a Friday night and had been drinking and was truculent, though of course there was no excuse for beating her or the boys, none whatsoever, so Glenn was always sorry afterwards.

Consequently, when Sally watched her third son dream, she chose to believe that it was a sign of his blessed contentment and felt relieved that at least someone in this poor and troubled family was a happy person, and for that reason she thought of him as her favorite child. She believed that he was not like his father and, because he was a boy, not like her, either. When she gave birth to a boy she could barely believe that it had come from her body. Her fourth child would be a daughter, Lena, in whom Sally would see herself recreated wholly, poor thing. That is what she called her, "poor thing." Then a year later, her fifth child would be born, a son they would name Rolfe, who Sally at first thought was like the first two, another chip off the old block, as Glenn said: and so for a few years he was—independent, troublesome, violent, male. Later, with excruciating difficulty, he would change, but no one in the family knew that, except possibly Wade.

The family lived from the start in an inherited house, Sally's uncle's place, a small run-down Cape farmhouse on 125 acres of rocky overgrown scrub four miles west of the center of Lawford on the north slope of Parker Mountain. Sally and

Glenn moved into the place right after they were married, ostensibly in order to take care of her sick and long-widowed childless uncle Elbourne, but in reality they moved in because they had no other place to live and Sally was already pregnant. By the time Glenn declared that the name of his firstborn son was going to be Elbourne, he had already talked the crippled increasingly senile old man into putting the house in his and Sally's name—in exchange for payment of three years' back taxes, Glenn explained, and for safety's sake. When, a year later, Uncle Elbourne died in his bed in the cold urine-smelling downstairs bedroom, Glenn and Sally Whitehouse were able to believe that they had made the old man's final days cheerful, a belief backed now by the name of their firstborn son and by their legal ownership of the house.

From such circumspect beginnings, then, did the ram-shackle old farm come eventually to be known as the White-house place, where we five Whitehouse kids were raised, where we argued and fought and suffered together and in our own gnarled fashion loved one another, the place that, finally, as soon as we were able, all five children fled—Elbourne and Charlie running to Vietnam, where they died, Lena to mar-riage with the Wonder Bread truck driver and obesity and charismatic Christianity and five squabbling children of her own, and I, Rolfe, whom the others regarded as the successful one, to the state university.

Wade, the dreamer, fled the Whitehouse place first for the young tenderhearted and beautiful Lillian Pittman; and a few years later, believing he was running from his marriage, he tried to follow his brothers and got sent to Korea instead; then he fled back to Lillian; and a few years after that, believing again that he was in flight from his marriage, he arrived at his trailer by Lake Minuit, Toby's Inn, Margie Fogg, his job with LaRiviere, his love of his daughter Jill.

Meanwhile, our father, Glenn Whitehouse, was forced to retire early, at sixty-three, when the Littleton Coats mill was sold, and he and our mother remained out there alone in the old Cape, which we children regarded with dark suspicion and rarely visited, especially not on holidays. The old couple grew slowly silent, passing whole long days and nights without say-ing a word to one another, Ma knitting afghans for Lena's children down in Revere and church bazaars here in town, Pop cutting and stacking wood for the winter, drinking steadily from midmorning until he fell asleep in his chair in front of the flickering eye of the television.

Usually, at three or four in the morning, the cold woke him with a start, and stumbling to the stove, he shoved a chunk of wood into it as if angry at the thing. He adjusted the damper, shut off the TV and shuffled to the kitchen, where in the dark he poured himself two fingers of Canadian Club and drank it down. Then he eased his brittle body to the bed that he still shared with his wife. He did not understand what had happened, why everyone, everyone except his wife, had gone away from him; and even she, who did understand what had happened, in her own way had long ago gone away from him too: and she lay next to him cold with rage, while he burned, burned.

But hadn't he always burned? Isn't that what people who knew him years ago said of him? That before he became a prematurely old man and drank only to stay drunk, Glenn Whitehouse had seemed even then to burn, and not just when he stumbled into bed, as now, and lay there awake till dawn— but all the time, day and night. He had been redheaded when younger, and red-faced, with eyes and lips like glowing coals, a man who went hatless and in his shirtsleeves when other men wrapped themselves in parkas. And when he drank, which was every few nights, even when Wade was a child and probably long before that, the man seemed to burst into flame. His normally dark low voice lifted and thinned, and suddenly his mouth filled to overflowing with words that tumbled past his large teeth into the cool night air of empty parking lots and the cabs of pickup trucks, spattering among hisses and steam and flashes of light, making his listeners laugh nervously and dance away and back again, fascinated and a little frightened. For despite his heat, Glenn Whitehouse, sober, in his manner and bearing was ordinarily a glum silent sort, a workingman who hated his job and whose cross impoverished family only served to remind him of his failings, a man who made friends with difficulty and kept them not at all.

In those early days, before he finally lost his ability to distinguish between being sober and drunk, while our father drank, and for as long as he kept on drinking, he became brilliantly and shamelessly incoherent. The danger, the violence, came late in the evening, when he stopped drinking, so that, while he was never one of those men who got into bar-room brawls and, when sober, he had not once raised a hand against his wife or children, his wife and his children nonetheless ran and hid from him when he first arrived home at night, especially on Friday nights, after he had been paid and had spent some of his pay at Toby's Inn or on a fifth of CC at the Littleton package store with the men riding back down from the mill to Lawford together. Ma and her children would come out of hiding only when one of the children had sneaked into the kitchen and had reported back that the old man was drinking again.

"It's okay," young Elbourne would say. "He's got his bottle out, and he's sitting at the table pretending to read the paper," he said, and he laughed.

Then one by one we drifted into the kitchen from the barn or the upstairs bedrooms to warm ourselves at the man's fire—Elbourne and Charlie, Wade and Lena, and Sally and even me, barely old enough to walk, seeking our father's heat.

As soon as he saw us, he began to speak. "Elbourne, my boyo! Elbourne, big boy! Get yourself over here by your dear old daddy and let's have a good look at you, eh? Big boy, what the hell have you been up to now, what the hell sort of trouble have you been getting yourself into? You love me, son? Does Big Boy love Daddy? Does he love his Pop? Sure he does.

"You probably don't know it, son, but I have ways of finding things out about you. You don't realize, you poor thing, but all your teachers, you see, all of them, oh yes, first they all see me in the store or down at Toby's or even up in Littleton, first they see me and then they come right out with it, Elbourne, my big boy bursting the seams of his jeans, so you must tell me yourself, you see, so I can go back to these funny folks, these teachers and preachers and so forth, and not seem quite so . . . quite so *ignorant,* yes, ignorant of my own child's puny adventures."

He spoke rapidly, not drawing a breath, it seemed, giving no one a chance to answer his questions or respond to his declarations. "I've got sons, goddammit, oh my God, have I got sons! I've got a hell of a bunch of sons, all of them going to be big men too, right, boys? Right, Elbourne? Charlie? Wade? Rolfe? You love me, boys? Do you love your daddy? Do you love your Pop? Of course you do. Sure you do.

"And what about you, daddy's girl? What about you? Where have you been all my life, eh? You love your daddy,

Lena? Come here, child. You love your Pop? Of course you do."

Lena came shyly toward him and let him lift her onto his lap, where she sat uncomfortably on his jumpy knees for a few seconds before wriggling back down as soon as the man had gone on to something else, usually his wife and our mother, whom he characterized as beautiful and wise and good. "Oh, Jesus, Sally, you are such a goddamned good person! I mean Good. Capital G. I truly mean it, the goddamned fucking truth! Sally, you are so much better than I am, I who am no good at all, you who are a good person, a truly good person, like a fucking saint. Beyond fucking com-pare. I'm sorry, excuse the language, but I mean it, and I'm sorry but there's no other way to say it, because you are so fucking good you don't even make me feel bad. You are. Which is about as good as anyone can be and still be human! And you are totally human, Sally. A woman human. Oh, Sally, Sally, Sally!"

Later on, after we smaller children, Lena and I, had been put to bed, Pop either ran out of whiskey or drank so much of it that when he stood, he nearly fell, and he permitted Ma to put him to bed in the downstairs bedroom in which old Uncle Elbourne had died and which, afterwards, they had painted and moved into themselves. The older boys and Wade, who was eleven now and stayed up as late as he wanted, watched television in the living room with Ma, who sat on the old greasy green sofa in her housecoat and slippers and ate homemade popcorn, while the boys sat on the floor and competed with one another's smartass comments on the television program.

Without turning around, they knew he was watching them from the doorway of the bedroom, and they went suddenly silent. All of them knew he was there and said nothing, Ma, Elbourne and Charlie, and even Wade. Although at that time Wade had never actually been hit by Pop, except of course for the usual spankings when he was little, he nonetheless had watched his older brothers being hit and heard Ma being hit late at night while the boys cowered in their beds and said not a word to one another until it was over, when they spoke rapidly of other things.

They went on watching the television show as if the man were not standing in the bedroom doorway behind them—it was *Gunsmoke*, with James Arness as Matt Dillon, a tall loose-limbed man whose big lantern-jawed face comforted Wade somehow, although it was like no face he knew personally. Even so, Wade let himself dream over that large kindly strong face, wishing not that his father looked like U.S. Marshal Matt Dillon but that his father knew such a man, that's all, had a friend whose good-natured strength would quiet him down and at the same time cheer him up a little, make his father less turbulent and unpredictable, less dangerous.

"Shut that goddamn thing off!" Pop said. He had a crumpled pack of Old Golds in his hand and was wearing only underwear, baggy dark-green boxer shorts and a tee shirt. Behind him, the bedroom was in darkness, and the man's small pale wiry body looked almost fragile in the dim light from the lamp on the low table next to the couch. He dropped his cigarettes, and when he bent down to pick them up, Wade saw the bald spot at the back of Pop's head, which he usually covered by combing his straight reddish hair from the left side all the way across to the right, and Wade decided that he liked looking at Pop this way. He would never have said it, he knew no one he could say such a strange thing to, but he thought at that moment that his father grabbing at the floor for a pack of cigarettes, knobby-kneed, all pointy elbows and shoulders, flat-chested and red-faced, with his one sign of vanity exposed, was cute-looking, a man you could not help liking, even when he was sour-faced and shouting at you.

Elbourne jumped to his feet from the floor beside the couch and snapped off the television set. "Okay, okay, for Christ's sake," he mumbled in a barely audible voice, and he headed for the stairs. Charlie silently followed.

"We'll keep it turned down," Ma said. She sat facing the fading gray image on the screen, one hand buried in the bowl of popcorn on her lap. "Wade," she said, "turn it back on. Just keep the sound low so your father can sleep."

Wade unlocked his crossed legs and got up and reached for the knob, and Pop said, "I said shut the fucking thing off. Shut. It. Off."

Wade thought for a second that Pop sounded like Marshal Dillon in Miss Kitty's bar daring a drunken gunfighter to reach for his gun. The boy held his hand still, six inches from the knob.

"Go ahead, it's all right," Ma said. "Just keep it low so your father can sleep." She drew several pieces of popcorn from the bowl and pushed them into her mouth and chewed slowly.

Pop took a step into the room and pulled a cigarette from the pack and placed it between his lips, and as he lit it, he said to Wade, "Go ahead, you little prick, don't do what your father tells you. Do what your mother tells you." He inhaled deeply and blew the smoke at his feet, as if he were now thinking of something else.

Wade moved his hand a few inches closer to the knob. Where were his brothers? Why had they given up so easily?

Ma, chewing on the popcorn, said to Wade, "Honey, turn on the show, will you?" Wade obeyed, and his mother turned around on the couch and said to his father, "Go on back to sleep, Glenn, we'll be—" when he passed her by quickly and reached out for the boy with both hands and shoved him hard, away from the television set and back against the couch. Wade let himself fall into a sitting position beside his mother; his father snapped the television off again.

"You little prick!" Pop yelled, his eyes narrowing, and he raised his fist over Wade's head.

"Don't!" Ma cried, and the fist came down.

There was no time to hide from the blow, no time to protect himself with his arms or even to turn away. Pop's huge fist descended and collided with the boy's cheekbone. Wade felt a terrible slow warmth wash thickly across his face, and then he felt nothing at all. He was lying on his side, his face slammed against the couch, which smelled like cigarette smoke and sour milk, when there came a second blow, this one low on his back, and he heard his mother shout, "Glenn! Stop!" His body was behind him somewhere and felt hot and soft and bright, as if it had burst into flame. There was nothing before his eyes but blackness, and he realized that he was burrowing his face into the couch, showing his father his backside as he dug with his paws like a terrified animal into the earth. He felt his father's rigid hands reach under his belly like claws and yank him back, flinging him to his feet, and when he opened his eyes he saw the man standing before him with his right hand cocked in a fist, his face twisted in disgust and resignation, as if he were performing a necessary but extremely unpleasant task for a boss.

"Glenn, stop!" Ma cried. "He didn't do anything." She was behind Pop, standing now but still holding the bowl of popcorn before her, as if she were his assistant and the bowl contained certain of his awful tools.

101

Pop held Wade with one hand by the front of his shirt, like Matt Dillon drawing a puny terrified punk up to his broad chest, and he took his left fist, swung it out to the side, opened it and brought it swiftly back, slapping the boy's face hard, as if with a board, then brought it back the other way, slapping him again and again, harder each time, although each time the boy felt it less, felt only the lava-like flow of heat that each blow left behind, until he thought he would explode from the heat, would blow up like a bomb, from the face outward.

At last the man stopped slapping him. He tossed the boy aside, onto the couch, like a bag of rags, and said, "You're just a little prick, remember that."

Wade looked up and saw that Pop was still smoking his cigarette. Ma had her hands on the man's shoulders and was steering him away from the couch, back toward the bedroom door, saying to him, "Just go on back to bed now, go on, go back to bed," she said. "You've done enough damage for one night. It's over. It's over."

"When I say do something, goddammit, I mean it," Pop said over his shoulder. His voice was high and thin, almost a whine. "I really mean it. When I say do something, I mean it."

"I know you do," she said. "I know."

Then the man was gone into the darkness of the bedroom, and the door was closed on him, and Ma was able to attend to her son's bleeding mouth and nose, his swelling cheeks. She reached toward him, to soothe and cool the heated flesh of his face, but he shoved her hands away, wildly, as if they were serpents, and backed wide-eyed from her to the stairs behind him, where he turned and saw his older brothers waiting for him, huddled in gloom on the stairs like gargoyles.

He moved slowly past the two, and a few minutes later, when he had undressed and climbed into his bed, they came along behind him. For a long time, our mother sat on the couch, listening to herself break apart inside, while everyone else in the house, even Wade, let pain be absorbed by sleep— cool gray, hard and dry as pumice stone, sleep.

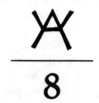

8

HOME MADE COOKING. Wade passed the sign and drew the grader carefully to the side of the road at the far end of Wickham's parking lot, where he shut off the engine, clambered down to the ground as if descending from a tree house and started to walk back toward the restaurant. The sign, custom made for Nick Wickham in pink neon by a bearded ponytailed glassblower over in White River Junction, bugged Wade.

Wade knew something was wrong with it, had said so to Nick the first time he saw it, but he had not been able to say what it was. It was only a few weeks before, early one morning stopping in for a cup of coffee before work, that he had first noticed the sign. Today, with the snowstorm, that morning seemed not weeks but an entire season ago, early autumn, with leaves flashing brass-flecked light in his eyes. He had driven his car into the lot and had seen Nick up on a stepladder attaching the new sign to the low roof of the restaurant.

"That don't look right," Wade had said. "It looks like it's spelled wrong or something."

Nick had glared down and said, "Fuck. Wade Whitehouse, it's people like you that keep this fucking town from prospering. You got a perpetual hair across your ass, pardon the expression. No matter what an individual does to improve things around here, you got to find fault with it."

"I'm not finding fault with it," Wade had said. "It's a goddamned good idea, putting up a neon sign and all. Good for you, good for the town. Looks real modern too, like those new restaurants they got down to Concord," he said. "Probably wasn't cheap, neither, was it?" he asked. "I mean, them hippie craftsmen, they can cost you an arm and a leg. You think you're getting a dish or something, you think you're getting something you can use, something of true value, you think. Only it turns out it's a goddamn work of art."

Nick got down to the ground and folded his ladder and stepped back a ways to admire his new sign. He smacked his lips, as if he had just eaten it. "This town," he said, "sucks."

Wade said, "Aw, c'mon, I was only just saying that there's something wrong with 'Home Made Cooking,' that's all. The sign's fine. The sign itself. It's just what it says that's wrong."

"How? Why? Tell me what the fuck's wrong with it. Jesus Christ. That thing cost me a hundred and fifty bucks."

"It don't matter," Wade said to Nick, and he clapped him on the shoulder. "It looks real . . . serious," he said. "It looks like you're in the goddamn restaurant business to stay. We're proud of you, Nick, we the citizens of Lawford, New Hampshire, we goddamn salute you, sir!" he said, and he reached to open the door. "Now I think I'll go in and have me some of that home made cooking you're advertising, if you don't mind."

Since that morning, every time Wade pulled into Wickham's parking lot—every time, in fact, that he passed the restaurant, whether he stopped in or not—he examined the neon sign and tried once again to figure out what was wrong with it. The sign made him nervous, embarrassed him slightly, as if it were a mirror in which he had caught a glimpse of himself with a silly grin on his face.

Nobody else seemed to find the sign peculiar or "wrong"; in fact, no one even spoke of it unless to compliment it. One evening Wade had leaned over the counter and asked Margie what she thought of Nick's new sign, asked her offhandedly, as if he himself held no opinion on the subject, and she had said, "Oh, well, the sign's terrific, I guess. But who needs it? Everybody who comes in here has been coming in here for years. They don't need a neon sign to tell them where it is or what's sold here. It's nice, though," she had said. "Better than what was there before."

"What was there before? I never saw anything there before."

She punched his arm and laughed. "That's the point." She patted his hand. "*Nothing* was there before," she said, and she reached across the counter and with both hands squeezed his cheeks. Hands: Margie Fogg had hands that went everywhere, all over you, faster than you could think about and before you could decide whether you wanted her to touch you or not. From back in the kitchen, Nick hollered for her to pick up her orders, for Christ's sake, before they froze, and she let go of Wade's cheeks and, rolling her eyes, slouched toward the kitchen in a parody of obedience.

Now Wade stood among the cars and pickup trucks in the snow-covered lot for a few seconds before going into the restaurant, and once again he studied the pink neon sign, pinker than usual in the falling snow, almost obscenely pink. Underwear pink, he thought, although he had never known a woman who wore pink underwear. Margie wore white cotton underpants and cream-colored bras. Lillian's underwear was beige or sometimes bronze-colored or dark gray. Taupe, she once told him. Who knew what color she wore now? Surely not Wade. Ho, ho, not he. But the sign was bubble-gum pink. Wade figured that hookers, probably, were the only women who wore bright-pink underpants—prostitutes, B-girls—and then he remembered one who had, a girl in Seoul, he even remembered her full name, Kim Chul Hee, and he quickly looked down from the Home Made Cooking sign and entered the restaurant.

Inside, clouds of cigarette smoke and intense chatter swirled from the booths along the wall, where men wearing luminous orange hunting vests and caps and plaid wool shirts were seated in groups of three and four. Coats, parkas and quilted jackets were strewn on chair backs and hooks around the room. A dozen or more men, their boots dripping puddles onto the floor, perched on stools with their elbows on the counter, smoking and talking intently, as if just before Wade entered something exciting had occurred here. Normally, the place was quiet as a tavern at this hour, no matter how many people were there.

Wade looked around the crowded room, his eyebrows

raised for a greeting, but no one seemed to notice him. Even Margie, standing at the booth at the far end with her empty tray propped against her outslung hip, did not notice him. She was listening to the conversation between the four young men seated before her: Chick Ward, whose purple Trans Am Wade had observed parked outside among the pickups and Wagoneers and Broncos like a fancy switchblade among sledgehammers; and two other guys, whom Wade did not recognize but who he assumed were from Littleton, where Chick often went to drive his car at night; and there was the kid Frankie LaCoy, who, like Chick, spent a lot of time up in Littleton, but for a different reason, because Littleton was where Frankie bought the grass he sold here in Lawford. All four were dressed for hunting and from the looks of their boots had been tramping through the woods since daybreak. There had not been any dead deer tied to the fenders of Chick's Trans Am out front—Wade had registered that on the way in—but why should there be? Chick was no hunter, except for women. You'd expect to see a couple of naked women trussed up and lashed to the fenders of the Trans Am, not white-tailed deer, right? That Chick Ward, he was obsessed.

Wade ambled over to the booth and laid one hand across Margie's broad shoulder and placed the other on Chick's. He liked sometimes to try doing with his hands what Margie seemed compelled to do with hers: it looked good when she did it; it made her seem connected to other people in a way that Wade envied.

Margie turned to him, and the four men ceased talking and looked up at him expectantly with sober expressions, even Frankie, who usually grinned and winked when he saw Wade, as if the two shared a delightful secret, which in a sense they did. Wade knew that Frankie was the only person who sold marijuana in Lawford, and Frankie knew that as long as he acted as if Wade did not know, Wade would let him alone.

This morning, however, Frankie looked up at Wade as if he wanted the older man to explain something to him, to unravel an irritating mystery. Chick Ward too. Chick usually ignored Wade, except to grunt hello and, suddenly flush-faced, scowling, to stare at his feet, like a guilty child, which Wade understood to be the result of an encounter they had had years ago, when Chick was still in high school and liked peeping through windows at middle-aged women getting ready for bed. The other two men, both bearded, with long dark hair spilling over their collars, did not know who Wade was, but even so, they peered up at him eagerly, as if he had brought them important news.

"Getcha deer yet?" Wade asked the group. He squeezed Margie's shoulder. There was something off, a beat or a note missing. People were not acting normal this morning, Wade thought, or else he was not seeing things right, as if he had a fever or were hung over or his toothache were distracting him. It was like watching a movie with the sound track out of sync. "Whaddaya say, boys?" he tried. "Some kinda snow."

He let go of Chick's shoulder, avoided his gaze and tapped a cigarette halfway loose of the pack and plucked it out with his lips. He squeezed Margie's shoulder a second time. There were mornings like this—infrequent, six or seven times a year, but frequent enough to trouble him—when, after having lost all memory of the final hour of the previous night at Toby's Inn, he strolled into Wickham's for coffee, and it was instantly clear to him that whatever he had said or done during that last hour of total darkness the night before, whatever it was that he could not remember, was known this morning to everyone in the place.

Margie said, "You okay?"

"Yeah, sure, why not?" Wade said. His heart was pounding, as if he were frightened, but he was not frightened, not yet. He was only a little confused. There was a slight, almost imperceptible break in the pattern of greeting, that was all. No big deal. Yet he was sweating, and he was smiling oddly, he knew, making remarks that did not quite add up, driving the pattern of greeting further and further off with every passing second. He could not stop himself. He felt the way he believed Frankie LaCoy felt all the time, which put him on a kind of defensive alert.

To no one in particular Wade said, "Good thing my kid went back down to Concord with her mother."

Frankie nodded in agreement and said, "Yeah." Then he said, "How's that?"

"The snow and all."

"Oh. Yeah."

Margie took a step back and looked into Wade's eyes, and he instantly turned away. Nick Wickham, wiping his hands on a towel, had come out of the kitchen and moved swiftly to refill several mugs of coffee for the men at the counter.

"Gimme a big one to go!" Wade called. Too loudly, he knew. "Cream, no sugar!" Wade suddenly wished that he had not stopped at the restaurant, that he had gone on plowing the road, alone, cold and content inside his dreams. Margie's concerned gaze and the slightly perplexed expression on Frankie's face and Chick's expectant look were all too uncomfortably familiar to him. Other people were in one world; he was in a second. And the distance between their worlds caused other people concern and perplexity and made them curious about him—for here he was alone in his world; and there they were gathered together in theirs.

He lit his cigarette and saw that his hands were trembling. Look at the bastards, shaking like little frozen dogs begging at the door to be let inside. Wade felt fragile, about to shatter. When he was sixteen he had felt this particular kind of fragility for the first time, and he had gone on rediscovering it, suddenly, with no apparent cause, ever since. One minute he was moving securely through time and space, in perfect coordination with other people; then, with no warning, he was out of step, was somehow removed from everyone else's sense of time and place, so that the slightest movement, word, facial expression or gesture contained enormous significance. The room filled with coded messages that he could not decode, and he slipped quickly into barely controlled hysteria.

Margie said, "Jill went home with her mother? I thought she was up for the weekend." Then she said, "Oh-h," and her hand reached out and touched his forearm. She put her tray down on the floor, leaning it against the side of the booth, and reached toward Wade as if to embrace him.

He stepped back and stared at a spot on her shoulder, as if she were his girlfriend Lillian Pittman and he were sixteen again, stopping her with his movement and the sudden rigidity of his face. He had told her about his father's beating him again, revealed it to her without planning or even wanting to, blurted out the information in the middle of a conversation about something else. "My father laid into me something wicked again last night," he said, and Lillian, sweet innocent Lillian, made that same move toward him, just like Margie, hands reaching out, her long narrow lovely face swarming, it seemed to him, with pity and bewilderment, and with perversely detached curiosity as well, for she knew nothing of violence then, and it seemed both the most horrible and the most inexplicable thing she could imagine. Entranced as much as repelled by what he had told her of it, she nonetheless knew nothing of the light and heat he felt when his father beat him, nothing of the profound clarity of feeling that emerged from the center of his chest when it happened, nothing of the exquisite joining of all his various parts that he experienced when his father swung the boy's lean body around and punched it and shoved it to the floor while his mother's face howled in the distance. He could in no way tell her of these things; he could barely know of them himself. All he could know was that he had left out of his account something that was crucial and filled him with shame, which is why he simultaneously moved toward her for solace and pushed her away.

"Just forget I said it," he murmured. "Just forget I said anything about it."

Margie let her arms drop to her sides. "About what?"

"You know. Jill."

She said, "C'mon, just a minute," and moving swiftly, slipped her arm around Wade's arm and turned him away from the booth toward the small pine-paneled back room where the video games and pinball machines were located, empty of players at this hour, shadowy and smelling of old cigarette smoke. Nick hollered, "Marge!" as she stepped through the door, and she shushed him with a wave.

Wade leaned against the Playboy machine, exhaled noisily and said, "Listen, Margie, I got to take care of business. Christ. I got to get . . ." He trailed off, and he spread his hands, as if in actuality he had nothing to do. Looming behind him was a brightly lit picture of Hugh Hefner in silk pajamas and bathrobe, pipe in smirking mouth, forelock dangling, and four naughtily unclad adolescent girls with provocative leers and outsized breasts like pink balloons slinging themselves around him. Wade shifted onto one elbow and seemed to study the picture. "Don't you shut these things off at night? Wastes a lot of electricity."

"Never mind that," she said. "Chick and Frankie and those boys were playing already this morning. Anyhow, I don't want to talk about that. And neither do you." She paused and placed her large hands on both his shoulders, as if blessing him. "What happened to Jill?" she asked.

"I got sick of arguing with her. Sent her home."

"Truth?"

"Yeah. Nothing happened. Nothing 'happened' to her." He suddenly pictured Jill crumpled on the highway, broken like a pumpkin under the flashing yellow light by the school, the car that hit her, a black BMW, racing away into darkness. "I'm . . . I'm going to start up one of those custody suits. I don't fucking give a shit," he said. "You know?" He was aware that his eyes were filling with tears, but he was not weeping: he was not sad.

"Don't be a horse's ass," she said. "You don't mean that."

"Yeah. Yeah, I do mean it."

"No, you don't. You're pissed, Wade, that's all. You ought to let yourself cool off from this one for a few days and then just sit down and for once have yourself a long talk with Lillian. Straight talk, I mean. You know? Work it out with her. Let her know honestly just how this kind of stuff makes you feel," she said. Then she added weakly, "Lillian's not out to get you, Wade. You know?"

"The hell she isn't. Lillian's been trying to nail me to a cross since the day I met her. Since fucking high school. No. I'm gonna hire me a fucking lawyer from Concord and get this thing, this divorce thing, rearranged. I am. I been thinking about it, a lot. I was too fucked up and all, when we got the divorce, so I just hid out and took whatever crumbs they were willing to toss me, her and that goddamned lawyer of hers." He held his nose with thumb and forefinger and yanked. "I didn't even have a regular divorce lawyer, that's how dumb and fucked up I was. I'm embarrassed to say it, but it's true. And now she can do any goddamned thing she wants, anything—move to Concord, get married. Move to fucking California, if she wants. Meanwhile, I still got to send her three hundred bucks a month child support or go directly to jail, do not pass go. Only, when it comes to actually being with my own kid, being a real father and all, I don't have a single say-so," he said. "It's like she *owns* Jill or something and only loans her out to me or something, and then only when she feels like it. And when she wants her back, she comes and gets her. Like last night. That's not right," he pronounced. "People aren't property. Nobody owns anybody, especially not kids. Right's right."

He stood up straight and drew Margie's hands off his shoulders and smiled. "Look, I got to get out of here. I got to get my coffee and climb back onto that goddamned grader.

Mr. Gordon LaRiviere's going to be royally pissed at me. Nick the Wick's probably pissed at you already."

"Nick the Wick," she said, smiling.

He looked directly into Margie's face. "That goddamned woman," he said. "Lillian thinks she and her goddamned husband can just drive up here and cart Jill off like that and leave me . . . leave me all alone like this. It's more than pissed, Margie. I'm a whole lot more than pissed. No shit. I been that plenty, and I know the difference. This is different." He spun around and headed for the door.

Margie shook her head sadly and followed him. As he approached the cash register at the end of the counter, Nick looked out from the kitchen and said, "Your coffee's by the register, Wade. What do you hear about Jack Hewitt and that guy he found? Who the fuck is the individual?" He called out, "Hey, Marge, for God's sake, honey, you got two orders sitting there getting cold!" Nick held a trio of white plates like playing cards in one hand and with the other rapidly shoveled pancakes off the griddle. "You hear anything more about that guy that shot himself? You talked to Jack?"

All along the counter, men looked up at Wade and waited for him to answer. Wade glanced beyond them and saw that most of the men in the booths were waiting too. "No. No, I mean, not since last night," he mumbled. "He took a guy named Twombley up to Parker Mountain early."

Nick handed the three plates of pancakes to Margie and came down the counter to Wade and rang up his coffee. "You heard, didn't you?" he said quietly.

"What?"

"About the fucking guy shooting himself." Nick pointed an index finger at one temple and pulled the trigger and said, "Bang. Least that's what it sounds like. Not on purpose, I mean. I assume accidental."

"Where . . . how'd you hear that?"

"CB. Little while ago. One of the boys on the way in, Chick, I think, picked up Jack on the CB calling for the state troopers. Jack told the staties he was up to Parker Mountain with a guy who shot himself, and wanted help. Couple of the boys started over from here to give him a hand, but the troopers were already all over the fucking place up there and sent them on back. I figured you'd know the whole story," he said. "I figured you'd know what really happened, I mean. The

111

fucking guy kill himself? This Twombley, who the fuck is he, anyhow?"

"No. I . . . I didn't know. I was . . . Jesus, where was I? I was out plowing—I been out in the grader all morning," Wade said. "And up the school before that," he quickly added. He felt vaguely guilty, as if he were somehow lying and were struggling to find an alibi, when all he was trying to do was answer the man's simple innocent question. He took a deep breath and tried again. "Twombley . . . Evan Twombley is summer people, from Massachusetts. He's got a place over on Lake Agaway. Friend of LaRiviere's or something, which is how Jack come to take him out hunting. For Gordon. It was his idea. Gordon's, I mean." Wade started for the door. "I shouldn't say any more about it. I was out plowing the whole time," he said, and he swung the door open and stepped into the blowing snow, where he paused for a second, as if to clear his head, turned and saw the pink neon sign on the low roof of the restaurant.

HOME MADE COOKING. It should be Home Cooking, Wade suddenly realized. Or Home Made Pies, or some damned thing. Stupid. He is stupid. She is stupid. We are all stupid.

9

WADE WANTED ONLY to get rid of the grader, shuck it, cast it away and never drive it again—huge lumbering ridiculous machine. It humiliated him. It was only a thing, but he despised it. It was inept, and slow. It belonged to LaRiviere, and driving it made Wade feel that he belonged to LaRiviere too, as if he were painted the same wimpy shade of blue and had that dumb motto on his back, OUR BUSINESS IS GOING IN THE HOLE!

He had an excuse to get off the machine now. Let LaRiviere find somebody else to finish the plowing; Wade had official business to attend to. Thanks to Twombley. The state troopers might turn away Chick and Frankie and their crummy friends from Littleton, but they would have to let him through. Let Wade through, he's okay. No matter if it *was* an accidental shooting, it still took place in his jurisdiction, and he was obliged to turn in a report to the Fish and Game Commission, so they would have to let him talk to Twombley, assuming Twombley could talk, and he would have to take statements from Jack and anyone else who happened to witness the shooting. Sonofabitch was probably half drunk or too hung over to handle his gun properly.

But as he climbed back up into the cab of the grader, Wade sighed. No, he would end up spending the whole damned day driving that damned grader. Gordon LaRiviere the well driller was also Gordon LaRiviere the chairman of the Board of Selectmen, who hired and fired the town cop. LaRiviere would tell Wade to make his goddamned investigation on his own time and turn in his report later. For now, until five o'clock this afternoon anyhow, Wade Whitehouse the snowplow driver belonged to Gordon LaRiviere the town road agent. Only then would he belong to the Board of Selectmen. And at no time would he belong to himself.

It was a quarter to eleven when Wade drew the grader off the road onto LaRiviere's parking lot. In the far corner near the shop, his own car sat huddled under a blanket of snow, and next to it was parked LaRiviere's pickup, a 4 × 4 Dodge with a roll bar and running lights like Jack's and a plow that LaRiviere made Wade repaint light blue after every major snowstorm, covering over the nicks in the paint made by stones and gravel scraped up while plowing.

LaRiviere was crazy. No other word for it, as far as Wade was concerned. He insisted on having everything he owned look simultaneously ready to use and never used. When LaRiviere drove out to inspect a well-drilling job, he paced around the site with his hands on his hips and his upper lip curled as if he had just spotted a pile of cat shit on the toe of his boot. Then he would stop the work and make Wade and Jack or whoever was drilling police the area, restack the pipe, lay the wrenches and tools down side by side in order of size. Only when the trucks, rigs, stock, tools and site had been arranged as if for sale in a showroom would he allow the men to go back to work.

Wade pulled the grader in next to the shop and shut off the motor and climbed stiffly down to the ground. The snow was falling lightly now, tiny hard particles that stung his face. He was cold, and it felt permanent. There was, he said to himself, no rational reason for a man to go on living in a climate like this when he did not have to. And Wade knew he did not have to. True, wherever he lived he would live just as badly, and true, in a perverse way he loved the town, but at least in some places he would be warm. He thought about it often, and usually he understood why he had not left Lawford and then left the state of New Hampshire and even left New England altogether. Sometimes, though, the only reason he had for not moving, even down to Concord, where Lillian had taken Jill, was that he no longer possessed the energy it would require. Perhaps he had never possessed it, even when he was young and freshly married, a high school kid, practically, or when he came back from Korea four years later and had a few bucks and was freshly married a second time. Lillian would have traipsed off with him, he knew, to Florida or Arizona, or maybe to one of those southeastern states like North Carolina. When he was in Korea he met men, Seabees, who told him that he could easily find a high-paying job using the same skills he had used drilling for water in northern New Hampshire drilling for oil instead in Texas or Oklahoma; if he had suggested that to Lillian—and had not kept the idea to himself, as if there were nowhere else on earth a man like him could find a job—she would have said, "How long do I have to pack?" And then everything would have been different. He thought the unaccustomed thing crossly: Oh, Lord, he was a fool! The others were stupid, maybe; but Wade was worse: he was a fool.

LaRiviere's not knowing about Twombley surprised him. When Wade told him what had occurred up on Parker Mountain, the little he knew, LaRiviere's normally red face went white, and the big man seemed to shrink inside his clothes.

"I figured you'd already heard," Wade mumbled. "Off the CB," he said, nodding toward the front office, where LaRiviere kept a small unit on the file cabinet next to Elaine Bernier's desk. "I thought you knew all about it."

"I hate that fucking squawk box!" LaRiviere said, glaring up at Wade from his chair. "I just use it to call out. What the fuck am I going to call Jack for, why would I call Jack this morning anyhow?" he snarled.

"They knew about it over to Wickham's, even."

"Forget that, for Christ's sake. What're you worrying me about that for? We got to get going, I got to get up there. Twombley. Jesus." He was puffing himself up now, enlarging his abnormally large body, for action, movement, control. His hair bristled like an angry dog's, and he rose from his chair and grabbed his blue down parka off the hook behind the door.

"C'mon, you drive; we'll take my truck. Put that fucking cigarette out, will you?" he said to Wade. He pushed past him and headed out the door.

Wade followed, flipping the key to the grader onto Elaine's desk. Outside, as they crossed the parking lot, he tossed his cigarette into a snowbank.

LaRiviere saw him and said, "Not there, for Christ's sake."

"Where, then?" Wade reached down and retrieved the still smoldering butt and held it out to LaRiviere as if offering it to him.

"Oh, Christ, Wade, how the hell do I know? Go inside, go use the fucking ashtray, but hurry the fuck up, I'm in a hurry. Jesus," he said, and he started trotting toward the pickup.

Wade ducked back into the office, rubbed the cigarette out in the large ashtray on the counter, directly under the No Smoking sign, and smiled uneasily at Elaine, who did not smile back. Elaine Bernier disliked Wade because she knew Gordon LaRiviere did not like Wade but needed him and thus was not free, as she was, to show his dislike. She considered her scowls and snide remarks a vital part of her job.

In the truck, Wade drove, while LaRiviere, grim and silent beside him, continued to puff himself up, tightening the last few creases in his broad flat face, swelling his chest and arms. Wade reached for the CB receiver and flicked it to the police channel as they sped north past Wickham's and passed out of town. They heard static and gibberish for a few seconds, then the gravelly voice of the dispatcher from Littleton telling car 12 to stay where it was, situation under control, ambulance already arrived.

"Fuck," LaRiviere said. "Turn it off."

Wade obeyed.

"All you heard was there was some kinda accident up there, right?"

"Yeah."

"That's all you heard?"

"Well, no," Wade said. "Twombley was shot. I heard that. Not Jack. He's okay."

"Fuck."

"No, Jack's okay. I assume."

"Fuck. You don't know how bad or anything?"

"You mean Twombley."

116

"Yes, Wade, I mean Twombley."

"No." Wade switched on the wipers. "I don't know how bad." The snow was spitting at them, but the sky had lightened to a creamy gray color. It would not last much longer.

"Fuck, fuck, fuck."

"He's probably okay. He more than likely just shot himself in the foot or something. That's what usually happens."

"I should have sent *you* out with him instead of Jack."

Wade was surprised. He glanced at LaRiviere, who was chewing his thumbnail. "Yeah, I wish you had," Wade said. "I'd rather be deer hunting instead of riding around freezing my ass on that fucking grader." He reached over and opened the ashtray in front of LaRiviere, who promptly deposited a sliver of thumbnail and went to work on the other one. Wade slid the ashtray closed.

"You ain't the hunter Jack is. And he can't drive the grader worth shit."

"Like hell," Wade said, although he knew LaRiviere was right on both counts. Jack hated the grader even more than Wade did and drove it with a careless anger that twice had got the thing turned onto its side in a ditch. And while Jack had not failed to kill a deer the opening day of every season since he was twelve, Wade had not taken a single shot at a deer in over a decade. For the last four years he had not bothered even to try. Not since Lillian and he split up the second time. Lots of things had gone out of him after that, among them the cheerful stubbornness that a man needed to keep on trudging into the woods with a gun year after year, despite the pattern of frustration and failure, in search of a flash of fur, a flag of a tail switching through the trees. Wade always made too much noise when he walked, as if warning the animals, a heavy-footed man with a body made more for carrying than for stalking, and he always figured the movement of animals wrongly, figuring them to move left instead of right, uphill instead of down, away instead of near: he would see the deer, look to where he thought it was going, and it would be gone. Then he would fire his gun at a stump four or five times, just to fire the damned thing, and scare every deer in hearing range deeper into hiding.

They passed the school, and Wade said, "You know that guy Mel Gordon, Twombley's son-in-law?"

"Yeah."

"Fucker almost ran me over this morning. Passed a stopped school bus."

"Big deal."

"I'd say so. I plan to nail the bastard."

LaRiviere shifted in his seat and studied Wade's profile for a second, then went back to working on his thumbnail. "Forget Mel Gordon," he said, reaching forward to open the ashtray. He slipped the sliver of fingernail in and closed it again, patting it once afterwards as if with approval.

"Like hell. I was standing there in front of the school, holding up traffic to let the buses in, you know, like I do, with kids crossing the road there and all, and this sonofabitch in his BMW gets impatient and cuts around the line and tear-asses right at me and then blows by like I'm not even there. Could've been a little kid crossing right then, for all he knew. Sonofabitch oughta lose his fucking license for something like that."

"So what are you gonna do, give him a lecture?"

"Shit, no. Summons him. Summons the bastard for a moving violation. I'd sure as hell call that a moving violation, wouldn't you?"

LaRiviere didn't answer. They had turned off Route 29 onto Parker Mountain Road, which was still unplowed, and were following in the tracks left by the half-dozen or so vehicles that had preceded them. Wade threw the truck into four-wheel drive, and the truck adhered to the rutted surface of the road as if magnetized by it. Drooping snow-covered pine trees whipped past. The remnants of ancient stone walls smoothed and softened by the snow drifted alongside the truck like loaves of new bread as it wound its way toward Saddleback Ridge, then out along the ridge and back and forth along the switchbacking road to the top of the mountain itself.

Both men were silent now, deep in their thoughts. Wade was replaying Mel Gordon's offense against his dignity and the law, but who knew what LaRiviere was thinking? When he is not fussing the world into neat little piles and squares and rows, you cannot know what is going through his mind. He is a man who plots and schemes, a secretive man with a bluff exterior who plans his moves way ahead of time and rarely makes one that he has not already made a hundred times in his imagination. He thinks of life more or less as a strict and, for

118

the winners, highly rewarding contest. In LaRiviere's world, you win and win big, or you lose and lose everything. Survival, mere survival, does not exist for him, except as a dismal loss, which is one of the several reasons he despised Wade. As far as LaRiviere was concerned, Wade merely survived, which meant that his life had no purpose other than to facilitate LaRiviere's. Either you are able to use people or they use you. Nothing in between. People who think they are in between and believe they are safe there are laughable. Like Wade.

They saw it before they heard it—all at once it loomed up in front of them, a huge white emergency vehicle with red lights flashing, and Wade wrenched the wheel hard to the right and drove the truck off the road into the shallow ditch, up onto the bank, and into a stone wall, where the plow clanged against the rocks and the truck stalled.

The ambulance flashed past without slowing and was gone. Snow filtered down from the trees like flour onto the windshield and broad hood of the truck. Wade said, "Sorry," and restarted the engine, shoved the truck into reverse and backed slowly onto the road.

"That must've been Twombley," LaRiviere said in a low almost reverential voice, as if he were in church. "Jesus. I bet that was Twombley." He sounded frightened and stared after the ambulance for a few seconds. "I hope you didn't ding the fucking plow," he said absently.

"You want me to follow them into Littleton, to the hospital?"

"No, not now. They probably won't let us see him right off."

"Probably."

"Let's get to the top and talk to Jack first," LaRiviere said, gathering himself together again. "Jack'll know what happened," he said. "He fucking better. Oh, if this could've been avoided, Wade, I'll put that kid's ass in a sling."

Wade started driving again, more cautiously this time, as if he expected a second ambulance to charge out of the snow and appear suddenly in front of them. He was puzzled by LaRiviere: what was Twombley to him anyhow, except a now-and-then business buddy? Wade, like most people in town, knew that LaRiviere had been buying and occasionally selling patches of real estate for years, on his own or in partnership with others, and no doubt Twombley had been one of his sometime partners in the purchase of pieces of land, over-grown hilly farmland, mostly, some of it with enough timber to harvest, but most of it nearly useless and apparently unprof-itable, except for where it adjoined a road, and a trailer park could be set up or a small house built on it and sold. Even so, despite any business connections they might have had, Twombley and LaRiviere were hardly what you would call asshole buddies. Besides, it was not like LaRiviere to show any feeling for another person, especially another man, unless it was anger or his usual impatience—except when he wanted something from the man, in which case he exuded charms more suited to a Moroccan rug bazaar than to the northern New Hampshire real estate market.

But this was not anger or impatience or phony affection he was expressing for Twombley; it was almost tenderness, protectiveness, concern. Wade liked it: he did not know why and maybe did not even know it was a fact, but he had loved crazy old Gordon LaRiviere since he was a kid, practically, when he first went to work for him right out of high school, and he always needed new reasons to explain his love of the man. LaRiviere's love of someone else, even a man like Evan Twombley, might be one.

They were silent the rest of the way. By the time they arrived at the top, where there were two cruisers drawn in neatly at the right side of the road opposite Jack's truck, it had stopped snowing altogether. Three troopers, one talking to Jack, a second with a German shepherd on a leash, the third with a Polaroid camera in his hand, stood at the front of Jack's truck, and a fourth trooper walked through the snow toward them from LaRiviere's cabin on the rise beyond.

To Wade, as he pulled in behind the cruisers, all the men looked oddly happy. They wore sly smiles on their faces, as if they had just won a bet with a fool. Jack had both fists placed against the hood of his truck and was shaking his head slowly back and forth, while two of the troopers, hands in pockets, watched and listened to the third talk to him. The talker glanced across the hood of the truck at Wade and LaRiviere as they came up to them, and went on talking.

"So I says to her, 'Lady, I don't give a shit if you're John F. Kennedy himself. I didn't vote for him when he was alive and I ain't voting for him now.' " The trooper was a tall wiry man in his late forties; his hair looked dyed with black shoe polish, and his high flat cheekbones gave his gray eyes a permanent squint. He had a low rumbling voice that stroked itself as he spoke. "Hello, Gordon," he said to LaRiviere. "Wade." Then he went on, " 'I clocked you at a hundred and five between Lincoln and Woodstock,' I says to her, and she reaches into this little leather bag she's got on the seat there and pulls out this fucking hundred-dollar bill, so I says to her, 'Ma'am, unless you're just trying to show me a picture of the late president, you better put that back, because up here bribing a police officer's a criminal offense.' "

Jack stood up straight and faced the man, smiling. "A hundred and five," he said. "That's wicked fast. What was she driving?" he asked. "Hey, Wade. Hello, Gordon," he added, casting a quick look their way.

"Maserati. One of those hundred-thousand-dollar wop cars you can't even get your feet into. Must be like driving in a condom."

Jack laughed and folded his arms over his chest and turned to face LaRiviere. "Well, Gordon," he said. Then, suddenly serious, he sighed. "You heard the news," he said.

"Some. I heard some. I heard Twombley got shot."

"He did," Jack said somberly, but almost as if he were merely announcing the man's departure, Wade thought. Though there was a slight note of regret in Jack's voice, it was as if Twombley had left early for lunch or a meeting in town before they had a chance to get their deer this morning. It was a serious event they were discussing: men from this region, when something disastrous happens and the thing must be spoken of, talk aslant and sometimes even joke in order to talk about it at all.

"Fuck," LaRiviere said. He exhaled loudly and looked off toward his cabin. "Fuck, fuck, fuck."

Wade reached down and patted the German shepherd on its wide head. "How you been?" he asked the tall black-haired trooper, a captain, Asa Brown, whom Wade had dealt with before. Wade did not particularly like Brown, and he was sure that Brown did not much like him, either. Actually, Wade thought Brown a dishonest braggart, and he believed that Brown thought Wade incompetent.

"Not bad, Wade. Not bad. Had me a run-in the other day with one of them Kennedy types. I was just telling Jack here.

Watch the dog, Wade. He takes a mind to, he'll tear your fucking hand off."

"Oh, he likes me," Wade said, but he withdrew his hand and shoved it into his coat pocket. "Doncha?"

Still regarding the view, LaRiviere said, "Twombley shot bad?"

"I'd say so," Jack said.

"Thirty-thirty at close range," Brown said.

"Jesus." LaRiviere whistled.

The men were silent for a few seconds. Then Wade said, "Will he make it?"

"Nope," Brown answered. "DOA. Dead on arrival."

The trooper with the dog, a burly blond kid in his early twenties wearing a pimply shaving rash on his throat like a pink ruff, said to Brown, "You want me to head on back now?"

"Yeah, might's well. Get started on the paperwork. I got to talk to the next of kin, I suppose."

LaRiviere looked at Jack. "You see it?"

"Nope. Heard it, though. We wasn't very far apart. I'd spotted this big buck, and then I heard the gun go off and turned around, and Twombley was gone. Disappeared. Then I looked over the little cliff we was using for a stand, and there the fucker was, deader'n shit."

"Blew the poor bastard wide open," Brown said. "Thirty-thirty. Soft-nosed bullets. He had a bigger hole in back than in front, hole you could put your head in. And he had a pretty big hole in the front too. You could've put your fist in that one."

"Well," LaRiviere said. "Well." He paused. "Think the snow's done?"

"Looks like it to me," Brown said, and he peered up at the creamy sky. "For today."

Jack looked straight ahead and at no one in particular. "It's a real early winter," he offered.

Wade said nothing. He was staring into Jack's impassive face, catching glimpses of light in the darkness there, flashes and glints of heated metal whirling in a blackened pit. The bits of light that he saw, the heat that he felt, he had never seen or felt in Jack before, and they surprised Wade. He had known the tall angular youth since the boy first showed promise as an athlete in grade school, that one summer Wade coached the Lawford Pony League team and, thanks to Jack, they went all the way to the state semifinals down in Manchester.

The trooper with the dog and his partner with the camera crossed the road and got into the lead cruiser, turned it around carefully and headed back down the mountain. The third trooper stood at ease a short ways behind Brown, as if awaiting further orders.

LaRiviere looked at his watch and said, "Well, shit. This's gonna be one fucking mess to clean up. Twombley's son-in-law and I suppose his daughter are up for the weekend. Didn't you say you seen him already this morning, Wade?"

"Yeah. I did. I seen them."

"You know where they're staying?" Brown asked LaRiviere.

"The family's got a place on the lake, out on the point on Agaway. Nice place. They come up summers and during the winter on weekends for skiing. You know, they go to Waterville mainly, and over to Franconia and Loon, for skiing. Nice place. Sauna, hot tub, the works. Cost a fucking penny, I'll tell you. Fellow from Concord built it for him. I dug the wells."

"*I* dug the wells," Wade said. "Over three hundred feet apiece, fourteen gallons a minute each."

LaRiviere stared at Wade with obvious irritation and opened his mouth to speak, then closed it.

"You know the place?" Brown asked the trooper behind him, ignoring Wade.

"I don't think so."

"No, I don't think you do, either," Brown said. "You want to talk to them, Gordon?" he asked. "Tell them about the old man's tragic demise? You know them. You knew the old man."

"Sure. What the fuck. My day's already ruined," he said. "Gimme the keys," he said to Wade. "You can go back with Jack."

Wade said okay and handed over the keys. Then he said, "I'm still going to give that bastard a summons, you know."

LaRiviere looked at him hard and was silent. His stare said, What the hell are you telling me now, you dumb stubborn bastard?

"I mean, it's too bad about Twombley and all, but shit, right's right," Wade said. He turned to Jack. "The fucking son-in-law, whatzizname, Mel Gordon, practically ran me over this morning, passed a stopped school bus and everything. In front of the school. He's goddamned lucky he didn't kill somebody's kid."

Jack didn't respond. He seemed to see straight through Wade to the snowy woods beyond.

Brown smiled his thin smile, like a garter snake. "I didn't know you was such a hardass, Wade," he said. "Give the guy a break. If you want, I'll tell him that by the way the local sheriff's pissed off, but because of the circumstances and all, he's letting this one go."

"I'm not a sheriff, Asa."

"I know."

LaRiviere said, "You still got a shitload of plowing to do, Wade."

"It ain't done, if that's what you mean."

For a few seconds everyone was silent. "Something bugging you, Wade?" LaRiviere said.

"A few things. Yeah."

"A few things. Well, right now we're not too interested. And as for a few things, there's a few things need taking care of first. Then you can be bugged all you want. On your own time, though, not mine."

LaRiviere wheeled and started across the road toward his truck. Brown and the other trooper followed, heading for the cruiser.

When LaRiviere had got his truck turned around, he drew it up next to Wade; he reached across the seat and cranked down the window. "I expect I'll see the grader gone by the time I get back to the shop, Wade. And for Christ's sake, forget giving a fucking ticket to Mel Gordon. His father-in-law's just killed himself. Use your fucking head," he said.

Wade said nothing.

In a low almost whispered voice, Jack asked, "You want me to do anything in particular at the shop?"

LaRiviere hesitated a second, then said, "You might's well take the rest of the day off. You look sort of fucked up to me. Which I can understand. You've already been paid for the day anyhow, right?"

"Well, not exactly. I mean, he never paid me."

"You'll get your money," LaRiviere said. "I'll see you get your money. Go on home. Get drunk or something. Start over tomorrow," he said. "And don't talk to any newspapers about this," he added. "Twombley's a big deal down in Massachusetts, you know."

"What'll I say?"

"Just tell them the truth, for Christ's sake, it was an accident. But forget the details. Tell them they should talk to the state police about it, if they want details. Tell them if they want details your lawyer says you shouldn't comment."

"My lawyer? I don't need no lawyer, do I?"

"No. No, of course not. Just say it, that's all." Then he rolled up the window and drove off, with the cruiser following close behind.

The two vehicles disappeared, and it was suddenly silent, except for a light wind sifting through the pines, the ragged call of a crow in the distance, the squeak of Wade's boots in the snow as he shifted his weight. He lit a cigarette and offered Jack one.

"I got my own," Jack said. He rummaged in his shirt pocket for his pack, got it out and took a light from Wade's yellow Bic.

"Did you smoke when you was playing ball?" Wade said. "Why's that?"

"I dunno. Just asking. I keep thinking about quitting."

"Yeah. I smoked since I was a kid. Sure I did."

"No shit? Even in school you smoked? I don't remember you smoking till you come back from New Britain."

"Sure. Coach never knew it. They had a rule. Not in the pros, of course, but in school."

"Even in Pony League? You were smoking then?"

"Yeah."

"Shit. You was only—what?—twelve then."

"I started when I was eleven."

"No shit. I never knew that. I was coaching Pony League then, remember? I didn't have no rules about it, but I didn't think I needed them."

Jack smiled slyly. "Sure, I remember." Then he laughed. "You were a shitty coach, Wade. Pretty good left fielder, but a shitty coach. You oughta play some Legion ball next summer."

"I know it."

They were silent and both looked toward LaRiviere's cabin in the pine grove on the rise beyond the snow-covered muskeg—the tall angular young man in the orange hunting vest and quilted jacket and the shorter man in the dark-blue trooper's jacket and watch cap, both men with hands stuck in pockets, cigarettes in mouths, eyes squinted against the bright light reflected off the snow. They looked like cousins or a younger and an older brother, blood relations separated by two decades, one man favoring the mother, the other favoring the father, two very different men connected by thin but unbreakable ties to a common past. They stood free of the truck and seemed to be waiting for someone to emerge from the cabin, a person bringing them important news—of a birth or a death or the arrival of the absolute truth.

Without looking at Jack, Wade said, "Where'd Twombley get shot?"

"In the chest."

"No, I mean whereabouts."

Jack pointed to his left, downhill through the scrub. "About a half mile in, along the old lumber road, down there where it looks out over the lake."

"You bring him up yourself? That's a steep climb."

"No, no. The ambulance guys, they lugged him up."

"He was dead right away?"

"Yeah. Sure." Jack turned to him and smiled. "What're you doing, playing cop?"

"No. I got to make a report to Fish and Game, of course, but I was just wondering, that's all. What'd he do, to shoot himself, I mean."

"I don't know. Fuck, I was watching a fat old buck with a rack like a fucking elk or something stroll past. I guess Twombley slipped on the snow or something, fell over a rock. Who the fuck knows? It's rough ground down there, and he wasn't used to the woods. With the snow and all, he could slip easy. Who knows? I just heard the gun go off. Bang! Like that, and he was gone, blown away." Jack flipped his cigarette butt into the snow a few yards in front of him.

The light breeze had shifted and was blowing into their faces. Now there was a pair of crows calling to each other, and Wade could see one of them, glossy purple-black and nervous, perched near the top of a red pine to the left of LaRiviere's cabin.

Wade said, "I've never seen a man shot and killed before. Not even in the service. It must be something. I saw plenty who'd already been shot, you know, shot dead or wounded, all fucked up in all kinds of ways. When I was an MP, mostly. Same as when I come back here. Even here I've seen a couple guys after they'd already been shot, but I never actually *saw* it. You know? It must be something, to see a man shoot himself."

"Well . . . I didn't actually *see* him do it. Like I said."

"Sure you did."

"What?"

"Saw him do it." Wade studied the crow as it leapt from branch to branch of the scraggly red pine. "Of course you did." Wade put himself behind Jack's eyes and turned from the sight of the huge buck in the draw below to look along the ridge at Evan Twombley twenty feet away, just to make sure, like a good guide, that Twombley could see the buck, too, and was ready to shoot it; he saw Twombley take a tentative step toward the edge of the drop-off, saw him flip off the safety of his .30/30 with his thumb; he saw him slip on a small rock or stick hidden under the snow, toss one hand, the hand with the gun in it, damn it, out to break his fall, twisting the rifle as he went down, his fingers somehow tangled around the trigger guard or even brushing the trigger as he tried both to keep himself from falling and to protect the rifle, and before he hit the ground, the gun went off, and the force of the bullet exploding into his chest sent him flying into the air backward and down into the draw—a rich and powerful fat man blown clean off the earth.

"What the fuck are you telling me, Wade? I never seen the guy get shot. I told you that."

Wade watched again as Twombley caught sight of the deer below, stumbled and turned his back in the direction of his fall; this time he fell with both hands shoving the fancy new rifle away from his chest, to keep it from being damaged or covered with snow, turning it somehow so that the tip of the barrel passed over his chest—when it fired straight into his chest, smashing his lungs and heart and backbone, splashing blood and bits of flesh over the snow and sending the body of the man tumbling this time, like a broken dummy, like trash, into the gully below.

"You must've seen him get shot," Wade said in a low voice. "I know you did."

"Let's get the fuck out of here," Jack said. "You're not making sense, man. This whole thing has got me rattled anyhow." He passed in front of Wade and climbed into the truck, slammed the door as if angry and started the engine.

Wade watched Twombley die a third time.

First, from behind Jack's eyes, he saw the huge buck

emerge from its hiding place in the birch copse at the left side of the draw and walk slowly along the draw directly into his and Evan Twombley's line of sight. Now Twombley could see the animal too, and suddenly excited, he patted the younger man on the shoulder, demanding, with gestures, his rifle back, for he had been unable to walk through the snow with it and had already dropped it once, and finally he had made his guide carry it for him. Wade brought the tip of the barrel up, shoved the stock against his right shoulder, aimed through the scope so that the bullet would hit the meat of the right shoulder from above, pass through the chest and exit from the left side of the animal's belly, killing it instantly and very cleanly with one shot. Twombley, mad with greed for the shot and the sudden knowledge that he was not going to get it, that his guide was taking it himself, grabbed the rifle with both hands and tried to tear it free, and the tip of the barrel swung around, and the gun went off. Twombley was tossed backward and over the precipice, his already dead body tumbling over the rocks and snow to the bottom, where it lay with its legs and arms splayed, as if it had been hurled from the sky, gushing blood into the snow. The echo of the gunshot died, and then the sounds of the huge buck leaping through the dense tangle of brush farther down drifted back, the clatter and crash of flight growing fainter and fainter, until the woods were silent again, except for the sigh of the wind through the trees and the mocking call of a crow somewhere above and behind, up by LaRiviere's cabin and the road.

Wade was startled by the blat of Jack's horn from the truck. He had already turned the vehicle around and was waving angrily for Wade to get in.

Slowly, Wade walked over to the truck and climbed up into the passenger's seat. He pointed at the three rifles in the rack attached to the window behind him. "Those're yours, right?"

"Yeah."

"One of them must be Twombley's, though."

Jack didn't answer.

"That there's your old twenty-gauge," Wade went on, laying his hand on the shotgun, "and that there's the new Browning you was showing off last night at the town hall." Then he placed his hand on the barrel of the third gun and held it tightly, as if he had captured it. "This must be Twombley's gun. Brand-new, almost. Very fancy tooling," he murmured. "Thirty-thirty, and only been fired one time," he said. "It's a beautiful piece of work, Twombley's gun. But what the hell, Jack, I guess you deserve it. Right's right."

Jack said, "Yeah, right's right," and started to drive slowly downhill, following in the tracks left by the police cruisers and LaRiviere's truck and before them the ambulance carrying Twombley's body to Littleton.

"Twombley sure as hell won't be shooting it again, will he?" Wade said.

"No," Jack said. "He sure as hell won't."

10

LATE THAT SAME NIGHT, Wade telephoned me to ask if the Boston TV stations had reported Evan Twombley's death. Yes, I told him, they had, but I had barely noticed: the death by gunshot of someone about to testify about union connections to organized crime, even though disguised as a New Hampshire hunting accident, was a common enough news item and was sufficiently distant from my daily life not to attract my attention.

"There was something," I said, "but I missed it. Why, did it happen up your way?"

"Yeah, and I know the guy. And the kid with him, Jack Hewitt. Who you probably know too, incidentally. He works for LaRiviere with me. That kid, he's my best friend, Rolfe," Wade said.

It was close to midnight, and Wade sounded slightly drunk, calling me, I imagined, from the phone booth at Toby's Inn, although I could not hear the jukebox thumping as usual in the background. I was in bed reading a new history of mankind, and this was not a conversation I found enthralling.

I had heard from Wade a half-dozen times that fall, and

I had seen him twice; both times he had driven down suddenly on a Saturday night. He had stood around in my kitchen drinking beer, rambling on about Lillian and Jill and LaRiviere—his problems—then had fallen like a tree onto my couch, only to return to Lawford the next morning after breakfast. I was sure, as we talked about Twombley, that I knew Wade's whole story by now, the way you do when you have heard a drunk man's story, even your drunken brother's—perhaps especially your drunken brother's—and did not require any new chapters.

"Wade," I said, "it's very late. Not for you, maybe, but we have different habits, you and I. You're at Toby's, and I'm in bed reading."

"No, no, no. Not tonight. I'm at home tonight, Rolfe. I'm not reading, maybe, but in fact I'm in bed too. Anyhow, I'm calling because I need you to listen. You're supposed to be such a smart guy, Rolfe. I've got a theory about this guy Twombley, and I need you to check me out on it." He was excited, more than usual, and that alarmed me, although I was not sure why, so I did not cut him off. I half listened to what he called his theory, which struck me as slightly crackbrained, the alcohol talking. It was a theory unsupported by evidence and full of unlikely motives and connections. It also did not take into account—since Wade had not seen the Boston news, and the New Hampshire stations had not mentioned the shooting at all (it being only one of so many hunting accidents that day)—the fact that Evan Twombley had been scheduled to testify before a congressional subcommittee that was investigating links between organized crime in New England and the construction industry. I remembered that much from the news and had my own theory.

I mentioned the investigation to him anyhow, and he said, "No shit," and went on as if I had offered nothing more than Twombley's middle name. For Wade, there was no connection, because he seemed to want badly to believe that his "best friend" had shot Evan Twombley—accidentally, of course—and was hiding the fact, which, he insisted, was what worried him. "What'll happen is, it'll come out that the bastard didn't shoot himself, Jack shot him. And then lied about it. And the kid'll get hung for it, Rolfe. They hang you up here for murder, you know."

"He won't hang if it was accidental," I said. "But you do think Jack Hewitt shot him, eh? Why?"

"Why do I think it, or why did he shoot him?"

"Both."

"Well, it was an accident," he said. "Naturally. But who knows how it happened? It happens all the time, though. You play with guns, somebody's going to get shot. Eventually. But as to why I myself think Jack did it. That's not so easy to say. It's like it's the only way I can see it happening. The only way I can imagine it. I think about Twombley getting shot, and all I see is Jack shooting him."

"So where's this theory of yours?"

He admitted that it was not so much a theory as a hunch. I could tell that I was disappointing him. Again.

I apologized for sounding so skeptical and explained that it seemed likely to me that if Twombley's death was not in fact self-inflicted, then he surely was killed by someone other than the local boy Jack Hewitt, who probably never even saw it happen anyhow. "They were out deer hunting, right? In the woods. Jack probably heard the gun go off, then came back and found Twombley's body and concluded the obvious, that the man had shot himself. And if he did not shoot himself, then whoever did it took care to use Twombley's own gun. Just in case."

Yes, yes, Wade agreed, grumpily, and then he started to drift a bit, and soon he was recounting another small humiliation at the hands of his ex-wife. This story, too, I had heard before, or a close version of it, but now, to my surprise, I was listening as if it were fresh and new to me. It was his account of Halloween and his quarrel with his daughter Jill, and I was fascinated by it. There was some odd connection in my mind between the two stories, between his version of Twombley's death and his version of Lillian's driving up to Lawford and removing Jill from his care. I did not then know how powerful the connection was, of course, but it was there, to be sure, just below the surface of the narrative, and I felt its presence strongly and responded to it, as if it had the power of logic.

I closed my history of mankind and sat up straight in bed and listened closely to Wade, while he slowly told of his adventures of the night before, presented them with a sad mournful slightly puzzled voice, his sentences ending pathetically with phrases like "You know?" and "I guess."

And then, finally, he closed the conversation—it was more monologue than conversation—by telling me how tired he

132

was, just exhausted, beat. "I get to feeling like a whipped dog some days, Rolfe," he said. "And some night I'm going to bite back. I swear it."

I said, "Haven't you already done a bit of that?"

"No. No, I haven't. Not really. I've growled a little, but I haven't bit."

We said good night then and hung up. I tried to resume reading but could not, and when I tried to sleep, I could not do that, either. I lay awake for hours, it seemed, with visions of whirling suddenly in the snow, aiming down the barrel of a gun, firing.

But let us return to the morning Twombley died, to Lawford, twelve or fifteen hours earlier. After Wade and Jack rode down from Parker Mountain together in Jack's truck, Jack dropped Wade off at LaRiviere's and, as LaRiviere had suggested, went home, while for the rest of the day Wade drove the blue grader. By the time he parked it back at LaRiviere's garage, it was late afternoon and dark, and the temperature was falling toward zero again.

He scraped his windshield and then, while he waited for his car to warm up, decided that it would be best for everyone, especially for Wade himself, if he drove straight home, if he cleaned up his trailer, for God's sake, and cooked a simple supper and went to bed sober and alone. He was right: his mood and his afflicted view of the events of the day promised nothing but trouble for anyone who happened to join him at bar, table or bed.

Then, as if to verify the wisdom of his decision, his tooth flared up again. Over the afternoon, it had gradually turned into a throbbing knot of pain below his right ear. As usual, the pain got worse and spread quickly across his face, until its center was as large and as definable a shape as a man's hand, with the heel and thumb of the hand running along his jaw-bone to his chin, the little finger tucked up behind his ear, the palm smack against his cheek and the other three fingers pressing against the bony ridge that encircled his right eye. The pain was yellow, it seemed to him, neither hot nor cold, and lay in a thin zone between his outer flesh and the bone, radiating woe in both directions.

He groaned aloud all the way home.

The place looked even worse to him now than it had when he left that morning—a midden heap, as if a motorcycle gang had been camped here all fall.

He shucked his coat and set to work, bagging all the trash and garbage, old newspapers, *TV Guides,* beer cans and bottles, food containers, empty cigarette packs, crusts of bread, tin cans, apple cores and milk cartons. He moved all the caked and crusted dishes, pots and pans in the general direction of the kitchen sink and all the dirty clothes to the hamper in the bathroom, where he paused for a second, shuddered at the sight, ran the faucets briefly and dumped a layer of Comet into the tub, toilet and lavatory, to be scrubbed later, after he finished cleaning the kitchen.

In his shirtsleeves, he lugged two large green plastic bags outside and shoved them into the barrel at the end of the driveway. Un-fucking-believable, that a grown man could let things get this bad! The cold air made the toothache shriek, so he raced back inside, where it lapsed swiftly back to a steady low-key whine, which distressed him, but at least the pain was steady and he could make mental adjustments to it that did not have to be undone and remade every fifteen or twenty seconds.

It was not long before he had the kitchen clean—dishes washed and dried and put away, counters wiped down, moldy and decomposing food removed from the refrigerator and tossed out, floor mopped. And then he was off to the bathroom, scrub-a-dub-dub, and to the bedroom, where he hauled from the closet the portable Hoover he had picked up the previous spring at a flea market down in Catamount, his first vacuum cleaner, and even though it seemed to suck dirt weakly, as if through a single bent straw, he was proud of owning it and enjoyed using it—a good thing, too, as it took him nearly an hour to vacuum the entire trailer.

At last, his home was clean. It smelled like water and soap, looked symmetrical and square, felt smooth, cool and dry to fingertips brushed along the kitchen counters. His tooth went on aching, but the privacy it gave, the way the pain walled him in, somehow comforted him, and although several times he thought of aspirin—Why not, for Christ's sake, Wade, do yourself a favor and take a couple aspirins, maybe even pack a second pair between your cheek and gum—he quickly dismissed the thought, as if ending his toothache, or even easing it somewhat, would expose him to a flurry of faces, voices and questions that he preferred not to meet right now. Or ever, for that matter. Although he did not like to think of the toothache's lasting forever.

In the refrigerator there were three bottles of Rolling Rock and no other beverage. He had thrown out the curdled milk, and the orange juice had soured. He thought: if he drank all three beers, he would still be going to bed sober tonight. Good: he would drink all three: if there had been six or eight, he would have been forced to drink tap water. He cracked open one of the beers, took a long pull from it and poked through the permafrost of the freezer compartment, disinterring a package of baby lima beans and a chicken breast shrouded in several layers of Saran Wrap. Then he started a pan of rice, dropped the Baggie of baby limas into a saucepan of boiling water and melted a chunk of butter in a skillet. He held the chicken breast under warm running water to get it unwrapped and tossed it into the skillet. The food smelled good: domestic, orderly and constant—a warm bright spot in the middle of the cold dark forest.

By the time he sat down at the table to eat, it was after ten. He chewed slowly, carefully, with his left and front teeth only, and managed to avoid antagonizing the rotted tooth, which growled quietly in the right corner of his mouth's cage.

The table, a card table, actually, with four folding chairs placed around it, was situated in the middle of the kitchen. While he ate his solitary meal, he looked down the length of the trailer and admired the place. Before sitting down, he had turned off all the overhead lights in the trailer—overhead lights always made Wade feel he was still at work in LaRiviere's shop—and now to all appearances he was at home and there could have been two or even three moderate adults just out of sight in the living room having a quiet reasonable conversation about money, and in the near bedroom, his own, there could have been another such adult, reading in bed, maybe, the way his brother Rolfe liked to end his day, while in the farther bedroom a child did her homework. The bathroom door was ajar and the light was on, as if a woman who had just finished brushing her hair were touching up her lipstick before going out.

There was nothing wrong with this place that a little tender loving care could not fix, he thought, and he nibbled his lima beans with his incisors, like a rodent.

He got up and went for another beer, lit a cigarette and walked back to his bedroom and turned on the radio. He moved the tuner up and down a few times until he found the easy-listening station in Littleton: Carly Simon was singing about a man who really knew how to make love good, so good that nobody did it better.

Jesus, that woman knows things, Wade thought, and he strolled back to the table and sat down again. Then he saw that he was smoking without having finished his meal yet and hurriedly rubbed the butt out in the ashtray. He resumed eating and thought, Whoa. This man's got to start thinking seriously about quitting cigarettes. Maybe this spring, after things settle down. The chicken was a little tough and dry, but it tasted fine to him, and as long as he cut it into tiny pieces and kept it on the left side of his mouth, he did not have any trouble chewing it.

Wade welcomed evenings like this; they were rare, and he almost credited it to the toothache. As if locked inside deep meditation, he was profoundly alone. His conscious mind, walled around by physical pain and the trailer and the snow and darkness beyond, was cleared of everything but the filmy shreds of a few simple fantasies, and though it was a long ways from happiness, it seemed as close to happiness as he had been able to get in weeks. Maybe longer. But he did not want to think about that right now; so he didn't.

When he had finished eating, he cleaned his dishes, dried them and put them away, and while standing by the sink, looked past his reflection in the window at the darkness outside and smoked a cigarette all the way down and drank off the third bottle of beer. He turned the thermostat back to sixty and went into his bedroom, shutting off the lights one by one behind him. He undressed and draped his clothes neatly over the back of the chair, got into bed and switched off the radio and the bedside light.

It was at this point in his evening, in bed, his home cleaned, a dinner cooked and eaten, relaxed and content and physically comfortable—relatively little toothache pain—that he suddenly sat up straight in the darkness and clapped his hands loudly against one another, as if applauding his own performance. He turned the light back on and picked up the telephone and dialed his brother Rolfe's number. Rolfe would understand, and he might have some useful information as well. Rolfe was a little weird, but he was plenty smart, and he was logical.

But, as we know, Wade's conversation with his younger brother did not go quite as he hoped. Two or three minutes into it, Wade was once again going on about Lillian and Jill, the kind of story that always left him angry and exhausted. And his tooth was raging again. He finally hung up the phone and snapped off the bedside light.

In seconds, he was asleep and dreaming.

Hours later, Wade dreamed this: There is a baby in his arms, swaddled like Jesus, only it is not Jesus, it is a girl baby, but not Jill, either, thank God, because it is blue with the cold, and it may be dead. *Oh no, do not let it be dead!* he pleads, and he examines the tiny puckered face and discovers first with relief and then with irritation that it is a doll, one of those lifelike dolls, with its face all screwed up as if about to cry, and as Wade comes up from under the water to the hole in the ice, he breaks the surface and thrusts the doll out ahead of him and throws the thing right at his Pop, who is fooled and thinks it is a real baby; Pop sticks out his drunken hands to catch it, his pale eyes wide open with fear that he will drop it, but by the time Wade has climbed out of the freezing water to stand dripping in his underwear on the ice, Pop has discovered that it is only a doll Wade has brought him; he shoves it back at him and stalks off, heading for the distant shore, where Wade can see the trailer park and Pop's old red Ford pickup next to the blue trailer at the end. Wade looks down at the thing in his arms and wonders whose baby is this, when he realizes suddenly that it is Jack Hewitt's baby. A son! Imagine that! Jack had a son! God damn! Wade observes that there are no women in this dream and that the girl babies are dolls. There must be something wrong with that. Men do not have babies, women do. But what about men?

What do men do? he cries, and he woke up, tears streaming down his face in the darkness of his trailer, his body as much as his mind cold to the bone, the toothache gone.

Early the next morning, but not too early, for he did not want to have to wake them, especially this morning, Wade drove out to Lake Agaway on the north side of town. He figured he would have to say something nice about Twombley, express his condolences to the next of kin, that sort of thing, and then get down to business with the son-in-law. Asa Brown and Gordon LaRiviere be damned: it wasn't their job to protect the children; it was his.

He passed Wickham's, noted that the parking lot was almost filled and that most of the cars were out-of-state. There was that stupid sign, HOME MADE COOKING, pale pink in the bright morning light. A few cars had the bodies of shot deer tied to roofs and fenders, and Wade decided that he would stop for breakfast later, after he had paid his visit to Mel Gordon, when there would be only a few people still at the restaurant and he could talk to Margie and make his important phone calls. That was how he thought of them—important. This morning at eight, Wade Whitehouse was a man with several important tasks, legal matters, by God, and he wanted Margie to see him, a competent man, engaged in completing them.

He would have liked to take her out to Twombley's place on Lake Agaway, so she could see him deal with Twombley's son-in-law, and he had almost called her when he first got out of bed, but he remembered that Margie worked Saturday mornings. That was okay; she would get off at noon and could ride down to Concord with him this afternoon to see the lawyer. Maybe she could even be with him when he talked to the lawyer. Although that might not look so good, he thought. Well, she could wait in a restaurant or do some shopping, and he could tell her all about it afterwards.

A quarter mile past Merritt's Shell Station, at the old mill, where there was a cluster of shanties huddled together as if for warmth, Wade turned left onto the winding narrow dirt road that led down to Lake Agaway. The sky was bright blue and cloudless, and patches of blinding sunlight flashed over the hood and windshield as he passed between stands of tall spruce and pine—trees that should have been cut and sold.

Wade made the observation every time he drove this road: these tall lovely blue-black trees should be lumbered on a regular rotating basis, and would be, too, if rich people did not own the land and did not prefer the decorative use of the trees to any other. It pissed him off.

The lake itself is not especially large, maybe two miles long and a half mile wide, and you cannot see it from the road, even though it lies only a few hundred yards off to your right and slightly downhill. It is a picturesque deep-water lake nestled between two ridges, with a north-looking glimpse of Franconia Notch and a south-looking view of Saddleback and Parker Mountain. Nice.

Five families own all the shoreline and acreage between the two ridges, summer people from Massachusetts—a physician, two manufacturers, one of whom was supposed to have invented the salt-and-pepper packets used on airplanes, a judge recently appointed to the Supreme Court and now spending most of his time in Washington, and Evan Twombley, the union official. The five families who preceded this five entered long ago into polite but legally precise association with one another to keep the land from being subdivided and to keep the five properties from ever being purchased by Jews or blacks—an agreement appended to the deed and called a covenant, as if made between Christians and a conservationist Protestant God who, only three years before, when Twombley bought his place from the last of the original five, had decided finally to recognize Catholics. Then, predictably, a problem arose. Though it was Evan Twombley, as the first Catholic so recognized, who had signed the deed with the covenant attached, it troubled folks that his son-in-law, Mel Gordon, once people got sight of him, was thought to be Jewish. It was too late by then, of course, to do anything—one could not withdraw the covenant—but as long as the place did not pass to the son-in-law, no one would worry. They did enjoy talking about it, however, giving themselves little frissons of anxiety.

By this morning, the other four families in the Lake Agaway Residents Association, as it was called, had learned of the death of their weekend neighbor Evan Twombley in a tragic hunting accident yesterday in Lawford, New Hampshire. One of them had a satellite dish and had heard it mentioned last night on the eleven o'clock news on Channel 4, and it was in both the Boston papers, sold at Golden's store, this morning. Well. A shame.

Perhaps Twombley's daughter and son-in-law would want to sell the place, which would be the preferred course of action, needless to say. If his daughter alone inherited it (a strong likelihood, thank heavens), no one would especially mind or object, so long as she did not turn around and put the deed in both her and her husband's names. The daughter was certainly not Jewish, and the children therefore could not be, since everyone knew that to be Jewish you needed a Jewish mother.

It was still possible, of course, that the Jew Mel Gordon would jointly inherit the property. If that happened, one could only hope that on reading the deed, the fellow would come to the restrictive clause at the end and would decide to say nothing about it, would go right ahead and simply sign the deed and let it go at that, quite as if he were not Jewish or black. Damn. If this Gordon fellow *had* been black, none of this would have happened, would it? Anyhow, his agreeing to the restrictive clause in the deed might turn out to be somewhat embarrassing for the Association, mightn't it? After all, you did not have to come right out and say it, and no one would be rude or crude enough to ask him, but everyone in the Association and everyone in town as well thought Mel Gordon was Jewish, which meant, of course, that he *was* Jewish. People are not wrong about these things. On the other hand, it was not clear that he was *not* Jewish, either, especially if he himself was unwilling to say so one way or the other. It didn't really matter, though, did it? Times change, don't they? This is surely not the sort of problem our parents had to face.

Wade pulled into the neatly plowed driveway and followed it down to the three-bay garage and parked. He got out of his car slowly, as if he had all the time in the world, and strolled around to the wide porch that faces the lake. The house is a large two-story wood-frame house covered with cedar shakes, built three years ago to look a hundred years old, as if indeed it were inherited.

LaRiviere had scoffed at the idea of spending so much to make a place look old. "If you're going to spend a quarter of a million bucks on a summer place, it ought to look like something brand spanking new, for Christ's sake."

But Wade liked the way it looked, and he believed that if he had the money, he would want his summer place to resemble this one, a house where several generations of smart successful kindhearted people had come to relax and be together with their children and parents and grown brothers and sisters, a place with a wide porch facing the lake, lots of old-fashioned wicker rockers on the porch where you sat in the twilight and told stories of favorite summers past, old silvery cedar shingles, two chimneys made of local stone, a steep-pitched roof with wide overhangs that slid the snow off the house to the ground before it either accumulated so much weight that it broke through or got held up by ice at the gutters and started lifting roof shingles and doing water damage when spring came.

He knocked on the glass pane of the storm door with what he felt was authority, and the inner door was opened at once.

A blond boy about eight years old with a large tousled head and thin stalklike neck pushed the aluminum-and-glass storm door open about six inches and with great seriousness examined Wade. The boy wore flannel pajamas with action pictures of Spider-Man printed on them. In one hand he held a bowl of pastel-colored cereal and milk that was slopping onto the floor; with the other he held on to the door.

"Your daddy home?" Wade asked.

The boy studied Wade's face and said nothing.

"Is your daddy here, son? I got to talk with your daddy."

As if dismissing him, the boy turned away and let go of the storm door, and the breeze off the lake shoved it closed in Wade's face. He could see into the living room, for the child had left the inner door wide open. Wade watched him trot to a television set in the far corner, where he plopped down on the carpeted floor and resumed watching cartoons and began to spoon the pastel-colored cereal into his mouth.

The living room was huge, open to the eaves, with a head-high stone fireplace at either end. A staircase led up to a deck, where several closed doors indicated bedrooms. Downstairs, there was a grand piano in a bay window, which instantly impressed Wade: he had never seen a grand piano inside a house before. When he thought about it, he realized that he had never seen a grand piano anywhere. Not in person.

He knocked on the glass again, but the boy continued to eat cereal and stare at cartoons as if Wade were not there. Finally, Wade drew the door open and stepped inside and closed the inner door behind him. "C'mon, son," he said. "Go and get your daddy for me."

"Sh-h-h!" the boy said, without looking at him. Then Wade saw that there was a second, smaller boy lying flat on the floor a few feet beyond him, his head propped up on tiny fists. He was blonder than his brother and wore underpants and a tee shirt and seemed to be shivering from the cold. He peeked over his brother's shoulder and scowled at Wade and said, "Sh-h-h, will ya?"

"Jesus H. Christ," Wade murmured, and he started to leave, when he heard a woman's voice above and behind him.

"Who are you?" It was a light tentative voice, the opposite of the boys' voices and the snarls emitted by the bare-chested muscular characters on the television screen; Wade turned and looked up and saw a thin silvery-blond woman standing just beyond the balustrade of the deck above him; he felt for a second that he was in a play, like *Romeo and Juliet,* and the next line was his and he did not know what it was.

He felt his face redden, and he took off his watch cap and held it in front of his crotch with both hands. The woman's face was long and bony but very delicate-looking, as if the bones underneath were fragile and her pale skin exceedingly thin. Her eyes were red-rimmed, and her shoulder-length blond hair was uncombed. She wore no makeup but was wrapped in a dark-green velour robe that made her face and thin hands and wrists seem to be covered with white powder. Wade had seen her numerous times before, of course, but she had always been tanned, wearing jeans and fancy sweaters, and in winter she wore ski togs. Usually he had observed her at a distance, in town or at the post office. When Twombley was building the house and Wade was out here drilling the wells, she had come up from Massachusetts twice with her husband and sons, but they had strolled through the half-constructed buildings and down by the lake without stopping to speak to him. This was the first time he had seen her up close, and it seemed to him that he was seeing her under disarmingly intimate circumstances.

He stammered, "I was . . . I'm Wade Whitehouse. I was wondering, is your husband here? I was wondering that."

"He's asleep. We were up very late," she said, as if she wished that she, too, were asleep.

"Well, yes, I'm . . . I want to say that I'm real sorry about your father, Mrs. Twombley."

"Gordon," she corrected him. "Thank you."

"Gordon. Sorry. Mrs. Gordon. Jesus, I'm sorry about that. Mrs. Gordon, right."

She gripped the rail as if for balance and said, "Do you think you could come back later on, when he'll be up?"

"Well, yeah, I suppose so. Sure. I mean, I don't want to intrude, you know, at a time like this and all. I just had a little business to settle with Mr. Gordon. I'm the local police officer, and there was something I wanted to speak with him about."

"Something concerning my father?" She took several steps along the deck toward the stairs.

"Oh, no, nothing about that. Jeez, no. It's a . . . it's a traffic thing," he said. "No big deal."

"Can't it wait, then?"

Wade thought, Yes, yes, it can wait, of course it can wait. It could wait until another morning, when she would be freshly wakened once again and this terrible thing concerning her father would have passed by; he could drive over here and talk with this fair woman at her breakfast table, while her husband and her children drove farther and farther north into the mountains, leaving her behind so that Wade could comfort her, take care of her, provide strength for her to draw upon in her time of affliction and grief, this intelligent beautiful sad needy woman who was unlike all the other women Wade had known and loved, he was sure.

He backed toward the door, gazing up at her, concentrating so narrowly on her pale form that he did not see the man emerge from a room at the far end of the balcony—Mel Gordon, dark-eyed, unshaven, short black hair pressed to his narrow skull. He was wearing a wool plaid robe, forest green and blue, the Gordon tartan. He crossed his arms over his chest and studied Wade for a second, and as Wade reached behind him for the doorknob, Gordon said, "Whitehouse. Next time, phone ahead."

"How's that?"

"I said, 'Next time, phone ahead.' "

The older of the two boys cut a look at his father and said, "Daddy, be quiet, will you?"

Wade smiled and looked down at his feet and shook his head slightly. "Jesus Christ," he murmured. Then he said, "Mr. Gordon, when I come all the way out to serve somebody a summons, I don't call ahead for an appointment."

Gordon's face knotted, and he moved quickly past his wife to the stairs. He said, "What the hell are you talking about?" He hurried down the stairs, as if to close a window against a storm, and when he reached the landing at the bottom, a few feet from where Wade stood by the door, he said,

"C'mon, Whitehouse, let's see it, this summons." He held out his hand and glared at Wade. "Let's see it."

"I got to write it out." Wade reached into his back pocket and drew out his fat pad of tickets and plucked a Bic ballpoint pen from his shirt pocket.

"What the hell are you talking about, Whitehouse?"

"I'm issuing you a ticket, Mr. Gordon. Moving violation." He pursed his lips and started to write.

"Moving violation! I just got out of bed, for Christ's sake, and you're telling me you're giving me a goddamn speeding ticket?" He barked a laugh. "Are you nuts? Is that it, Whitehouse? You're nuts? I think you're nuts."

Wade went on writing. "Yesterday morning, you passed a stopped school bus, which was flashing its lights, and then you passed a traffic officer holding traffic for pedestrians at a crosswalk," Wade said without looking up. "Looked to me like you was speeding too. That's a thirty-five-mile-per-hour zone. But I'll let that one go by this time."

Above them, the pale woman in the dark-green velour robe turned and retreated to one of the bedrooms. Wade glanced up and saw her disappear. The two men would duel down here below, and when only one of them remained, he would mount the stairs to her tower, where he would enter her darkened room. She would not know which of the two men in her life was crossing the room toward her.

Mel Gordon reached out and grabbed Wade's writing hand, startling him. "Hold on!" Gordon said.

Wade wrenched his hand free. "Don't ever put your hands on me, Mr. Gordon," he said.

"You're talking about a goddamned traffic ticket, aren't you? From yesterday."

"Yup."

"From when I passed you at the school, where you had decided to hold up traffic for a goddamn half hour while you dreamed of becoming a traffic cop or something." Gordon had stepped back now and was smiling broadly with amused disbelief. A surly pelt of black chest hairs filled in the V of chest exposed by his robe, and the pelt grew almost to his throat. He is the kind of man who has shaved twice a day since early adolescence and thinks all men do. "You going to advise me of my rights, Officer Whitehouse?"

"Don't give me a hard time, Mr. Gordon. Just take the

damn ticket and pay the fine by mail, or go to local court next month and fight it, I don't care. I'm just—"

"Doing your fucking job. I know. I watch television too."

"Yes. Doing my job. Here's your ticket," he said, and he tore it off the pad and handed the sheet to Gordon.

"You are something. You are really something."

"Yeah. Well, so are you, Mr. Gordon. Something." He smiled. "And your kids? They're rude to strangers," he added, tossing the boys a hard look, as if they were bugs.

"Hey!" Gordon said. "You might insult my wife, too, while you're at it." He took a step toward Wade. "Why the hell not? After all, you probably know all about her father's accident. Must be something about that you can make a crack on, if you really give it some thought. Why not, Whitehouse? Why not touch all the bases while you're here?" He smiled meanly.

"Yeah, well, I know about her father. I'm sorry about that."

Gordon held the ticket out in front of him with one hand and folded it neatly in half and tucked it into Wade's shirt pocket. He was no longer smiling. "You get the hell out of my house now, asshole. And know this—you are going to be a *lucky* asshole if I haven't got you fired before the day is out." He yanked open the door, turned Wade toward it and said, "I can put your country ass out of work with one phone call, Whitehouse, and I'm just pissed enough to do it now." He placed a hand against Wade's stiffened shoulder and moved the man through the doorway to the porch, then slammed the door shut behind him.

For a few seconds, Wade stood out there on the open porch, facing across the white ice-covered lake toward the black line of trees and hills beyond. He patted his shirt pocket, where the folded ticket seemed to give off heat, and then zipped his jacket against the steady breeze that blew across the lake. His mind was filled with the image of the blond woman on the balcony above him, her beautifully fatigued face, her tall slender form as she gazed down and with her eyes asked him to come up the stairs and save her.

11

WHEN HE THOUGHT ABOUT IT—which, while driving
back to town from Lake Agaway, he did—Wade realized that
there was no one in town he could go to for advice concerning
the hiring of an attorney. He would never again use the last
lawyer he had hired, the guy who got him stuck like this in the
first place. That had been a shot in the dark, a lawyer from the
Littleton yellow pages, and he had obviously missed. Now,
however, Wade knew what he was doing, yes-by-God, and he
needed an attorney who would reflect that knowledge.

There were a few people in Lawford who could recommend someone to him—Alma Pittman, Chub Merritt, Gordon
LaRiviere—but Wade did not particularly want anyone in
town to know what he was up to. Except for Rolfe, who was
too long too far out of town and state and could not help him
find a lawyer but might advise him generally; and there was
Margie, of course, who was different from everyone else in
town, because she alone happened to love him—or if she did
not love him exactly, she could be brought to love him, he
believed, by kindnesses returned, something he had up to now
been reluctant to provide.

It was an out-of-balance affair, in which one party, Margie, was a finer human being than the other. But both parties knew it and accepted it, so that the worst thing that could happen, Wade believed, was that Margie someday would find a man who returned her kindnesses and she would leave Wade for such a man. But Wade expected that he would not feel much worse about things then than he did now. Which was possibly why he refused to move in closer to Margie, why he kept his gaze slightly averted at all times, even while making love to her. It did not keep her a stranger, exactly, but it kept her from becoming a wife.

Back in town now, Wade drove past LaRiviere's, and as he passed he remembered drilling a well once for a man who was a Concord attorney, a guy named J. Battle Hand, whom neither Wade nor LaRiviere himself had ever actually met, but from what he could see, the man was successful: he had bought a large chunk of very expensive land down near Catamount and had built a Swiss-style chalet on the southern slope of a huge hill where there was a ski resort going up on the backside of the hill—condos, restaurants, shops, bars, saunas, a Ramada Inn, a half-dozen different ski slopes and tows: the works. And this guy, J. Battle Hand, owned the undeveloped half of the hill and evidently had no plans to do anything with it but plunk his own vacation home down in the middle of it, setting it in a stand of thick white birches with a lovely long view of the hills of central New Hampshire, only a mile and a quarter from where people drove whole days from Massachusetts and points south to get to.

By Wade's and Lawford's standards, and even by the standards of the much larger town of Catamount, the house was palatial. LaRiviere's bid on the well had come in slightly high, but he had been hired anyhow, probably because of his reputation for being able to set up and drill on slopes that discouraged most flatland well drillers. LaRiviere could drive out to a hilly site when they got ready to set up the rig and in seconds could find the one piece of ground where the rig could be backed into place and the drill sent into the ground vertically. It was uncanny, at least to Wade, who inevitably had picked someplace else to drill. LaRiviere would survey the ground with a quick gaze, note Wade's spot, pick another, then humiliate Wade by first having Jack Hewitt or Jimmy Dame park the rig where Wade had suggested. Every time, no matter how they jacked it, the rig ended up tilted at an angle that could not be corrected by the drill. Then LaRiviere would have Jack bring the truck down a few yards and to the left a ways, where a batch of chokecherry bushes had obscured the surface of the ground, and sure enough, the rig sat level as a cake in an oven, and the drill bit, lowered into place, aimed straight down to the center of the earth.

Though he had never met the man, Wade remembered J. Battle Hand clearly, mainly because of his name, which struck him as a lawyer-like name, the name of a man who fought like a tiger for his clients, who believed in justice and in absolute right and absolute wrong and would not defend a person unless he first believed in that person's innocence and in the righteousness of his cause. It was clear, too, that he had become wealthy this way. J. Battle Hand was precisely the kind of attorney Wade needed for bringing a custody suit against his ex-wife. He needed a good rich man. Or, better, a rich good man.

He pulled in at Wickham's, looked around for Margie and discovered what he had forgotten—she had worked yesterday, the first day of hunting season, and had today off. Nick told him that she had phoned in a message for Wade to call her if he came in. Half the booths and tables were filled with deer hunters, most of them local. These were not the fanatics and out-of-towners who had crowded the place yesterday morning. In one day the intensity of the hunt had been sufficiently diluted that here, along the sidelines, most of the observers and participants were able to affect little more than passive involvement with the killing still going on in the woods. It was not all that different from any other Saturday morning at Wickham's. Two of the pickups parked in front had dead deer in the back, but they looked more like cargo than trophy. The town seemed to have settled into a seasonal rhythm, the deer-hunting season, which was as natural and unconscious an aspect of life as winter or spring: one simply went out and acted "natural," and in that way one was able to behave appropriately too. Easy.

Wade got Nick to change a dollar bill, and he headed through the nearly empty restaurant to the game room in back. Nick himself was serving at the counter this morning; he had a high school girl waiting tables, a plump girl with a uniform two sizes too small for her and a face made up to look like a Las Vegas showgirl's. Back in the game room, where the pay phone was located, a pair of teenaged boys were playing donkey ball and smoking cigarettes. Wade dropped a coin in, got Concord information and the number of J. Battle Hand, attorney at law, and dialed it.

It occurred to Wade that J. Battle Hand might not be in his office on a Saturday morning, he might be over in Catamount skiing, or lounging in front of a fire in his huge living room, so he was pleased and a little surprised to have a secretary ask him who was calling and then to say, "Just one moment, please, Mr. Whitehouse," and then to find himself instantly and easily speaking with the man he wanted to represent him in what Wade regarded as the most complicated, ambitious, possibly reckless but nonetheless righteous thing he had ever undertaken: the attempt to gain regular and easy access to his own child. This might not be all that hard, after all, he thought, and he noticed that his hands had stopped shaking and his toothache had gone back to a dry rattle in his mouth. It had not bothered him much this morning anyhow, but it had been there nonetheless, like unpleasant background noise, a next-door neighbor playing his radio a little too loud.

Hand's voice was low, calm, authoritative, just as Wade had hoped he would sound. He said, "I see," many times, while Wade quickly explained what he wished Hand to do for him. When the lawyer suggested that, before they do anything, Wade come in to his office and talk, Wade explained that he worked up in Lawford and had trouble getting off on weekdays; he would like to come in today, sometime this afternoon, if possible. Hand said fine, how was two o'clock, and that was that.

No, sir, this was not going to be as hard or as confusing as he had expected. They had not talked about how much it would cost, of course, but Wade could tell from the sound of the man's voice that Attorney Hand was a reasonable man. Whatever it cost Wade, it would be worth it to have Jill back in his life, and he could pay it out over years, if necessary. He could take out a bank loan, maybe, a second mortgage on the trailer, if he had to—and no doubt he would have to, for he had no savings whatsoever.

Then Wade called Margie. As soon as he heard her voice, he wanted a cigarette. He patted his shirt pocket and found that he was out. "Shit," he said.

"What?"

"Wait a minute, I got to get a pack of cigarettes. Can you hold on?"

"Hurry up. I'm baking."

"Be right back," he said. He was suddenly frantic for a cigarette; the need was as physical and immediate as the need to urinate. He placed the receiver on top of the phone box and hurried out to the cash register and bought a pack of Camel Lights from Nick. By the time he got back to Margie, he was already smoking, his lungs and face feeling soothed and familiar again.

"I got to quit these things," he said to her, but he could not imagine being able to endure for more than a minute the agitated unfamiliarity that smoking eliminated. It was a singular and specific kind of psychic pain, which had been caused by the cigarettes in the first place, and they were the singular specific remedy for it. If there were available to him a similar remedy for the general pain, a wide-body potion that eliminated the overall agitation and unfamiliarity that he believed he suffered every waking moment of his life, and if that potion were programmed to kill him in an even shorter and more exact time than the cigarettes were, Wade surely would have taken that remedy too. The final result may be death, but addiction is about eliminating pain with what causes the pain in the first place, and death was coming along anyway, so what the hell. But there was no such general remedy that he knew of, and though he did not always think so, he was probably lucky there was none. It was perhaps sufficient that at present it was only the cigarettes that were killing him.

While he spoke to Margie, he kept thinking of Mel Gordon's wife, the dead Evan Twombley's living daughter, standing between him and Mel Gordon like an angelic shield, protecting him from Gordon's dark fury, and when Margie said that she could not spend the afternoon with him in Concord, she had to finish baking pies for Nick Wickham, Wade was almost glad. For the moment, his image of Margie Fogg could not compete with his image of Mel Gordon's wife.

"It's probably just as well," he said. "I got to see my lawyer at two anyhow."

"So. You're really going to do that. The custody thing."

"Yep."

"Oh, God. I think you'll be sorry. I think you'll wish you had never opened this whole thing up again, Wade."

"Maybe. But I'd be a hell of a lot sorrier if I just let it go. Kids grow up fast," he said. "And then it's over. You get old, and the kids are grown into strangers. Look at my old man and me."

"Your father," she said. "Your father was not like you. That's why you and he are strangers."

"That's the whole point. My father . . . well, I don't want to get into that."

"And Lillian, she's not like your mother, either. Lillian's going to fight this like a she-bear. Believe me."

"Yeah," he said. "I know. But that's the whole point too. If Lillian *was* like my mother, I wouldn't be doing any of this in the first place, you know." He lit a second cigarette off the first and inhaled deeply. "Besides, me and my old man, we aren't really strangers."

"No."

"In fact," he said, "I was kind of thinking of going up there tomorrow. I haven't been by to see them in months. You feel like coming?"

"Sure," she said in a flat voice. She was giving up on Wade: his inconsistency was patterned and self-serving, and there was no way in for her. She might as well just let him be who he is and enjoy him for that as much as possible. More and more often these days, she found herself regarding Wade from a distance. She knew what it meant: sooner or later she would not want to sleep with him anymore. Right now, however, she was lonely, she was, and she felt imprisoned by her body, she did, and she wanted out, badly, and sleeping with Wade, even if only on occasion, provided her with brief reprieves, like conjugal visits, and she was not about to give that up. She was not.

"Wade," she said, and she said his name in a low voice that was instantly meaningful to him, like the start of a catechism, and they began their old ritual sequence:

"Yes."

"Can you come by my place tonight?"

"Yes."

"Will you?"

"Yes, I will."

"Do you want to?"

"Yes, I do."

"What will you do with me, Wade?"

He cupped his hand over the mouthpiece and cast a glance at the teenagers playing donkey ball in the corner of the room. In a low voice, he said, "I'll do everything you want me to do."

"Everything?"

"Everything. And a few things you don't want me to do."

"Ah-h-h," she said. "You're not at home now, are you?"

"No."

"So we can't do it over the phone," she said.

"No. We can't. I'd look . . . I'd look pretty silly if we did. I'm in Nick's back room."

"You wouldn't look silly. Not to me you wouldn't. I love to see you do that," she said. "You know what I'm doing now, don't you?"

"Yes. Yes, I do. I surely do. But I'm not going to listen anymore," he said. "Besides, I thought you were baking."

"Ummm. I am."

"I'm gonna hang up on you. Before I make a fool of myself in public. I'll come by later," he said. "I'll come by and make a fool of myself in private. If that's okay by you."

She assured him that, yes, it was fine by her, and they said goodbye and hung up. Wade sighed heavily, and the two boys looked over at him and stared for a second.

"Hello, Wade," the taller one said. "Getcha deer yet?"

"Nope," he said. "I give up hunting five years ago, boys. Give it up for women. You oughta try it. Great for your sex life," he said, and he hitched up his pants and headed out the door, his mind refilling with the golden light cast by his image of Mel Gordon's wife.

The office of J. Battle Hand was on the first floor of a white Federal town house on South Main Street in Concord. It had snowed only a few inches in Concord the day before, and then it had rained, which had washed away the accumulated snow, but it was cold under a low dark-gray midafternoon sky, as if it were going to snow again, and the sidewalks were smeared here and there with half-frozen puddles.

Wade was unused to sidewalks and made his way carefully from his car to the steps of the building, up the steps and in, where he passed a door that announced the presence of a women's health center, whatever the hell that was, and an accountant's office, and walked to the back, where he entered a carpeted outer office and was greeted by a smart-looking young woman with a boy's haircut and one dangling earring and long thin arms. She looked up from her red typewriter and smiled at him.

He took off his cap and wished suddenly that he had changed his clothes before coming down from Lawford. Maybe he should have worn his sport coat and necktie and his dress pants. He felt huge and awkward in the room, all thick neck and wrists. Country.

The young woman raised her eyebrows, as if expecting him to tell her what he had come to repair. The furnace? A broken water pipe on the second floor?

"I . . . I got an appointment," Wade said. "With Mr. Hand."

"Your name?" She stopped smiling.

"Whitehouse."

She checked a pad on the desk, punched a key on the phone and said into the receiver, "A Mr. Whitehouse to see you." Then silence, and she hung up and got up from her desk and motioned for Wade to follow her.

She was tall, as tall as he, and wore a black-and-white-checked miniskirt and smoky stockings that made her legs look slender and firm. Wade followed her calves and the backs of her knees, and they led him into a second office. The woman told him to take off his coat and sit down and said that Mr. Hand would be right with him. She offered him a cup of coffee, but he declined, because he knew his hands were trembling. Then she left him, closing the door behind her.

There were two dark-green leather chairs and a matching sofa in the windowless room, and the walls were lined with the red and blue spines of thick books. There was a second door, in the far corner of the room, and Wade settled into the chair that faced it and waited. His toothache was clanging away, but he felt pretty good.

After a few seconds he began to hope that Mr. Hand, for unknown reasons, would not appear and that somehow Wade could sit right where he was forever, outside of time, safely beyond his past and just this side of his future. He was warm enough and comfortable enough, and there was an ashtray on the low table next to him, so he could smoke. Which he did.

He was halfway through the cigarette, when he heard a

click, and the door swung open and in, and to his astonishment a person in a wheelchair entered. It was a rubber-tired wheelchair with a tiny electric motor powering it, all chrome bars and spokes. The man driving the chair was slumped off to his left, flicking buttons on a control box with the fingers of his left hand. He brought the chair swiftly through the doorway, turned it abruptly, as if it were a remote-controlled toy car, toward Wade, then drove it forward to within a few feet of Wade's chair, where it stopped suddenly and parked.

The driver looked like a ventriloquist's dummy dressed in a dark pin-striped suit. His head was disproportionately large, and his face, in alarming contrast to the slumped inertness of his body, was bright and expressive. He had dark hair, gray at the temples, a square sharply defined forehead and brow and large pale-blue eyes. His skin was waxy white and taut, like paper-thin porcelain, the skin of a person who has long endured great pain, and when he smiled to greet Wade, it was almost a grimace, which seemed to require a mighty and consciously engaged physical exertion, as if he had to will his facial muscles to move one at a time.

But move they did, and when they did, his face lit up with intelligence and, Wade thought, humor. Maybe the man had deliberately prepared this surprise, had costumed and masked himself and sat in his wheelchair for hours behind that door waiting for Wade to arrive. Wade wanted to laugh out loud, to say, "Wow, hell of a getup there, Mr. Hand! Happy Halloween and trick-or-treat and all that, eh?" He wanted to reassure the man that the masquerade had worked, that he was indeed surprised, and he was scared too.

"Mr. Whitehouse," the man in the wheelchair said. "Good to meet you." It was the same voice Wade had heard on the phone, a deep baritone, smooth and cultivated.

Wade shifted his cigarette from his right hand to his left and started to extend the right, then plopped it back onto his knee. He swallowed and said, "Howdy."

"I heard you had some serious snow up your way yesterday."

Wade nodded, and the man went on. "There's practically two different climates between here and there. What is it, forty, forty-five, fifty miles, and when you get snow, we get rain. At least till mid-December. Then we both get snowed on. I think I prefer the snow, though, to this dreary rain," he said.

"Yeah," Wade said. "Yeah, I prefer the snow." He lapsed into silence again.

"Do you ski?"

"No. I never did. I never did try that."

"Well," the lawyer said, suddenly looking serious. "Let's talk about this suit you're proposing, shall we?" With his right hand he wrestled a yellow legal pad from a slot on the side of his chair onto his lap, drew a pen from his shirt pocket and prepared to write.

But Wade was not ready to talk about Lillian and Jill yet; in fact, he had almost forgotten why he had driven down here in the first place. He wanted to know what was wrong with Hand, what injury or disease had made off with his body. He wanted to know what the man could and could not do, how he could work as a lawyer, for God's sake, or how he managed to drive a car, get dressed, cut his food. How he was with a woman.

He had never seen a man like this up close, and now he was about to hire him to do a very complex and mysterious job for him. Wade was about to place himself in a dependent relation to a man who said he preferred snow to rain but surely could not go out in the snow, a man who, even with his fancy rubber-tired battery-powered chair, could not get around in the stuff, but who nonetheless had built a huge vacation house on the side of a mountain where it snowed six months a year. He was a cripple who lived on a goddamned ski slope!

He suddenly thought of Evan Twombley, an overweight city fellow with his new gun up on Parker Mountain in the snow, hunting for a deer to kill and then getting killed himself. He thought of Jack Hewitt, lean and in all the necessary ways expert, moving swiftly, silently, through the drifts and brush and over the rock-strewn trails of the mountain, with the fat red-faced man struggling along behind. This man, J. Battle Hand, in the world of normal men and women, was like Twombley in the snowy woods, and Wade was like Jack somehow.

Maybe here, though, among these books, it was J. Battle Hand who was the lean mean expert, and Wade who was like Twombley, red-faced and puffing to keep up and, unless he was damned careful, likely to shoot himself. Or get shot. For less than a second, like a slide inexplicably shown out of order, Wade saw Jack Hewitt shoot Evan Twombley, a wash of falling snow, the abrupt tilt of the hill, the fat man going over, blood against the white ground.

Then he was in Attorney Hand's office again, wondering how the man was able to plead cases in court. Actually, Wade thought, if I was sitting on a jury and this guy wheeled up in front of me and started defending his client, I would be inclined to believe whatever he said. It was hard to think that a man with so little use of his body, a man whose body was such an undeniable truth, could lie to you about anything. This man, J. Battle Hand, could say anything he wanted and be believed.

Wade brightened a little: Lillian would hire some slick gray-haired guy like that lawyer she hired for the divorce, tall and good-looking, smooth as a goddamn presidential candidate, and Attorney Hand would roll back and forth in front of the judge and make mincemeat of the guy. Not like last time, when Wade had entered the courtroom with Bob Chagnon from Littleton, all rumpled and nervously sweating and talking too fast in his north-country French-accented English, until even Wade felt embarrassed for him. Lillian had looked down and smiled. Wade had seen her and had suddenly wanted to tell his lawyer to shut the fuck up, for Christ's sake. Stop talking, now, before everyone in the room ends up believing what Wade himself already knew, that in this twice-destroyed marriage Lillian had been the smart and competent one, and Wade had been dumb and out of control, an uneducated irresponsible irrational man prone to violence and alcoholism. Look at his lawyer, for Christ's sake, look at the man he hires to represent him—a half-assed half-drunk Canuck who can barely talk English and ends up telling the judge that when Wade hit Lillian those times it was because she deserved it! "Your Honor, the woman egged him on," Chagnon had said.

No wonder he lost everything. Wade was lucky the judge did not send him to jail, and the judge told him so.

Wade sat back in the green leather chair, crossed his legs and lit another cigarette and began explaining to his new attorney why he wanted to gain custody of his child. Lillian was turning Jill against him, he said, and, more and more, the woman was making it difficult for Wade to see Jill or for Jill to visit him. First she had moved to Concord, and now she was talking about moving even farther south, or out west, maybe, as soon as her new husband got himself transferred, and if that was tough for Wade, well, too bad. This was not exactly true, but Wade figured it soon would be. She could move to Florida if she wanted to, and there was nothing he could do about it.

The lawyer said nothing and seemed to be waiting for Wade to continue.

But on the other hand, maybe he did not really need custody, Wade offered. Maybe all he needed were guarantees of regular visits with Jill during the school year and then summers and holidays. Maybe that would be enough. All he really wanted was to be a good father. He wanted to have a daughter, and he *had* one, by God, but the girl's mother was doing everything she could to deny that fact. Wade figured that if he asked for custody and offered Lillian regular visits and summers and holidays with Jill, the judge might be willing to do the opposite, to let Lillian keep custody and give *him* the regular visits and summers and holidays. What did Mr. Hand think of that strategy? he wondered.

"Not all that bad," Hand said. "If you have a sympathetic judge. It's risky, though. You don't want to ask for the moon and then lose everything because of the asking. Sometimes you're better off asking for exactly what you want, instead of what you think you deserve. If you know what I mean. You're still unmarried, I take it. It would help if you were married and there were someone at home while you're at work."

"Well, yeah. Now I am. Unmarried, I mean. But that's going to change," Wade said. "Soon."

"How soon?"

"Oh, by this spring anyhow. Probably before. There's this woman, she and I been talking about getting married for a long time. Nice woman," he added.

"Good," Hand said, and he wrote on his pad for a few seconds, using only his fingertips, the weight of his hand holding the pad flat against his leg.

Then he asked Wade about Lillian's character. Did she and her husband provide a good life for Jill? Did they have any alcohol or drug problems that he knew of? Any sexual problems or habits that might be upsetting to the child? "That sort of thing would help," he said to Wade. "Especially if we're going for custody. In fact, without hard evidence of sexual misconduct or drug or alcohol abuse, we probably should not even ask for custody in this state. And even then, it would be an uphill fight. You understand," he said.

Wade understood. In fact, he was starting to feel foolish

in this quest of his. What was it that kept him from making his anger and frustration understood? What kept him from finding the words and then the legal means to articulate the pain he felt at the loss of his child? That was all he really wanted. He wanted to be a good father; and he wanted everyone to know it.

No, he said, Lillian did not have any alcohol or drug problems that he knew of, and neither did her husband. And they took good care of Jill. He had to admit that. And he could not imagine any sexual misconduct that Lillian or her husband would be guilty of, at least nothing that would be harmful to a child. "It looks pretty hopeless, don't it?" he said.

"Well, no, not exactly. I need to see your divorce decree. We surely can try to have the father's visitation rights redrawn so that you can be assured of ample and regular access to your daughter. Jill is her name?"

"Yes."

"Fine, then." He bent his chest toward his hand and shoved the pen into his shirt pocket, then slid the legal pad into the carrier on the side of the chair, flicked a button on the box with the fingertips of his left hand and moved his chair back a few feet. The motor made a quiet humming sound as the chair moved and a click when it stopped. "You'll send me a copy of the divorce decree as soon as you get home?"

"Yeah, sure."

"And I'll need a five-hundred-dollar retainer. You might enclose that," he said.

"Jesus," Wade said, and he knew he had begun to sweat. "How much," he began, "how much will the whole thing cost?"

"Hard to say, exactly. If we go for custody, we'll have to take depositions, maybe even subpoena a few people as witnesses, hire a social worker and a child psychiatrist to examine Jill and visit your home and your ex-wife's home, and so on. It could add up. Ten or twelve thousand dollars. It could drag on. And then, even if we win, she might appeal. But you must understand that we can't go looking for custody without acting serious about it, even if what we expect is something much less. On the other hand, if we just want to get your visitation rights redrawn, assuming they're unduly restrictive at present, which the divorce decree will tell me, then it probably won't cost more than twenty-five hundred dollars."

"Oh." Wade felt dizzy and hot; his hands were trembling again, and he knew his toothache was about to return in full force.

"You're a workingman. A well driller, you mentioned."

"And a police officer," Wade interrupted him. "I'm the town police officer."

"Ah. That'll help," he said. "Say, didn't you have a shooting up your way yesterday? Some kind of hunting accident? A man from Massachusetts. Some kind of union official, right?"

"Yeah."

"You know much about it? Sounded a little . . . unlikely to me."

"How's that?"

"Oh, I don't know. Big-time union official out hunting with his guide, and somehow he shoots himself. You always wonder a little about these stories. Who was the guide? Local man, I suppose."

"Yeah. Kid named Jack Hewitt. Used to be a ballplayer, got drafted by the Red Sox a few years back, then ruined his arm. You might've read about him in the papers. Nice kid. It was an accident, though. No doubt about it. Kid like Jack wouldn't have any reason to kill a guy like Twombley anyhow."

"Money," the lawyer said, smiling. "There's always money."

"Yeah. Money. Yeah, there's always that. But it's hard to imagine," Wade said.

"Yes, well, speaking of which," the lawyer said, "my point in asking about your job is, can you manage the costs of a custody suit? Because you might be better off legally, as well as financially, just to go for the . . ."

"I know, I know," Wade said, standing up and pulling on his coat. "I guess . . . I guess the custody suit business is just my way of showing how pissed off I am at my ex-wife. I'm not as dumb as I probably look. I'll do whatever you recommend," he said. "And it looks like you're recommending me to forget the whole goddamned custody business."

He made for the door, opened it and over his shoulder said to the lawyer, "I'll send you the divorce decree on Monday. And the five hundred."

The lawyer looked impassively at him and said nothing.

Wade walked through the outer office, then stopped in

the doorway and peered back for a second and watched the lawyer's chair scoot out the door opposite him, as if rushing him off to another meeting. The lawyer's swift and purposeful mobility in his chair frightened Wade somehow. He tried to smile at the receptionist or secretary or whatever she was, but she was busily typing; she wore a headset and showed no sign of knowing Wade was even in the room. He closed the door carefully and moved on.

At the end of the hall, he almost bumped into two girls coming out of the women's health center. They were giggling teenagers, kids, only a few years older than Jill, in scarlet lipstick and powder-blue eye shadow. They wore jeans, half-unbuttoned blouses and quilted down vests.

They probably just got fitted for diaphragms, Wade thought, and it was an embarrassing thought for him, although he did not know why and did not go any further with it than that. He restrained himself from judging the girls, though for a second he wanted to scold them, and he merely said, " 'Scuse me," and stood back a second and watched them leave, switching their behinds, heads held high, hands patting their healthy hair in anticipation of the cold wind outside. As he got into his car, he thought, Those girls probably just had abortions! Jesus H. Christ. What a world.

12

WADE DROVE THE LENGTH of Main Street, halfway to the prison north of Concord, then turned around and drove all the way back. Specks of snow were coming down. It was two forty-five, and Wade felt himself drifting swiftly toward a familiar form of hysteria: a tangible panic. His particular desire, to conduct a successful custody suit against Lillian, now looked like a naive delusion, and his more general and long-lived desire, to be a good father, was starting to feel like a simpleminded obsession. There was a waxing and waning connection between the two desires, he knew, a hydraulic connection, so that when one was strong, the other weakened. When both weakened, however, as now, Wade dropped through the floor of depression into panic.

To fight off the panic, he decided that he wanted to see Jill. What the hell, it was a Saturday afternoon, he was coincidentally in Concord, and he needed to explain some things to the child. Why not call up and arrange to spend the rest of the afternoon with her? He also hoped that, after the fiasco at the Halloween party, she would be able to reassure him somewhat. Surely, his company was not so bad, so boring, that she could

not enjoy herself with him. It was more or less a communication problem. They had missed each other's signals the other
night; that was all. He could apologize, and she could apologize, and everything would be swell.

Besides, it was his right, goddammit, especially after Lillian and her husband had driven up to Lawford Thursday
night and taken her away from him. When you take a man's
child from him, you take much more than the child, so that the
man tends to forget about regaining the child and instead
focuses on regaining the other—self-respect, pride, sense of
autonomy, that sort of thing. The child becomes emblematic.
This was happening to Wade, of course; and he dimly perceived it. But he was powerless to stop it.

He called from a phone booth in the parking lot of the K mart
in the shopping mall east of Main Street. The snow was coming
down harder now and might amount to something, he observed, thinking warily of the drive home. The afternoon sky
had darkened and lowered, and the day seemed to be easing
into evening already. Shoppers, mostly women and children,
occasionally a man, hurried back and forth between their cars
and the store.

He let the phone ring an even dozen times before giving
up. Hell, it's barely three, he thought: too early to head back
to Lawford and see Margie, but still early enough to wait
around awhile and then take Jill out for supper at a Pizza Hut.
She would like that. Meanwhile, he decided, he would go
someplace for a beer, maybe try one of those fancy new bars
in the renovated old warehouses behind the Eagle Hotel he
had heard about, where there were supposed to be lots of
single men and women hanging out, swingers or yuppies or
whatever the hell they call them these days. He would not
mind a look at that. Then he would try to call Jill again.

He parked on North Main Street in front of the hotel and,
passing under phony gas lanterns, strolled through the
bricked-over alley to The Stone Warehouse in back, walked in
without hesitation or a preliminary look around the place—as
if, though not exactly a regular, he came here frequently—and,
using tunnel vision, zeroed in on the bar. He ordered a draft
from a tall good-looking youth with slicked-back hair and then
turned, glass in hand, and slowly perused the place.

The room was large, with mostly empty booths and rough tables covered with red-and-white-checked tablecloths. Large potted ferns, ornate brass coatracks and spittoons cluttered the aisles, and on the walls old-fashioned farm tools had been hung, scythes and sickles, hay rakes, even horse collars, and elaborately framed pictures of New England couples dead a hundred years, dour and disapproving. Who would have thought junk like that could look good? But it did.

The place smelled of raw wood, beer and roasted peanuts, a downright pleasant smell, he thought. Not like Toby's Inn. Wade looked down the bar, where a pair of young large-bellied men were watching the Celtics on TV and munching peanuts, and then he noticed that the floor by the bar was covered with peanut shells. A waitress approached the bar, and the shells crackled under her feet like insects.

Next to him on his right, three young women were seated and talking intently, smoking cigarettes with a kind of fury and every few seconds sipping in unison at their large beige drinks. Wade studied them, slyly, he thought, and tried to overhear their conversation, which he soon discovered concerned a man whom one or all three of them worked for. They were in their early thirties, he guessed. Two of the women wore jeans and plaid flannel shirts and cowboy boots; the third also wore jeans, but with tennis shoes and a washed-out yellow tee shirt with GANJA UNIVERSITY printed across the front. When Wade saw that she was not wearing a bra, he tried not to look at her anymore. She was a long-haired blond; the other two were brunettes and had short hair. Wade thought that maybe those two were sisters.

He ordered another beer. The Celtics were leading the Detroit Pistons by twelve at the half. Maybe he ought to try calling Jill again. He pulled his coat off and hung it on the brass rack behind him and went looking for a pay phone, which he found at the bottom of the stairs leading to the rest rooms.

Again, he let the phone ring a dozen times, in case she was just coming in the front door, he thought, and then realized he had visualized not Jill but Lillian, visualized her unlocking the front door, her arms wrapped around grocery bags, key in hand, the phone ringing. He hung up and came back to the bar.

He cast a glance at the breasts of the young woman in the yellow tee shirt, then asked the bartender for a basket of peanuts and started to concentrate on cracking them open and popping the nuts into his mouth. The women, he realized, were talking about the size of a man's penis. He listened closely: there was no doubt about it: three attractive young women were laughing about some man's small penis! He did not dare look over; he just bore down on the shells, splitting them open between his thumbs and sweeping them onto the floor, faster and faster, as if he were ravenous.

Two of the women, the blond and one of the brunettes, had slept with the man, whoever he was, and they were regaling the third woman by comparing his organ to a thumb, a mouse, a clothespin—a peanut, for God's sake! "I mean, you could've knocked me over with a feather when I got a look at it!" the blond said. Wade pushed the basket of peanuts away and ordered another beer.

"He's sort of amazing, though," the brunette said. "I mean, he gets a whole lot of mileage out of that thing. Wouldn't you say?" she asked the blond.

"Oh, jeez, yes." She laughed. "Miles and miles," she added, and then she shrieked, "Except that you think you're never going to get there!" They all laughed loudly, and then one of the brunettes noticed Wade and hushed the others. Wade turned on his stool and tried to see what was happening with the Celtics.

"How's Bird doing?" he called down the bar.

One of the big-bellied pair at the end turned slowly and said, "Oh-for-seven, three fouls."

Wade said, "Shit," as if he cared, got up and took his beer to the end of the bar and sat down. "Whatsascore?"

Without turning around, the man said, "I dunno. Seventy-something–sixty-something. Celts by six or seven."

"Aw *right!*" Wade said, and he checked into the game with the same intensity he had devoted to shelling the peanuts. He lit a cigarette and tried to concentrate on the game, but his tooth was starting in again, a low throb that threatened to build quickly, and he was feeling once again like a double exposure: everything the other people said and did was half a beat off the rhythm of everything he said and did, so that the others seemed almost to be members of a different species than he, as if their species had a slightly different metabolism than his and relied on a related but different means of communication than his, so that everyone else in the room seemed to be sharing everyday knowledge and secrets that he was biologically incapable of experiencing. Knowledge and secrets: everyone had them; and Wade Whitehouse had neither.

He looked into the mirror behind the bar and tried to watch himself, as if he were a stranger, look strangely back, and then he saw over his shoulder and behind, coming into the bar from outside, where it was snowing hard now, his ex-wife, Lillian! She brushed snow off her shoulder in that quick impatient way of hers, as if taking the snow personally. He kept her in view in the mirror, saw her ask something of the woman at the cash register and then disappear down the stairs toward the rest rooms.

She must have come in to pee, Wade thought. Maybe Jill was waiting outside in the car. He checked his watch: four-twenty: still plenty of time to take Jill out for pizza. Wade slid off his stool and walked to the cash register and started down the stairs after Lillian, when he saw the back of her long lavender coat and realized that she was using the phone. He halted several steps above her; he moved out of her line of sight and listened.

"That doesn't matter," she snapped. "I've only got a couple of hours and that's it. So *please,*" she said, and her voice had shifted into a tone that Wade recognized and swelled to: it was intimate and soft, almost sexual. "I'll be in the lot behind The Stone Warehouse. In the Audi," she said. And then she said, "Hurry," and Wade spun and moved quickly up the stairs, crossed back to the bar and resumed watching the mirror.

A second later, he saw Lillian emerge from the stairwell, nod and smile quickly to the woman at the cash register and leave. Wade grabbed his coat and hat and signaled to the bartender that he wanted to pay. The bartender flipped over the check—*$8.25! Jesus H. Christ!*—and Wade gave the man his ten-dollar bill and made for the door. It took him a moment to determine where the parking lot was and how to get there from the front of the Eagle Hotel, and then he jogged back to his car.

The traffic was light—a few cars sloshed past, windshield wipers clacking and headlights on. Wade made a U-turn on North Main and drove back to Depot Street, turned left and left again and drove past the parking lot, where he spotted the silver Audi in the far corner.

He did not think she could recognize his car in the snow,

165

but even so, he went beyond the lot a ways and parked it out of sight beside a big green Dempster Dumpster about fifty yards away. He was on a slope above the lot now and facing the backside of the Audi. The rear window was covered with wet sticky snow, and he could not see inside, but he was sure she was there, waiting. For what, goddammit? For whom?

With the motor and wipers off, his own windshield was quickly covered over, and he felt suddenly as if he were inside a cave, looking at the walls. He opened the door and stepped out, moved to the other side of the Dumpster, lit a cigarette and waited. Like a cop, he thought. Well, why not? He *was* a cop, was he not? Damn straight. And Lillian, was she a suspected criminal, or was she just his ex-wife meeting some guy on the sly, and if that was all, then was Wade merely perversely curious, a kind of Peeping Tom?

He knew it was a man she was meeting, no doubt about it: he had heard it in her voice: *"Please,"* she had said, and "Hurry."

The pain from his tooth was cutting like a bandsaw up the side of his face, and he placed the palm of his hand against it, as if to shush it, keep the noise down, while he moved carefully away from the Dumpster and then down the shallow embankment to the parking lot, where he slipped along the side of the building to a darkened doorway, the back door to the restaurant upstairs, and stepped in out of the snow. He had a good angle on the Audi from there and could not be observed from the car without some effort: he was still behind the vehicle, but to the side now and only thirty feet away; he could easily see Lillian sitting behind the wheel, smoking.

Was she smoking? But Lillian did not smoke anymore, he remembered. In fact, she made a big deal of it, told him repeatedly and with disgust that she could smell it in Jill's clothing and hair whenever she came back from being with him. He looked closer. She was smoking, all right, but it was not a regular cigarette; no, sir, it was not tobacco. He could tell from the way she held it between thumb and forefinger and then examined it after she had inhaled that she was smoking marijuana.

He was shocked. And suddenly he was panting, and his legs were watery with an eroticized rage that confused him. There was nothing wrong with smoking a joint; hell, he did it himself now and then. Whenever someone offered it to him, actually. But the sight of her doing it now, combined as it was with her waiting in a parking lot to meet someone he knew must be her boyfriend, her *lover,* made him feel sexually betrayed in a very peculiar way. It was peculiar, Wade knew, that he felt betrayed at all, as if she were stepping out on *him,* her ex-husband, and not the man she was married to (a decent enough guy, Wade thought for the first time, though still a bit of a jerk), but it also turned Wade on sexually. It was as if he had inadvertently come upon her secret stash of pornography. Manacles, dildos, whips. He was thrilled, erotically charged, and he was enraged, and he was ashamed.

He closed his eyes for a few seconds and leaned against the cut-stone wall behind him, and when he opened them he saw a car ease through the falling snow into the parking lot. It was a dark-green Mercedes sedan driven by a man who, Wade knew at once, was here to meet Lillian. The car drew up next to Lillian's Audi, and she instantly got out, walked purposefully around the front and got in.

The headlights reflected off the wall of the warehouse and cast light back into the car, and Wade could see Lillian and the man clearly, as if they were up on a stage, while they kissed. It was a long serious kiss, but slightly formal too, done without their arms around one another: they were a man and a woman who had been lovers for a long time and who knew that their kiss was only a preliminary and did not have to stand for everything else. Then, when they drew apart, Lillian handed what was left of her joint to the man, and he relit it and inhaled deeply, and Wade realized that he knew him.

The man backed the Mercedes away from the wall, and his face disappeared into darkness again, but Wade had seen him; he knew absolutely who he was. There could be no doubt. The face was one Wade would never forget: it had shamed him, and then it had haunted him, and Wade had come to despise it. The face was smooth and symmetrical, as large as an actor's, with square chin, wide brow, long straight nose. The man's hair was dark, with distinguished flecks of gray, combed straight back. And he was taller than Wade by six inches, at least, and appeared to be in good condition, the kind of condition you buy from a health club, Wade had once observed. His name was Cotter, Jackson Cotter, of Cotter, Wilcox and Browne, and he was from an old Concord political family, and no doubt he was married, had three beautiful children and lived in a big Victorian house up on the west end. And here he was having an affair with Lillian, who three years before had been his client in what he no doubt regarded as a simple but slightly unpleasant upstate divorce case.

Jackson Cotter turned his big green Mercedes around and headed out of the parking lot to the street, turned left and disappeared. Wade realized that his mouth was open, and he closed it. He felt wonderful. Jesus, he felt great! He was standing alone in a darkened doorway next to a restaurant parking lot in downtown Concord in a snowstorm, and he felt more purely cheerful than he had felt in years. Maybe ever. He clapped his hands together as if applauding, stepped from the doorway and strode into the falling snow.

A minute later, he was back in The Stone Warehouse shoving a quarter into the pay phone at the bottom of the stairs. This time, after three rings, someone answered: it was Lillian's husband, Bob Horner; he caught Wade by surprise. Wade pictured the man with an apron tied around his waist and almost laughed, but he quickly recovered and said in what he felt was his normal manner of speaking to Horner on such occasions, "This's Wade. Is Jill around?"

Horner was silent for a few seconds. Then he said, "Ah . . . no. No, Wade, she's not here."

"Jeez, that's too bad. She out with her mom someplace?"

"No. No, Jill's with a friend."

"You expect her back soon? I'm in town, you see. In Concord. And I was hoping maybe I could scoot by and take her out for a pizza or something."

Horner hesitated, then said, "It's kind of late, Wade . . . and she's . . . Jill's staying overnight with a friend tonight."

"Oh-h." Wade hoped he sounded disappointed.

"Yeah, well, maybe if she'd known you were going to be in town . . ."

"I didn't know myself," Wade said. "But next time I'll call ahead," he offered.

Horner said that was a good idea and he would tell Jill that he had called. Then he said, "Wade, maybe I shouldn't mention this, but I was wondering . . ."

"What?"

"Well, I don't want to stir things up again, but . . . look,

I lost my hat the other night up there. In Lawford. I was wondering if maybe somebody picked it up. You didn't see it, did you? After we left."

Wade said, "Your hat? You had a hat?"

"Yes." His voice had turned cold; he knew Wade was lying. "A green felt hat."

"Jeez, Bob, I don't remember any hat. But I'll keep an eye out for it. Maybe somebody else snagged it. You never know."

Horner said thanks and then hurriedly got off the phone.

Smiling broadly, Wade hung up, mounted the stairs and stood at the cash register for a second. He noticed that the three young women and the two guys at the bar had left; the place was almost empty now. There were only a few diners sitting at the tables, and the waitresses were standing around in the back, talking to one another.

The cashier, a stout middle-aged woman filing her nails, said to him, "How much snow out there?"

"Oh, inch or two, I guess. Not much."

"Enough to keep everybody home, though," she said.

"Yeah. Which is where I ought to be getting," Wade said.

"It's too early for winter," the woman observed.

"Yeah. Yeah, it is," Wade said, and he pulled his watch cap down over his ears. "But I like it," he said, and he waved and went out the door.

"Drive careful," the woman called after him, but he didn't hear her.

Making love with Margie that night was especially easy for Wade. Not that it was ever difficult; it was just that sometimes Wade would rather be left alone to think his own thoughts, to use his skull as a wall that kept him in and other people out.

But being in bed with Margie made Wade feel safe and free in ways that he rarely felt—not at work, certainly, thanks to LaRiviere, and not when he was at home alone, either, and not when he was with Jill, and not once with Lillian in all those years of being married to her. When he was drinking late at Toby's he sometimes got to feeling safe, but never free.

No, it was only with Margie, and only in bed with her, that he felt the way he imagined he should have as a child but could not, because of his father, mostly, but also his mother, who could not protect him. And thus, when he lay down beside

Margie and they began to make love to one another, he often hesitated, held back slightly, as if loitering, while she plunged on ahead. Then she would grow impatient and would urge him to hurry up, for God's sake, let us not hang around here any longer than we have to, my friend, and he would come forward toward her, and that would be that.

Tonight, though, he loitered not at all. He had arrived at Margie's house around eight-thirty, his drive north from Concord slowed somewhat by the snow. All the way up, he had pictured Margie naked and turning softly in her bed beneath him, her arms flung back, mouth open, legs wrapped tightly around his hips, her sweet soft skin smooth and pliant, her large slow body suddenly vulnerable, swift and intrepidly intimate, the way Wade believed only women could be, and when he walked across her back porch into the warm kitchen, he was already tumescent, oh boy, ready to go; and she was ready too, perhaps having numerous times that afternoon and evening imagined him naked and in bed as well, his tough thick body arched intently over her at that exquisite moment when he first entered her, so mysteriously male and powerful in that precise way, in the way of his maleness, that to give herself over to the power, to succumb willingly to the sheer physical force of his body, was to enter deeply into the mystery, which she did instantly, for that was where she wanted to be.

They had talked awhile in the kitchen: she served him a bowl of beef stew and chunks of the homemade bread she was so proud of and that Wade loved; and while he ate and she sat opposite him at the table, watching, he told her what had happened in Concord, his disappointing meeting with the lawyer (he neglected to mention the wheelchair) and his exhilarating discovery later. He did not tell her about his phone conversation with Lillian's husband.

And then they went straight to her darkened bedroom. He lit the candle by the side of the bed, as he always did, and in seconds they both had their clothes off, the covers kicked back, and were wordlessly wrapped in one another's warm skin. She came quickly, and then a minute later came a second time, more powerfully, gulping and crying out several times, until he, too, was inundated by the orgasm, and he suddenly found himself coming and heard himself moan along with her and then sigh.

They lay on their backs—feet, hips and shoulders touching—in silence for a long while. Finally, in a low flat voice, as if talking to himself, Wade said, "I've been thinking a lot about Jack Hewitt. I'm worried about him," he went on. "About that business yesterday, with him and that guy Twombley."

Her voice, too, came from a distance, from another room in the large old house. "Jack's sort of sensitive, I guess. More than most. But he'll be okay in a few weeks. Maybe even sooner."

"There's something funny about that shooting. There's lots funny about it, actually."

"I heard he was drunk as a coot last night and got into a big fight at Toby's with Hettie when she wanted to drive him home. He got mad and drove off without her. Left her standing in the parking lot."

"I'm sure, I'm positive, that it didn't happen the way Jack says it did. It could have, of course, but it didn't. I know he's lying."

She went on as if she hadn't heard him. "Jack's turned into one of those men who are permanently angry, I think. He used to be a sweet kid, but it's like, when he found out that he couldn't play baseball anymore, he changed. He used to be so sweet," she said. "Now he's like everyone else."

"I've been wondering if maybe Jack shot Twombley, instead of Twombley shooting himself. I've even been wondering if maybe Jack shot him on purpose."

Now she heard him. "*Wade!* How can you even think such a thing? Why would Jack Hewitt do that, shoot Twombley on purpose?"

"Money."

"Jack doesn't need money."

"Everybody needs money," he said. "Except guys like Twombley and that sonofabitch son-in-law of his. People like that."

"Still, Jack wouldn't kill somebody for it. Besides, who would pay him to do such a terrible thing?"

"I don't know. Lots of people, probably. Guy like Evan Twombley, big-time union official and all, he's probably got lots of people want him dead. Believe me, those construction unions are full of mean motherfuckers. Down in Massachusetts all those unions do business with the Mafia, you know. My brother told me some stuff."

She gave a laugh. "The Mafia wouldn't hire a kid like Jack

Hewitt to do their business for them."

"No. I guess not. Still . . . I just know Jack's lying about how it happened. I can tell. He just seemed too . . . too tight or something, too slick, when he told it. I know that kid, I know what he's like inside. He's a lot like I was when I was his age, you know."

"Yes. I suppose he is. But you never would've done something like that, shot somebody for money."

"No, I guess not. Not for money. But there were times back then, when I was a kid, when I might've shot somebody if I'd been given half a damned excuse. I used to be pretty fucked up, you know."

"But you're not now," she said, and she smiled in the darkness.

Wade lapsed into silence and for a moment thought about his recent days and nights, wondering how to characterize them. Fucked up? Not fucked up? What kind of life did he lead, anyhow? What kind of man had he become in his forties?

He rolled over onto his side and, propped on one elbow, rested his head in the flat of his hand and studied Margie's broad face. Her eyes were closed. She breathed lightly through her mouth, which curved into the residue of an ironic smile. To him, her face was wide open, bravely unprotected; her mouth was relaxed, and her lips parted, so that her upper front teeth protruded slightly and looked like a schoolgirl's new teeth to Wade; the two vertical lines that usually creased her forehead were gone, as if erased, and she might have been a mischievous child pretending to be asleep: her skin seemed to glisten in the half light of the room, and Wade reached over and brushed away a moist strand of her hair, then leaned down and kissed her on the exact center of her forehead.

"I can see what you looked like when you were a kid. Exactly," he whispered.

She kept her eyes closed and said, "You knew me when I was a kid."

"Yeah. Yeah, I did, but I never knew what you looked like. Not really. I mean, I never really studied your face, like now. So I never was able to see you as a kid, a little girl, when you actually were a little kid. Until now, this way."

"What way?"

"After making love. I like it. It's nice to be able to see that in a grown-up person. And strange," he said, and added, "It's scary, sort of."

"Yes. It is nice. And strange," she said. After a few seconds, she added, "I don't think it's the same for women, though." She opened her eyes, and the vertical creases in her brow reappeared, and Wade's view of her as a child got blocked. "I mean, women can see the little boy in the man pretty easily, you know. But I think we see it mostly when the man doesn't know we're watching. It happens when he's paying attention to something else. Like watching sports on TV or fixing his car or something."

"What about after making love?"

"Well . . . I think mostly men try to hide the boy in themselves. They think it's a sign of weakness or something, so they try to hide it. Maybe especially when they're making love. You, for instance," she said, and punched him lightly on the shoulder. "After we make love, you look like you just climbed a mountain or something. Triumphant. The conquering hero! Tarzan beating his chest." She laughed, and he laughed with her, but hesitantly.

"Oh, you try to be cool about it," she went on, "but you're proud of yourself. I can tell. And you should be," she added, and she punched him again. "Frankly, though," she said, and she peered out from under her eyelashes, "frankly, though, you needn't be proud. Because I'm easy. Real easy."

"For me."

"Oh yes, only for you. Very hard for anybody else."

Wade laughed and slid out of bed and padded barefoot and naked down the hall to the refrigerator and pulled out a bottle of Rolling Rock. By the time he got back to the bedroom, the bottle was half empty. "Want some?" he asked, and passed it over to her.

She said, "Thanks," propped herself up and took a delicate sip.

Wade lay on his back, folded his arms behind his head and peered into the cloudy darkness above him. The candle beside the bed was guttering; on the wall the flickery shadows of his elbows and arms looked like tepees and campfires.

Margie sipped at the beer and studied the shadows and decided once again, as she always did at times like this, when

Wade was peaceful and sweet and smart, that she loved him.

"Do you still think," he said, "do you think I ought to forget this custody thing? After what I saw tonight, with Lillian and that lawyer of hers? Illegal drugs and illicit sex, you know."

Margie was silent for a moment. She sighed and said, "Wade, you got to be able to prove those things. But really, I don't know what I think. It's not me who's the father, it's you."

"Yeah, I am. And that's the whole problem in a nutshell," he said. "I'm *supposed* to be the father, but I'm not able to. Not unless I make a huge fight over it. A goddamned war. Thing is, Margie, now it's a war I believe I can win."

"You're obsessed with this, aren't you?"

He thought about the word for a few seconds—*obsessed, obsessed, obsessed*—and said, "Yes. Yes, I am. I am obsessed with it. It may be the only thing I've wanted in my life so far that I've been clear about wanting. Totally absolutely clear."

She took a sip of beer and said, "Then . . . I guess you have to go ahead and do it."

He was silent. Then he said, "There's another thing I've been thinking a lot about lately," and he took the bottle from her hands, finished it off in one long swallow and set it on the floor beside the bed. He slipped one arm under her head and reached around her with the other and heard himself say words as if a stranger were speaking and he had no idea what words the stranger would say next. "I don't know how you feel about the idea, Margie, because we've never talked about it before. Maybe because we've been too scared of the idea to talk about it. But I've been thinking lately, I've been thinking that maybe we should get married sometime. You and me."

"Oh, Wade," she said, sounding vaguely disappointed.

'I been just thinking about it, that's all," he said rapidly. "It's not like a marriage proposal or anything, just a thought. An idea. Something for you and me to talk about and think about. You know?"

"All right," she said. And she waited a moment and said, "I'll think about it."

"Good." He kissed her on the lips, then rolled away from her and blew out the candle. When he lay back down, he could hear her low slow breathing, and after a few seconds, he tried catching her rhythm with his, as he did when they made love, and got it, so that soon they were breathing in harmony, walking along together, stride matching stride, brave and in love and crossing a grassy meadow together with blue sky overhead, drifting puffs of white clouds, soaring birds above and sunshine warming their heads and shoulders, and neither of them, ever again, alone.

13

THE SHRILL RING of the telephone tumbled Wade from light and heat—a blond dream of a beach town in summer—tossed him into darkness and cold, a bed and a room he could not at first recognize. The wrangling jangle of a telephone: he did not know where the damned thing was; it kept on ringing, still coming at him from all sides; some kind of maddened bird or rabid bat darting around his head in the darkness.

Then it stopped, and Wade heard Margie's voice, realized he was in her bed, her house, phone, darkness, cold. He was naked, and the covers had slipped down to his waist, and his chest and shoulders and arms were chilled. He shivered his way under the covers and listened to her sleep-thickened voice.

"What? Who is this? Oh, yeah, he's here. Wait a second," she said, and she bumped Wade on the shoulder with the receiver. "It's Gordon LaRiviere. He's rip-shit about something." She peered at the clock radio on the table beside the bed. "Christ. Four o'clock."

Wade placed the receiver against his face, said, "Hello?" and remembered: the snow. Oh, Jesus, yes. It had been snowing all night, and here he was lying in bed, sound asleep. He had acted like any other citizen with a right to go to bed at night expecting the roads to be plowed in the morning when he woke up and made ready to drive himself and the family to church. Why had he forgotten? How had he been able to spend the night as if he did not work for LaRiviere?

It was the first time since LaRiviere got the contract to plow the town roads that this had happened to Wade; it alarmed him. What will you do next, when you have forgotten something this routine? It puzzled him; it made no sense. His life was essentially so simple and reactive that to do everything that was expected of him, Wade almost did not have to think: if it snowed, he went to LaRiviere's garage and took either the truck or the grader and plowed the roads until they were clear; if the roads were covered with ice, he hooked the sander to the truck or grader and sanded the roads; and, of course, if it was a school day, he showed up at the school at seven-thirty and directed traffic at the crossing. After that, Monday through Friday, he spent the day doing whatever LaRiviere told him to—drill a well in Catamount, estimate a job in Littleton, clean the gear and stack pipe in the shop. Simple. A wholly reactive life.

Now, for the first time in that life, it had snowed and Wade had not reacted. A strange kind of memory lapse: he had behaved as if last night had been merely an ordinary clear cold Saturday night in November instead of a snowy one; and he had ended up in bed with Margie Fogg—because his daughter was not with him this weekend and Margie had made it clear that she wanted him to make love to her; and then he had fallen asleep—because he was sleepy. Only to find that somehow in the last eight or ten hours he seemed to have stepped out of his life and into some other person's life, a stranger's. And this scared him even more than LaRiviere's predictable and justifiable wrath did. He realized that his hands were sweating. What the hell was going on with him? Maybe he really was fucked up, just like when he was in his twenties. Just like Jack. He had thought everything was going to be fine.

"Wade!" LaRiviere bellowed. "Boy, I hope to Christ you're through getting your dick wet! You think maybe you could do a little work for me before the fucking sun comes up?"

"I . . . I didn't realize . . ."

"No, I guess you didn't. It's only been snowing since sup-pertime. Where the fuck you been, Florida? For Christ's sake, Wade, you know the goddamn drill. You know what to do on a goddamn night like this. You *plow!* You drive into town, and you take out the fucking plow, just like Jimmy did at eleven last night, and you plow, goddammit." He paused for breath and started in again. "You plow till all the fucking roads in this town are cleared. And then I pay you for it. And then the town pays me. Very simple, Wade. I am the road agent, and I got a goddamn responsibility to the town, for which they pay me, and you got a responsibility to me, for which I pay you. That's the drill. Got it?" He was panting. Wade pictured him red-faced and rounded in his rumpled pajamas at his kitchen table.

Wade said, "Jimmy's already gone out?"

"Wade, it's fucking after four A.M.! He's been out since eleven last night."

"I suppose he's got the truck, and I get to go out in the grader again."

"You think he oughta swap, maybe? Where the fuck you been the last five hours, tell me that! No, I'll goddamn tell *you* where you been: while Jimmy's been out there plowing snow, you been tucked in bed plowing Margie Fogg!"

"You're crossing a line," Wade said quietly.

"You already crossed, you've crossed just about every god-damn line you can in this town and still get by, so don't start warning me, buddy. You got fifteen minutes. You got fifteen minutes to get your ass down here to the shop and put that fucking grader out on the road. I spent the whole last hour on the phone and the CB trying to find out where the hell you were. Ever since Jimmy called in that none of your roads were plowed yet and he ain't seen you anywhere."

"I'll be there," Wade said, and he sighed loudly.

"Fifteen minutes. You got fifteen minutes, or you're fired, Wade. From *everything*. You're supposed to be on call twenty-four hours a day. You're the town cop, and you plow the town roads. It's like that. I had a short talk with Mel Gordon, by the way. But we'll settle that later, you and me. Right now, Wade, you haul your ass on down here to the shop."

"I said I'll be there," Wade said in a dead voice, and he reached across Margie and slid the receiver into its cradle.

"He's really pissed," she said. "Isn't he?"

"Yep." Wade slid out of the bed and yanked his clothes on.

"He probably ought to be, though. I mean, I never really thought of it," she said. "The plowing. How come you didn't just do it? What happened?"

"I forgot."

"Forgot? You forgot it was snowing?"

"No, no, I knew it was snowing, all right. I just forgot that I was the one who had to plow it off the roads. Sometimes," he said, "sometimes you just forget who you are. Especially when you're sick of who you are," he added, and he walked quickly from the bedroom, and Margie thought, Oh boy, trouble.

It was cold, but not uncomfortably so, and Wade was almost glad to be outdoors. Sometime earlier, probably around midnight, while he slept, the snow had stopped falling, and the sky had cleared. Now, as Wade drove toward town from Margie's house, he could feel morning coming on, and he suddenly felt glad to be out of Margie's bed and alone in his car with the heater fan clattering, the woods on either side of the road dark and impenetrable behind a white skirt of snow, the car headlights splashing bright light ahead of him, like a wave washing up on a beach.

LaRiviere sat glowering out his kitchen window when Wade drove into the lot and parked his car next to the grader, but he did not come out to holler or to threaten him, and Wade simply went about his business and drove back out in the grader. He knew his route, and he knew that it would take him four to five hours in this snow, barely six inches of light powder. There was no school today: he would not have to worry about being out in front of the school in time to direct traffic and could just go on plowing until the job was done.

It was not long before Wade began actually to enjoy himself; it was almost fun, huddled up there in the grader alone in the cockpit with the four headlamps peering like monstrous eyes over the top of the huge front tires, casting nets of light across the smooth soft unbroken snow. The pain from his tooth was steady and familiar, like an old friend, and Wade felt calm and competent and not at all lonely.

Headed north on Main Street, he chugged past Alma Pittman's house. Under a white mantle, the house was dark as a tomb, and Wade imagined the tall thin woman lying in her bed in the upstairs bedroom where she had slept alone her whole life, straight out and on her back, her hands crossed over her flat chest—not as if dead, exactly, but in a state of suspended animation, waiting for dawnlight, when she would rise, dress, make herself a pot of tea and go back to her work of keeping the town records. For as long as Wade could remember, back into his childhood, Alma Pittman had been the town clerk. She ran for the post, with only token opposition, every year, her election a simple annual renewal, as if no one else could be trusted to log the births and deaths, record the marriages and divorces, list the sales and resales of land and houses, register the voters and issue the permits and licenses for hunting and fishing and calculate and collect the taxes and fees, and in that way connect the town to the larger communities—the county, the state and even the nation—and make the people of Lawford into citizens, make them into more than a lost tribe, more than a sad jumble of families huddled in a remote northern valley against the cold and the dark.

Wade knew the inside of Alma Pittman's house well: she was his ex-wife's aunt, and after Lillian's father had died and her mother had remarried and moved up to Littleton, Lillian, who still had two years of high school left, had moved in with her aunt. That was the summer Wade got his driver's license, and every Sunday he drove Lillian out to the Riverside Cemetery, where she placed wildflowers in a plastic vase by her father's gravestone and then stood silently for a few moments at the foot of his grave, wringing her hands and fighting off tears. She followed the routine precisely every Sunday afternoon, as if the whole enterprise—wildflowers, silence, hand wringing, heaving chest and wet eyes—were a spiritual exercise, a weekly purification rite that had nothing to do with her father.

To Wade that summer, Lillian was a nun touched by tragedy. She was tall and slender, still a girl, with long oak-colored hair that, brushed a hundred strokes every night and fifty more in the morning, hung straight as rain almost to her waist. Her father had been a housepainter who had not drawn a sober breath in years, people said. The previous autumn he had been painting the flagpole at the newly built elementary school, and in sight of half the children in town he had fallen from the top of the pole, had smashed his back and skull and had died right there on the playground.

I was in the first grade then, my first year at school, and

had been among the fifty or sixty kids who had seen the man fall (or heard it, or were close enough to have seen it but did not—I am not sure even today whether I actually did see it) and told the story over and over at supper—"I'm out there at third base, so I got this wicked good view of the flagpole, which is right behind the batter's cage, and all of a sudden, it's like a plane crashing, *eerroo-oom!* Whap!"

Finally, after a week of it, Wade had snapped at me, "Hey, c'mon, Rolfe, we all know the story. Whyn't you think of something new to say? Besides, it's kind of disgusting when we're eating."

Pop had held his fork in midair between his plate and mouth and said, "Leave him be, Wade. Don't be such a candy-ass, anyhow. Rolfe probably won't ever see nothing that stupid again."

"I hope not," Ma had said.

Wade had shut up, but sensing the source of my brother's discomfort, I did not tell the story again.

The following spring, Lillian's mother married Tom Smith, a divorced drinking buddy of Lillian's father, another housepainter, who lived up in Littleton and owned a triple-decker apartment house there. The woman took her two younger daughters to Littleton with her, leaving Lillian behind, to complete high school and live with her spinster aunt, Alma Pittman, the hardworking dour pinch-faced older sister of her dead father, a woman who was regarded as necessary to the town but a little overeducated, because she had studied accounting for two years at Plymouth State before coming back to Lawford during the war to take care of her ailing parents.

Lillian did not particularly like her cheerless aunt, but the woman left her alone, gave her a room upstairs and allowed Wade to come over whenever he wanted and even let them spend hours alone in Lillian's room with the door closed, where they passionately kissed and hugged and groped through each other's clothing to their virginal bodies. And after a while, exhausted, they would cease to struggle with the angels of their adolescent consciences; they fell away panting and talked in whispers of their fears and longings; and sometimes they came downstairs and sat side by side on the couch, with Alma in her ladder-back rocker, and the three of them watched television together. And though Wade and Lillian did not actually make love in those steamy sessions upstairs (perhaps *because* they never actually made love), it was during those summer months, when Wade was sixteen years old and Lillian fifteen, that they decided to marry as soon as they graduated from high school. It was the same summer that Wade first spoke to anyone of our father's violence.

In the years that our father had been beating him, Wade had not spoken of it to anyone, not to his friends at school or on the football and baseball teams, who often joked, the way boys in cars or in locker rooms will, about how their old man used to beat the shit out of them but he damn well better not try it now or he will damn well get his ass kicked. And he could not imagine talking about it with our mother, though at times it seemed clear that she wanted him to. Whenever she brought the subject up, he felt his heart race, as if she had asked him something about his sex life or told him something about hers, and he always said, "I don't want to talk about it."

Our sister, Lena, suffered only her father's verbal assaults, so Wade knew she could not possibly understand. It was bad for her, but different. And though he sometimes wanted to warn me, now seven and not yet beaten by the man, Wade felt somehow that if no one spoke of it, if no one acknowledged it, then it might never happen again. It might turn out to be ancient history.

As for his older brothers, they seemed to Wade to regard our father's occasional, predictable and, for the most part, avoidable attacks as just one more of the many brutalities of our life so far, as one small corner of the rough terrain of childhood, something we were supposed to endure and then pass through and become scornful of, which was why, goddammit, Elbourne had gone, and next month Charlie was going, straight into the army without even waiting to graduate from high school. So that if Wade had spoken of it to them, he would only have been pointing out his inadequacies, revealing to his older brothers, as to himself, his lesser status as a human being.

Besides, for Wade, even when he believed he was thinking clearly about it, the beatings were still too confusing and complicated to talk about with Elbourne and Charlie. All Elbourne would say is, "Don't come to me with your problems, Wade. You're big enough now to wipe the floor with the sonofabitch, if you want to. Do like I did. After that, believe me, he'll never lay a hand on you." And Charlie would say,

"You don't even have to wipe the floor with him, you just got to make him think you're *willing* to. Like I did. After that, he'll back off. Remember?" And Wade did remember.

It was four years earlier, and one spring weekend our father decided to save the barn, which had been falling down for a decade, by tearing off the fallen part and rebuilding the rest with whatever timbers and boards he could salvage from the half-collapsed back loft and the old cow stalls below. The framing timbers were still for the most part unrotted, and many of the aged wide pine boards, silvery gray and bearded with splinters, were reusable, and our father's notion of shortening the barn by thirty feet and squaring up the rest, with no expenditure except for nails, was an attractive one—even to his sons, who knew they would have to provide the free labor.

Elbourne got out of it—he was sixteen and had a weekend job already, pumping gas for Chub Merritt, but Charlie, who was fourteen then and large for his age, had nothing better to do on a cloudy April Saturday, and Wade, though only twelve, was able to pull nails and haul boards and timbers alongside a grown man. I have no memory of the event. I was too young to help in any way and probably stayed inside the whole day.

Wade and Charlie liked the idea: the barn had been ugly to them for years, an embarrassment, even before the roof had collapsed at the rear from the weight of the snow one particularly bad winter, and they had learned to avert their gaze from the decrepit leaning unpainted structure, to pretend that it was not sagging there in the lot between the house and the woods. Now they could look at it and imagine a crisply squared handsome old barn made tight against the weather and clean enough inside to use as a garage and workshop.

Pop had told them at breakfast, "I figure a couple, three weekends is all, and we'll have us a brand-new barn built out of the old one. We can store a winter's wood in it then, and you boys want to work on some goddamned old clunker there, no problem."

Wade and Charlie had gone out to the barn and had started ripping off and hauling boards from the back to the front before Pop had even finished breakfast: it was rare that people in the Whitehouse family worked on something together, and each of the boys was secretly pleased by the chance to work alongside his father and brother on a project that so clearly would benefit them all. In a short while, Pop had joined them, had set up his table saw a short ways outside the barn door and was cutting the boards to size and nailing them over old gaps and holes. He was no carpenter, but it was not a difficult job, and by noon they could see a difference: most of the skeleton of the rear half of the barn had been exposed, and most of the holes in the front had been covered over.

They broke for lunch, leftover macaroni and cheese, and the boys sat at the table so they could look over Pop's wispy red hair and out the window behind him to the barn, and while they ate they kept glancing up to admire what they had done so far. They finished eating before Pop did and returned to work, and when he joined them he was lugging a six-pack of Schlitz, which he set on the ground next to his table saw. He popped open the first and said, "Might's well make this enjoyable." He said it glumly, as if he believed it was impossible to make anything enjoyable.

The boys said nothing. They looked at each other, then resumed pulling down the boards and knocking out the bent rusted nails and hauling the boards forward and stacking them neatly a few feet from the saw, where Pop went on measuring, and trimming them and nailing them into place. A cutting breeze had come up, and the smooth gray sky had roughened and lowered somewhat. At one point, the saw stopped its whine, and Wade heard the wind hiss through the pines, reminding him of winter, and he suddenly smelled wood smoke. He looked over at the house and saw a silver ribbon of smoke unravel from the chimney and knew that Ma had started a fire in the kitchen stove, and for the first time that day he wished he were not doing what he was doing.

Then it started to rain, a cold prickly windblown rain, and Pop hollered for the boys to come help him haul the table saw and extension cord inside the barn. They got the saw inside, and the three of them stood silently in the cold gloom and listened to the rain drum against the roof. Ancient rotted hay in the lofts overhead smelled sourly of failure and disappointment to all three of them, and Pop polished off the last of the six-pack and said, "Fuck it, let's call it a day."

"Maybe it'll stop in a few minutes," Charlie said. Besides, he pointed out, the extension cord to the house was long enough for them to run the saw inside the barn as well as out, and a lot of the boards and some of the framing could be pulled down without going out in the rain.

Pop rummaged through his jacket pocket and pulled out his cigarettes and lit one. The familiar smell of the cigarette relaxed Wade, and he leaned back against the wall and inhaled and wished he were old enough to carry his own cigarettes. He had smoked numerous times at school, and he liked it, liked the taste and smell, the way it made him slightly dizzy for a few seconds, then calm, and he liked the way he thought a butt dangling from his mouth made him look—like a grown man. But he knew that if he started carrying his own cigarettes around and pulling one out and smoking it at times like this, Pop would not object; he would only laugh at him.

Above them, swallows made a quiet gurgling sound from somewhere in the mossy darkness of the rafters, and Wade remembered summer afternoons, when the hay was dry and not so ancient and sour as now, wrestling in the lofts with his older brothers, the three boys pretending they were pirates boarding a Spanish galleon, where they fought in the rigging over the division of the spoils: the jewels for Elbourne, the doubloons for Charlie, and for Wade . . . whatever was left over. He tried dollars, and they laughed at him for his stupidity, no dollars in those days; he tried watches and rings, and Charlie said those were jewels; and so somehow he got his pick of the women, which seemed like nothing worthwhile to him, so he refused, and before he knew why or how, he was made to walk the plank, his brothers behind him poking him with their wooden swords, as, blindfolded, he edged his way along a beam high up in the barn, felt the end of it with his toes, stopped, got shoved from behind by the point of one of the swords and was falling through space, in blackness pitching into the hay, scratchy and full of dust, hugging him like a huge pillow.

"Charlie," Pop said. "How much arm you got on you?"

"Huh?"

"You know something, Charlie-boy, you been getting awful big for your britches lately. So I was wondering how much arm you got on you. Wondering if you think you can put your old man's arm down." He smiled playfully, and Charlie grinned.

"Why? You want to arm wrestle?"

" 'Why? You want to arm wrestle?' " the man mimicked the boy. "Of *course* I want to arm wrestle. Just to set you right on who's still the boss here, who says when we go in and so forth. Come on," he said, "let's go," and he rolled up his right sleeve.

Charlie looked around him. "Where?"

"Right here. On the saw." Our father reached under the steel tabletop and cranked down the jagged eight-inch blade, made it disappear below the slot, so that the flat of the table was waist-high between him and Charlie. He leaned over and placed the point of his right elbow on the table next to the blade slot, his hand open and grasping at air.

"Come on, let's go," the man said, grinning. "Keep your elbow the other side of the blade slot, though. You cross it, you lose. And keep your other hand behind your back, like I am," he said, and he grandly swung his left hand behind him and smacked it against the small of his back. "You're not allowed to hold on to anything for leverage."

"You worried, Pop?" Charlie looked over at Wade and smiled and rolled his eyes. Both boys knew that the man was going to beat him easily, which made Pop's obsession with the rules of the game amusing: it was one of the few aspects of his character that they liked, this occasional pointless fastidiousness, which may have been all he had for a moral code. Whenever the family saw him subject himself to it, we were comforted.

"Shit no. No, I'm not worried. I just don't want you claiming later that I didn't beat you fair and square. Right's right, boy. For both of us. So come on, let's get to it," Pop said, and he smiled warmly into his son's round face.

Charlie rolled up his sleeve and placed his right elbow on the steel table. "Cold," he observed, and he grabbed Pop's hand. They were the same height, Charlie maybe an inch or two taller, but the boy was skinnier than the man, and his arm and hand were still a boy's.

"Wade, you give the signal," Pop said, and Wade came around to stand at the end of the table, like an umpire. "You ready to get whipped, Charlie?" the man asked.

"Yep."

Wade said, "One. Two. Three. Go."

The man's arm stiffened, and the muscles and ligaments swelled, as the boy pulled on it with his own. Our father smiled and said, "You know what they call this where I come from?"

Charlie was holding his breath and trying with all his

strength to pull our father's arm off the vertical; he could not speak: he shook his head no.

"Twisting wrists," the man said, calmly, as if he were talking to his son on the phone. Then he slowly twisted the boy's hand in his and drew it a few inches toward him and smiled again. He was not only stronger than his son, he was smarter.

But suddenly Charlie twisted back, surprising our father, and he found himself able to draw the man's bulging arm a few inches toward his own chest, off the vertical, and then he twisted his wrist back the other way and discovered that he had leverage on the man, and instead of pulling on his arm, he was pushing it.

Wade was thrilled, astonished, and then he was frightened, and he imagined the saw blade coming up, whirring between their elbows, rising slowly as they grunted over it, inching closer and closer to where their arms joined at the wrists. He wanted them to let go, to let their clasped hands come unglued, before they were sliced neatly apart by the saw. He took a step back from the table and tried to look away from his father and brother, but he could not move his gaze.

Pop still smiled, but now it seemed forced, pasted onto his face. "You . . . think . . . you got . . . me . . . eh?" he said, as he fought back against the force of his son's arm, shoulder, back and legs, for now Charlie believed that he actually might beat our father in this game, and he had thrown his entire body into it. He said nothing, kept pushing down on our father's declining arm.

The rain fell against the roof of the barn; the swallows chuckled in the rafters. Down below, in the center of the open space between the lofts and stalls, the two bent figures faced each other intently over a small steel table, while Wade stood at the end of the table, bearing witness.

Wade suddenly clapped his hands together and blurted, "Come on, Charlie! Come on!"

Our father looked over at Wade and glared, and he redoubled his effort, twisting Charlie's wrist and hand back toward him, then quickly away, so that he was able to shift the strain on his own arm and start to pull with the full strength of his bicep and shoulder, drawing the boy's arm slowly back to a vertical position, where once again their clasped hands were held suspended above the slot that hid the blade of the saw.

They stayed there, each unable to move the other, the veins in their foreheads standing out, faces and arms reddening from the effort. Neither of them smiled or said a word. They grunted now and again, and their breath came in hard gasps.

Then Charlie's other hand, the left, wandered back toward the table, as if curious and a little stupid, and it lay on the table palm down. And when Pop saw it there, he said, "Hold it! Hold it!" He let go of Charlie's right hand and lifted his elbow off the table and stood up straight. He brushed his hair back with both hands and said, "You cheated. It's a default."

Charlie looked at his left hand in disgust. "Aw, c'mon, Pop, I could've just put it back. All you had to do was say. I didn't get no advantage."

"Sorry, Charlie. Rules is rules, m' boy," Pop said, and he smiled cheerfully, turned and walked out the huge open door and peered up at the sky. "Still raining," he called back, "and looks like it's going to keep on. I'm going in, where it's warm," he said, and he hitched up his baggy pants and disappeared from view.

The boys were silent for a moment. Charlie said, "I could have beat him, you know. I was beating him."

"Yeah."

"He knows it, too. He knows I was beating him."

"Yeah. He does."

"The bastard."

"Yeah. The bastard."

They stood in the middle of the barn floor a few minutes longer, listening to the rain and the swallows and staring out the rear of the barn, which was wide open to the dark-gray sky and the meadow and pinewoods at the far side of the building, where they had ripped down all the boards. They knew that now the job would never be done, that tomorrow our father would find other things for himself to do and other chores for them, and the barn would stay the way it was, its ribs and spine exposed to the weather, the rest slowly rotting off, as rain blew in and snow fell. It would be like a huge long-dead animal come upon in the woods when the snow melts, half in the ground and half out, half bones and half flesh and fur, and when you walk up on it, you see what it is and remember what it was, and you look away.

14

LILLIAN WANTED TO SEE Wade's face, but he kept as much of it as he could out of sight: he wore sunglasses and a Red Sox cap pulled down low, and as he drove he kept glancing out the window on his left and talked to her without looking at her. They were on the way to the Riverside Cemetery, their regular Sunday afternoon visit to her father's grave, and Wade had picked her up at her aunt Alma's, as usual, right after lunch. It was a bright sunny day with a cloudless blue sky and high dry air, and in spite of the somber occasion, Lillian had come out of her aunt's house whistling a song from *South Pacific.*

She stopped whistling as soon as she got into the car, Wade's ten-year-old Ford sedan, which he had salvaged from the parts of three different Fords. They had all been wrecks, bought from Chub Merritt last fall when Wade was fifteen for a hundred bucks apiece and worked on at home throughout the winter and spring in what remained of the old barn behind the house. He had got his license in May but did not drive the car until late June, not until he had it running smoothly and had painted it cherry red, with his initials, WW, pin-striped onto the front doors just below the window frame, a gold monogram slanted to the right and made to look like lightning bolts.

"Wade, what's the matter with your face?" she asked, and tried to see.

He turned his face to his left and said, "Nothing's the matter."

She saw, however, that his cheeks were swollen and discolored; she instantly knew that behind the dark glasses his eyes were blackened. "Oh, Wade!" she cried. "You got into a fight!"

He denied it, but she persisted. He had promised he would not drink or fight. He had promised. Many times they had decided together that these were stupid activities, drinking and fighting, fine for their stupid insensitive friends to indulge in, perhaps, but not for Wade Whitehouse and Lillian Pittman, who were superior to all that, who were finer, nobler, more intelligent than their friends. Because they had each other, they did not need anyone else; they believed that. They did not need their parents, though she did wish her father were still alive—he would have understood and admired Wade; and not their friends; and not any of their teachers at school, who were dull and hopelessly out of touch with what was important and moving to teenagers; and not her aunt Alma or Gordon LaRiviere, Wade's new boss, or anyone else in town, either. They needed only each other, exclusively and totally, and they had each other, more or less, so they were free to ignore everyone else, which meant, among other things, that Wade did not have to drive around at night with the other boys his age drinking beer and getting into brawls in Catamount or at the Moonlight Club down in Sunapee or with summer kids from Massachusetts at the Weirs in Laconia. He had promised. He hated that stuff, he had told her, just as much as she did. It was stupid. It was brutal. It was humiliating.

It was also dangerous and, if they were fighting over a girl, as they often were, sexual; consequently Lillian and Wade kept track of who had fought whom over the weekend. They listened to Monday morning hallway gossip as eagerly as their classmates did, and sometimes Lillian secretly imagined Wade getting into a fight with, say, Jimmy Dame, who had told her once in the hallway that she had great tits, why didn't she show them off more? And when she told him what Jimmy had said to her, Wade had secretly imagined slamming him up against the lockers and punching him once, twice, three times, quick hard hits to the chin that snapped Jimmy's head back against the lockers, making a loud metallic clang every time Wade hit him.

Lillian reached across the seat to Wade and brushed his cheek with her fingertips.

He pulled away and said, *"Don't!"*

At the bend in the Minuit River, where the land rises gradually from the eastern bank to a high meadow, Wade turned off the road and drove along the rutted lane that leads uphill to the cemetery. The light fell in planes tinged with pink, great broad sheets of it that reflected off the dry mint-green leaves of maples and oaks and the meadow grass shuddering in the breeze. Where the meadow bellies and the rise eases somewhat, the lane passes through a cut-stone gate into the cemetery, and Wade pulled the old Ford off to the right and parked it.

Lillian got quickly out, taking her bouquet of daisies and Indian paintbrush with her, and strode away from the car. Wade watched her cross in front of him again, fifty feet farther into the rows of graves, and pass between the Emerson and Locke family plots, graves that went back a hundred and fifty years. Lillian did not cross the graves; she always walked along the proper paths laid between them, taking sharp rights and lefts, until she had zigzagged her way to the far corner of the cemetery and stood at last at the foot of her father's grave. A small red-granite stone marked it: *Samuel Laurence Pittman 1924–1964.*

Wade sat in the car and let the sun beat down on his face and chest, let it warm and soothe him, while through his sunglasses he watched Lillian remove the old dead stems and leaves from the plastic vase next to the gravestone and replace them with the new. She walked quickly to a spigot in the ground a short distance away and returned with the flowers in water and gently set the vase down to the right of the marker, adjusting it carefully, as if making it easier for her father to admire them. Then she stood, clasping her hands together at her waist, like a woman in prayer, and looked steadily at the gravestone, as if it were her favorite portrait of her father.

Wade thought, I wish my father was dead. Dead and buried. He savored the image: he drives out here on Sundays, just like his girlfriend, Lillian, dutiful and loving, and he stands at the foot of his father's grave for hours at a time, contemplating the man's confinement down there, locked inside a heavy wooden coffin, buried under six feet of dirt with a three-hundred-pound headstone on top, just to make sure.

Wade was still young, and Elbourne and Charlie had not died yet, so he imagined death as either absence or confinement or, in some cases, both, which was what he wanted for our father, both. He wanted the furious redheaded man gone to someplace else, and he wanted him imprisoned there, locked up, manacled, bound so that he could not ball those hard fists of his and could not lash out with them, could not swing his arms, kick his feet, grab and push and toss and kick a person. The man would have to lie in his box flat on his back, arms crossed over his chest and wrapped tightly, legs bound at the ankles, and then the cover is thumped down and padlocked, and maybe a chain is wrapped around the coffin and padlocked, like Houdini's. Then the coffin is lowered by a backhoe into the grave, which has been dug extra deep, so that you cannot see the bottom without shining a flashlight directly into it, even during the day. And then dirt gets shoved into the grave, rocks and all, and afterwards the backhoe is driven back and forth over the filled-in grave, flattening and smoothing and tamping down the dirt with the weight of the machine. Sod is placed over the raw dirt, and soon it has woven its roots into the roots of the grass surrounding the grave, making a tough green quilt to cover it. And finally Wade lowers the gravestone from the backhoe, a huge boulder dug out of the woods up behind the cemetery, a gray boulder as big as a car.

Wade shuts off the engine of the backhoe and clambers down from his seat and comes and stands at the side of the boulder, places a hand on it as if it is the shoulder of an old friend, and he listens for the sound of movement, any kind of movement, from below, almost hoping to hear something, a crumbling of clods of dirt, the scrape of a rock against another. He hears his father squirm. The sound stops, and now all he can hear is the breeze off the valley below sweeping over the grassy meadow to the trees. A pair of blue jays call raucously in the distance to one another. A dog from the village barks, once. Then silence. Delicious silence.

Lillian had returned to the car and sat next to him, staring straight ahead, clearly ready to leave the cemetery. She shifted restlessly in the seat but said nothing. Then Wade turned to her and pulled off the sunglasses, and in a voice that was almost a whisper, he said, "I didn't get into any fight. It was my father. My father did this to me."

His legs felt like sand, and his hands were trembling. Quickly, he replaced the sunglasses; he looked through them and out over the hood of the car and held on to the steering wheel with both hands, as if he were driving at great speed. Outside the open window, the soft wind blew, and the sun was shining; the meadow grass glowed green and gold, and from the pine trees at the far side of the cemetery, the same pair of jays called.

Lillian reached both hands toward Wade's face, and when, without looking at her, he pulled away, she dropped her hands back to her lap and studied them for a second. She said, "I don't . . . I don't understand." She looked at his face again. "You mean, he *hit* you?" She could not picture it, could not visualize any scene in which Wade, who seemed so large and male to her, so impregnable, like a stone wall, could be struck and hurt by his father, who was actually smaller than Wade and seemed old and fragile compared to him.

Wade said, "Yes. He hit me."

"How could he . . . do that? I don't understand, Wade."

"Simple. He just hit me. He does that."

"What . . . what about your mother?"

"She doesn't hit me."

"I mean, doesn't she . . . stop him? Can't she *say* something?"

Wade barked a laugh. "Sure. She can say any damned thing she wants. So long as she doesn't mind getting belted for it herself."

"I . . . I don't understand, Wade."

"I know you don't," he said.

She was silent for a second, and then suddenly she was weeping, tears running down her cheeks, and she felt so sorry for this boy that she thought she would break. "Oh, Wade, couldn't you stop him? Why? Why did he do that? It's awful," she said, and she reached once again for him, and again he cringed and pulled away, but this time she persisted, placing one hand on his shoulder and with the fingertips of her other hand touching his cheek and then removing the sunglasses. She caught her breath at the sight of him, and said, "Oh-h!"

He let her examine him, as if he were a sideshow freak, and said nothing. He drew his cigarettes from his shirt pocket and with trembling hand lit one and inhaled deeply. See the freak smoke a cigarette. See his hand shake. See how his lips and mouth function normally, while the rest of his face is misshapen and discolored. Read this map of pain and humiliation.

He said quietly, "Bang, bang, bang," and then he, too, was weeping, great wrenching sobs surging from his stomach and chest, and he brought his face forward and placed his forehead against the cool rim of the steering wheel.

Lillian wrapped her arms around his shoulders. How she hated that man Glenn Whitehouse, who had done this awful thing to a boy. Wade was a boy to her at this moment, a child injured by his parent and betrayed and abandoned at the deepest level imaginable. She knew, too, that Wade's pain went on and on, way beyond her imaginings, for she had never been beaten by her father or mother, and though her father may indeed have never drawn a sober breath, as everyone in town said, he had also never raised his hand, or even his voice, against anyone. Her father was weak and sweet, and he had not frightened a soul. The most alarming moments she had endured with her father came on those rare occasions when she realized that, if he was not drunk, he was thinking about getting drunk and so was not in fact present to her, did not actually see or hear her in the room. Those moments made her feel as if she did not exist and so lonely that she got dizzy and had to sit down and babble to him, make him lift his head and smile benignly at her, a big sleepy horse of a man, while she chattered on about school, about her sisters and her mother, making up events and whole conversations with neighbors, teachers, friends, madly filling with words the hole in the universe that he made with his presence, until, at last, her father rose from the kitchen table, patted her on the head and said, "I love you a whole lot, Lily, a whole lot," and went out the door, leaving her alone in the kitchen, a speck of bright matter whirling through a dark turbulent sky. And now her father was dead, and she believed that she did not feel that pain anymore, because she missed him so.

They sat in Wade's car for a long time, while the sun moved across the summer sky and touched the topmost branches of the trees and the air began to cool. In a quiet dispassionate voice, Wade tried telling it to her as if it had happened to someone else. It was the only way he could tell it without crying.

He had come home last night late, after having gone to the movies in Littleton with Lillian, where they had stopped by for a short visit with her mother and stepfather and her sisters, and when he got home and had walked into the kitchen, tired, sleepy, head still buzzing with memories of his and his girlfriend's hot good-night kisses, he had been greeted by the sight of his mother, hair wildly streaming, in her flannel nightdress, rushing across the room to him. She was terrified, eyes red from crying, arms extended, and she swiftly got behind Wade, between his bulky body and the closed door, and wrapped her arms around his middle and clung to him.

Pop sat at the kitchen table with a smile on his face that the boy found oddly calming: Nothing is wrong, it said. But Ma was sobbing hysterically, clutching him from behind, and suddenly Wade was afraid of his father's smile. Nothing is wrong, it continued saying. We men understand how women are: hysterical, weird. She will calm down in a minute, and you will see that she is all worked up over nothing again.

Wade turned his back on his father and held his mother to him, wrapping her in his arms and smothering her sob against his chest. "What happened?" Wade asked her. "What happened, Ma? What's the matter?"

He heard Pop growl, *"That* is none of your goddamned business, mis-ter." He was drunk, mean drunk, dangerous as a trapped animal. Far more than the sight of his mother crazed, it was the way his father spoke, the way he emphasized the wrong words in his sentence—the first, "that," and the last, "mis-ter," hanging on to it, savoring its flavor—that set off Wade's alarms and made him stiffen with fear.

Wade glanced back over his shoulder and made sure Pop was still seated at the table: he was pouring himself a drink from the bottle of Canadian Club. Wade saw through the doorway beyond into the living room, and huddled at the bottom of the stairs at the far side of the room were his little brother Rolfe and his sister Lena in pajamas. Lena sucked her thumb ferociously, and Rolfe, without smiling, flipped a wave to his brother.

"Come on, Ma," Wade said, "let's just call it a night, okay? Come on," he said gently, turning her toward the door into the living room. "Why don't you ease on to bed now, okay? I'll be right here." He heard his father snort.

"He just starts picking on me," Ma cried. "Picking and picking, over nothing. Nothing." She shuffled a few steps toward the door. Wade had one arm around her tiny shoulders and held one of her hands with the other, as if inviting her onto the dance floor.

Slowly, carefully, he moved her out of the room, while she continued to talk brokenly. "It starts with nothing, nothing . . . and he, he gets mad at me. It was only for supper, he was mad because the casserole . . . it was a nice supper, it was, but he was late, so we ate without him. You know, you were here. He was late, and the casserole got all dried out, and he was mad because we didn't wait for him. I explained, Wade, I told him you had a movie date and all, and he was late."

Wade said, "I know, I know. It's all right now." He tried to hush her as they moved one small step at a time across the living room toward the door to the bedroom, Uncle Elbourne's room, they still called it, after all these years, as if our mother and father had never taken true possession of it, even though they had conceived all but one of their children in that room.

"And then when I try to argue with him . . . all I did was try to explain, but he just gets madder and madder and starts yelling at me for all kinds of things. About money, and you kids. Wade, he blames me for *everything!* Nothing I say . . . nothing I say . . ."

"I know, Ma," Wade said. "It's okay now, it's over." They entered the darkened bedroom, and Wade turned on the lamp on the dresser by the door and closed the door behind them. He eased her over to the bed, drew back the covers, and when she had climbed into the bed, brought the blankets back over her. She looked like a sick child, her fingers clutching at the top of the blankets, her face looking mournfully up at him: so helpless and frail, so confused, so pathetically dependent, that—though he wanted to weep for her—he was filled instead with terror: he knew that he could not help her but had to try.

He whispered, "Did he hit you, Ma? Did Pop hit you?"

She shook her head no, turned down her mouth and stuck out her lower lip and started crying.

"Ma, he didn't hit you, did he? Tell me the truth." Her face didn't show any evidence of having been hit, but that did not mean much, Wade knew. He could have hit her someplace where it would not show.

She caught her breath and said in a whisper, "No. No, he hasn't done that in a long time. He stopped . . . he stopped doing that. Not since that last time . . . with you, when you got fresh. Oh, you poor thing!" she said, and she started crying again.

Wade said, "He hasn't done it since then? What about the other kids? I'm not here a lot, you know."

"You boys are all too big now," she said.

"No, I mean Rolfe and Lena." He looked back nervously at the closed door.

She shook her head. "No. He doesn't do that now."

"You're sure?" Wade did not believe her. "What about tonight?"

She looked up at him, and her eyes filled again. "I thought . . . I was afraid. I *thought* he was going to do it again," she said. "That's when you came in. He had his fist up, he was going to do it. Just because . . . I was all upset, he was saying terrible things, things about me. I know it's just the alcohol in him that's talking and I shouldn't react, but I can't help it, the things he says upset me so, and I start crying and answering back, and that's what he can't stand. Answering back. Questioning his authority. He loses his temper."

"What did he say?" Wade asked; then he said, "No, never mind. I don't want to know. He's drunk. It doesn't matter what he said, does it?" He smiled down at her and patted her hands. "You try to sleep now. Everything's over now. He'll be off on some other tangent, and in a minute he'll be hollering at me for coming in late. You watch," Wade said, and he smiled.

He backed away from the bed and, still facing her, turned out the light, then reached behind him for the doorknob, opened the door and stepped out, closing it carefully, quietly, as if she had already fallen asleep. He looked over at his little sister and brother and flapped the backs of both hands for them to scoot upstairs to bed. Somberly, they obeyed and were gone.

When Wade returned to the kitchen, Pop was standing by the sink, studying the half-filled glass in his hand as if he'd spotted a crack in it. "You get an earful?" he asked Wade.

"What do you mean?"

" 'What do you mean?' You know what I mean. Did you get an earful?"

Wade stood on the other side of the table with his arms folded across his chest. He said, "Listen, Pop, I don't care what you guys fight about, it's your business. I just don't want—"

"What? You just don't *want* what? Let's hear it." He put the glass down on the counter next to him and glared at his son. "Pissant," he said.

Wade took in a deep breath. "I guess I just don't want you to ever hit her again."

Pop stepped forward suddenly and said, "Guess. You guess." He moved toward the table, then around it on the right, and Wade swiftly moved around it on the left, until they had reversed positions—Wade had his back to the kitchen sink, and his father was on the other side of the table, with his back to the door.

"She tell you I hit her?" Glenn said. "She tell you that?"

"I'm not talking about tonight. I'm talking about the future. And the past doesn't matter. That's all," Wade added weakly. "The future."

"You're telling *me?* You are trying to tell *me* what I'm supposed to be afraid of? You think I'm afraid of *you?*" He showed his large teeth and made a quick move toward Wade, and when Wade jumped, he stopped and folded his arms over his chest and laughed. "Jesus H. Christ," he said. "What a candy-ass."

Without thinking it, Wade reached behind him into the dishrack, and his hand wrapped itself, as if of its own volition, around the handle of the skillet, heavy, black, cast iron, and he lifted it free of the rack and swung it around in front of him. The sound of his heart pounded in his ears like a hammer against steel, and he heard his voice, high and thin in the distance, say to his father, "If you touch her or me, or any of us, again, I'll fucking kill you."

His father quietly said, "Jesus." He sounded like a man who had just broken a shoelace.

"I mean it. I'll kill you." He lifted the skillet in his right hand and held it out and just off his shoulder, like a Ping-Pong paddle, and he suddenly felt ridiculous.

Without hesitation, Pop walked quickly around the table, came up to his son and punched him straight in the face, sending the boy careening back against the counter and the skillet to the floor. Grabbing him by his shirtfront, Pop hauled the boy back in front of him and punched him a second time and a third. A fourth blow caught him square on the forehead and propelled him along the counter to the corner of the room, where he stood with his hands covering his face. "Come on!" his father said, and he advanced on him again. "Come on, fight back like a man! Come on, little boy, let's see what you're made of!"

Wade yanked his hands away and thrust his face open-eyed at his father and cried, "I'm not made of what you're made of!" and Pop hit him again, slamming Wade's head back against the wall. Wade covered his face with his hands once more, and he began to cry.

Pop turned away in disgust. "You sure as shit ain't," he said, and he walked over to the door, where he turned back to Wade and said, "Next time you start telling your father what to do and what not to do, make goddamned sure you can back it up, buddy-boy." Then he went out, slamming the door behind him.

Wade let himself slide slowly down to the floor, where he sat with his legs straight out, his head slumped on one shoulder, his arms flopped across his lap—a marionette with its strings cut.

It was like being asleep, he told Lillian, only he was not really sleeping. He did not know how long he remained there on the floor—hours, maybe—but at some point he heard his father's pickup turn into the yard. He got up from the floor, wobbly-legged, and quickly made his way to the stairs, and by the time he heard his father bump his way into the kitchen, Wade was standing in the darkness in the middle of his bedroom. He listened to the man's clumsy drunken movements below, heard him at last go into Uncle Elbourne's room and close the door. Then, slowly, his face on fire, Wade took off his shirt and jeans and loafers and socks and got into his bed.

Lillian held his hands to her own face, as if to rub into her cheeks and brow the heat and pain that filled Wade's face. "Did your mother see you this morning? Does she know?"

"No. I left early, before anyone was up," he said. "I didn't want her to know. I didn't want anyone to know. Not even you."

"Oh, Wade. Why?"

He started to try to say it, and he spoke the word "shame," but when he heard himself say the word, he knew that it meant something different to her, so he tightened his lips into a line and shook his head from side to side. "It's over now, that's all that matters. I only wish," he said, "I wish I'd killed him when I had the chance. I should've busted his head open with that frying pan," he said.

"Why didn't you? Why didn't you fight back? You're bigger than he is."

Wade looked at her and withdrew his hands quickly and slapped them onto the steering wheel rim. "Don't," he said. "Don't ever ask me that again. You don't understand. Nobody can understand. Okay?"

She said, "Okay. I'm . . . I'm sorry. I didn't mean . . ."

"Never mind 'I didn't mean' or 'I'm sorry.' Just don't ever ask me that again," he said, and he started the motor of the old Ford. He reached over and flipped on the radio and ran the dial up and down for a few seconds, until he caught the Burlington station. It was a Supremes song, and he could not make out the words, but he liked the way the music sounded, tight and fast and clear, like a stream in spring, filled with snowmelt.

By the time they got back to town and were parked in front of Lillian's aunt's house, it was dark. "Do you want to come in for supper?" she asked. "I know Aunt Alma won't—"

He said, "Lillian. No. Jesus."

"I'm sorry. I forgot."

"Well, I didn't," he said. "I can't. Ever."

"I meant about how you look," she said. She reached over and once again touched his swollen cheeks and brow, gently, as if verifying the truth of his story by touching his wounds. Then she got out of the car and went inside.

15

IN TERMS OF THE SOCIAL FORCES at play, in terms of our native environment, one might say, my life was not different from Wade's. We were raised alike, until I left home and went down to the university, where, if I was not exactly transplanted, I grew and throve as if placed in the sun and under the care of a more kindly and talented gardener than any I had known so far. Since that time, however, because of the similarity of our early lives, every thought, memory and dream of my brother Wade has brought with it the painful unanswerable question "Why me, Lord?" Why me and not Wade? In my dreams of Wade, in my memories and thoughts of him, we are interchangeable.

After all, I was no more or less adapted than Wade to the soil and climate we were both born into—stingy soil, rocky and thin, and a mean climate. By the age of eighteen I was as much a tough little lichen as he and should have shriveled, should have curled up at the edges and died at the university, as he believed he would, which is why it never occurred to him to apply to the university when he was eighteen. And later, in the affluent suburban town where I have lived now for almost a decade, I should have been, as Wade would have been, merely a curious exhibit of foreign flora at the local museum of natural history or a figure in a diorama depicting life among the less advantaged peoples to the north. Yet here I am, a teacher, no less, a veritable pillar of a privileged community, member of benevolent and fraternal orders, welcome guest in the white colonial homes of physicians, dentists, real estate brokers and auto dealers. I even attend church regularly. Episcopal.

It makes no sense. Which is why the question "Why me, Lord?" has plagued my adult life. It makes me feel permanently and universally displaced, as much here as up in the village of Lawford. As if I were Chinese in Switzerland or Welsh in Brazil. We struggle to change our place in society, and all we manage to do is displace ourselves. It should be a simple matter: it is what this country was invented to do—to change our lives. Lift yourself up by the bootstraps, young fellow. Make yourself upwardly mobile, my dear. Rise like cream to the top, m' boy.

And in a way it is a simple matter, if, like most people, a person is intelligent, organized and energetic. Certainly most of the people in the Whitehouse family possessed those qualities, especially as children. After all, every year thousands, maybe millions, of good citizens do change their lives for the better, in terms of class, just as I have done, and as my brother did not. From log cabin to president: it is our dominant myth. We live by it, generation after generation. Do not look back, look ahead. Keep your eye on the sparrow, your shoulder to the wheel, your feet on the ground. That is what I have done; it is how I have lived my life so far. And it is how my brother Wade lived his life too. That is why I ask, Why me, Lord?

Why did I apply to the university, when no one else in my graduating high school class aspired to an education higher than that offered at hairstyling or welding school in Littleton? Elbourne and Charlie joined the army. Wade, who was a better student than I, on graduation simply turned his summer job with LaRiviere into a full-time job and considered himself lucky. Lena got pregnant and married. But I left our parents' home in a radically different way than my brothers and sister, for reasons I still cannot name, and when I got down there to the university and discovered that I did not know how to talk or dress or eat in the acceptable way, did not know how to write or read or speak in class, did not even know how to smile, why did I endure such inadequacy and not go running home to where my inadequacies were regarded as virtues and skills? Wade, had he got as far as enrolling, would have been expelled in a week for brawling in the cafeteria or would have quickly flunked out. Why did I go on, to graduate school in Boston, to the study of history—that place where no one lives, where everyone is dead now—to become a teacher, of all things, when all I wanted, all I want now, is to be left alone? I am not ambitious, I am not bookish, I am not even unusually intelligent, and I have no special gift. So why me, Lord?

I asked it, of course, whenever I happened to see Wade himself or when he called me on the telephone. But I also ask it when I find myself seated at dinner next to the attractive unmarried woman poet from Chicago with the interesting new haircut who is visiting her older sister, who happens to be the wife of my ophthalmologist, a man who knows no one more suitable as a dinner companion for his sister-in-law than I. And I ask it in the middle of the high school parking lot as I watch my scrubbed well-fed elaborately dressed and coiffed students pile into their new Japanese cars and race away to the beaches, ski slopes and dance bars. I ask it when I read in my morning newspaper another account of the death of a child at the hands of her mother's drunken boyfriend. I ask it while driving in my car when I come to the outskirts of town where the hills and forests begin and I turn my car around and head back south into town. Why me and not Wade—and why Wade and not me?

It is depressing, at least to me, to linger over such questions, and distracting. After all, this is not my story, it is Wade's. I am but the witness, the compiler; I am the investigator and the chronicler; and I should get on with my work.

When we last saw Wade, he had left Margie's warm bed and was plowing the town roads at dawn on a Sunday. You no doubt will have noticed by now that we often leave him there, perched up on the grader with snow blowing in his face, dreaming of his past or future, adrift on a wave of feeling that carries him away from his present life. That is a characteristic tableau for him, perhaps an emblematic one. He is alone, and while he is of the town and plays an essential role in its life, he is not in the town exactly, is not going intently about his private business like everyone else. Gordon LaRiviere, in pajamas, is seated at his kitchen table drinking coffee and balancing his personal checkbook, while his wife sleeps. Alma Pittman is dressed and making a pot of tea and wondering if it is too early in the season to shop in Littleton for the Christmas cards that she likes to have ready to mail to every taxpayer in town the day after Thanksgiving. Chub Merritt is down at the garage already, on his back underneath Hank Lank's truck, fixing an oil leak. Nick Wickham has opened the restaurant, and his first customers, a pair of deer hunters from Manchester, have just shucked their orange coats and sat down at the counter, briskly rubbing their cold hands. While at the north end of town, in the drafty old house she rents from her ex-husband's parents, Margie Fogg, naked, lies awake in her bed, pondering Wade's suggestion that she marry him.

She has lived alone in this house for almost five years now, but she lived there with her husband, Harvey, and his parents for the previous five years as well. They had wanted children, she and Harvey, but had been unable to conceive one, and they had wanted their own house, but Harvey was a carpenter without much work and she worked part time then, tinting photographs of babies and graduating seniors for a Littleton studio photographer, and they could never seem to get enough money together for a down payment. Then Harvey fell in love with a twenty-two-year-old waitress at Toby's Inn, and he left Margie, to live with the waitress and her two small children in a trailer out on Route 29, and six months later she had his baby. Harvey's parents felt sorry for Margie and ashamed of their son and let Margie live on in their house, and when they decided to move to a retirement village near Lakeland, Florida, they took out a second mortgage on the house and let Margie make the payments to the bank as rent.

It was not a bad deal, but Margie was not happy in the big old house, a ramshackle colonial that got shabbier every year, as paint peeled, shutters fell, shingles blew off and the furnace broke. She repainted the downstairs rooms and closed off the second floor, so that she would not have to heat it in winter and did not have to go on sleeping in the same bedroom she had shared with her husband. His leaving her for the waitress had not afflicted her nearly as much as her in-laws supposed. Harvey had been a boastful insecure man, and from the start their sexual connection had been at best problematic. He wanted

204

children, "a real family," as he put it, and blamed her for their not producing any and consequently treated her as if she were depriving him of an essential right. It made him bossy and sarcastic and filled him with self-pity, which saddened her: she remembered Harvey Fogg when he was a teenaged boy, skinny and shy and eager to please, surprised and nervously passionate when, at nineteen, he discovered that she loved him and married her for it.

Then, a year before Harvey left her, Wade had come into her life—sort of. She had not intended or expected it, but they had become the kind of friends who are bound by unhappy marriages—they could talk to each other as to no one else of the hurt their marriages were causing them—and for a few months they sustained a jumpy distracted love affair, until both decided to try to save their marriages and broke it off. They were not in love with each other and knew it. Wade was in love with Lillian, he thought: he had already divorced her once and married her again, and besides, they had Jill now. And Margie, secretly, loved only her memory of Harvey as a teenaged boy. Sometimes she was afraid that the only man she could ever love would be a teenaged boy, shy and fragile, awkward in his passion and openly embarrassed by it. She found herself increasingly attracted to the boys who came into the restaurant, and though she hid her interest in them, she could not keep herself from lingering at their tables, talking and joking and teasing them about their clothes and hair, their sweet male pretensions. The boys thought of her as motherly but still young and sexual and flirted with her as they wished they could flirt with girls their own age or with their mothers. They said things to her that combined tenderness and bravado, and she made them think they were brilliant.

Later, when both their spouses had left them, Margie and Wade gradually resumed their old friendship, and the sex, licit now, was easeful and generous without the fervent anxiety of before. Once a week or so, they slept together, always in her bed. For Wade, it was not the way it had been with Lillian, fraught with mystery and often capable of astonishing him with the thoughts it provoked. Instead, it was what he assumed sex was for most people. For Margie, making love with Wade was slightly boring but necessary, and it always made her feel better afterwards, like exercise.

Marrying Wade, however, was something she had not

thought about once, not in all the years she had known him, which might seem strange: she was a single woman in her late thirties in a town where such a woman was suspect, and Wade was the one man in town whose company she enjoyed. Wade was smart, everyone knew that, and not bad-looking, and he could be funny when he wanted to, and he worked hard, although he did not make much money, and a chunk of that went to his ex-wife. He drank too much, sure, but most men did, especially unmarried unhappy men. And he had that reputation for violence, his sudden bursts of anger. But most of the unmarried unhappy men she knew had that same reputation: it seemed to go with the territory. They were disconnected men, cut off from what calmed them—a home, children, a loving loyal woman who comforted and reassured them when everyone else treated them as if they were useless and expendable. Of course, Wade had once possessed all that, and he had still been violent, not down at Toby's Inn, as now, but worse, at home and against his own wife. Remember, Margie thought, Wade Whitehouse was a wife-beater.

It was *known,* by rumor and surmise, the way it usually happens in a village, without the principals ever telling anyone. Lillian's mother lived up in Littleton with her second husband, and people remembered that when Lillian was married to Wade she had left him several times for a week or two and had gone to stay with her mother. And people knew that there were three or four other times when she and Jill had left the house they shared with Wade and had stayed overnight in town at Alma Pittman's. Later, on her return home, when out in public with her husband, Lillian had acted like a POW— dutiful but sullen, slow-moving, careful: most people, though they do not say it and may not even think it, associate this kind of behavior in wives with domestic violence. And when Wade and Lillian had got divorced the second time, rumors drifted back down from Littleton, rumors possibly started by Wade's lawyer, Bob Chagnon, that the reason Wade got slapped with heavy child-support payments and lost the house to Lillian and could see his daughter only once a month was that he had admitted to having lost his temper on several occasions and hit his wife with his fists. Wade could have denied it: she had no proof: there were no medical records to be subpoenaed; and Alma had refused to get mixed up in marital problems, as she put it; her mother, after all, was her mother, and Lillian had wanted to spare her the pain of having to say in public what her daughter had revealed to her in secrecy and shame; Jill, of course, was too young to be questioned about it. Fortunately for all of them, Wade had simply hung his head and confessed that, yes, in the heat of a quarrel, he had hit her. People shook their heads sadly when they heard this, but they understood: Lillian was a hard case, a demanding intelligent woman with a lot of mouth on her, a woman who made most people feel that she thought she was somehow superior to them, and no doubt she made Wade feel that way too. A man should never hit a woman, but sometimes it is understandable. Right? It happens, doesn't it? It happens.

Margie agreed. Lillian was a demanding woman, and Wade was a stubborn man: no wonder they came to blows. Margie herself was not demanding, however; and that was then, this was now. That was Lillian Pittman; and she was Marjorie Fogg. They were not interchangeable parts. Wade would never hit *her*.

As for his drinking, Margie believed that it was immaterial, and besides, if he had a good woman to come home to, Wade would come home, instead of hanging out after work at Toby's Inn till all hours with kids like Jack Hewitt and Hettie Rodgers. Instead, he would be home telling Margie jokes over supper and watching TV with her afterwards and making love to her in bed before falling peacefully to sleep. So it *was* possible that she and Wade could have a happy life together, certainly a life happier than this one they were leading alone.

They drove out together that Sunday afternoon to visit Glenn and Sally Whitehouse, our parents. It had stopped snowing, and the sky was bright blue, the snow blinding white and falling from the trees in fantails as the temperature rose. The woods crackled with the sound of distant gunfire.

The old Whitehouse place, as it is still called in Lawford, is less than four miles from town, out on Parker Mountain Road, and Wade rarely went there. He counted on seeing Ma and Pop now and then by accident in town, at town meeting or at Golden's store or at the post office. That was enough, he felt, to keep him in touch with them, and besides, they never actually invited him out to visit, any more than they asked me. They knew better, after years of our finding excuses not to come, than to ask anymore. When the Whitehouse children leave home, even if only to move down the road, they do not return willingly. Our mother knew why, but our father would not. I often wonder if she hated him for having driven her children so far away. It has also occurred to me that perhaps he only did what she wanted him to do. Naturally, I have never spoken of this to Wade or Lena.

Wade pulled off the plowed road onto the unplowed driveway and parked his car by the side porch. The house looked abandoned, closed up, as if no one lived there anymore. There were no fresh car tracks or footprints in the snow leading to the road, and the windows were dark, half covered with flapping sheets of polyurethane.

Wade got out of the car and sniffed the air, but smelled no wood smoke. Margie got out and looked at the house for a second and said, "Are you sure they're home? Did you call?"

"No. But the truck's here," he noted, and pointed at the snow-covered pickup parked at the side of the house. "Looks like they've stayed inside since the snow started." His face crinkled with concern, and he hurried to the porch door.

They stamped their feet loudly on the porch floor, and Wade reached for the doorknob and pulled, but the door would not open. "The fuck?" he said.

"What's the matter?"

"Door's locked. That's peculiar." He tried again, but the door did not give. He stepped to the side, cupped his hands around his face and peered through a porch window into the dark kitchen, where everything looked normal—a few dirty dishes in the sink, coffeepot on the wood stove, Merritt's Shell Station calendar on the wall showing November.

Margie came along beside him and looked into the room and said, "Do you think they're okay?"

"Of course!" he snapped. "I would've heard."

"How?"

"I don't know, for Christ's sake!" he said, and he turned back to the door and knocked loudly on it. In silence, Margie came and stood behind him. After a few seconds, they heard the door being unlocked at last, and when it swung open, they saw Pop standing in the gloom of the room, a puzzled look on his face, as if he did not recognize his son. He wore long underwear and a pair of stained woolen trousers held up by green suspenders, and he had a pair of ancient slippers on his bare feet. His thin white hair was disheveled, and his face was unshaven and gray. He looked elderly and fragile, and he said nothing to Wade, just turned and shuffled away from the open door toward the stove, which he bent over and opened, as if to check the fire.

"Pop?" Wade said from the doorway. "Pop, you okay?"

The old man did not respond. He clanked the door of the cold stove closed and walked slowly to the woodbox and started to pull out a batch of old newspaper and several pieces of kindling. Wade looked at Margie and sucked his lips against his teeth, nodded for her to enter ahead of him, and the two of them came inside and closed the door.

Silently, Pop built the fire, while Wade and Margie watched, their breath puffing out in small clouds in front of them. The kitchen was as cold as it was outdoors, but dark, and consequently it seemed colder. "Jesus, Pop, how the hell can you stand the cold, dressed like that?" The old man did not answer.

Wade looked into the living room and saw nothing amiss; the door to the bedroom beyond, however, was shut. "Where's Ma?" Wade asked.

Pop struck a match on the top of the stove and lit the fire, then stood stiffly up and for the first time looked at his son and the woman with him. "Sleeping," he said.

Wade unzipped his coat but did not take it off. Dragging a chair from next to the table, he sat down and crossed one leg casually over the other. "This's Margie Fogg, Pop. You remember her, don't you?"

Pop looked steadily at Margie for a second. "Yes. From Wickham's," he said. "Been a while."

Margie crossed the kitchen and shook the old man's hand, but his gaze had drifted away from her and seemed focused on some point halfway into the living room beyond.

"You want some coffee or tea?" he blurted, as if suddenly realizing that they were in the room with him. "Or a beer?"

As if joking, Wade laughed lightly and said, "What I'd like is to know how you and Ma are doing. I haven't seen you in town in a while, and I was wondering." His voice was high and tight, the way it always was when he talked to his father.

"Oh. Well, we're all right, I guess. Your ma is fine. She's sleeping. You want me to get her?" Pop asked.

Wade said yes, and the old man shuffled from the room.

Quickly, Margie moved close to the stove and held her hands out to it, as the fire crackled and popped through the kindling. She unzipped her down jacket, then changed her mind and zipped it back up. Wade got a chunk of heavier wood from the woodbox and tossed it into the stove and stood next to her.

"Jesus," he whispered.

Margie said nothing. She could see that Wade was frightened but knew that he did not want to say it.

"This house. Lots of memories associated with this house. Not much has changed, I'll tell you that. Except that the place is getting more and more decrepit. They're too old for this house," he said.

Then Pop was back, alone. The bedroom door was still shut. "Where's Ma?" Wade asked, his voice high and tight again, like a scared adolescent's.

"She's coming. I told her you was here." The old man took the coffeepot from the stove and rinsed it out at the sink, handling it clumsily, as if he were unfamiliar with its shape and parts.

"Here, Mr. Whitehouse, let me do that," Margie said, and she plucked the coffeepot from his gnarled hands and proceeded briskly to clean it out. Pop backed away, hesitated a minute, then brought her a can of coffee and set it next to her on the drainboard, where there was a half-empty bottle of Canadian Club.

Time passed, and still Ma did not appear. Margie got the coffee perking, cleaned the few dishes in the sink and put four cups out on the table, while Wade smoked a cigarette and moved restlessly around the room, from the window to the door to the living room and back to the table, where he sat down for a moment before jumping up again. He and Pop did not speak to one another, but Margie filled the silence by asking the old man a few questions, and he answered her slowly and vaguely.

"How have you been heating the house?" she inquired, as if idly curious. "Not with just this stove."

"No. There's a furnace."

"You're not using it today? It's awful cold inside, don't you think?"

"Yes. It's . . . broke, I guess. Didn't kick in last night. There's an electric heater in the bedroom."

"Maybe Wade can take a look at it," Margie suggested. "Would that be okay? Your pipes'll freeze. You're lucky they're not frozen already."

"Yes. Fine."

"Wade," Margie said, "could you do that? Check the furnace? They shouldn't be way out here with just this stove for heat."

Wade looked at her as if he had not heard and said, "Yeah, sure. Listen, Pop, I'm going to see if Ma's all right," he said suddenly, and he moved toward the door. He hated the sound of his voice. Pop raised a hand, as if to stop him, then let it fall slowly to his side, and Wade left the room.

Wade hesitated briefly at the doorway, then crossed the living room to the bedroom, where he paused for a second and knocked lightly on the door. In a voice just above a whisper, he said, "Ma? It's Wade. Can I come in?"

There was no answer. Margie had come to stand in the doorway between the kitchen and the living room, while behind her, Pop, his hands buried in his pockets, looked down at the stove.

Wade slowly opened the door a few inches and saw that the room was dark. It was as cold and damp as a cave, and his breath puffed out in front of him. The window shades were pulled down, but he could make out the furniture in the room, positioned where it had always been—the sagging double bed against the far wall, the bed tables and lamps beside it, the cluttered old high-top dressers that had belonged to Uncle Elbourne, Sally's sewing chair and table by the window. Around the floor several articles of clothing were scattered, Glenn's shoes and dingy bathrobe, Sally's cardigan sweater, and on the floor next to the sewing chair there were a cut-glass ashtray spilling over with butts and ashes and a brown whiskey bottle and a tumbler with about an inch of whiskey in it.

Wade could see Ma in the bed, on the far side, where she always slept, covered with a heap of blankets. He walked to the foot of the bed and looked down at her. She lay on her side, facing away from him, and all he could make out was the outline of her body, but he knew that she was dead. He thought the words, *Ma's dead*—when suddenly he heard a click and a loud whir from the floor beside him, and he leapt away, as if startled by a growling watchdog. It was the fan of a small electric heater coming on, and the spring coils began to glow like evil red grins behind the fan, and a hot wind blew at his ankles.

Stepping carefully away from the thing, he crossed to the head of the bed, where he could see the woman clearly. Beneath a mound of blankets and afghans, she wore her wool coat over her flannel nightgown and lay curled on her side like a child, with her tiny hands in mittens fisted near her throat, as if in enraged prayer. Her eyes were closed, and her mouth was open slightly. Her skin was chalk white and dry-looking, almost powdery, as if her face would crumble to the touch. Her body resembled a feather-light husk more than an actual human body, and it seemed incapable of holding up the weight of the blankets that covered her to the shoulders and wrists. "Oh, Lord," Wade whispered. "Oh, Lord." He came forward and sat down on the floor, cross-legged, like a small boy, facing her.

Margie stood at the door, watching in silence, instantly comprehending. The room was icebox cold, and she could see her own breath, and she knew that the old woman had frozen to death in bed. She closed the door and walked slowly back to the kitchen, where Pop stood staring down at the stove.

"Coffee's perked," he said in a low voice.

Margie got a potholder and plucked the pot from the stove and filled a cup for herself and one for Pop. When she handed it to him, she said, "Mr. Whitehouse, when did she die?"

Holding the steaming cup in his shaky hands, he looked up into her eyes as if confused by her question. "Die? I don't know," he said. "She's dead, then."

"Yes."

"I wasn't there, I was out here most of the time. It was snowing, and cold, and the furnace wouldn't kick in."

"Did you check on her?"

"Yes, I checked on her. But she was asleep. She had the electric heater in there, and I had the wood stove out here, so it wasn't all that cold. The cold don't bother me as much as her, though. Which is why I give her the heater."

"Don't you have a telephone?" She looked around the room for one.

"Yes. In the living room." He pointed feebly to the door.

"Well, why didn't you call someone to fix the furnace? Wade or somebody?"

"Wade," the man said, as if it were the name of a stranger. "I thought she was all right," he went on. "I thought till this morning she was all right. I was . . . I fell asleep out here, and then I woke up and went in to the bedroom, but she didn't wake up. So I sat in there with her for a long time. Until you and Wade come by." He drew a chair out from the table with the toe of his foot and sat down and sipped noisily at his coffee.

"Are you sad, Mr. Whitehouse?" Margie asked.

He looked at his coffee. "Sad. Yes. Sad. I wish, I wish it was me in there instead of her." He put his cup down and placed his large red hands on his knees. "That's what makes me sad. I'm the one should've froze to death."

Margie turned and walked to the sink and placed her cup and saucer on the drainboard. She reached over and grabbed the half-empty bottle of Canadian Club and a water glass and carried them back to the table and placed them next to the man. "You are right," she said firmly. Then she left him alone in the room and went into the living room, looking for the telephone.

16

THE DAY OF THE FUNERAL was almost springlike: one rose in the early morning and crossed to the window, opened it and listened in vain for birdsong and scrutinized the bare trees for buds. The snowline crossed New Hampshire from west to east near Manchester, a third of the way up the state, and as the temperature rose, the line retreated northward to about Concord, where it would finally settle by midmorning over snow too deep to melt quickly.

In the woods and on the fields on both sides of the interstate, the snow thickened, softened and compacted under the weight of its own melt, making it difficult for the deer hunters out there, the latecomers and the persistent ones who had not yet shot their deer. North of Concord and west of the Merrimack Valley, the land lifted gradually into humpbacked hills, and there were few houses and farms visible from the highway, and only occasionally now, from the church spires poking through treetops, could one infer from his car the presence of small towns, like Warner and Andover, with a north-country souvenir shop, motel and filling station huddled together at the infrequent cloverleafs and exits. It is poor and lonely but undeniably lovely country; yet in spite of its loveliness, there is an overabundance of madness and despair in those settlements and towns. So much deprivation and so much natural beauty combine in a life to make it sad and angry beyond belief to an outsider.

As I drove north to Lawford on that unseasonably warm November morning, I reflected not so much on the fact of our mother's death as on Wade's having chosen to include in his report of that death the announcement of his forthcoming marriage to Margie Fogg, whom at that time I had not met. When he told me over the telephone that our mother had died and told me how she had died, I felt myself flee, and then I watched myself do it. I fled to a place of safety where I had lived, it sometimes seemed, for most of my childhood and youth and where, it had always been clear to me, Wade never went himself. If I lived for the most part with only a slight and tangential and always tentative connection to my exterior life, Wade lived almost wholly out there on his skin, with no interior space for him to retreat to, even in a crisis or at a time of emotional stress or conflict. Perhaps we were merely mirror images of each other, our apposite modes of life twinned versions of the same radical accommodation to an intolerable reality. It was as if beneath Wade's skin there were nothing but solid rock, an entire planet solid to the core that could not be penetrated by consciousness; while beneath mine there was only empty space that one could tumble through, rolling over and over in a plummet toward a cold and distant black star. Away, away—and free, free.

Wade called me, as usual, late at night. Even before answering the phone, I knew it was he—no one else calls me at that hour—and I was ready to listen to another chapter in one or both of his ongoing sagas, which by now, as I have said, I was more than casually interested in. There was possibly a third story that connected the first two, but mainly there was the detective story concerning the shooting of Evan Twombley, and there was the family melodrama about Wade's custody fight with Lillian.

But not this time. Wade was telling a different story tonight, or so it seemed then, one in which I myself was a character, for he had called to tell me that early that morning or sometime during the previous night our mother had died, and he had discovered the body when he had gone over to visit her and our father with Margie Fogg. Pop was okay but kind of out of it, he told me. Worse than usual, maybe, though no drunker than usual.

Naturally, I wanted to know the details, and he provided them, his voice growing thinner and thinner as he talked, as if the connection were fading. He spoke very rapidly, and I could barely make out what he was telling me anyhow, but I was moving away fast, which made it worse. I was in my old free-fall, losing contact, and soon I would be in deep space, unable to hear any human voice or perceive anyone's emotion, even my own. I heard him say something urgent and slightly, almost inappropriately, gay about his friend Margie Fogg and the old house and Pop, and then he mentioned the funeral. I heard the word, funeral, and a few sentences about our sister Lena, but his words were coming to me from a much greater distance now and rapidly, like electronic signals blipping across a screen, and then there was nothing but static, and finally not even that. Silence, except for the cold wind blowing across millions of miles of empty space.

It was not until later—months later, actually—that I had as-sembled enough information to let me understand what, in his remarks about Margie and the old house and our father, Wade was trying to describe to me. That Sunday afternoon out at the house, Margie had called the fire department, and the emer-gency vehicle—a five-year-old rusted Dodge van outfitted with oxygen, splints, bandages and plasma and driven by Jimmy Dame, with Hector Eastman riding shotgun—had raced out from the Lawford fire station. The two told Wade and Margie to stand back and had tried mouth-to-mouth resus-citation first, as they were trained to do, and then quickly gave up and carried Ma out of the house on a stretcher to the van and drove off to the Littleton Hospital, where she could be legally pronounced dead. Cause of death: hypothermia. Time of death: sometime between 1 and 7 A.M., Sunday, November 2.

After Ma's body was out of the house, Wade slowly came back to himself. Pop had not once left his chair in the kitchen and throughout had continued to drink whiskey, a half inch at a time, from a water glass. Margie stayed away from the old man and tried to comfort Wade, which, oddly, was not difficult.

He said, "I knew the second we pulled up in the car that something was wrong, and the only thing I could think of was that Ma was dead. I don't know why, but that was the only thing I could think of." He and Margie were sitting side by side on the sagging green sofa in the living room, the dead eye of the television staring at them. The room was still cold, in spite of the fire in the kitchen stove, and they had their coats on.

"It's like I almost expected it," he continued. "So that when I went into the bedroom and found her like that, I wasn't surprised or shocked or anything. It's strange, isn't it?"

She said yes, but sometimes people had premonitions about things like this. So, yes, she said, it was strange, but not unusual. She stroked his back in slow circles across his shoulder blades, as if he were a child, and laid her other hand tenderly on his knee, and wondered what was really going through Wade's head. His family relations, she believed, were very different from hers. To her, Wade seemed intensely involved with his various family members, even with his father, whereas she was not. She had a younger sister she thought was a lesbian, who was in the navy and stationed in the Philippines, and her older brother managed a video rental outlet in Catamount and had a wife and seven kids who kept him too busy to participate in her life in any regular way. Since both of her parents were still alive up in Littleton, she did not really know what Wade was feeling about his mother's death, but God, it must be awful. Her mother, whom she never saw anymore (she had Alzheimer's and had not recognized Margie in years), lived in an old motel converted into a nursing home and financed by the state; her father, whom she dutifully visited once a month, lived alone in a dark small filthy apartment over the Knights of Columbus hall and spent a lot of time in the VA hospital in Manchester. He had been a lifelong cigarette smoker and had lost one lung to cancer and was still smoking and coughing with every third breath. Margie knew that soon one and then both of her parents would die, and she wondered what she would feel then. Abandoned? Relieved? Angry? All three, probably. Maybe that was how Wade felt today, and maybe that was why he seemed to be feeling none of them. You must feel frightened too, she reasoned, terrified—because when your parent dies, you know that, even if you squeeze out a normal three score and ten, you are next. That seemed to be what Wade was feeling most, now that she thought about it—

frightened. It must get in the way of grief, that thick mix of abandonment, relief and anger, which no doubt came later, when you got used to the idea of being the next one to die.

"I guess I'm the one who has to take care of things now," Wade said. "Being the oldest and all."

"What things?"

"The funeral. Calling folks, Rolfe and Lena and so on. And Pop. I've got to do something about Pop," he said, and he turned in the couch and peered back into the kitchen at the old man, who seemed lost in his thoughts or, without thoughts, was merely counting out the seconds until he felt it was appropriate for him to take another sip of whiskey. Sixty-one, sixty-two, sixty-three . . .

"After us kids left home and he had to retire—from the drinking, I suppose—after that he was Ma's problem. Now . . . well, now I guess he's mine."

"He's a problem, all right," Margie said.

Wade lit a cigarette and inhaled deeply. "I think," he said, his brow furrowed, as he stared thoughtfully at the burning cigarette in his hand, "I think maybe I ought to move out here to the house. Put my trailer up for sale. I'm going to need some money I don't have, for that custody suit business, you know. And there's no way Pop can live out here alone."

Margie said, "He's not easy, Wade. He's especially never been easy for you."

"He's old. And Jesus, look at him, he's out of it. But give him his bottle, put him by the fire or in front of the television, and he's okay. I can move in upstairs, fix the place up a little, clean and paint the place, get the furnace working, and so forth. You know. Make it nice." The picture in his head was filling out quickly with details: he saw the house renovated, almost elegant in its New England farmhouse simplicity, with his father peacefully semiconscious and more or less confined to Uncle Elbourne's room and the kitchen and living room, and Wade free to do with the rest of the house whatever he pleased, as if it were his own. Rolfe surely would not object, and Lena would be relieved to hear it. One of the upstairs bedrooms could be decorated nicely for Jill, and he could share the other with Margie.

"What do you think?" he asked her.

"About what?"

"About living here with me."

218

"With you, maybe. With you and your father, though?"

"He'll be all right," Wade said firmly. "I promise you. I can control him. He's like a child now, a kid who's lost his mother, almost."

"Are you talking about getting married, Wade? You and me? Like you were last night?"

"Well . . . yeah. Yes, I guess I am."

Margie got up from the sofa and crossed the room to the doorway to the kitchen, where she stood looking at the old man. Slowly, he turned his head and looked back at her. He was like an old bony abandoned dog—skinny neck, dark sad eyes, slack mouth and slumped shoulders.

"How are you doing, Mr. Whitehouse?" she said.

His eyes filled with tears, and he opened his mouth to answer but was unable to make words come. He moved his head from side to side, like a gate, and lifted his open hands to the woman as if asking for coins. She walked forward and embraced him and stroked his tousled white hair. "I know, I know, you poor thing," she said. "It's hard. It's very hard."

Then suddenly Wade was beside her, and he wrapped his large arms around both of them, enclosing his father and the woman he would soon marry. He held the old man he would take care of from now on and the woman who would be his helpmate and partner in life, the woman whose presence in his life, in this old house way out in the woods, would help make Wade's life a proper father's life, one he could happily bring his daughter home to at last.

By the time I arrived at the house, three days later, Wade and Margie had already moved in. It was eleven in the morning, and the funeral was scheduled for one in the afternoon—at the First Congregational Church, Reverend Howard Doughty officiating.

Wade had been a busy fellow, I later learned. Sunday night, he had fixed the furnace and stayed over at the house with Pop, sleeping on the couch. Before going to bed, while Pop sat and drank by the fire in the kitchen, Wade went through our parents' scattered papers and dug up, among other useful things, the documentation that he needed to make the insurance claim and finance the funeral, burial and gravestone. The next morning, he arranged all three. He notified the *Littleton Register* and the remaining members of the family—Lena and Clyde down in Massachusetts and Lillian and, of course, Jill, although he asked Lillian to "break the news to her," as he put it, when she got home from school. Then he telephoned the dozen or so people in Lawford whom Ma would have wanted at her funeral, leaving it to them and to the newspaper to pass the word on to the outer circle of friends and acquaintances.

Though Wade managed to direct traffic at the school Monday morning, he did not go in to work—when he called to explain, LaRiviere was surprisingly understanding and sympathetic, Wade thought. By noon, he had put his trailer up for sale, and that afternoon he carted his and Margie's clothes and personal belongings out to the house and stashed them in the larger of the two upstairs bedrooms. When Margie arrived, after work at Wickham's, the two of them cleaned the house thoroughly. Ma's effects—her clothes and personal papers and photographs and her knitting tools and yarns; there was not much else—they boxed and stored in the attic.

Tuesday morning, he directed traffic at the school and then drove to work as usual, and when he walked into the shop, LaRiviere told Wade, in front of Jack Hewitt and Jimmy Dame, that he could forget about well drilling for the rest of the winter, Jack could handle the work they had left till the ground froze, while Wade worked inside. "Learning the business from the business end," LaRiviere said, with a beefy arm slung over Wade's shoulder. Wade slipped from under the arm and stepped away, suspicious: this was a very different tone from the one Wade had long ago grown used to.

Jack glowered and lunged into the cold to finish the well they had started the previous week in Catamount, and Wade, as instructed, pulled off his coat and, clipboard in hand, started to make an inventory of all of LaRiviere's material stock, equipment and tools. "I want to know my assets, Wade," LaRiviere said in a confiding tone, "and I want *you* to know them too. I want to know what we need for a year's work and don't have on hand, buddy, and then I want you to sit yourself down and order it." When Wade asked him if he could have Wednesday off, for the funeral, LaRiviere told him not to worry about it, and then added that from now on Wade was going to be paid a salary, instead of by the hour, same as if he were working a forty-hour week, whether he put in forty hours or not. And not to worry, buddy, about being paid for Monday and Wednesday this week: it was done. Wade almost heard him say "partner."

He wants something from me, Wade thought, and I won't find out what it is unless I smile and go along with him.

During his lunch break, Wade mailed his divorce decree and a check for five hundred dollars, borrowed the day before from Pop's modest savings account, to Attorney Hand, and afterwards, by telephone from Wickham's, he informed Hand that he would soon be getting married and was moving with his fiancée into his father's "farm." He also mentioned, as if in passing, his discovery that Lillian was having an extramarital love affair with Hand's colleague Jackson Cotter, and Attorney Hand said that was a very interesting aspect to the case. "Tantalizing," he said, and Wade could almost hear him smack his lips, the way he had almost heard LaRiviere say "partner."

By Wednesday, the day of the funeral, so much had happened in Wade's life that it seemed Ma had been dead for months.

Out at the house, the freshly plowed driveway and a specially cleared parking area by the side porch were full of cars, as if a celebration were going on. I parked my Volvo behind what I assumed was the minister's car—a maroon station wagon with REV on the vanity plates—and got out and stretched and smelled the silvery wood smoke drifting from the kitchen chimney. I heard the sounds of distant gunfire crackle erratically against the wind in the pines, and I suddenly remembered that the forests and fields just beyond the house and in the hills and valleys for miles around were still dangerously populated by deer hunters.

There were a few cars and a blue pickup truck, LaRiviere's, that I did not recognize and several that I knew— Wade's Ford with the police bubble on top and Pop's old pickup, still covered with snow and parked in the deep drift at the side of the house, as if stuck there permanently. I spotted the VW microbus that belonged to Lena and her husband, their fifteen-year-old recidivist hippie van plastered with born-again Christian bumper stickers instead of peace signs. The emblem of the Rapture—a black arrow shaped like a fishhook descending in a silver field against a vertical arrow ascending—and the cryptic question "Are You Ready for the Rapture?" and "Warning: Driver of This Vehicle May Disappear at Any Moment!" along with the more usual crosses and fishes in profile and mottoes like "Jesus Saves" and "Christ Died for Our Sins" were stuck all over the sides of the van, as if the vehicle were a huge cerulean cereal box promoting apocalypse and everlasting life and promising redeemable gift certificates inside.

Lena and her husband, Clyde, had made Christ their personal savior, apparently the result of a visit from Him—a type of house call was the way they explained it—one night of despair four or five years earlier, and while the chaos of their life had not changed one iota, it had gained significant meaning, since they and their five children were now devoted to the life of the spirit and the next world instead of to the body and this one. Their disheveled and deprived daily lives were now regarded as evidence not of incompetence, as in the past, but of their new priorities. I did not pretend to understand the nature of the conversion experience, of being "saved," one way or the other, or the teachings of the Bible Believers' Evangelistical Association, to which they belonged, but it was clear to me that whereas before they had been depressed and frightened, for what seemed very good reasons, such as poverty, ignorance, powerlessness, etc., they were now optimistic and unafraid. Of course, according to the pamphlets Lena mailed to me from time to time, what they were looking forward to was the imminent end of the world, to earthquake and famine, to seas turned to blood, to plagues of sores, to legions of demons and the writhing demise of the antichrist, events that those of us who were not scheduled for rescue by the Rapture might find even more depressing and frightening than poverty, ignorance and powerlessness.

As I moved from my car toward the house, I passed the three younger of Lena's and Clyde's children, who were pushing huge snowballs through the soft wet snow of the front yard. Though they wore sneakers and thin jackets and were hatless and without mittens and their clothes were wet and their hands and faces bright red from the cold, they were evidently happy and, in spite of running noses, seemed healthy. They saw me coming along the driveway and waved, and I waved back.

A boy, the largest of the three, six or seven years old, smiled sweetly and said, "Hi. Who're you?"

"I'm your uncle Rolfe," I said, and I smiled. "You don't remember me, eh?" In fact, we had never met, which fact embarrassed me slightly. I did not know his name—Stephen or Eben, or maybe Claude—and did not care to ask it.

"Nope, but I heard of you," he said.

"What are you building there? A snowman?"

All three laughed as if I had said something hilariously funny. "No!" the boy exclaimed. "A citadel!"

"Oh."

His sister, her puffy cheeks chapped scarlet from the wet snow, said, "Are you here to say goodbye to Grandma?"

"Grandma's in hell!" the youngest one shouted. He appeared to be a male child but was wearing some kind of kilt made from an adult's woolen scarf, so one could not be sure.

The other boy somberly said, "That's why we say goodbye."

"We're going to be in heaven with Jesus," the little girl explained to me, "and Grandma's in hell with Satan, who is Jesus' enemy. That's why we have to say goodbye, Uncle Rolfe."

"Grandma wasn't saved," her brother said, a note of regret touching his voice.

"I see."

"Are you saved, Uncle Rolfe?" the girl asked.

"No, I'm not."

"Then you'll be cast into hell with Grandma."

"Yes, I guess I will. Me and Grandma and Uncle Wade and Grandpa. We'll all be there together," I said. "And when we die, you'll have to come and say goodbye to us too, won't you?"

The older boy nodded his head up and down. This was a drag, families breaking up all the time. He did not understand it and wished that it could be different, but he did not want to spend eternity in hell, no, sir, he did not, no matter who was there.

As if bored by me, the three went back to building their citadel of snow, and I continued on to the house. Before I had a chance to knock, the door was opened by an attractive woman who introduced herself as Margie Fogg and shook my hand warmly. She gazed straight into my face, and I liked her at once.

Wade stood in the center of the crowded kitchen, looking competent and serious, if a little uncomfortable. He was wearing a white shirt and tightly knotted jet-black tie and navy-blue gabardine sport coat, with dark-brown slacks and shoes, and his face and hands were red and seemed huge and constricted by his mismatched clothing. In one hand he held a can of Schlitz and in the other a cigarette. The room was hot from the wood stove, crowded and close. I saw faces I recognized—Lena and Clyde and their two older children, adolescents whom I had not seen in years, and in the corner by the stove, Pop—and I saw the faces of three strangers, everyone standing, as if waiting to be called to attention and given marching orders.

Wade first, I thought—the easiest. And I reached out with both hands and placed them on his muscular shoulders and drew him to me. We hugged, self-consciously, with our butts sticking out so as to keep light shining between our bodies from shoulders to toes. That is the way we men are, we New England men, we Whitehouse men, Wade and I: we want light between us at all times.

He said my name, and I said his, and we let go of one another and withdrew. Not ready yet to deal with Lena and Clyde and their strange-looking children—both the boy and the girl had modified Mohawk haircuts and resembled barnyard fowl with acne, Rhode Island reds, maybe—and certainly not ready to greet Pop, I first introduced myself to the strangers in the room, who turned out to be the Reverend Doughty, a slender blond man in his thirties wearing horn-rimmed glasses and an avocado-green double-knit suit, and Gordon LaRiviere, appropriately somber, mentioning that he remembered me from my high school days and offering gruff condolences as we shook hands, and a skinny young man in a black suit who was a representative of Morrison's Funeral Home in Littleton, on hand, I guessed, to escort the rest of us to the church on time.

It was unclear to me why LaRiviere was there or why he was behaving in such a solicitous manner toward Wade: "How you holding up, Wade?" he asked at one point, when Wade, after tossing his empty beer can into the trash, stood for a second with his back to the rest of us and stared after it.

Wade turned quickly and said, "I'm fine, fine." He checked his watch. "Shouldn't we get this show on the road, now that Rolfe's here?" he asked the room.

No one knew. We all looked to him for an answer.

He shrugged. "Pointless to stand around in the church with nothing to do, I guess."

"What about Jill?" I asked. "Is Lillian bringing her?"

In a low voice, Margie said that they would be at the church.

Wade walked quickly to the refrigerator and pulled out another beer. "Anyone else want one?" he asked. "Rolfe?"

"No, thanks," I said. "I don't drink."

"Yeah, right. I guess I forgot."

Indeed. My question about Lillian and Jill had irritated him. He knew better than anyone else in the family that I had not drunk anything alcoholic since college and in fact had drunk almost not at all even then. We never discussed it, Wade and I, any more than we discussed his drinking, but I think we both knew that they were equal and opposite reactions to the same force.

I nodded to Lena's and Clyde's children, both the girl, Sonny, and the boy, Gerald, noted their matching dark-red tufts of hair, gray scalps, crosses dangling from their earlobes and around their scrawny necks, and passed them by swiftly on my way to Lena, huge as a purple tent in her muumuu, with a black scarf covering most of her hair, which, to my surprise, had turned almost completely gray. She looked shockingly older than when I had last seen her: how many years had it been—seven, eight? I could not remember, I suddenly realized, how many years it had been since I last stood in the same room with my father, brother and sister. I knew that I would never again stand in a room with them and my mother, certainly not in heaven and not in hell, either.

Lena wore no makeup or jewelry, and her hair was chopped off bluntly at shoulder length. There was nothing about her person that was designed to disguise, or to distract one from, her girth and plainness, and she showed no signs of being either happy or sad to see me—merely grim acceptance. Embracing her was like hugging a barrel, and I instantly let go and stepped away and almost with relief shook the hand of her husband, Clyde, which felt like a piece of firewood, dry, heavy, dead to the touch.

Clyde is a tall thick-hipped pear-shaped man with a large pointed Adam's apple and small shoulders and chest, so that his body seems to be constructed of the lower half of a fat man and the upper half of a thin man welded together at the waist. Clyde's appearance, too, surprised me, for he now looked a full decade older than Wade, whose age he was. His face was drawn in and tight, puckered around blue eyes and a flat red-lipped mouth. He said, "Hello, Rolfe. It's good you came now. We were about to pray. Will you join us in prayer, Rolfe?" His eyes blazed intently into mine, and I looked to Wade, whose expressionless face seemed to be saying, No help here, buddy, you are on your own, and on to Margie, who looked sharply away from me, as if embarrassed.

"Well," I said, "I just got here. Give me a minute, will you?" I tried to smile graciously, but Clyde did not meet my smile. I stepped to my father then and found myself actually glad to see him there—small, silent, inattentive, like the only child in a room full of angry adults.

"This is nuts," Wade muttered.

"Wade," Margie said sharply.

When I hugged my father, the force of my embrace caused his head to bob like a puppet's, and I drew away from him, afraid. Wade was right—it was nuts.

Clyde was already down on his knees, and his two children had followed with alacrity, like acolytes, earnest assistants at the rite.

"Dear Lord Jesus," Clyde began, his eyes jammed shut, head tilted toward the ceiling. "O my Lord Jesus in heaven! We come to thee on our knees today begging forgiveness for our sins and thanking thee for the blessing and the undeserved gift of thy salvation. We thank thee, Lord Jesus. For everlasting life by thy side in heaven, we thank thee, O Jesus, Lord of the Heavenly Hosts, whose blood was shed so that we may live!"

The boy, eyes tightly shut, moaned, "Praise the Lord!" and the girl followed, as did Lena, who was still positioning herself on her knees, not an easy job, given her bulk and awkwardness. Behind me, the Reverend Doughty, in a quiet shy voice, added his more restrained Praise the Lord, and I turned and watched him get down on his knees too, somewhat reluctantly, perhaps, but obediently, just in case.

What were the rest of us to do but follow suit? First the young man from the funeral home—more accustomed, perhaps, to scenes like this than we were—got down on his knees, and then Margie and Gordon LaRiviere, and finally Wade got down—all of them watching Clyde warily, as if playing Simon Says and expecting the next command to be a trick. That left only Pop standing, and me.

Pop's gaze, for the first time since I had entered the house, had taken on a hard focus, and he directed it at everyone in the room, one by one, until it landed on me. I shrugged, as if to say, Why not? and hitched my trousers by the crease and got down on my knees with the others, expecting Pop to do the same.

He shook his head slowly from side to side—in disbelief? disapproval? disgust? I could not tell. Meanwhile, Clyde's prayer went on, full of praise and gratitude for Jesus' having interceded in the natural order of things by eliminating death for those sinners willing to turn their lives over to Him. As he prayed, Clyde glared up at the ceiling, as if at an accuser, while Lena and her children held their eyes tightly closed, their lips moving over a tumbling flow of words that were inaudible to the rest of us. Reverend Doughty, his hands clasped before his chest, seemed to be posing for a photograph, and though his eyes were open, he looked at nothing in particular and everything in general. Gordon LaRiviere, head bowed, eyes closed, hands appropriately clasped, had the appearance of a man who hoped he was not being seen by anyone he knew. Margie and Wade, too, were clearly going through the motions, nothing more, with their heads slightly bowed, eyes open, expressions reserved, all-purpose and noncommittal, and I tried to follow their example.

Turning away from us, Pop walked to the sink and took down from the cabinet his bottle of Canadian Club. He carefully poured a substantial drink into a glass, then spun around and took a gulp from the glass and set it down and crossed his arms over his chest and watched us. He said something, but I could not hear him over Clyde's loud prayer and the numerous Amens and Praise the Lords that punctuated it. No one but me seemed to be observing Pop. He smirked in a way I remembered, and suddenly I felt not embarrassed but wildly ashamed to be seen this way, on my knees, hands pressed together, in the midst of fervent prayer. I saw us—me, Wade and Lena in particular, but the others as well—the way Pop saw us, and I cringed and tried to make myself smaller, hoping for invisibility, the way I had as a child. I could feel his wrath building, could almost smell it, a gray smell, like an electrical fire starting to smolder, when he spoke again, loud enough this time for me to make out his words: "Not worth a hair on her head," he said.

The prayer went on, however, as if he had merely said "Praise the Lord." There was a little more volume, perhaps, for Clyde now had tears running down his cheeks, and it looked as if Lena was about to join him. Reverend Doughty seemed to have caught the rhythm of it, his eyes clamped shut, his body swaying back and forth, his hands wringing with the beginnings of fervor, and even LaRiviere and the mortician seemed tied to the form of the prayer. I cut a glance at Margie and Wade, but they were both staring down at the floor in front of them, as if hoping for a trapdoor to open. Again Pop said it, louder still: "Not worth a goddamned hair on her head!"

Wade turned around and looked at him, puzzled. He scowled and shook his head no, as if to a fidgety child, and resumed his prayerful stance. Clyde rolled on. "Jesus, we beseech thee, thy children beseech thee, to please look down on this woman, our mother and friend, O Lord, and make her example known to us. Make her vivid to us, Lord! We know that it is too late for her to be saved, but let her be an example unto those of us who have forsaken thee. Make her vivid to us! Let her sufferings in hell, where she must burn even now, serve as a warning to those of us who still have time, Lord. Make her vivid to us who are dead in spirit only and who still have time to allow thee to enter us, to cleanse us and to lift us up into everlasting life!"

With bottle and glass in hand, Pop stepped elaborately over the legs of the people in his path and made his way to the living room door, where he stopped short and in a voice that was practically a shout announced, "Not a one of you is worth a goddamned hair on that good woman's head!"

Wade said, "Pop!" and he stood up. His face was white, and in a trembling voice, he said, "Don't do this now, Pop."

Clyde stopped praying, but he held his position, eyes shut, tears sliding down his cheeks. Lena and her children froze too, in silence, waiting. Margie dropped her hands to her sides but stayed on her knees, while LaRiviere slowly got up, and the mortician and Reverend Doughty followed.

"Maybe I'll head on over to the church," LaRiviere said, and edged toward the door.

"This is a difficult time," Reverend Doughty said, backing away. "Emotions run high at a time like this."

The mortician nodded with compassion and followed LaRiviere to the door, where he said, "I'll wait in the car," and all three men stepped outside and closed the door behind them.

Those of us left in the room were standing now. Our father's face had reddened with rage and he began to sputter, a furious small man spattering us with his words, the way he had done it years ago, when we were children and were terrified of him, and now here we were, Wade and I and Lena, terrified again, as if we were still children, even including Margie, I realized, when I looked at her drawn white face, and Clyde too, whose eyes were opened at last, and the boy and the girl, who had moved around behind their parents and peered over their shoulders, wide-eyed, mouths slack.

Wade took a step toward our father and said, "Listen, it's no big deal, Pop," and our father swiftly put his bottle and glass on the floor and clenched his fists and came forward a few feet, his bony face shoved out in front of him like a battering ram.

"Come on, smart guy. Tell me how it's no big deal," he growled. "Tell me how a single one of you is worth a single hair on that woman's gray head."

He was right, and I knew it. And I was sure that Wade and Margie knew it, and that probably even Lena and Clyde and their children knew it too. Our mother *was* worth more than we. For she had suffered our father more than we. He was telling this to us, and he was proving it too. Our mother had endured our father's wrath long after we had fled from it, endured it all the way to her death, and now here he was demonstrating it before us, his wrath, with his claim that we were morally inferior to her. The form of his claim, in that it was a form of wrath, was the proof of his claim.

I hung my head in shame and backed away, hoping that my example would influence the others—as I had done when we were children at times like this. It was something I had learned from my mother, this silent coercion. I had not used it for years.

In a shaky thin voice, Lena said, "Pop, Jesus is more powerful than any demon, and there is a demon in you, Pop. Give yourself to Jesus, and rid yourself of this demon."

"Praise the Lord," Clyde whispered.

"Go fuck yourself!" Pop snarled, and Lena stumbled backward, as if blown by the force of his words. She began to whimper, then to blubber, and her husband put his arms around her and moved her toward the door, with the boy and the girl close behind. As they passed through the door to the porch, all four looked fearfully back at our father—a brick-red taut little man standing in the middle of the room with his fists clenched—as if they feared he would come charging after them or were about to hurl one of his raging demons into them.

But he had not once taken his eyes off Wade. That was who he wanted. The rest of us did not matter to him. Margie placed both hands on Wade's shoulders and tried to draw him to her, but he wrenched himself loose and took another step toward our father. I moved in the opposite direction and in a low voice said, "Wade, just leave it."

Pop, in that awful mocking tone of his, said, "Listen to your little brother. 'Wade, just leave it.' Candy-asses. All of you. That's what I've got for children, Jesus freaks and candy-asses. 'Wade, just leave it.' 'Praise the Lord.' 'Just leave it.' 'Praise the Lord.'"

Wade stepped forward, fists clenched, and suddenly Margie moved around and got in front of him, where she tried to push him back with one hand and reach out toward Pop with the other. Pop struck her hand away with his fist, and her face went gray, her mouth opened in amazement. Wade reached over her and grabbed one of Pop's wrists and yanked him once toward him. Margie screamed, she actually screamed, and Wade let go of our father, but it was too late. The old man was flailing away at his son with his fists, his blows bouncing off Margie's shoulders and neck, hitting Wade on the arms. I reached in and tried to grab Wade by the shoulders and pull him away, but he was too powerful for me and merely shrugged me off. He shoved Margie out of his way and locked our father into his arms. They panted furiously into each other's face, glaring. Wade walked our father in a bear hug backward to the wall, where he pushed him with his chest and bounced the old man's frail and suddenly flaccid body against the wall. He released him, and our father collapsed onto the floor.

Breathing heavily, Wade got down on his knees, as if to pray again. He looked into the old man's face, which glowered back, as if out of a cave. "If you ever touch her again," Wade said, "I'll kill you. I swear it."

The old man stared coldly at his son and said nothing.

Margie said, "Wade, it doesn't matter now. None of it matters."

From across the room, I watched them, the woman and

the two men, as if they were characters in a play, and the play were half over and I had just entered the theater. Slowly, the old man got to his feet, and the younger man stood up, and the woman turned around, and all three faced me. The old man moved into line next to the woman, who now stood in the middle. They were breathing heavily and sweating. They looked from one to the other, shedding their roles and regaining themselves and in the process recognizing each other's self. It was as if they had been possessed. They smiled at each other, shyly and almost with relief. Then the three of them looked out toward me and linked hands, and, I swear it, they bowed low. That is how I saw it. What else could I do? I applauded.

The mortician opened the door from the porch and announced that it was time to leave for the church.

"Okay," Wade said. "We'll be right there."

Pop looked around him as if searching for something. Putting an arm over his shoulder, Margie said, "You want your coat? It's not very cold today."

"No, no," he said. He seemed confused. "I thought . . . I was looking for Sally," he blurted, and his eyes filled with tears.

"Oh, Glenn," Margie said, and she hugged the old man.

Wade clapped him affectionately on the shoulder, then looked over at me, as if thinking, The poor sonofabitch. We keep forgetting that no matter what their life was like together, no matter how bad it was for Ma, it was the only life he had. The poor old sonofabitch probably loved her. There was no reason for Rolfe to make fun of him by clapping like that.

Wade's hand moved to his jaw and touched it tenderly: his tooth had quieted down a bit for days, and now here it was again, buzzing like a stirred-up hornet's nest. "You got any aspirin?" he asked Margie.

She shook her head no, and Wade reached down to the floor and retrieved Pop's whiskey bottle and glass. There was a half inch of whiskey still in the glass, and he drank it off himself.

"Toothache," he said, and put the bottle and glass down on the counter next to the sink.

"When are you going to get that thing fixed?" Margie asked.

"Soon. Soon. Soon as I've got half a day to kill," he said, and he went to the door and held it open.

Margie walked Pop to the door slowly, carefully, as if he were breakable. He took tiny steps and seemed afraid of falling. How could this pathetic man cause such trouble in a family? Margie wondered, as she moved him across the room toward Wade. He was as weak as a child and as easily controlled. He had thrown a tantrum, that was all, which was perfectly understandable, under the circumstances. There was no need to get physical with him, to manhandle him the way Wade had, or run away from him as Lena had done, or just go limp, like Rolfe. It amazed her that they seemed so frightened of him. It was as if they still thought of themselves as small children and for that reason still saw him as a powerful and violent man, when of course, as anyone could see, it was he who was the child and they, Rolfe and Lena and Wade, who were the adults. Strange. And that business of Rolfe's, the clapping, it was strange too. He was weird, even weirder in his own tight-assed way than Lena. Margie was starting to like the old man, even to feel protective toward him, though she could not imagine why that should be so.

Glenn Whitehouse passed through the door to the porch and stood there for a second, gazing out over the snow-covered yard. He saw the citadel the children had built, a biblical ruin in the snow. Lena's and Clyde's van was gone, as were the vehicles belonging to LaRiviere and the minister. The mortician stood by the open rear door of a black Buick sedan.

Pop turned to Wade and said, "Who's going in the funeral car?" He did not want to ride in that car, but he knew that he had to. It looked like a death car, and he was afraid that if he rode in that car alone, with only the dummy from the funeral home up front driving, he might not arrive at his destination. He did not know where he would end up, but it would not be at the church with the other people. Maybe Wade or Margie would ride with him, or maybe even Rolfe, though Rolfe made him feel self-conscious when he was with him alone. Something about that boy set Pop off. He made him feel he was supposed to say something, as if there was a question the boy wanted answered and the first test was for him to figure out what the damned question was. He was cold, that boy, not like

Wade, who was pissed off all the time, but you always knew where you stood with him, or even Lena, who might be a Jesus freak married to a Jesus freak, but she was not cold, that was for sure. The woman had feelings. But Rolfe did not. Or at least he did not seem to have any feelings. He was the strange one, not Wade or Lena.

"I'll ride with you, Pop," I said. Wade agreed and said that he and Margie would follow along in his car. Pop and I got into the back seat of the Buick, and the driver closed the door and got into the front. Pop sat silent and still, looking straight ahead. I wanted to ask him a question, it burned in my chest, but I could not for the life of me name it. I looked at him while we rode, hoping somehow that the sight of his face in profile would bring the question to me, but it did not.

17

THE FUNERAL AND THE BURIAL were relatively uneventful, thanks no doubt to Pop's earlier outburst and Wade's reaction to it. Reverend Doughty performed the obsequies with amiable competence, as if officiating at a retirement. No one wept over the coffin—Wade had insisted that it be a closed-coffin service: "There's no way you can improve on a body that's been frozen to death," he told the mortician, "unless you keep it in the freezer and have the funeral there. Which you cannot do." The mortician agreed, but with reluctance. It would have been easy to have presented the body beautifully: it had died so peacefully. Oh, well, the winter was young. Soon there would be plenty of bodies that had frozen to death in their sleep, and the bereaved would not be quite as belligerent as this one.

Lillian and her husband Bob Horner and Jill arrived at the funeral a few moments after it had started, and Wade did not see them until he and three others—Gordon LaRiviere, our brother-in-law Clyde and I—carried the coffin from the church to the hearse. Lillian and Horner had seated themselves by the aisle in the last row of the church, with Jill between them, gazing in wonderment at the coffin, and as Wade passed their aisle, he nodded somberly. Jill did not take her eyes off the coffin. Horner returned the nod, but Lillian, whose eyes appeared to be red from weeping, pursed her lips, as if sending Wade a kiss. Wade seemed surprised and puzzled by Lillian's gesture and stared after her and almost stumbled at the door of the vestry.

And at the burial, no one shed more than a few perfunctory tears. It was held at the Riverside Cemetery, high on the slope near the ridge, where Elbourne and Charlie, whose remains had been shipped back from Vietnam two decades earlier, were buried. At the head of each grave, a tiny VFW flag fluttered next to a small gray-blue granite stone with the boy's name and birth and death date carved into it. Our mother's open grave lay just beyond her firstborn son's, shockingly dark and deep against the white blanket of snow, a quick entry to another world, where neither snow nor sunlight ever fell.

At one point, after Reverend Doughty had said his final benign and appropriately ecumenical prayer and the coffin was at last ready for the descent, Wade crossed from where he had been standing with me and Margie and Pop to the opposite side of the grave, where Lillian and Jill and Bob Horner stood alongside most of the twelve or fifteen townspeople who had attended. As he passed one of the several floral arrangements provided by the funeral home, he plucked a long-stemmed white carnation, which he handed to Jill. Leaning down beside her, he whispered into her ear, and she stepped forward and laid the flower across the coffin.

Then Wade returned to the bouquet and drew out four more flowers, which he presented in turn to Lena, me and Pop, keeping one for himself. He nodded to Lena, and she followed Jill's example; as did I. Then Wade placed his own flower on the coffin.

We all looked at Pop, who stood blinking in the sunlight, his flower held in front of him as if he were about to smell it. It was strange moment. We were suddenly and unexpectedly aware of our mother's presence in a way that until this moment we had either denied or had been denied. Her sad battered life seemed to come clear to us, and for a few seconds we were unable to look away from her suffering. We had looked away, averted our gaze, for so many reasons, but mostly because we all three believed at bottom that we could have and should have saved her from our father's terrible violence, the permanent wrath that he seemed unable to breathe without. But somehow, the sight of that shrunken old man holding the flower before him in trembling hands, unsure of what to do with it, made us briefly forgive ourselves, perhaps, and allowed us to see him as she must have seen him, which is to say, allowed us to love him, and to know that she loved him and that there was no way we could have saved her from him, not Lena, surely, and not I, and not Wade. And not even the old man himself could have saved her from the violence that he had inflicted on her and on us. If he had taken himself out behind the barn one morning during his life with her and shot himself in the head, inflicted on himself in one awful blow all the violence he had battered us with during the years we lived with him, it still would not have released us, for our mother loved him, and so did we, and that awful blow would have been inflicted on us as well. His violence and wrath were our violence and wrath: there had been no way out of it.

As if she were sitting up in her coffin with her arms reaching toward her husband, our mother drew our father slowly forward. He tottered a bit, blinked away tears, and held out the carnation, a pathetic and vain plea for forgiveness impossible to give, and placed it over the others. Then he withdrew, and the young mortician flipped the lever, and the coffin slowly descended into the grave, and our mother was gone.

One by one, the townspeople returned to their cars and pickup trucks parked below on the lane and drove off, until only we family members, including Lillian and Jill and Bob Horner and, of course, Margie Fogg, who had one large arm around Pop's shoulders, remained at the gravesite.

Wade looked down at Jill, smiled and then hugged her closely. She let herself be held for a few seconds and stepped away.

"I'm glad you're here," Wade said to her. "Can you stay for a while?" He looked at Lillian for an answer.

She hesitated, as if she herself would like to stay on and were trying to think of a way to say it that would not mislead him. But then she shook her head no.

Wade inhaled deeply and held his breath, making a hard bubble in his chest, and looked off toward the ridge. "You ever come to your father's grave anymore?" he asked Lillian.

She turned and followed his gaze up the slope. "No, not anymore. It's too . . . it's too far."

She was remembering what Wade wanted her to remember, those summer Sunday afternoons when they were teenagers newly in love and the future was endless and full of hope for them—together and alone. They were going to turn into a marvelous man and powerful woman and brilliant couple: they were going to become successful at *everything*, but especially at love. And here they were, and now Wade wanted her to know, in the same way he knew, what in the intervening years had been lost and, if possible, to grieve with him for a moment. This might be the last time they could share something as tender and powerful as grief over their broken dreams.

But Lillian did not know that, because she did not know yet about Wade's new lawyer, so she offered Wade only a quick pat on the shoulder and said, "Wade, I'm sorry about your mother. I always liked her and felt sorry for her." She glanced sharply over at our father; he had been turned by Margie; she was moving him with care down the slope toward Wade's car.

"Come on, honey," Lillian said to Jill. "We've got to get back by four for your ice-skating lesson."

"I'm taking ice-skating, Daddy!" Jill said, suddenly brightening.

"Great. Figure skating, I suppose." He wondered where in hell she could take figure-skating lessons up here. Nowhere, probably.

"And ice ballet."

"Great."

She smiled warmly at him, and waved, and moved off with her mother and her stepfather, who, Wade realized, had a new Tyrolean hat, just like the other.

For a few moments, Wade stood alone by our mother's grave. I watched his dark slump-shouldered figure from the black Buick down below, with Pop sitting in silence beside me. Wade seemed terribly lonely to me then. He must still love that woman, I thought. How painful it must be for him, to have his mother buried and to stand and watch the woman he loves and his only child walk away from him. I was glad that I did not have to endure such pain.

* * *

Not surprisingly, Lena and her family headed back down to Massachusetts right after the burial. I rode out to the house with Wade and Margie and Pop, however, because my car was parked out there, but also to talk over a few financial matters with Wade. It was clear that Wade now intended to take responsibility for the house and for Pop, but it was a little vague to me as to who would bear the costs for this. Far better, I felt, to discuss and clarify these changes now than to let debts, real or imagined, and resentments, just or unjust, accumulate.

We left Margie with Pop in the kitchen and walked outside to the porch. It was midafternoon but already growing dark and, with the sunlight gone, getting cold fast. A pair of snow shovels leaned against the wall of the porch, and Wade grabbed one and handed me the other.

"Let's dig out Pop's truck before the skin of the snow freezes up," he said.

I said okay and followed him around to the side of the house, where we commenced to break apart the drift that had nearly buried the vehicle. The snow had thickened during the day and was heavy, packed tightly by its own weight, and we were able to cut it into neat blocks that flew solidly through the air when we heaved them. It was pleasant warming work, and the talk came easily to us, perhaps because the tensions of the funeral were now behind us and we were able to mourn privately and alone.

Wade seemed grateful for my interest in his plans. He would pay for all the funeral expenses with a small insurance policy that our mother had taken out years ago. He had checked the deed and other papers he had found in her dresser drawers and learned that there was no mortgage or lien on the house. He was not sure about the taxes but would stop by and ask Alma Pittman tomorrow, he assured me. Wade explained that he planned to live in the house and pay for any renovations or repairs himself, along with the taxes and insurance, and when Pop died, which he said could be tomorrow or twenty years from now, he would probably want to buy out my and Lena's two thirds, after having the place properly appraised, of course. I said that I was agreeable to the arrangement, and I was sure Lena would feel the same. Pop had his social security check, a bit more than five hundred dollars a month, which Wade said should more than cover his expenses for food and booze. It all sounded reasonable and even kind.

"What about Margie?" I asked.

"What about her?"

We had ceased work for a minute, and we were leaning on our shovel handles, face to face. "Well, do you plan to get married?"

"Yes," he said, although they had not yet set a date for it. Meanwhile, she would be living with him. "She'll probably quit her job and stay out here at the place with Pop," he added. "We leave him alone here, he'll set the damned place on fire. And of course Jill will be here a lot, so it'll be good to have Margie around then. Things are going to change there, by the way," he said, and he briefly updated me on his legal maneuvers. "I got an appointment Saturday in Concord with my lawyer, and after that all hell's going to break loose for a while. And dammit, it's worth it," he said. But then he sighed, as if it were *not* worth it, and we went back to work.

In a short while, we had the truck free of the snow and had driven it out to the cleared part of the driveway while we cleaned up the area. Then Wade suggested that we shovel out the driveway all the way to the barn, so he could put Pop's truck inside and leave it till spring. "Or whenever. I don't want the bastard driving drunk, and he's always drunk now, so it's best to put the damned thing out of the snow, in the barn. Empty the gas tank and hide the keys."

The barn was still more or less intact at the front, although open to the weather in back, where the roof had collapsed and where years ago Pop and Wade and Charlie had torn off most of the boards in Pop's short-lived attempt to close up the building. When we had cleared the driveway from the front of the house around to the back, all the way to the large open door of the barn, Wade got in Pop's truck and drove it inside. It was dark by now, and the truck headlights illuminated the skeletal interior of the structure. It looked like the backstage area of a long-unused opera house.

I walked behind the truck, and when I entered the barn, with the light bouncing and sliding off the lofts and beams overhead, I was suddenly out of the winter wind and early darkness and found myself surprisingly comfortable there; I wanted to stay, to make my home in the wreckage and rot of the old building; I liked the barn, decrepit and falling down, better than the house.

Wade kept the motor running for a few moments, as if he, too, were reluctant to break the spell cast by the lights and the strange interior space of the barn. He got out and stood beside me and, with me, looked up at the roof, at the old empty haylofts and through the exposed beams and timbers at the back at the dark sky beyond. There was a familial comfort to the place, and one could almost smell the cattle and other livestock that had once been housed here. But there was also a mystery to the place, as if an unpunished crime had been committed in this space.

Pop's shaky old red truck, a Ford stake-body rusted out at the fenders and the bottom of the cab, idled quietly, while Wade and I walked in careful silence through the splash of light, touching the splintery unpainted wood of the walls, as if looking for clues. Wade lit a cigarette and stopped walking and, with his back to me, stared out the open end of the barn at the brush-cluttered field behind it. The lights from the truck sent a wash of pale light over the snow to the far woods. Beyond the woods the land rose sharply on the left toward Parker Mountain and fell away on the right toward Saddleback Ridge. The old farm lay halfway between them and in years past, when the land was cleared of trees, must have offered lovely views out here. There were over a hundred acres of high sloping brushy fields and woodlands that had belonged once to Uncle Elbourne and then to Pop and now, in a way, to Wade. The dark hillside and woods stirred me profoundly in a way I could not name, and Wade must have felt as I did, for we continued to stare out from the wreck of the barn in silence.

"Wade," I said. "That was a nice gesture, with the flowers, at the cemetery."

"Yeah, well, it seemed like something was . . . needed. You know. For Ma."

"I was wondering, I wondered if maybe you felt the way I did, when we put the flowers on top of the coffin."

"How's that?"

"Well, sort of like she was there, for just a minute longer, giving us some kind of message. About Pop. About taking care of Pop, maybe." This was not working: Wade and I are incapable of talking about the things that matter most to us. Still, it seemed important to try.

"Taking care of Pop, eh? *You* want to take care of him? Be my guest. I suppose what I'm doing for him is what Ma would have wanted, but if it was up to me alone, I'd take the bastard out behind the barn and shoot him. I kid you not."

"Well, it was a nice gesture anyway, with the flowers."

"Thanks," he said, his back still to me.

We stood in silence for a moment longer, and then, finally, I turned toward the truck and suggested that we go back inside the house.

"Not yet, not till I burn out the little gas that's left in the tank. You go in if you want. I got to stay here until it stalls out, or the battery'll run dead. I guess I ought to shut off the head-lights, though," he said, clearly not wanting to. "There's a kerosene lantern I saw a minute ago over by the side of the door, where we came in. Whyn't you light that?" he said.

I did as he instructed, while he climbed into the cab and flicked off the headlights; and then we had a soft pale-yellow light filling the cavernous space. The truck motor chugged on, and I felt as if we were inside a ship at night, crossing a northern sea, looking out into darkness and cold with a steady wind in our faces.

I do not know where the thought came from, but suddenly I remembered the shooting of Evan Twombley, and I asked Wade if he had heard anything new about it in the last few days.

He said no and seemed oddly reluctant to talk about it, as if embarrassed by his earlier obsessive interest in the case. "I guess it was an accident, like everybody thinks."

"Like everybody *wants* to think, you mean," I said.

"Yeah. Yeah, I suppose so. But don't get me all started up on that again. It doesn't go anywhere, and whenever I get to thinking on it, I get crazy, like a dog worrying at a flea it can't scratch. It feels better if I just let it alone," he said.

"You want to know what I think happened?"

Wade said no, then yes, and walked around to the passenger's side of the truck and opened the door and groped in the dark through the glove compartment. I had taken up a position on the tailgate, and when he returned and sat down beside me, he was carrying a nearly full bottle of Canadian Club. "I've been finding them all over the damned place," he said, and he unscrewed the cap, sniffed the contents and took a slug from the bottle. "In the basement, in the attic, under the bathroom sink. I didn't realize how bad he'd got." He started to pass the bottle to me, then withdrew it. "Sorry," he said.

"Wade, I think your first response to the Twombley shooting was the correct one."

"Which is?"

"That it was not an accident."

"Then who shot him?"

"Well, your friend, I think. Jack Hewitt."

"Motive, Rolfe. You got to have motive."

"For Jack? Money."

"Okay. Money. Jack always needs money, and he's had big ideas about life ever since he got all that attention for being a ballplayer. But come on, who the hell would pay Jack that kind of money? Bonus-baby money."

"Easy. Who benefits if Twombley is suddenly dead?"

"Oh, the mob, I suppose. The Mafia or the Cosa Nostra or whatever the hell they call them these days. But those guys, they don't need to hire a hick from the sticks. They've got their own talent, guys with lots of experience. Specialists."

"Right. They would not deal with a guy like Jack. I know that. Who else benefits?"

"I don't know, Rolfe. You tell me."

"Okay, I will. It is likely that there are people running the union who do not want Twombley to testify in Washington about connections between the union and organized crime. Twombley was the president, but his son-in-law is the vice-president and treasurer, and he will probably be the next president. I saw that in the papers. What's his name, Mel Gordon?"

"Gordon, yeah. The guy with the BMW I told you about. I told you about him, didn't I?"

"Yes. So listen, here is my theory. It is quite possible, it is even likely, that Twombley was unaware of connections between the union and the mob, money-laundering operations, say, where cash skimmed from Las Vegas or from drugs gets into the pension fund and then in turn gets invested in real estate deals, for example, or, what the hell, mutual funds. Sound and very legal investments. That could happen without his knowing. Until, prompted by a federal inquiry, he starts nosing around himself."

242

Wade took another drink from the bottle and set it down next to him on the tailgate. He looked at me and said, "Tooth-ache," then lit a cigarette and stared out the open door at the backside of the house, where now and then we could see Mar-gie pass by the kitchen window, walking from the sink to the stove.

Wade said, "So you think Mel Gordon would want to get rid of him, but he wouldn't want it to look like a hit, a profes-sional killing. Because that would only confirm the Mafia con-nection and make people dig deeper."

"Right. But a hunting accident, now *that* would be per-fect."

"Yep," he said. "I guess it would. It's true, y' know. Show a kid like Jack enough money, and he just might do something like that. And it's obviously the easiest way in the world to shoot somebody and get away with it. Shit, in this state, even if you admit that you shot somebody in the woods, so long as you say it was accidental, you might get fined fifty bucks and your hunting license gets pulled for the season. Jack, fucking Jack. He probably claimed the guy shot himself, instead of saying he shot him himself accidentally, because it was the first day of the season and Jack hadn't got his own deer yet and didn't want his license pulled."

"That, and his reputation as a guide."

Wade laughed lightly. "I don't know, Rolfe. It's all a little too neat for me." Then he turned serious again. "Nothing in life is ever that neat."

"Some things are," I said.

"Only in books."

This was a criticism of me, I knew, the bookish one, as Wade would have it, the one who did not know about real life, which he regarded as his area of expertise. He may not have been to college, as he was fond of pointing out, but he had been in the army and had been a cop, and he had seen some things that would surprise you about human nature. Whereas I, by his lights, had lived a privileged and protected and therefore, when it came to human nature, an ignorant life.

"It is what happened," I said. "And not because it's so neat, but in spite of it. And I know you agree with me."

He stood up and walked to the door and stared down the driveway past the house to the road. "You're trying to make me crazy with this, Rolfe. It gets me so fucking mad, when I think about Jack shooting this guy Twombley, and Mel Gordon paying him for it, to kill his own father-in-law, for God's sake, the father of his own wife—it gets me so mad I can't stand it. I feel like hitting something, pounding the shit out of it. You sit there, calmly laying it out like that—I don't know how the hell you do it. Doesn't it piss you off?"

"No," I said. "Not particularly."

"Well, it makes me crazy. And I can't do a damned thing about it. The kid gets to kill the guy, and Mel Gordon gets to buy the death of his own father-in-law, and that's the end of it. Nobody gets *punished* for it. It's not right."

"You don't care about that, do you?" I said. "Punishment?"

"Sure I do! Right's right, goddammit. Don't you care about that, about what's right?"

"No, not when it has got nothing to do with me. All I care about is what really happened. What the truth is. I am a student of history, remember."

"Yeah, I remember." We were silent for a few moments. Wade sat back down beside me on the tailgate and took another drink of whiskey. The truck sputtered, and then the motor coughed and stopped.

"Out of gas," Wade said in a low voice. He got up and turned off the ignition and returned. "Let's go in," he said. He sounded dispirited.

"I should be getting on home. It's a long drive, and I have school tomorrow."

"You coming in to say goodbye to Pop?" He lifted the chimney on the lantern and blew out the flame, dousing us in darkness.

"You think he will notice one way or the other?"

"Nope."

"Then I'll skip it." I told him that I liked Margie, she was very attractive and seemed kind, and I suggested that he bring her with him the next time he came down to visit. He said he would and shook my hand, and I walked to my car alone. From the road, while my car warmed up, I watched Wade walk onto the porch and go inside the house, and I did not know it then, but when the door closed, it was the last time I would see my brother.

* * *

During the long drive home, I played back to myself that odd eerily lit scene in the barn, troubled by it somehow and feeling vaguely guilty, as if in an important way I had misrepresented myself. It was as if I had cast myself in a role that I was unsuited for, a role that was better suited for Wade to play, and in doing so, I had thrown Wade off his lines and intentions, had changed his motives and thus, to the detriment of the play itself, had affected his actions. It was a usurpation of sorts, for me to speculate with such bland confidence about the cause of Twombley's death, and though I did not realize it at the time, by reawakening and giving a hard focus to Wade's involvement with that event, I was sending Wade off in a direction of inquiry that he should never have pursued.

I know that now, of course, with the benefit of hindsight. But back in November, the day we buried our mother and the night we dug our father's truck out of the snow and stored it in the old collapsing barn, I myself must have needed Wade's obsession with Twombley's death, and I myself must have wanted Jack Hewitt and Mel Gordon, two men I had not even met, punished for killing him. I had no way of knowing what Wade would do with my highly speculative theory—let us face it, a hypothesis based on intuition and the flimsiest of evidence, fortified with little more than my pretended knowledge of how large unions function—but I did know that Wade would accept my version of events, that it would become the truth for him and that he would apply to that truth a range and intensity of emotion that was denied me.

That night Wade slept fitfully, floating in and out of dark dreams and barely conscious fantasies, and he woke gloomy, dour and in a hurry to get to work. He directed traffic at the school with impatience and a glower for everyone he saw, even the children. It was a sunny day, cloudless and relatively warm, but Wade held his head down and his shoulders hunched, as if pummeled by a northeaster. By the time he arrived at LaRiviere's, he had fixed his mind onto a single question: What was LaRiviere's connection to the killing of Evan Twombley?

Where prior to our conversation in the barn Wade had

viewed LaRiviere's uncharacteristic benevolence and sudden generosity with some puzzlement and gratitude, he now clearly saw his boss as behaving suspiciously. LaRiviere's putting Wade on salary and offering him an inside job, and his somewhat unctuous presence at the house before the funeral and his surprising offer to be the fourth pallbearer, when, after more than twenty years of being Wade's employer, he barely knew our mother's first name—all that had struck Wade at the time merely as odd but, in a sense, typical: he was used to thinking of LaRiviere as odd. My conversation with him in the barn, however, had created for Wade a new order, as it were, a microcosmic system in which all the parts now had to fit, especially the odd ones, the puzzling and inconsistent parts, and to Wade, LaRiviere's recent behavior was exactly that. A mere symmetry, a small observed order, placed like a black box in a corner of one's turbulent or afflicted life, can make one's accustomed high tolerance of chaos no longer possible.

Wade walked into the shop and saw Jack and Jimmy Dame ready to head out, the drilling rig loaded with steel pipe, gleaming and clean as if it were brand-new, straight out of a trade-journal advertisement. Jimmy was walking around the front of the truck taking swipes at real and imagined specks of dirt with a rag, while Jack sat up inside the cab, smoking a cigarette and reading the sports page of the *Manchester Union-Leader*.

"Put out that fucking cigarette!" It was LaRiviere from the office door, and his face was red and swollen, like an angry frog's.

Jack grimaced, took one last deep drag and reached for the ashtray on the dashboard, moving slowly.

"Not there, asshole. Flush it!"

Jack swung down from the truck, saw Wade standing just inside the door and, expressionless, walked across the shop to the lavatory. Wade thought, This is a smart little piece of theater, everything normal, the usual craziness from LaRiviere, the usual surly response from Jack, who is probably half hung over, or at least trying to look that way to me, the two of them going through their routines so that I will think that everything is normal. He could imagine them agreeing privately before he arrived: LaRiviere would catch Jack smoking in the shop just as Wade came through the door, and Jack would react with his everyday sour compliance.

Wade knew that somehow LaRiviere was a part of the killing of Evan Twombley. He had to be: LaRiviere was the one who had provided Twombley with Jack as a guide in the first place, and he had advised Twombley to go hunting on his land up on Parker Mountain, to use his cabin up there if he wanted, and when Wade had told LaRiviere about the shooting, he had acted odd about it, making Wade drive him up to the mountain lickety-split and seeming almost relieved when he heard the state police version of the event. For a second Wade entertained the notion that the police captain, Asa Brown, was somehow involved, but then dismissed it: he only thought it because he did not like Asa Brown personally and wanted him somehow involved.

It was harder with LaRiviere and Jack: in a way, he loved LaRiviere, had worked for him since he was a high school kid, except when he was in the army, and at times had thought of him as the kind of father he wished had been his, the kind of father he thought he actually deserved; and Jack he viewed as a little brother, almost, a man who was a lot like himself twenty years earlier—a smart good-looking kid with a brash sociability, stuck in a small town, maybe, but making the most of it. No, he did not want LaRiviere and Jack involved in this sorry business, and when he looked at the two men, the one blustering about cigarette butts and cleanliness, the other dropping his butt into the toilet as if dropping a coin into a fountain, he felt a form of grief, a turbulent mixture of abandonment, rage and guilt. Toward Asa Brown, however, all he felt was the all-too-familiar cold-edged resentment that insecure people feel toward those who humiliate them. No way that Asa Brown was involved in this Twombley business.

Wade said to LaRiviere, "Morning, Gordon," and went to his locker and hung up his coat and hat.

LaRiviere smiled broadly, tossed Wade a wave and retreated to the office.

As Wade picked up his clipboard and inventory sheets and prepared to resume counting wrenches and fittings, Jack passed him and said, "I'm fucking out of here, man."

"Catamount?"

"No, I mean this fucking job. This job sucks. Working outside in winter sucks. I'm fucking out of here." He stalked to the truck and climbed back up into the cab, where Jimmy waited in the driver's seat. Jack cranked down the window and hollered to Wade, "Open the garage door, will you?"

Instead, Wade strolled around to Jack's side of the truck and in a smooth low voice said, "Why don't you quit now, Jack, if you want out so bad?"

Jack sighed and leaned his head back against the seat. "Wade, just open the door. We're already late, and Gordon's got a hair across his ass."

"No, I mean it—why don't you quit this job? You've got enough money now, don't you? Head out to California, my man. Start over. Surf's up, Jack, but you, you're back here digging wells in the snow."

"What do you mean, I've got enough money? I'm as broke as you are."

Wade smiled broadly, then turned and ambled across the shop and hit the electric door opener, and the door lifted with a rattle and slid overhead. As the truck exited from the garage, Jack leaned out the open window and shouted to Wade, "You're looney tunes! You know that? Fucking looney tunes!"

"Like a fox!" Wade hollered after, as the truck lumbered across the parking lot toward the road. Wade started to turn back to the switch, when he saw the familiar black BMW enter the parking lot from the road, and as the truck passed on its way out, the BMW stopped. The truck stopped, and Jack lowered his window again, and Wade saw him exchange a few words with the driver of the BMW, then move on.

Wade stood at the garage door and watched Mel Gordon park his car next to the building and walk briskly around to the open door, where the man saw and recognized Wade.

Their eyes met, and then (significantly, Wade thought) Mel Gordon looked away at once and passed Wade by. Wade turned and followed him with his gaze as he headed straight for the office door. The door opened for a second, and Wade saw Elaine Bernier, seated behind her desk, greet Mel Gordon with a delighted smile.

"Mr. Gordon!" she exclaimed.

"The boss in?" he asked in a cheerful voice.

"Yes indeedy!"

Mel Gordon turned and drew the door closed behind him, catching Wade's glare as he pulled it to, returning it with a glare of his own, then slamming the door shut.

With a smile and a whistle, Wade punched the button, and the overhead door slid down and slammed against the concrete floor. His chest was warm and filled with what felt peculiarly like joy, the way it felt when he discovered Lillian meeting her lover in Concord. The world was full of secrets, secrets and conspiracies and lies, plots and evil designs and elaborate deceptions, and knowing them—and now he knew them all—filled Wade's heart with inexpressible joy.

18

BY MIDMORNING, the sky had clouded over, and then snow fell again—large flakes, like bits of paper, that got smaller as the front moved in and the temperature dropped. Wade continued with the inventory, counting and listing fittings, pipe, tools and equipment in careful order—boring tedious work, much of it performed while squatting in front of undercounter wooden bins half filled with loose copper trees, galvanized ninety-degree elbows or brass gate valves. It was warm inside the shop, however, and brightly lit and, of course, spotlessly clean, and Wade would much rather have been here than down in Catamount, drilling a well in half-frozen ground. Which, without LaRiviere's sudden and still puzzling change of attitude toward him, is exactly what he would have been doing.

Once an hour or so, he went into the closet-sized lavatory, shut the door and smoked a cigarette, and it was evidently during one of those breaks that Mel Gordon, having finished his business with LaRiviere, had departed from the shop: when Wade quit for lunch and walked out to the parking lot to drive over to Wickham's, the BMW was gone and its tracks had disappeared.

He got into his car and turned the key in the ignition, thinking at that moment mainly about his toothache—promising himself, yet again, that he had to get the damned thing fixed, drilled, pulled, whatever the hell it took, because this was ridiculous, a grown man walking around with a perpetual toothache in the age of modern dentistry, for God's sake—when he realized that he was getting no response from the car. He turned the key again, heard a faint click, then nothing, except the tick of the new snow falling on the roof and hood.

He hated this car. Hated it. He was supposed to be a cop, on call twenty-four hours a day, but he had to rely on an unreliable eight-year-old Fairlane with a slippery clutch, a throw-out bearing that constantly chattered and now, he was sure, a bad starter motor.

LaRiviere's new Dodge 4×4 sat next to Wade's car, and he decided to take it: what the hell, why not? Let the man show him just how far he could go. Pull his chain, rattle his cage, shake the man up a little.

He got out of his car and reached for the door handle of LaRiviere's pickup, when he saw the motto OUR BUSINESS IS GOING IN THE HOLE! and as if Wade were programmed, old habit kicked in, and he found himself walking into the office to ask LaRiviere for permission to use the truck.

He told LaRiviere about the starter motor, it had been giving him trouble on and off for the last month, but before he had a chance to make the switch and ask for the use of LaRiviere's own vehicle, LaRiviere flipped Wade the keys. "Take my pickup. I can use the Town Car; it needs some use anyhow. Tell you what you ought to do, is have Chub Merritt tow your shitbox in this afternoon, and you drive the pickup until he gets yours fixed. You ever think of buying a new car, Wade?" he suddenly asked, squinting over his desk at him, drumming his fingers as if sending messages through the wood.

"On what you pay me?"

LaRiviere ignored the remark. He pressed his intercom and hollered into it, "Elaine! Call Chub Merritt and have him come tow Wade's car in and check out the starter motor."

"What?" her high hard voice came back, the tone colored more by disbelief than by not having heard him.

LaRiviere repeated his order and added that he wanted

Chub to bill the company for the job. "Consider it a company expense, Wade. Better yet, I'll bill the town. We'll charge it against the police budget. You ever think about buying a new car, Wade? You're the town police officer, you know, and the town police officer ought to have a decent vehicle, wouldn't you say?"

"I would."

"Maybe we could sneak that through the budget next town meeting, a new car for Wade Whitehouse. Get you a full-sized Olds or something, or a Bronco, not one of them little K-cars that fucking Lee Iacocca makes. That guy gets to me, you know?" he went on, swiveling his chair around and swinging his legs up onto the desktop. "First he goes broke, then he gets the taxpayers to bail him out, then he comes on like Captain Capitalism, like he's running for fucking president. Him and that guy Donald Trump. Fucking guys feed at the public trough, and when they get rich from it, they turn into Republicans. I always liked it that you're a Democrat, Wade. You and me," he said, smiling broadly and, to Wade, looking a whole lot like Lee Iacocca himself. "It's good talking politics now and then. So what do you say, you want a new car or not?"

"Sure I do. What do I have to do for it?"

"Nothing. Nothing you're not doing right now, Wade. I been thinking lately, you don't get enough appreciation around here, and it's time we changed things a little, that's all."

"I saw Mel Gordon here this morning," Wade said.

"So?"

"He say anything more about that summons I gave him? Tried to give him, actually. Sonofabitch wouldn't accept it."

LaRiviere sighed and furrowed his brow with large concern. "Wade, that was not smart, going out there right after the man's father-in-law shot himself. Let's let that one go, okay? Call it a favor to me."

"To you? Why?"

"Mel's doing some business with me. It's nice to do favors for people you do business with. Besides, he was all upset that day. He was in a hurry, and the way I understand it, you were holding everybody up at the school. No big deal, Wade."

Wade had a cigarette out and was tapping the end against his watch crystal. "That was before Twombley was shot."

"Don't light that in here. I'm allergic."

"I won't. Wasn't that before he could have known about Twombley?"

"What the fuck difference does it make, Wade? Just lay off, will you? Try to be sensible, for Christ's sake." He shifted in his chair, brought his legs down and picked up a pencil, as if going back to work. "Look, take my truck, enjoy yourself, and stop worrying about Mel Gordon, will you?" He smiled. End of interview.

Wade said sure and turned to leave. As he reached for the door, LaRiviere, in a quiet offhand way, said, "What about your folks' place out there, Wade? What're you planning to do with it?"

"Nothing. Live there. Want to buy my trailer back?"

"Maybe. What the hell, I put those trailers in to sell them, and I sold all of them once already and a few of them twice. But I was wondering, I wondered if you thought of selling your folks' place."

"You interested?"

"Could be."

"You and Mel Gordon?"

"Could be."

"Why shouldn't I be the guy who holds on to the place and sell it myself down the line? Why should you guys make all the money? Anyhow, I can't sell it to you. I need the place, and my old man, he needs the place."

"Okay, okay. Just asking."

"I got it. Just asking." Wade stuck the cigarette between his lips and pulled a Bic lighter from his pocket.

"Out! Out!" LaRiviere hollered, waving both hands at him.

Wade grinned, then closed the door and left the shop.

He did not light his cigarette until he had driven LaRiviere's pickup into the parking lot at Wickham's and had noticed, with his usual irritation, Nick's neon sign, HOME MADE COOKING. He sat in the truck, peering over the raised plow at the sign on the low roof of the restaurant, the words bright pink through the falling snow. He inhaled deeply, the smoke hit the bottom of his lungs, and it suddenly came to him: the sonofabitch LaRiviere, he *was* in it, after all! They're *all* in it! LaRiviere, Mel Gordon, Jack—all of them. Mel Gordon was in the real estate business with LaRiviere, using union funds,

253

probably, to buy up all the loose real estate in the area, for God knows what, since it was barely worth paying taxes on, most of it, and Twombley found out about it, so they used Jack to get rid of him.

Wade sat in the truck, smoking, and several times he ran it through, sorting out the connections, isolating the missing pieces, trying to separate what he knew from what he did not know. He did not know *(a)* the exact financial connection between Mel Gordon and LaRiviere, but he was sure it involved union funds and possibly organized-crime money; and he did not know *(b)* why anyone would want to buy up all the loose land and old farms in town and out along Saddleback and Parker Mountain, when no one else had wanted it for generations; and he did not know *(c)* why he cared so intensely about who killed Twombley, why it made him so angry that he could feel his heart start to pound and his body get rigid with rage, so angry that he wanted to hit someone with his fists.

He found himself dreaming an image of himself, stepping forward with his fists cocked, leaning into the blow, driving his fists forward into the body and face of a person who had no face, no gender, even. Just a person, a person being hit by Wade Whitehouse.

As of today, Margie was no longer working days at Wickham's; she was out at the house taking care of Pop, until Wade got home, when she was to drive into town and wait tables till Nick closed up the place at nine. They had agreed to try it temporarily, but after they got married, Wade said, he did not want her working at all. She had said, "What am I supposed to do, then, clean house and cook all day and night too? I did that once, Wade, and I don't think it works for me. Maybe, but I don't think so."

Wade's response had been to point out that someone had to stay with Pop; they could not leave him alone anymore; and at night and on weekends, when he was not working himself, Wade would not want to sit home alone waiting for her to get through at Wickham's.

They had not been quarreling, exactly, so much as thinking aloud over breakfast. Neither of them had imagined that it might so quickly turn out to be difficult to mesh their lives smoothly. To Wade, the idea of wedding Margie's life to his had simply meant that he would work at his job and Margie would take care of the house and hearth, which happened to include an alcoholic old man and soon a ten-year-old girl. To Margie, the idea of moving in with Wade had meant that she did not have to worry quite so much about money and did not have to be lonely all the time. In spite of their strenuous and failed first marriages, they both held firmly in their minds that image of the family in which the man goes to his job all day and comes home at night, and the woman stays home and takes care of the house and any children or sick or infirm adults who happen to be there, and everybody is happy.

What went wrong in her own family and in Wade's, as in their first marriages and in most of the marriages that they knew about, causing so much suffering to both the parents and to all the children, was a failure of individual character— Wade's father, her father, his mother, her mother, and so on— and, of course, bad luck. The way to make a marriage work, they both believed, was to improve your character and take advantage of your luck. The first they believed they had control over; the second you took your chances with. So that when one agreed, or refused, to marry a person one loved, one was making a statement about that person's character and was expressing his or her attitude toward luck at that particular point in his or her life.

Margie thought highly of Wade, and she had felt lucky lately: just when her life had seemed to be freezing over her, trapping her beneath it in solitude and poverty, the man she enjoyed being with, a decent man with a steady job, had come into possession of a house and had expressed a strong desire to marry her. Wade had felt lucky lately too: there was the dumb luck of finding out about his ex-wife's affair with her lawyer just as he was about to launch a custody suit against her; there was the luck of LaRiviere's decision, whatever his reasons, to treat him fairly; there was the luck of the house dropping into his lap, as it were, although that was because of bad luck, his mother's death; and there was the luck of having a woman he felt comfortable with, a decent woman with good sense, willing and able to marry him.

So why not get married? For fifty or a hundred thousand years, men and women had been marrying for these reasons; why not Wade Whitehouse and Margie Fogg? In fact, the force of these conditions, character and luck, was so strong that for

them not to marry would take enormous effort, a kind of radical willfulness or downright perversity that neither of them
seemed to possess. They would either have to deny the influence over their lives of character and luck, or they would have
to admit that one or the other or both of them were bad people
incapable of improving themselves or else merely people afflicted by misfortune.

Late in the afternoon, Jack Hewitt and Jimmy Dame
drove into the parking lot, pulled the drilling rig up to the
garage door and honked for Wade to open the door. It was
snowing fairly heavily by now and gave all appearances of
continuing into the night, and while Jack and Jimmy hosed
down the rig and put tools away, Jimmy chanted, "O-ver-time,
o-ver-time, won't you give me o-ver-time?" and Jack looked
grimly at his watch now and then and at the door, as if planning his escape.

At four-thirty, Wade was ready to leave for home, so Margie could get to work at five, as she had promised Nick Wickham, and when LaRiviere came yawning out of his office to set
up the plowing detail, Wade explained how and why he would
not be available for overtime tonight. Probably not for quite
a while, maybe not all winter, he added, what with his new
responsibilities at home.

"You ought to sell that place and move into town, Wade,"
LaRiviere said, winking.

"Not mine to sell."

"Talk your dad into it, then."

"That man can't be talked into anything, Gordon, except
another bottle of CC. You know that."

"You can do it, Wade," LaRiviere said, draping an arm
good-naturedly over Wade's shoulders. "Jack, what say you
take the grader out tonight? Jimmy's used to the dump truck
and the V-plow."

"Can't do it. I got a date." Jack stood by the door, ready
to leave, his black lunch box in one hand, a rolled-up newspaper in the other. Jimmy was already down at the far end of the
garage, at the board where the keys to all of LaRiviere's vehicles and locks were hung, still singing, "O-ver-time, o-ver-
time."

"Jack!" LaRiviere barked. "Break your fucking date. We
got a job to do."

256

"*You* got a job to do, Gordon, not me," Jack said, and he walked out the door.

"*Sonofabitch!*" LaRiviere said, as if amazed.

Wade thought, What a pair of actors these guys are. Who would have thought they could play their roles this well? If he had not known what he knew, he would have been completely fooled by this routine.

"You sure you can't take out the grader tonight, Wade?" LaRiviere asked.

"Tell you what," Wade said. "Let me plow the roads out my way with your truck, not the grader. You know, from the turnoff up to my father's place from here, then on out Parker Mountain Road and the side roads in between, which you don't really need the grader for anyhow. That way, I can do it. I can pick up my old man at the house when I go by and let him ride along with me, and Margie can go into work a little late tonight."

LaRiviere seemed to give the matter some thought, then said, "Just be careful and don't ding the plow, and if you do, touch it up in the morning."

"Gotcha," Wade said. "What're you going to do about Jack?" he asked. "Fire him? You would've fired me, Gordon, up till a few days ago. You know that, don't you?"

"Well . . . things change, Wade. Jack, though, I guess he's still fucked up from the Twombley thing. Christ, everybody's a little fucked up these days. Anyhow, I need Jack for a while longer—till the ground freezes too tight to drill."

"It's already froze tighter'n a nun's cunt," Jimmy chirped. He had come up on the conversation after Jack's departure and stood by the door, ready to plow, hat pulled down, gloves on, collar up. "We busted one bit this afternoon and give up on the second before we busted it too. You were lucky to get your mom buried," he told Wade. "When did they dig the hole? Monday? They must've used a backhoe for it. I bet they used a backhoe."

"Shit," LaRiviere said, calculating the cost of the broken bit. "Jesus, winter's early this year."

"Jack wants to quit anyhow," Wade said. "He's ready to fly the coop. He's ready to go where it's warm."

"He can't leave the fucking state till they hold a hearing on the Twombley thing."

Wade smiled broadly. "A hearing? Why? Asa Brown think maybe Twombley didn't shoot himself?"

"Don't be an asshole, Wade. It's just a legality they got to go through, for Christ's sake. They got to decide whether to pull his license or not. Get off that one, will you? Everybody knows what you got cooked up in your brain about the Twombley thing. It's crazy, Wade, so forget it, will you? Jack's got enough on his mind from this thing, without you going around with all your goddamned suspicions. We aren't stupid, you know. Right?" LaRiviere asked Jimmy, who stood next to him now, facing Wade.

"Yeah," Jimmy said. "Jack's pretty pissed at you, Wade. He knows what you got in your mind, all cooked up, like Gordon says. He thinks you're acting nuts these days. He told me."

"I'll bet he does," Wade said.

LaRiviere asked Jimmy if he could handle all the roads except those at the Parker Mountain end of town, and Jimmy said sure, he wanted the o-ver-time, and it wasn't a real hard snow, four or five inches maximum. It was too cold to snow much, he said, and no wind. Good weather for deep-freezing the lakes, which meant ice fishing by Saturday. He grinned at the thought of holing up in a bobhouse for the weekend, away from his wife and children. He was a man whose desire to stay away from his large squabbling family was both justified and satisfied by his need to support them, a neat circle that left him guilt-free and alone and his wife and children fed and happy, for they did not want him around much anyhow, since it was clear that when he was home, he was only trying to figure out how to get away again.

Wade said fine, it was done, then, and hurried out to LaRiviere's truck: he wanted to get to the house by five o'-clock, so Margie would not be more than a half hour late for work, which would probably irritate her, but what the hell, he had an excuse. He thought of calling her, but that would only delay his arrival another five minutes and make her that much more cross with him. She was a punctual woman, a neat and orderly woman, and he was none of those things. She said it was as if he had been born twenty minutes late and had spent his life so far running on that clock instead of the one everyone else ran on.

Wade's sloppiness and disorder Margie regarded as characteristic of males in general, so she rarely commented on that. Men were slobs. LaRiviere, who, from Margie's perspective, was merely a man who loved everything to be neat and clean, was regarded by most people as crazy on the subject, almost unmanly, which she felt only proved her point. If LaRiviere had been a woman, like Alma Pittman, who was just as fanatical about neatness as he was, then people would have thought him normal, as they did her.

Wade's perpetual tardiness, however, Margie did not understand: it was as if he were doing it to get even with the world for some ancient secret wrong. It certainly kept the world mad at him—his ex-wife, his daughter, Gordon LaRiviere, his brother Rolfe: anyone who allowed himself or herself to schedule a meeting with Wade started that meeting a little bit mad at him, as if he had opened it with a small insult.

Wade turned left on Route 29 by the Hoyt place on Parker Mountain Road and dropped the plow, angled it fifteen degrees to the right, then crossed the bridge and made his way slowly home. When he arrived at the house, it was five twenty-five. The porch light was on, and he saw that Margie's car, her gray Rabbit, was gone. Damn, he thought, she should not have left the old man here alone. He cut into the driveway, plowing it out with a single swipe, and parked the truck. He liked LaRiviere's truck; it still smelled brand-new, and when he drove it, he felt above the world and isolated from it: the cab was tight and dry, with no rattles or bumps in the road intruding on his thoughts. He especially liked driving it at night, with the twin banks of headlights and the running lights on, the plow out in front of the wide flat hood like a weapon, dipping and rising as he moved through these narrow back roads, lights flashing against the snowbanks and spilling out ahead of him to the next curve and the darkness beyond.

When he went inside the house, Wade stood in the kitchen by the door and called out, "Pop!" No answer. Sonofabitch is probably passed out, he thought, and he cringed at the idea of having to haul his drunken father into semiwakefulness, shove him into his coat, like putting a child into a snowsuit, and lug him outside and up into the truck with him. He never should have agreed to do this plowing for LaRiviere. It was not his problem, it was LaRiviere's, and Jack's.

But they had wanted to play cat and mouse with him, go through routines designed to make him think everything was normal, that Jack was, as usual, both stubborn and impetuous and LaRiviere was easily pissed off and quickly forgiving. If Wade had said, "Sorry, Gordon, I'm not plowing tonight," LaRiviere simply would have called down to Toby's Inn, Wade knew, and asked for Jack. He imagined the two of them talking about it, LaRiviere in his office, Jack on the wall phone in the dark hallway that led from the bar to the men's room in back.

LaRiviere: "He didn't buy it. He's onto us."

Jack: "Shit! What are we going to do?"

LaRiviere: "I don't know. Maybe I can buy him off. I'll have to talk to Mel Gordon."

Jack: "Shit! You can't buy Wade off."

LaRiviere: "We bought you."

Jack: "Wade Whitehouse is not Jack Hewitt."

LaRiviere: "Yeah, well, I still got to get the roads plowed tonight. So get back here and take out the fucking grader."

Jack: "Shit! The grader?"

LaRiviere: "That's right, the grader."

Jack: "Shit!"

A second time, Wade hollered for his father. Still no answer. And then he saw the note on the kitchen table, next to one of the two place settings: *Wade, I had to leave for work. Thanks for being on time. Don't worry, I have Pop with me. Come pick him up at Nick's when you get home. Supper is in the oven for you both. Margie.*

Despite the evidence of Margie's anger, Wade was relieved by her note. He stuffed the piece of paper into his pocket, and when he stepped out to the porch, he saw headlights flash past, a 4×4 pickup with its plow in the air, and although it was moving fast, Wade instantly recognized the vehicle: it was Jack's burgundy Ford, leaving high snowy fantails behind it as it passed the house without slowing and disappeared at the curve, heading uphill toward Parker Mountain.

Wade climbed up into the driver's seat of LaRiviere's blue Dodge and started the motor, listened to the throaty rumble of the mufflers for a few seconds and flicked on the headlights, splashing a field of white over the yard. Then, with the plow up, he drove slowly out to the road, where, instead of turning left and downhill toward town, he turned right and started following Jack's tracks in the fresh snow. There were no side roads off this road out here, except for the lumber trails that crisscrossed through the woods, and no houses beyond the

Whitehouse place, except for a few closed-up summer cabins and, back in the woods, a couple of hunting camps, like LaRiviere's, on the near side of the mountain. It made no sense for Jack to be out here tonight.

Driving fast now, but not too fast, because he did not want to overtake Jack suddenly if he stopped or slowed, Wade peered through the lightly falling snow for the lights of Jack's truck. He shut down his own running lights and used the low beams, hoping that Jack was not looking back in his mirror: he wondered if Jack had noticed him standing there on the porch when he passed the house. If not, then Jack had no reason to think anyone was following him.

Suddenly, as Wade came over a low rise where the road dropped and ran between a pair of low frozen marshes, he saw Jack's truck a hundred yards ahead of him, and he hit the brakes, went into a short slide, and came to a halt. Jack was outside the truck and had been standing a few feet into the bushes beyond the snowbank, but he had seen Wade and was scrambling back into his truck now. He slammed the door shut and drove quickly on.

Wade pulled back onto the road and slowly moved ahead and stopped just behind where Jack had been parked, illuminating his tire tracks and footprints with the headlights. He could see that Jack had gone beyond the spot twenty or thirty feet, had stopped his truck and backed up, and had got out and walked around on the side of the road by the snowbank. Very peculiar, Wade thought. What the hell was he looking for? Incriminating evidence? Shell casings? Was this the scene of the crime? The woods beyond the frozen marsh on both sides of the road were dark and impenetrable. Wade knew the land rose abruptly just beyond the woods and that he was in a draw between a pair of long ridges that ran off the mountain toward Saddleback: there was nothing to see from here, except woods, even during the day.

Puzzled, he put the truck in gear and drove on, moving faster now and not as cautiously as before, because he knew Jack had spotted him, although he probably had not identified the truck as LaRiviere's. Still, Jack might be trying to elude him: there was no more reason for Wade or anyone else to be out here on a Thursday night than there was for Jack, unless you happened to be pursuing Jack.

Which Wade now knew he was indeed doing, pursuing

261

Jack. He switched on the running lights and his high beams and turned on the CB scanner, in case Jack was using it— whom would he call? LaRiviere? Mel Gordon?—and pressed down on the accelerator, moving swiftly and skillfully through power slides on the curves, the plow blade rising and falling out in front of the truck, like the steel prow of a boat in a storm, when the road dipped and pitched and rose again, higher each time, as it neared the top of Parker Mountain.

It had stopped snowing altogether now—Jimmy was right: it was too cold to snow—and Wade could see clearly ahead of him. The tracks of Jack's truck still extended out there in front of him, but he saw no lights in the distance: it was as if Jack had passed by an hour ago and not mere seconds; as if Wade were out here on the mountain road alone; as if he had made the whole thing up, had not seen Jack pass by his house and had not come upon his truck parked by the side of the road back there at the marshes, had not seen him hustle back into the truck and race away. There was nowhere to go up here. The road would gradually narrow, and just this side of the crest it would pass LaRiviere's cabin. Then, on the other side of the mountain, where the land descended through dense spruce and pine woods toward a spatter of small shallow ponds and lakes, the road would turn into a lumber trail switchbacking down the mountain, connecting eventually to Route 29, ten or twelve miles south of Lawford, where the road crossed under the interstate through a cloverleaf.

A few hundred yards before LaRiviere's cabin, Wade slowed and cut back his lights again, relying only on his low beams, and as he neared the turnoff by the muskeg in front of the cabin, the very place where Jack had parked the day he shot Twombley, where the ambulance and Asa Brown and the state troopers had parked, he saw Jack's truck, backed off the road on the left, with all its lights out, ready to head out and blow by him. Fifty yards from the muskeg, Wade moved his truck over slightly to the left and filled the road, so Jack could not pass him when he pulled back onto the road—when suddenly Jack's truck seemed to leap onto the road. But it turned the other way, toward the top of the mountain, full speed, with all its lights on.

Wade hit the gas pedal, and his tires spun, and the truck jumped to speed, and now the pair of trucks were separated by only a few yards, as they raced along the narrow winding road, up to the top of the mountain, flashing past the low stunted trees that grew up here, and then they were over the top, beyond the road. They were on the rocky switchbacking lumber trail, scrambling and leaping downhill, into gulleys and back out, lurching from side to side as the trail twisted and pitched through fallen trees and great heaps of brush. Both trucks were four-wheel-drive vehicles with oversized snow tires, their chassis kicked high with extra-long shackles, and they navigated the difficult terrain rapidly and with relative ease, though at this speed it was dangerous, and they had to dart out of the way as huge snow-covered boulders and tree stumps suddenly appeared out of the darkness before them. With the plows out in front slashing through the brush, the trucks lurched rapidly downhill, and soon they were in deep woods again, and the slope was not so steep. Where the trail switched to avoid a deep gully, Jack braked, and Wade clipped the rear bumper of Jack's truck with his plow and sent the vehicle spinning to the edge of the gully. Somehow, Jack regained control of it, the wheels crunched into the frozen soil, tossing clods of dirt and snow into the air, and he was gone again, racing ahead, with Wade drawing up right behind, his plow just a few feet from the dangling bumper of Jack's truck.

Then, unexpectedly, the ground leveled off, and the trucks were running alongside a shallow beaver pond, with sumac and chokecherry flashing past. At the far end of the pond, the trail swerved left, away from the beaver dam and the brook beyond, too abruptly for Jack to make the turn, and his truck crashed through a stand of skinny birches straight onto the pond, its momentum carrying it swiftly over the surface of the thick ice, its headlights sending huge pale swirls out ahead of it. Wade pulled up at the shore, and he watched Jack's truck slide across the ice like a leaf on a slow-moving river, until it came to a stop halfway across the pond, facing Wade's truck, with its headlights gazing back over the snow-covered surface of the glass-smooth ice. Wade dropped his truck into first gear, edged it to the shore, then down onto the ice, and slowly he drove directly into the glare of Jack's headlights, drawing carefully closer as if toward a fire, until finally the vehicles were face to face, plow blade to plow blade.

Jack opened his door and stuck his head out and shouted, "You crazy sonofabitch! You'll sink us both! Get off the fucking ice! Get off!" he cried, waving Wade away frantically.

But Wade refused to budge. Jack backed his truck away a few feet, and Wade came forward. Behind Jack, on the far side of the pond, was an impenetrable pinewoods; he could not retreat there. And he could not push Wade out of the way; both trucks were the same size, and neither had traction on the ice.

Again Jack swung open his door, and this time he stepped down to the ice. He was clearly enraged, but he seemed almost in tears with frustration, and he swung himself in circles with fists balled, while the ice creaked and groaned under the weight of the two trucks.

Slowly Wade stepped down from LaRiviere's truck and stood beside it for a few seconds, watching Jack twirl in rage and pain. It was cold, close to zero, and a sharp wind had come up, slicing through the pine trees and over the ice, lifting the light snow into low swirling curtains, and Jack passed in and out of Wade's line of sight as waves of blowing snow passed between them. He seemed to be clothed in gold, glowing in the strange vibrating light, there and then not there, like a ghost or a warrior from a dream, when suddenly Wade realized that Jack was holding a rifle. He disappeared behind another cloud of the windblown snow, and when he appeared again, he was aiming the rifle at Wade, shouting words at him that Wade could not at first make out—then he heard him—he wanted Wade to close the door of his truck and move away from it, to walk out onto the ice into the darkness. He cried in an unnaturally high and very frightened voice, "I'll shoot you, Wade! I swear it, I'll fucking shoot you dead if you don't move away from the truck!"

Wade closed the door to the truck and backed away from it a few steps. The ice was dry, and with the snow blown off it was too slippery to walk on except with extreme care, and he moved slowly, gingerly, so as not to fall. Jack shouted for him to keep moving, keep moving, goddammit, and he obeyed, step by step, until he was outside the circle of light that surrounded the two vehicles. Then Jack climbed back up into his truck. Quickly he opened the window on the passenger's side and switched a flashlight beam into Wade's eyes. "Don't move!" Jack shouted. "I'll shoot you dead if you move!" He backed his truck carefully away from the other, then moved around it and drove across the pond toward the lumber trail at the edge, clambered up onto the bank, and was quickly gone.

Wade stood in the darkness, listening to the wind rush through the pine trees behind him and to the low rumbling sound of the truck motor, and then he heard a third sound, like dry sticks broken over a knee, the snap of the ice under the truck starting to let go. Instinctively, Wade backed away, until he was only a few feet from the shore, where he stood and watched the ice out in the middle of the pond break into thick sheets and huge tipped planes all around the truck, when, as if a gigantic hand were reaching up from under the ice and yanking the chassis from underneath, the truck sank, front end first, then the entire vehicle, descending slowly, as if through ash, until it settled on the bottom, leaving the top of the cab, the roll bar and the running lights exposed, silent but with the headlights still glowing under the water, as if a chemical fire were burning there.

In a few seconds, the lights went out altogether, and Wade stood on the shore of the pond in total darkness. The wind blew steadily from behind him, the only sound in his ears. He knew he was maybe four miles from Route 29, if he followed the lumber trail out to the road, where Jack had gone. He could get up onto the interstate there, and maybe hitch a ride back to town, and if he was lucky he would get to Nick's before nine. A half moon had appeared from behind the clouds and seemed likely to stay and able to provide enough light for him to follow Jack's tire tracks in the snow. Wade did not want to think about anything more than that, getting back to town, and for the next few hours, although his tooth ached and his ears and hands felt as if they had turned to crystal in the cold, that is what he thought about.

IT WAS NOT DIFFICULT to imagine later how the rest of that night went for Wade: he left evidence behind him, a trail of sorts, and among the people he saw or spoke with that night and during the next two days (I myself turned out to be one of the latter), there was not much disagreement.

He made his way from the pond out of the woods by following the tire tracks of Jack's truck in moonlight and, once up on the interstate, hitched a ride from the second car that passed him heading north. It was a new Bronco with a hearty pair of deer hunters from Lynn, Massachusetts, who had taken Friday off and had driven up after work, as they did every year, for the long last weekend of the season.

They took him to Toby's Inn, where they had reserved a room weeks earlier, which is how, with considerable effort, I was able to locate them down in Lynn months later and learn about the strange man they had noticed back in November standing on the shoulder of the highway, hitchhiking in the cold night in the middle of nowhere. He scrambled into the back of the car and shivered, and when he spoke his teeth chattered, and when they pulled into the lot at Toby's to drop him off, he was still suffering from the cold, it seemed. He said little, blaming his presence out there on a car breakdown, and added that he had to meet his wife at Wickham's Restaurant in Lawford by nine or he would be in big trouble.

The two deer hunters laughed knowingly, as married men will when another married man reveals his status in a way that makes a wife sound like a nagging mother and a grown man like a mischievous boy, and suggested that he join them for a drink at Toby's, where he could phone his wife, if he wanted to, and have her pick him up there. They did not want his company so much as they wanted to ask him where the locals were finding deer this year: they came to the area every year to hunt and knew that the natives in these upcountry villages had a much better notion of where to hunt than they themselves ever could, but they did not know that such information never left town. Their view of country people was that they like to please strangers, which of course was flattering to themselves. I did not disabuse them of this notion: I was interested only in obtaining from them as complete a picture of Wade that night as was available to me, and the hunters' high opinions of themselves, in spite of their eventual failure to sight a single deer over that long weekend, kept them from censoring their memories of their brief encounter with my brother.

He was not dressed for the weather, they thought; he wore no gloves or boots, but that was consistent with his story about his car's having broken down and his having to hitch a ride into town to meet his wife, who apparently had her own car. He seemed more than cold, however, and huddled shivering in the back of the warm Bronco like a man who was terrified of something. Like a man who had seen a ghost, was the phrase both men used.

When they pulled into the parking lot at Toby's Inn, a guy in a dump truck was plowing, and Wade ducked his head and turned deliberately away from the guy, as if he did not want to be seen by him. He hung back in the car when the others got out, and they thought at first that he had changed his mind about having a drink with them, so they asked him again to join them. He mumbled, "Maybe one," and slowly got out of the truck, hunkering his head down behind his collar, as if still hiding from the man plowing out the lot, but then suddenly he said no, and without saying so much as thank you or goodbye, walked straight toward the plowman and climbed up inside the truck as if they had agreed to meet there.

What the deer hunters did not realize is that they had parked beside a burgundy 4×4 pickup truck, a fancy new vehicle with the rear bumper half torn off, and that when they went into the dark pine-paneled bar and restaurant, the young good-looking kid they saw at the bar, talking wildly to a couple of young women and two or three local men about some nut chasing him through the woods, was Jack Hewitt. Nor did it occur to them that the nut who had chased him was the gray-faced trembling man they had just let off outside. They took a booth, ordered "Toby-burgers" and beers, and studied with optimistic envy the stuffed and mounted heads of antlered deer and moose hanging on the walls. Tomorrow, by Saturday at the latest, they were sure they would have their own trophies strapped to the roof of the Bronco, racing back south to Lynn, Massachusetts, where they knew a taxidermist over in Saugus who could stuff a whole deer, if you got it to him quickly enough, could mount it in a lifelike re-creation of the way it looked at the very instant you shot it, hind feet kicking the air, white tail flagged, eyes wild with terror and pain, and you could put it in your basement recreation room if you wanted to.

Wade yanked shut the door of the dump truck and said, "You headed back to town now?"

"Yep. I'm headed to the shop. Want a lift to the shop?" Jimmy asked. He shoved half a cubic yard of packed snow hard against the head-high bank at the end of the parking lot, banged the truck into reverse, lifted the plow and backed away from the snowbank and stopped.

"No. Wickham's."

"Margie over there?"

"Yeah. And my old man," Wade added.

"Thought he was going out with you in Gordon's pickup."

"She brought him in with her."

"You cold? Heater's on full blast."

"No. I'm fine."

"Heard about you chasing Jack over· the backside of Parker Mountain."

Wade was silent. He rubbed his eyes with his fingertips.

Then, like a child, he put his fingers into his mouth and sucked them.

Jimmy moved the truck out onto the road and dropped the plow again and headed south into town, scudding the unplowed snow on the right lane off the road. "You got folks pretty scared, Wade. And pissed. More pissed than scared, actually. Jack, I mean he's wicked bullshit."

"I expect so."

"What the hell did Jack do, to get you on his case so hard? He's a decent kid. A little bit cocky, maybe, but—"

"He happen to tell you what he was doing up there tonight?"

"He might've. It wasn't so bad; maybe just looking to jack himself a deer was all. Not something to chase him all over the damn county for. Considering."

"Jacking deer, eh? He said that?"

"Might've. Maybe he was just checking tracks, for later. You know, when he gets his license back. He knows them woods pretty good up there; maybe he was just checking out some deer trails in the fresh snow, see if his big ol' buck was still up there."

"Maybe he was up to something a little more interesting than that."

"Well, it don't matter a rat's ass to me. You're the cop, you can do the worrying about who does what and where and when. All that. Course, it's none of my beeswax, Wade, but if I was you, I'd cool it on Jack for a spell. Gordon's going to—"

"Just drive, for Christ's sake."

"Okeydokey."

They rode in silence for a ways, past the school, past Merritt's Shell Station, and as they entered the village center, a few hundred yards from Wickham's, Wade said, "Jack tell you about Gordon's truck going through the ice?"

Jimmy whistled a single long descending note. "Well, no, Wade, he did not. He did say you was out on the ice, said he had to pull a fucking gun on you to back you off him." He paused, then said, "Gordon's truck went through, eh?"

Wade did not answer.

"Guess it's still too early for ice fishing."

"Yeah."

"You know Gordon's going to want your ass in a sling for this one. If I was you, Wade, I'd move to Florida. Tonight."

"But you're not."

"Nope, I'm not. Thank Christ."

"You think Gordon knows yet?"

"Wade, you're the only one to tell it, and so far, it looks like nobody but me knows. Unless they heard it from you. Except for the business about chasing Jack around the fucking mountain, and by now probably everybody in Toby's knows that part of the story. If I was you, Wade, I wouldn't tell Gordon about this in person. Course, I'm not you. Like you said. But I'd let him find out on his own, let him blow his stack for a while, and then come around later, when he's cooled off some."

They pulled into Wickham's parking lot, where there were only a few cars, including Margie's gray Rabbit. What Wade should do, Jimmy said, was stay out of sight for a few days. Don't even answer the phone. He himself would go down and get the truck out of the pond in the morning. "Can I get in there with Merritt's tow truck? If I can do that, I can put the winch on her and yank the fucker out from the shore."

Wade said he thought Merritt's truck could get into the pond from Route 29 on the old lumber trail. He would not have to come down from the top.

Jimmy said fine, he would break the news to LaRiviere himself, after he got the pickup safely into Merritt's garage, and Chub Merritt would probably have it running by Monday. "Slicker'n shit. That Chub, he's clever as a sheep when it comes to cars. Dumb as a stick otherwise."

Wade had stopped trembling by now. "I guess I owe you one, Jimmy."

Jimmy grinned. "I guess you do. But don't worry, I'll be putting my time in. Overtime."

"Yeah," Wade said. "That's all that matters to you, isn't it?"

"Nope. But it's enough to think about, ol' buddy. Keeps a fellow out of trouble."

Margie was angry. She looked up at Wade when he came in, stared at him for a second as if he were a stranger who reminded her of someone she once knew, and went directly back to filling the napkin holders. Nick hollered from the kitchen,

270

"We're closed!" then, peering out the open door, saw that it was Wade who had entered and said, "Your father's back here, Wade."

And indeed he was. The fire was in his face, and the small shriveled man was now taut and reckless with energy. Wade knew instantly what had happened: Pop had stopped drinking several hours earlier: no doubt, when Margie took him from the house and brought him into work with her, she had insisted that he leave his bottle of whiskey behind. Then he had not been able to locate anything more to drink at Nick's, and because of the cold and the snow earlier, had been forced to stay there in the kitchen with Nick, and slowly, like charcoal igniting at the edges and spreading into the center, he had started to burn, and now he glowed red, as if he were indeed, as Lena believed, possessed by a demon.

He stood in the center of the small cluttered kitchen with a dish towel in one hand and a soup pan in the other, and when he saw Wade standing in the doorway to the kitchen, he waved the pan at him and shouted, "Aha! The return of the prodigal son!"

"About fucking time too," Nick mumbled, swiping at the counter with a sponge.

"Look! I've got me a new job, second cook and bottle-washer, by God!" Suddenly Pop's face went from glee to a sneer, and his voice switched timbre and pitch, hardening into a saw blade and dropping down a register: "So don't worry yourself about me, you sonofabitch, I can take care of myself."

"Jesus Christ, Pop," Wade said. "Come on, let's go home. I'm sorry, Nick, I got waylaid. My car—"

"I guess the fuck you got waylaid," Pop said. "You follow your prick around like it was your goddamn nose. Don't you? You're a fucking hound dog, Wade. You always were."

"Can it, Whitehouse," Nick said, and he looked at Wade and said, "Get him the hell out of here, will you? It was funny at first, but I'm tired."

"And let's go home, you say, eh? What home are you talking about, my prodigal son? *Your* home? Or *my* home? Let's have us a little talk about that one, eh? You been making some pret-ty sly moves lately, and don't think I ain't been watching you, because I goddamn well have been watching you. Your mother's dead, Wade, so she can't make any excuses

271

for you anymore! You've got to deal with me now, mister! On your fucking own. Your mother can't protect you anymore. No more sugar tit, asshole!"

"Oh, Pop, for Christ's sake!" Wade moved toward the man with both hands outstretched, as if reaching for a small delicate thing in the air, and Pop leapt backward knocking over a stack of pans.

He laughed and stuck out his red tongue at Wade and said, "You think you can take me now, don't you? Come on, try me! Come on."

Nick moved quickly between them and said to Wade, "Let me help you get him out of here, so nobody gets hurt."

Margie now stood at the door, her coat on, and she moved away from the door and held it open, as Wade and Nick each grabbed one of Pop's flailing arms and scooted him across the floor and past her. Pop was shouting, denouncing Wade and Nick both, moving inside his body like a cat thrashing inside a bag, as the two men dragged the bag outside to the parking lot and shoved it into the back seat of Margie's car.

"You better sit back there with him," Nick said in a low voice, "and let Margie drive. He'll cool out. Won't he?"

"Yes," Wade said. He reached into the back seat and grabbed both his father's wrists, and holding them tightly, he climbed into the car and situated himself next to the man. "He'll cool out when he gets hold of his fucking bottle. *His* sugar tit."

Margie walked to the car from the restaurant, carrying Pop's coat and hat, and as she passed Nick, he stopped her and touched her cheek and saw that she was weeping. "Jesus, Marge," Nick whispered. "Get out of this. Fast."

She nodded and pulled away, got into the driver's seat and started the car. Inside, in the darkness of the back, Wade had clamped his hands on his father's bony wrists, and the two men stared silently into each other's eyes while Margie backed the car from the lot and headed north out of town. When she reached the Hoyt place and turned onto Parker Mountain Road, Wade leaned in close until he could feel his father's hot breath on his face, and he whispered, "I wish you would die."

The old man spat directly into Wade's face, and Wade let go of one wrist for an instant and slapped him hard on the side of his forehead, then grabbed the wrist again. Margie shrieked, "Stop it! Stop it! Just stop it!"

And they did. They glared into each other's face all the way home, but Pop did not struggle against Wade, who nonetheless kept the man's wrists locked firmly in his grip until Margie had parked the car in the yard and had rushed inside the house. Then, finally, Wade let go of Pop—first one wrist, then the other, like releasing snakes—and got out of the car, walked up onto the porch and went inside, firmly shutting the door behind him. A few seconds later, Pop came in too.

Wade clumped up the stairs, saw that Margie had shut the bedroom door. He went into the bathroom. He peed, zipped up and then stood before the sink and washed his hands slowly and deliberately, lathering them gently with soap and warm water as if they were small dirty animals he felt tenderly toward. When he had finished and was wiping his hands dry on a towel, he looked into the mirror and startled himself with the image of his own face. He told me, the following morning, that he looked like a stranger to himself, as if someone had sneaked in behind him and got caught accidentally by the mirror. "No shit, Rolfe, I just glanced up and there he was, only it was me, of course. But it was like I had never seen myself before that moment, so it was a stranger's face. Hard to explain. You fly on automatic pilot, like I was doing all night, and you disappear, you go off to God knows where, while your body stays home. And then you accidentally happen to see your body, or your face, or whatever, and you don't know who the hell it belongs to. Strange. It was the business with the old man, I know, and how incredibly pissed at him I was, and also chasing Jack Hewitt like that, and then the goddamned truck going through the ice, not to mention Margie's being so upset—one thing piled on top of another, until there I was, standing in front of a mirror and not knowing who the hell I was looking at.

"So I went back downstairs and saw that Pop had gone into his room and closed the door, and then in a sense I was alone in the house, which was fine with me. I had had enough of other people for one night. Sometimes other people are hell, pure hell. Sometimes I think you've got the right idea, Rolfe, living alone as far from this damned town as you can and never coming back here except when you have to.

"I got me a beer and stoked the fire in the stove and turned off all the lights and sat there in the kitchen for a while, trying to calm myself down a little, trying to forget about Jack and Twombley and all that, trying to forget about LaRiviere's truck. I tried not to think about Margie, even, and Pop, I tried not to think about him. But in that house, where we were all raised, knowing that Pop was in the next room, it's impossible not to think about Pop and about Ma's dying. That's the trouble with being in that house now. You can understand that."

I allowed that I could, indeed, understand, but he did not hear me, really; he just rattled on. He had called me late in the morning, a Friday, which was unusual, and had caught me at home, and he was in a manic mood, it seemed, calling me, I surmised, because he needed to talk about all this and no one else would listen. I listened, and, yes, I did understand, for I myself have felt as he did then, although not in nearly fifteen years. But I could remember all too easily how it felt to be filled with strangely powerful information—dark fears and anger and dangerous obsessions—with no one to reveal them to. I remembered how it felt to look at yourself in a mirror and see a stranger looking back.

"Anyhow," he went on, "I was sitting there in the dark, watching the fire glow through the cracks in the stove, you know how it does, and I suddenly remembered that summer when we didn't have a water heater and had to take our baths in the kitchen, in that big galvanized tub, with water heated on the stove. You were maybe five or six. I think I was sixteen, because I was in high school then and on the baseball team; that was the first year I made all-state, and I got special privileges, so I could drive by the school and say I was working out and use the showers there. I think Elbourne and Charlie did the same as me, took their baths someplace else. But you and Lena and Ma and Pop, you all had to bathe in the kitchen so we wouldn't have to lug big tubs of hot water up the stairs to the bathroom. The water heater was broke, or some damn thing, but we didn't have enough money to get a new one till that fall, and I guess because it was summer and the house was warm, nobody really minded too much. Do you remember that?"

I had no memory of it, which is not surprising: the machines we lived with—water heaters, furnaces, pumps, cars, trucks and refrigerators—were always old and decrepit, held together with tape and baling wire, and were always breaking down, and we frequently got along without one or more of them for months before we had enough money to fix or replace them. As a child of six, I would have been neither inconvenienced nor thrilled by having to bathe in a galvanized tub in the kitchen once a week. A forgettable experience.

"Well, I remember one afternoon, it must have been a Saturday, because Pop was home and that was when you took your baths anyhow, and you and Lena had already taken your baths. You got sent upstairs, as usual, while Ma took hers. I don't know where I was, probably working for LaRiviere by then. Yeah, that was the summer I went to work for Gordon the first time. Anyhow, it was just you two and Ma and Pop who were at home. And you got it into your head to sneak down the stairs and out the door, the door off the living room, without anyone seeing you, except Lena, of course, who probably knew what you were up to. And you tippy-toed around the outside of the house to the porch and peeked through the window there into the kitchen, where Ma was taking her bath. It wasn't exactly innocent, of course, but what the hell, you were only a little kid. . . ."

I tried to interrupt him, but he just rolled on with his story, so I let him finish.

"Well, Pop, he must have seen you from the living room or something, because he went out the back door himself and tippy-toed right up behind you, while you were staring at Ma, getting a real eyeful, probably, and he reached down and grabbed you right off the ground. Scared the bejesus out of you.

"And the old man, he lugged you screaming back into the house, by the living room door, of course, and he whaled on you, he truly lost it. You were only a little kid, and he knocked you around like you were me or Elbourne or Charlie, although by then he had laid off those two. He just lost it. I came home later, but I didn't know anything was wrong, except that you had been a bad little boy and were upstairs in your bedroom being punished for it.

"But the next day I noticed that you weren't around for breakfast, and then later in the day it came out, what you'd done, and what Pop had done. Ma was as usual real confused and upset, and Lena was scared shitless and wasn't talking, but by afternoon Ma was worried because you were actually spitting blood and breathing funny. It was obvious the fucker had broken your ribs or something. I told Ma we had to take you into Littleton to the hospital, and she said okay, but we first had to concoct a story about your falling from the hayloft in the barn. We told the doctor you'd been playing in the barn, where you weren't supposed to be, and you'd rolled off the loft to the floor and had banged yourself against some old boards or something out there when you fell. I don't think the doctor bought it, but he bandaged you up, and you were okay by the end of the summer."

"Wade, I hate to disappoint you," I said quietly, "but it never happened. Not to me."

"Of *course* it happened! Why would I lie about it?"

"You would not lie, necessarily. But you have got the story confused somewhat. What you described certainly did happen, but before I was born, and it happened to you, not to me. At least, that is how I heard the story, which I heard when I was about five or six, from you, or maybe it was from Charlie or Elbourne and he was telling it about you. Yes, it was Elbourne—it was he who told me. And you are right about the broken water heater and the baths in the kitchen. I remember now that we were bathing in the kitchen the summer I turned six, the summer Elbourne had enlisted and was home after basic training before leaving for Vietnam, so he must have been twenty. Charlie was out of the house by then, holing up in Littleton, and you were working for LaRiviere. But it was Elbourne who told the story, by way of a friendly warning, I suspect."

Wade interrupted and insisted that I had it all wrong: a person should know, after all, whether something as interesting and dramatic as being beaten by his old man and having to go to the hospital for it actually happened to him. And it did not happen to him, he said: I was the child in the story, not he.

"No, you were the child, although I was a child when I heard the story, and I heard it from Elbourne, who was hanging out upstairs in the big bedroom where you guys slept. It was evening, I think, not afternoon, and Lena and I had already bathed down in the kitchen, and I was in my pajamas, and I started to walk downstairs, probably to get a cookie or something, you know, when Elbourne caught me at the head of the stairs, reached out and grabbed me from behind and lifted me right up—he was huge, you know, way bigger than you or Charlie or Pop, even—and he carried me into his room, very good-naturedly, and teased me about sneaking down the stairs to catch Ma taking a bath, which of course embarrassed me terribly. Then he went on to tell me what had happened to you years before, when you were my age. The story was essentially the same one you just told, except for the business about the hospital and the lie told to the doctors—that bit about your falling from the loft in the barn. I never heard that one before."

Wade said that he had never heard *this* one before and laughed.

"Well, I remember it vividly, because the story terrified me. Up until then I had only seen Pop get mad, or heard him late at night from my bed, going against you or Ma, when he was drunk, and I had figured that Lena and I were somehow safe from him, although I was scared of him, of course. I guess I thought that somehow the drinking and anger were a part of your and Ma's relationship with him and that it had nothing to do with me or Lena. Not particularly intelligent of me, I know, but I was only a child then. So when Elbourne told me what Pop had done to you when you, too, were a child, I was suddenly terrified. And from then on, I was careful. I was a careful child, and I was a careful adolescent, and I guess now I am a careful adult. It may have been a high price to pay, never having been carefree, but at least I managed to avoid being afflicted by that man's violence."

Wade laughed again. "That's what you think," he said.

Then he changed the subject. He went back to the reason he had called me in the first place, which, as it turned out, had nothing to do with Pop or Wade's misadventures with LaRiviere's truck but concerned instead, once again, Evan Twombley, Mel Gordon, Gordon LaRiviere and Jack Hewitt—Wade's hobbyhorse.

The next morning, shortly after seven, Wade drove away from the house in Margie's car, gone at the usual time on a weekday to direct traffic at the school, as if everything were normal, in spite of numerous signs to the contrary: Margie either had feigned sleep or had stayed asleep when he had come to bed and had kept her back to him all night long, and in the morning, when he awoke, she appeared not to, and while he washed and shaved and dressed, she stayed in bed, head buried in the pillow. He had acted his part, not turning on the bedroom light

277

while he dressed, tiptoeing out and closing the door quietly, leaving a note for her on the kitchen table when he left: *I've gone to the school, borrowed your car, will check back later.* Pop, too, had stayed in his room until after Wade had left. Pop's habit was to rise at six, regardless of how late he had gone to bed the night before and how drunk: for Pop, there was now sufficient alcohol in his veins and cells that most of his acts had been reduced to the level of compulsion or involuntary reflex actions, giving, at best, only the appearance of volition.

At the school, Wade parked Margie's car next to the principal's, where he usually parked. Lugene said hello and nice day to him, and Wade, as always, said yeah and took up his post under the blinking yellow light in the middle of the road. The sky was peach-colored in the east, deep blue and starry in the west, with a light breeze in Wade's face. It was going to be a fine day, clear and warm: yesterday's snow had signaled the arrival of a front, and a high-pressure area seemed to be settling in for a spell.

The buses came and went, unloading their cargoes and heading back over the country roads for more. There was not much traffic otherwise: a few out-of-state cars with end-of-the-season deer hunters on the prowl, Hank Lank on his way to work, Bud Swette in his red-white-and-blue mail-delivery jeep, Chick Ward yawning past in his Trans Am, flipping a wave at Wade, Pearl Diehler, as she often did when she failed to get her kids fed and dressed in time, driving them in to school in her old rusted-out station wagon, smiling easily, naturally, normally, as she passed Wade. Wade liked Pearl, liked the way she seemed to be completely identified with motherhood: he never saw her without her two small children in tow. She was the good mother, to Wade and to most everyone else in town as well. Wade was feeling pretty kindly toward the whole town this morning: everything seemed to be operating on schedule and as usual, and he was able to fit his moves automatically in with everyone else's for a change. It allowed him, like his father, both to act and to give the appearance of volition, without having to think about it.

Then it was time to go to work. He got into Margie's car and swung out onto the road in the direction of LaRiviere's shop. He had not driven more than a hundred yards beyond the school, when he looked into his rearview mirror and saw coming along behind him, just now passing under the yellow blinking light, Merritt's tow truck. Wade was across from Alma Pittman's house and quickly pulled into her driveway and watched as the truck passed by, driven by Jimmy Dame, with LaRiviere's blue pickup dangling behind like a huge dead fish.

Then it was gone, and Wade sat in the car facing Alma's barn door, his tooth aching as if with deliberate fury, his body seeming to weigh against the seat like an ingot and his mind filling rapidly with images retrieved from the times years ago when he had pulled into this very driveway and had sat out here in his old red Ford for a few moments, suffering like a dog hit by a car, before gathering his scattered mind and bruised body together and going inside to see Lillian and try once again to lie to her and, at the same time, with the same words, tell her the truth.

He had failed, of course. His need was an impossible need for either of them to satisfy. They could not even have named it. Every time he tried, during those two years that she lived with her aunt while finishing high school, to say what his young life was truly like, he had failed, and eventually he had stopped trying to make her understand what he himself could not understand. But his failure and his ongoing need drove him closer to her nonetheless, and when in their senior year of high school they began to talk of marriage, a number of powerful tangled strands in his life were neatly and inextricably braided together: his pain and shame, his secret exhilaration and the heat and drama of it, his pathetic fear of his father and incomprehensible anger at his mother, and his inability to imagine himself—a wretched youth, alone—without a family: he would become his own father; and Lillian would become his mother: they would get married in the month of June, a week after graduation. He would be the good father; she would be the good mother; they would have a beloved child.

Wade saw movement at the window, and a second later the front door opened and Alma poked her head outside, looking puzzled. Stepping from the car, Wade called, "Hello, Alma! It's me. I'm just turning around."

She nodded somberly, a tall woman in green twill trousers and plaid flannel shirt, mannish and abrupt, a woman who kept herself aloof from the town but seemed to love it nevertheless. She drew the glass storm door closed and started to shut the inner door, when Wade, instead of getting back in the car, abruptly strode across the driveway and up the narrow freshly shoveled pathway to the door. Alma swung the door open again, and Wade entered the house.

She offered him a cup of tea, and he accepted and followed her into the kitchen, a large room in the back with her office adjacent to it, heated by a wood stove and still familiar to him after all these years, still filled with the distinctive smells of a compulsively neat solitary woman's cooking that he remembered from his youth and that he had admired and desired for his own kitchen, after he and Lillian were married. But their kitchen had smelled instead of larger, more gregarious meals—pot roast, baked beans, spaghetti and coffee and cigarettes and beer—and never the clean dry smell of baked bread and tea and raspberry jam.

Wade sat at the table and looked past Alma into her office, while she put water to boil. A large file was open, and on her desk, next to a crisp new computer, were several open boxes of three-by-five color-coded cards.

"You got yourself a computer, Alma."

"Yes," she said. "Been putting all my files on it. You take sugar and milk?"

"No. Black."

She asked him if he would like her to toast him a muffin or a piece of bread, and he declined both: he was not sure why he had come in, after all, or how long he wanted to stay, so he preferred not to entertain any further questions concerning his desires. He knew that he wanted to be inside Alma's house and in her trim efficient company, and he had accepted her offer of tea in order to accomplish it, but he knew nothing beyond that.

Alma put his cup and saucer in front of him and said to him, "Are you all right, Wade?"

"Yeah, sure. Why? I mean, I got a toothache, I got a few things bugging me, like everybody else. But I'm okay."

"Well, you look . . . sad. Upset. I don't mean to pry. I'm sorry about your mother, Wade. It was a nice funeral."

"Yes, well, thanks. I guess that's over now, though. Life goes on," he said. "Doesn't it?"

She agreed, sat down and stirred milk into her cup.

"Alma, I think there's some dirty business going on in this town," Wade said quickly. "I know there is."

"There always has been," she said.

280

"Well, this is maybe worse than what you and I are used to."

"Maybe. But I've gotten used to quite a lot of dirty business in this town over the years. And you, you see it all, or at least hear about it, don't you? You're the town police officer."

"Oh, come on, Alma, this is different than a little public drunkenness or vandalism or maybe someone beating on his wife or a couple of the boys pounding on each other down at Toby's. What I'm talking about," he said, lowering his voice, "I'm talking about murder. Among other things."

Alma looked across the table at Wade in silence, no expression on her face other than that of patience, as if she were waiting to hear about a strange dream he had last night. She slowly stirred her tea and looked at Wade's agitated face. Finally, she said, "Who?"

"Evan Twombley, the union boss who got shot last week."

"Did he murder somebody, or did somebody murder him?"

"He was murdered."

"Oh? Who did it?"

Wade told her.

"I doubt that," she said calmly, and she smiled, like a woman listening to a favorite nephew's tall stories. Which was how, later, she explained it to me. Wade, she reported, always was pretty imaginative, and he was upset that week, because of his mother's dying, among other things. So she had listened tolerantly, passively, to his jumbled account of how Jack Hewitt had been hired by Mel Gordon to make Twombley's death look accidentally self-inflicted. Wade also insisted that Gordon LaRiviere was involved somehow, but the nature of the connection was not yet clear to him. It would all come out, he said, if Jack, who Wade believed was the weak link, told the truth. Also, Wade felt, if Jack told the truth, confessed his part in the murder of Evan Twombley and revealed what he knew of the roles played by the other two, then Jack might get off light, and somewhere down the line he could start his life over. "He could be free by the time he's my age," Wade said.

Alma reached across the table and patted Wade's jumpy hand. "Wade," she said, "sometimes things are simpler than you think. Let me ask you a question."

"You don't believe me."

"About Jack Hewitt? No, I don't. But there is something to what you're nosing into. Just tell me this: Have you checked out the tax bill on your father's place lately?"

Wade said, "Well, actually, yes. I mean, no, but I was wondering about my father's taxes, if he'd paid them this year."

"Nope," she said. "He hasn't. Not for two years, as a matter of fact. One more year, he gets a warning to pay all the taxes due plus penalties, or the place gets seized by the town and auctioned. Of course, it almost never comes to that. The taxes are low, and even with the deflated price of real estate around here, people can always sell their property for more than what they owe, so either they do that or they go to the bank and borrow. Anyhow, it's a good thing to be checking on, I suppose, now that your mother's gone. And I figured you'd be doing that soon."

"Yeah, I thought so too. I was thinking of paying his bill when the insurance comes in."

"Anybody offer to buy that place lately, do you know?" she asked idly.

Wade said, "As a matter of fact, yes. LaRiviere."

Alma put her cup down and stood. "Come here a minute, Wade," she said.

He followed her into the office, a small winterized sun porch furnished sparely and efficiently with several tall filing cabinets, a desk and a high-tech black workstand for her computer. She sat down in front of the computer and drew a swivel chair in next to her and motioned for Wade to sit down. Flipping a pair of diskettes into the machine, she punched a bunch of keys expertly, and suddenly in front of Wade the screen was filled with rows of tiny figures and names, which could have been the computer's own packing and parts list, for all he knew. They meant nothing to him.

Alma turned in her chair and looked at him with sly satisfaction. "That ought to tell you something," she said.

Wade squinted and tried to read the words and numbers before him. He saw a few names he recognized—Hector Eastman, Sam and Barbara Forque, old Bob Ward, called Robert W. Ward, Jr., here—but nothing else on the screen made sense to him, and the names by themselves, of course, made no sense. "What is it, some kind of back-tax roll?"

"You might say that. No, this is a list of all the real estate transactions in town for this past year. Most of it is unused land," she explained. "Most of it bought for a little bit more than the back taxes owed." She pointed out the various columns on the sheet and their meanings—original owner, taxes owed, size of the property and buildings thereon if any, purchaser, purchase price, date of sale, and so on.

"Ah!" Wade exclaimed, as if now he understood what he was looking at.

"That's this year's sales so far." She punched a pair of keys, and the screen rolled. "Here's the record for three years ago." There were five lines across the screen, the rest blank. "Some difference, eh?" Then she switched back to the current year. "Check out this here column," she instructed, pointing at the list of purchasers.

Wade leaned forward and saw that all but four of the purchases had been made by something called the Northcountry Development Corporation. The remaining four, he noticed, were house lots close to town where in the past summer trailers had been set down. In those cases the seller was Gordon LaRiviere. Nothing unusual there.

"What's Northcountry Development Corporation?" Wade said. He lit a cigarette and looked around for an ashtray.

Alma got up from her chair and went into the kitchen and returned with a clean ashtray and handed it to him. "Keep it in your lap," she said. "I wondered that myself, Wade. So I went down to Concord one day and checked it out, since it's a matter of public record. It's registered in New Hampshire, all right, with a Lawford post office box for an address. And the president is Melvin Gordon, and the vice-president and treasurer is Gordon LaRiviere. Those two boys are buying up the mountain, Wade. Cheap, too. LaRiviere is a selectman and keeps track of the tax records, and that way he knows just what to offer for a piece of otherwise useless land. And since nobody else is offering these days, he gets it at his price. His partner probably puts up the money. LaRiviere surely doesn't have enough on his own to buy this much. Look," she said, pointing at the column that showed the size of the plots. "Two hundred and forty acres. A hundred and seventy-one. Eighty acres. And total up the purchase prices, if you want. I did. Three hundred and sixty-four thousand dollars, for this year alone. I believe that's out of Gordon LaRiviere's league."

"What about Evan Twombley?" Wade asked. "Was his

name on the incorporation papers anywhere?"

"Nope. Just the two Gordons. Wade, please forget that business with Twombley and Jack Hewitt. It's just a story you've concocted in your head. There's something more important going on that you're ignoring. Come here," she said. "I want to show you what I mean." She got up and crossed to the back of the office, where a surveyor's map of the township was tacked to the wall.

Wade followed, and Alma, using her finger as a pointer, traced the curving line of Parker Mountain Road out from Route 29. "All those lots bought by Northcountry Development Corporation, they connect to one another. Starting here, where the Lake Agaway Homeowners Association owns about a thousand acres, which is where your friend the late Mr. Twombley once had a place and where your other friend Melvin Gordon and Mr. Twombley's daughter now have a place. These two boys, Melvin Gordon and Gordon LaRiviere, on the QT, have bought up everything on both sides of the road, piece by piece, all the way across Saddleback and up the mountain and down the other side. They've bought up that whole end of town. Except for this place here," she said, and she placed her finger on a dot close to the road. "Which, according to the tax records, totals one hundred and twenty-five acres, with a three-bedroom house and a barn. Right?"

"Right," Wade said, exhaling slowly. "Except that the barn's about caved in now."

"No matter. It's still a building you're taxed for."

"What's the current bill—how much is due the town for the place?" Wade asked.

"Little less than twelve hundred dollars, including penalties. Not much, compared to most of those properties the two Gordons bought. I shouldn't have showed you this, but you can probably get a pretty penny for that place in a year or two, if you pay the taxes now and hold on to it."

"Yes," Wade said. He was panting visibly, Alma later reported, surprisingly upset by what she had shown him, and she suddenly wished that she had kept quiet about the Northcountry Development Corporation, because he banged his fist against the map and said, "See! That *proves* LaRiviere's involved in this! Jack, he's just a kid! He's just a pawn they used to get rid of the old man!" Twombley, Wade explained, must have found out that his son-in-law was siphoning union funds into land in northern New Hampshire, probably laundering organized-crime money somehow, and tried to put a stop to it because the union was being investigated.

"No," Alma said, "it's much simpler than that." What the map and the figures proved, she asserted, was that Gordon LaRiviere was going to become a very rich man by using his position as selectman to exploit his neighbors. "These boys are probably in the ski resort business," she told Wade. "And a year or two from now, you won't recognize this town."

Wade did not hear her and said not another word. He grabbed his coat and hat and made for the door without so much as a thank you. From the living room window, she watched him hurry out to Margie's car, get in and drive off. It was the last time she saw Wade, she told me, and she knew that something terrible was about to happen, and she felt intricately involved in it, just as, by the time it happened, we all would feel.

20

YOU WILL SAY that I should have known terrible things were about to happen, and perhaps I should have. But even so, what could I have done to stop them? By Friday, Wade was being driven by forces that were as powerful as they were difficult to identify—for me and for Margie, who were best situated to observe them, and certainly for people like Alma Pittman or Gordon LaRiviere or Asa Brown. We had no choice, it seemed, but to react as we did to Wade's actions that day and the next. In doing so, we were able later to claim something like innocence, or at least blamelessness, but by the same token, we were unable to affect his actions. To have behaved differently would have required each of us to be prescient if not omniscient and perhaps hard-hearted as well.

I cannot blame Gordon LaRiviere for his reaction to Wade that morning, although, given what I know now, it may well have been what drove Wade to his bizarre and violent actions later that day and that evening. In fact, when Wade, after having left Alma Pittman's, slammed his way into LaRiviere's shop, ignoring Jack Hewitt and Jimmy Dame, and strode into LaRiviere's office, pushing right past Elaine Bernier's attempts to stop him, LaRiviere did what I myself would have done under the same circumstances.

Wade came into the office already shouting. "You sneaky sonofabitch!" he bellowed. "I've got your number now, Gordon! All these years," he said, panting, his eyes ablaze with a strange mixture of fury and sadness, "all these years I worked for you, since I was a kid, goddammit, and I thought you were a decent man. I thought you were a decent man, Gordon! I actually went around feeling grateful to you! Can you fucking believe that! Grateful!" He pounded both fists on LaRiviere's desk, bam, bam, bam, like an enraged child.

Jimmy and Jack had appeared at the door behind Wade, while Elaine Bernier, her face gray with fear, fluttered in the outer office beyond them. LaRiviere calmly stood up, raising himself to his not inconsiderable height and swelling his body like a tent, and said, "Wade, you're done." He held out one hand, palm up. "Let me have the shop keys."

Wade looked around and saw Jack and Jimmy, both as grim as executioners, and he laughed. "You two, you don't get it, do you? You think you're free, but you're like slaves, that's all. You're this man's slaves," he said, and his voice changed again, became plaintive and soft. "Oh, Jack, don't you see what this man has done to you? Jesus Christ, Jack, you've turned into his slave. Don't you see that?"

Jack regarded Wade as if the man were made of wood.

"The key, Wade," LaRiviere said.

"Yeah, sure. You can have the key, all right. It's the key that's kept me chained and locked to you all these years," he said. "I give it back with pleasure!" He pulled his key ring from his pocket and worked one key free of it and dropped it into LaRiviere's extended hand. "Now I'm free." He stared into LaRiviere's unblinking eyes and said, "See how easy it is, Jack? All you got to do is give back what the man gave you, and you're free of him."

He turned, and Jack and Jimmy parted to let him pass. Elaine Bernier dodged to the side, and Wade walked through the outer office and was gone. Free.

From LaRiviere's, as far as we know, Wade drove straight home. It was midmorning by then, a sweetly bright day, warm enough to start the snow melting. Pop was out back, stacking firewood and splitting kindling for the stove, something he did almost every day at this hour, early enough for him to wield an ax with relative safety. He worked slowly, methodically, a brittle cautious man who seemed much older than he was, and he did not look up when Wade drove into the yard and parked Margie's car by the porch.

Margie was in the kitchen, drinking coffee and reading a week-old newspaper, and when Wade strode into the room, she folded the paper and looked up, ready now to talk with him about last night, about whatever it was that had happened in the back seat of the car: she did not know, really, what was going on between him and his father, but it was an ancient war, and she knew it was painful for Wade, and she was prepared to understand and sympathize. And as for the business of his being late, perhaps that could be explained: his car was obviously not here, so it must have broken down last night on the way home from work, too far from town to phone, and he had to walk all the way home in the snow, and somehow she had missed him on the road when she drove in to Wickham's, had driven right past him, poor guy, so that he had to turn around and walk back into town and was unable to get there until nine. Something like that, she was sure, had happened, and then at the restaurant and later in the car, when Pop had started in with his wild drunk-talk, Wade was probably so angry and feeling so guilty, too, that he just lost control, and that was why he slapped the old man.

But when she looked up from her newspaper and saw Wade, all these thoughts flew away, for she knew instantly that he was someone to be afraid of. His movements were abrupt and erratic, and his face was red and stiffly contorted, as if he were wearing a mask made from a badly photographed portrait of himself, and he was trembling: his hands shook; she could see the tremors from across the room as he pulled off his coat and draped it over a chair by the wall.

"I've got to talk to my brother," he announced. "Did you get my note? Yes, you did, I see it there. Listen, there's lots going on right now, and I've got to talk to Rolfe about some things," he said. "Everything okay? You got to go to work today, don't you?"

Margie nodded yes and watched him carefully, as Wade headed into the living room and grabbed up the telephone from the table next to the television set. "I'll only be a few minutes!" he called.

And that, of course, was when he telephoned me, at a time when I am not usually at home, but I happened on this occasion to have called in sick: it was a Friday, and I was suffering from some kind of mental exhaustion of my own, perhaps a delayed reaction to the funeral and my trip to Lawford, perhaps because of an obscure and complex and no doubt unconscious involvement with what Wade was going through—although at that time I was only marginally aware of what Wade was experiencing. At any rate, I had wakened that morning feeling unnaturally gloomy and peculiarly weak, unable to stand without my legs turning to water, so I had called the school and asked that a substitute take my classes for the day. Then, midmorning, the phone rang, and it was Wade.

It was an unusually long conversation. Wade was garrulous and intense at first, rapidly filling me in on the events of the previous evening. He left out, of course, certain details that would have put him in an unfavorable light, such as the slapping incident in the car, details that I obtained months later from various sources—Margie, Nick Wickham, Jimmy Dame, the deer hunters from Lynn, Massachusetts. Then he told me the story, his version, of the bathtub incident, which I found somewhat disconcerting, since it was so far from my own version of that story and because it happened to be about me. And finally he got to the apparent point of his call, to tell me what he had learned at Alma Pittman's this morning—he did not mention his being fired by Gordon LaRiviere—and to ask my advice on how to use this new information. "I know what it *means*," he said. "I'm just running out of ways to use it."

"For what?" I asked.

"What do you mean, 'for what?' To help Jack, of course, and to nail those sonsofbitches, the two Gordons, as old Alma calls them. Jesus Christ, Rolfe, whose side are you on in this?"

"Yours, naturally," I assured him. But his intensity and the ferocity of his feelings alarmed me. And his chaos and apparent lack of focus, in spite of his obsession with this case, were causing me to react carefully. He switched from topic to topic, tone to tone: one minute he would be railing against Mel Gordon, the next he would be complaining about his toothache, which had persisted for weeks now; he spoke with anxious sympathy about Jack Hewitt, seeming almost to identify with the man, and then rambled on at tedious length about his car's being in the garage and having to borrow Margie's car and being unable to leave Pop alone in the house for very long; he turned bitter for a few moments as he spoke about Lillian and his custody suit, as he referred to it, and then practically wept when he recounted how Lillian was keeping him from being a good father to his own daughter.

It was an anxiety-producing conversation, to say the least, and I felt one of my old migraines coming on, as if a penlight inside my skull were being shined directly at my eyes from behind. I wanted to get away from him, so I took over the conversation and spoke with perhaps more authority than I normally would have. I do believe, however, that this was precisely what Wade wanted me to do and why he had called me in the first place. While he was talking, once it became evident to me that he had become hopelessly confused, I made notes on the yellow pad I keep by the phone, numbering his individual problems and putting them into relation to one another: this is, after all, one of the ways I solve my own problems, by naming them and by placing them in order, so that solving the least of my problems leads finally to the solution of the largest. Why not try to solve Wade's problems the same way? Thus, when I decided to take over the conversation, I was able to speak with clarity and force. He listened and, for all I know, may have been taking notes himself, because as it turned out, he followed my advice to the letter. Which is why I feel today less than innocent, less than blameless for what eventually happened. Of course, I had no way of knowing how Wade would botch things, no way of predicting how simple circumstances would thwart him and no way of anticipating the forms he would eventually discover to express his increasingly violent feelings.

Wade got off the phone with me and, as I had suggested, immediately called Merritt's garage to arrange to pick up his car. It was Chick Ward who answered, and when Wade said he was calling about his car, Chick laughed, a sneering knowing laugh, and said, "Wade, old buddy, there's good news and bad news. Which do you want first?"

"Just give me the facts, Chick. I'm in a hurry."

"Okay, the good news, old buddy, is we haven't got to your car yet. It only came in yesterday afternoon, you know. That's the good news, you understand." His voice was loud, as if he were talking for the benefit of an audience of listeners other than Wade.

"What the hell are you up to?"

"You want the bad news?" Wade could picture Chick grinning at the other end, standing in the garage and flashing a knowing wink at Chub Merritt and anyone else who happened to be there resuscitating LaRiviere's drowned pickup truck.

"Just tell me when you'll have it fixed. It's the starter motor, I'm pretty sure, it's been giving me trouble—"

"The bad news," Chick said, interrupting him, "is, the reason we ain't got to your car yet is we got a problem here with a truck somebody drove through the ice last night. Figured you'd know something about that, Wade."

Wade was silent for a second. "Yeah," he said. "I know about that."

"Yep. Figured. Chub also says to tell you that Gordon LaRiviere won't let you bill your job back to him. You'll have to pay for it yourself. Probably come to a couple hundred bucks, if it's a starter motor, like you say."

Wade said nothing. Money . . . he had none. No job, no money, no car, nothing.

"That okay with you, Wade?"

"Yeah. That's fine with me."

"Oh, I got some more of the bad news, Wade. You want to hear it?"

"Not particularly, you sonofabitch."

"Hey, I'm just the messenger, you know. I just work here."

"Tell me."

"Well, Chub, he says you're fired, Wade."

"Fired! He can't! He can't fire me! LaRiviere already did that this morning."

"Oh, yeah, Wade, he can. He's one of the selectmen, and he said to tell you to turn your badge in and clean out your office down to the town hall and leave your office key with his wife there. She'll be in the Board of Selectmen's office all day. He says he'll pull the CB and the police light off your car while he's got it down here. I guess they're town property, Wade."

"Let me talk to Chub," Wade said. "There's some things he ought to know. Put Chub on."

Chick muffled the phone for a few seconds, then came back on and said, "Chub says, he says to tell you he's too busy drying out your ex-boss's pickup truck to talk to you. Sorry."

"Look, you sonofabitch, put Chub on! I know a few things he ought to know, goddammit. Before he fires me, he should know what I know about a few people in this town. You put him on, you hear?"

Again, Chick muffled the phone. A moment passed, and then Wade heard the receiver click, and a dial tone buzzed in his ear.

Slowly, Wade laid the receiver back in its cradle. So Chub was in it too! Chub Merritt was working with them. He was probably taking a cut from Gordon LaRiviere and Mel Gordon, and as one of the selectmen, he had as much access to the tax records as LaRiviere did, so his job was to keep quiet about Northcountry Development Corporation and, among other things, help keep Wade out of the way.

The throb in his jaw seemed to continue the buzz of the dial tone, distracting him abruptly from his mania—for by now it was that, a mania—and made him remember my second piece of advice, to call a dentist, for heaven's sake, and get that tooth pulled. Take care of the little things first, the things that are distracting and handicapping you in your attempts to take care of the big things. Get your own car back, get your tooth pulled, let Pop take care of himself while you get your facts in order, and take your facts over the heads of the locals, whom you cannot trust, straight to the state police. Let the state police go to work on this. And then maybe try to get Jack Hewitt to turn himself in. But do it calmly, peacefully, rationally. Do not chase him around the countryside or go up against him in a bar or in LaRiviere's shop, where there will be other people around. Talk to his girlfriend or his father, talk to somebody he trusts, and explain what is at stake for him here. Jack no longer trusts you, Wade, so you might have to let someone else convince him that he must confess his crime and incriminate the others. Save that young man, and break the others. And while you are doing that, instruct J. Battle Hand to pursue your case against Lillian. Now that you have given him information that not only tarnishes Lillian's good-mother image but also implicates her own attorney, your Mr. Hand should be able to cut a deal that will force Lillian to give you back your rights as a father. In a few short weeks, before Christmas, maybe even before Thanksgiving, Wade, everything that now seems out of control and chaotic will be under control and orderly, and you and the fine woman who will soon be your wife and your lovely daughter Jill and your father will sit down to Thanksgiving dinner in the old family homestead together, and you will offer up a prayer to thank the Lord for all that He has given to you this year. And maybe I myself will join you at that table.

With the phone book in his lap, Wade flipped through the yellow pages and checked the Littleton listings for dentists: there were four, and he called one after the other in alphabetical order, asking, and then begging and finally shouting, for an appointment that afternoon. All four refused to see him. Two of them—I later learned, having called them myself—remembered hanging up in the middle of his rant, convinced that he was either crazy or dangerous or both.

Wade slammed down the phone, tossed the telephone book across the room, and when he stood up and turned around, he saw Margie standing by the door, watching him, mouth open, ashen-faced.

"What?" he said.

"What on earth is happening to you, Wade? Why are you acting this way?"

"What do you mean? It's my tooth! My fucking tooth! I can't even think anymore because of it!"

"Wade, I heard you talking. You got fired this morning, didn't you?"

"Look, that's just temporary, believe me. There's so much shit going to hit the fan in the next few days, my getting fired by LaRiviere and Chub Merritt won't matter a bit. Those sonsofbitches are going to be out of business and doing time before I'm through." He paced around the room while he talked, and clamped his hand against his throbbing jaw, as if making sure that it was still attached to him. Behind Margie, Pop came into the kitchen from outside with a half-dozen chunks of wood in his arms and dumped them noisily into the woodbox. "There's a lot of stuff I haven't told you or told anyone yet, but by God, I'm going to blow this town wide open now," Wade said. "Don't worry, I'll get another

293

job. I can find work doing lots of things around here. People are going to need me, anyhow. After this is over, and people see what's been going on behind their backs, they'll make me into a goddamned hero. You wait: when this blows, people will need me. Like the way Jill needs me, right? You'll see, I'll deliver. And I'll be the best goddamned father for her who ever lived. You need me. Even Pop, for Christ's sake, he needs me. So don't worry, I'll have a job, a good job, when this is over, and I'll take care of this house, fix it up, make it nice for all of us. And this town needs me too. They don't know it yet, but they do. The same as Jill and you and Pop. I'll be the town cop again, don't worry. Maybe now they think they can send me howling into a corner, like a kicked dog or some damned thing, some small irritating thing in the way, but by God, it'll be different soon."

Slowly, as if being shoved back by the force of his words, Margie retreated from the room toward the kitchen, where she lifted her coat from the hook by the door and picked up her pocketbook, and while Wade paced and ranted on behind her, gesturing and explaining quite as if she were still standing at the living room door, she stepped outside.

She hurried down the steps and got into her car, started the motor and backed out to the road, thinking, The man's crazy. One's a drunk, and the other's crazy. What on earth am I doing here? She could leave, she thought: her furniture was still in her old place in town, and she had not yet written to her ex-husband's parents in Florida to tell them that she had moved out. But all her clothes, her linens and personal belongings, photographs, papers, were in Wade's house, which was how she thought of the house now. Somehow the place smelled like Wade and looked like him: once a fine piece of country workmanship, symmetrical, handsomely proportioned, attractively located, the house was now broken down, disheveled, barely functional.

Wade was turning into his father, she suddenly realized. Wade, sober, sounded and acted the way his father did drunk. And his father was being eased out of existence altogether. She could see what was happening. She did not intend to turn into Wade's mother. She would stay in the house one more night, she decided, and tomorrow, when Wade went down to Concord to see that lawyer of his, she would move out.

The pain was worse than it had ever been: it had turned scarlet, had painted half of the inside of his face, was smeared from the point of his chin to his temple and was eating its way in toward the center. Wade's vision was affected now, and he saw things in discontinuous flutters and flashes—Pop was in the kitchen shucking his jacket; the television set was turned on, the horizontal control out of whack, the picture flipping again and again; Pop was seated on the couch in front of the television; was in the kitchen; was adjusting the horizontal control. Noises were unnaturally loud, followed by strange bits of silence: the sound of Pop opening the kitchen cabinet, unscrewing the top of his bottle, pouring whiskey into a glass and drinking it down—Wade heard it all clearly and at high volume, as if Pop had a microphone attached to him; and then the television came on, loud at first, suddenly silent, loud again; and the sound of Pop dropping an armload of wood into the woodbox, like a rock slide, punctuated by a hollow silence.

Pop was watching wrestling, his hands clapped onto his knees as if to hold them still, while Wade chased the pain in his face around the room, from window to window to door, as if his face were a dog in a pen looking for a way out. Pop said something about a dish antenna, he wished he had one of those dish antennas, they should buy one of those dish antennas, how much did a dish antenna cost, did Wade know how much people paid for those dish antennas you see all over town these days? *Shut up!* Wade shouted. *Just shut the fuck up!* The television audience was screaming, as a huge nearly naked man wearing a mask picked up another man and tossed him to the mat and leapt onto him, and the crowd shrieked with joy. Then the picture flipped again, and Pop got out of his seat and adjusted the knob and said he wished he had one of those dish antennas and sat back down, while the man with the mask flew through the air with his feet out and slammed the other man in the back, sending him staggering across the ring against the ropes, and the audience went crazy, booing, screaming, clapping hands, some even standing on their seats and shaking their fists. Then silence, as Wade stood by the window and looked out across the snow-covered backyard to the half-collapsed barn. A crow—in sharp black profile, like a silhouette, perched on a rafter—turned its head slowly, as if it knew

295

it was being watched, until its beak was aimed at Wade like an accusing finger: *You!* Wade turned away, and the sound of the television bored into his head, the screams of the audience, the grunts and thuds of the wrestlers, the hearty voice of the announcer, strands of loud noise winding around one another and making a single shaft that drilled into his brain: Pop was out in the kitchen again; the television went silent; Wade heard the bottle being opened, the whiskey splashing into the glass, the sound of his father's mouth, lips, tongue, throat, as he swallowed. *Leave that fucking bottle out!* Wade shouted, and he strode into the kitchen, passed Pop coming the other way, grabbed the bottle from the counter and hurried outdoors.

The bright light of the sun against the snow blinded him, and he stood for a few seconds on the porch and struggled to see: he heard the wind sigh in the pines across the road, heard the crow call from the barn out back, heard gunfire from a distant clearing in the woods. Soon the blaze of light started to crack and crumble, and at last it fell apart in chunks of white that floated across Wade's field of vision. He stepped from the porch to the ground and walked around the porch to the woodshed attached to the end of the house, a three-sided lean-to open to the driveway, where Pop split, stacked and stored his firewood, and tools were kept on a rough workbench.

Wade entered the woodshed and once again could not see, blinded this time by darkness instead of light. He set the bottle on the bench and felt along the length of it, touching a hammer, tin cans filled with nails and screws, a rasp, a small monkey wrench, a gas can and parts of a chainsaw, a file, a splitting wedge, and finally, as the darkness softened to a gray haze, he reached the pair of channel-lock pliers that he knew were there—he had seen them the other night, Sunday, when he had come out here with a flashlight looking for tools to repair the furnace: Pop's tools, scattered and rusting, a drunk's tools, Wade had thought then.

He uncapped the bottle of whiskey and opened his mouth—it hurt just to open it—and took a bite of whiskey the size of a tea bag and sloshed it around inside his mouth and swallowed: but he felt and tasted nothing, no grainy burn in his mouth or chest; nothing except the cold steel ripsaw of pain emanating from his jaw. He opened his mouth wider and touched the beak of the long-handled pliers to his front teeth, pulled his lip away with his fingers, forcing a cadaverous grin onto his mouth, and moved the pliers toward the dark star of pain back there. The jaws of the pliers angled away from the handles, like the head of a long-necked bird, and he managed for a second to lock them onto one of his molars, then released it and clamped them on the adjacent tooth. He withdrew the pliers and set them back down on the bench. The pain roared in his ears, like a train in a tunnel, and he felt tears on his cheeks.

He took another bite of whiskey, grabbed up the pliers and the bottle and walked quickly from the shed into the white wall of light outside, weeping and stumbling as he crossed the driveway and made his way to the porch without seeing, going on memory now—until he was back inside the house and could see his way through the gloom of the kitchen into the living room, where Pop sat in front of the television: the grunting huge men slammed their pink bodies against each other and the crowd shrieked with pleasure; Wade hurried past Pop, up the stairs and into the bathroom.

He set the bottle down on the toilet tank and looked into the mirror and saw a disheveled gray-faced stranger with tears streaming down his cheeks look back at him. He opened the stranger's mouth and with his left hand yanked back the lips on the right side, then took the pliers and reached in. He turned the face slightly to the side, so that he could see into it, pried the mouth open still further, and locked the pliers onto the largest molar in the back, squeezed and pulled. He heard the tooth grind against the cold steel of the pliers, as if the tooth were grabbing onto the bone, and he dug further into the gum with the mouth of the pliers and squeezed tightly again and pulled harder, steadily. It shifted in its bed, and he moved his left hand into place behind his right, and with both hands, one keeping the pressure on the tooth, the other lifting and guiding the pliers straight up against the jaw, he pulled, and the tooth came out, wet, bloody, rotted, clattering in the sink. He put the pliers down and reached for the whiskey.

When he passed Pop, he set the whiskey bottle down with pointed emphasis on the table beside him. Pop looked at the bottle for a second and up at Wade, and their eyes met and suddenly flared with hatred.

Neither man said a word. Abruptly, as if dismissing him,

Pop looked back at the television. Wade grabbed his coat and hat from the hook in the kitchen, put them on and went outside, moving quickly through the sheets of bright light to the woodshed, where he picked up the gas can and headed on to the barn. His face felt aflame to him, burning from the inside out, as if the hole in his jaw were the chimney of a volcano about to erupt. Removing the tooth had opened a shaft, a dark tunnel, and sparks, cinders, hot gases flew up and scorched his mouth: he opened his mouth and spat a clot of hot blood into the snow and imagined it hissing behind him.

Inside the barn, it was dark and sepulchral. Wade emptied the gas from the can into Pop's truck and tossed the can aside. He stepped up on the running board and got into the driver's seat, took the key from his coat pocket, where it had remained since Wednesday, and after a few tries, got the motor running. The old truck shuddered and shook, and Wade backed it slowly out the huge barn door and along the narrow snowbanked lane that he and I had shoveled clear only two nights before, until he had it out on the road, where he aimed it toward town, worked the stickshift into first gear, and drove off.

21

ASA BROWN WORKED OUT of the Clinton County state police headquarters, a low concrete-and-yellow-brick building on the interstate a few miles north of Lawford. By the time Wade parked Pop's shaky old stake-body truck between a pair of cruisers in the lot, it was midafternoon and nearly dark. The sky was like gray suede, and a light breeze brushed snow off the banks onto the pavement, where it swirled and curled into low white berms.

Wade got out and for a few seconds stood by the open door of the truck and studied the large dark green Fords next to it and remembered that once long ago he had considered becoming a state trooper. It was after he had returned from his hitch in the army, after Korea, and it had seemed logical to him, since he had been an MP in the army, to take the exam and study at the trooper academy down in Concord and become a statie, by God, ride around all day in one of those cruisers wearing reflector shades and a trooper hat and busting heads down in Laconia when all the bikers came in for the motorcycle races every summer, driving the governor home from the statehouse for lunch, chasing coked-out Massachusetts drivers on the interstate speeding south after a long weekend on the ski slopes. It would have been better than what he had done instead.

He had not even tried to become a state trooper. He had come home to Lawford from Korea obsessed with what he called "unfinished business," by which he meant his love for Lillian, from whom he was then legally divorced. A year later, he was married to her a second time, his unfinished business finished, as it were, but by then he was working for LaRiviere again and building the little yellow house out on Lebanon Road for him and Lillian to live in, and he could not figure out how to become a state trooper and still hold down a full-time job and build a house nights and weekends. So he did not take the exam, which he knew he could easily pass. He remained a well driller and became the town cop instead and built the house for himself and Lillian and the family they wanted to raise.

When they got married the first time, right after graduating high school, they were both technically still virgins. A cynic might say they got married in order to sleep with each other and got divorced when they had gotten used to sleeping with each other and never should have remarried, and that would be part of the truth. But things are never as simple as cynics believe, especially with regard to bright adolescents in love. Wade Whitehouse and Lillian Pittman, through their openness and intimacy with one another, had separated themselves, by the age of sixteen, from the kids and adults around them and had protected each other while they made themselves more sensitive and passionate than those kids, until they came to depend on one another for an essential recognition of their more tender qualities and their intelligence.

Without Lillian, without her recognition and protection, Wade would have been forced to regard himself as no different from the boys and men who surrounded him, boys his age like Jimmy Dame and Hector Eastman and grown men like Pop and Gordon LaRiviere—deliberately roughened and coarse, cultivating their violence for one another to admire and shrink from, growing up with a defensive willed stupidity and then encouraging their sons to follow. Without Lillian's recognition and protection, Wade, who was very good at being male in this world, a hearty bluff athletic sort of guy with a mean streak, would have been unable to resist the influence of the males who surrounded him. The loneliness would have been too much to bear.

It was the same with Lillian: she did not want to become like her mother and all the women she knew in town, a sad oppressed lot whose only humor was self-deprecating, whose greatest fear was of the men they lived with, whose children were their ballast but weighed down their lives like stones in a shroud. Wade recognized the young thing in her, the bright delicacy of feeling and thought that every other girl her age she knew was intent on snuffing out, and she treasured him for that. She married him for that.

They married also for sex, naturally, but they never did grow used to sleeping with each other, as the cynic would have us believe. Before they were married, they made love passionately every chance they had and became sweetly familiar with each other's bodies, knew the other's response to the touch of hands and fingertips, lips, tongue and teeth as well as they knew their own. But true consummation, the act itself, did not take place until after they were married and lived in one of the small apartments over Golden's General Store, and when it did, to their great surprise, pleasure and gratitude, it was a simple continuation and extension of what they had been doing all along. It was not different; it was more. And they never stopped loving to touch each other with their hands and tongues and mouths, so that, in bed in the dark, when Wade finally rose up and covered Lillian's smooth and lively body and entered it, the pleasure of his entry and the force of it, the long sweet swing of it, was for both of them an irresistible crescendo that never failed to surprise and thrill them with its ability, like gravity, to control them.

No, he did not leave her because he had grown used to sleeping with her. When Wade left Lillian and joined the army—hoping to follow Elbourne and Charlie to Vietnam but getting sent instead to Korea—it was because at the age of twenty-one he had come to believe that by marrying so young, he had ended his life prematurely. It was the last, perhaps the only, chance he had to start over. His knowledge of himself, of his golden interior, thanks to Lillian, was of a boy whose life was not yet defined, whose potential was large but had in no way been realized. He possessed this knowledge because Lillian's love had kept the young thing in him alive long after it had died in everyone else he knew, just as his love for her had kept the young thing in her alive too. But despite that, here he was, living like a trapped adult, a man much older than he, a man whose life was already determined in every important way—by the job at LaRiviere's, by the small dark apartment filled with other people's castoffs, by the village of Lawford itself, all of it hemmed in by the dark hills and forests. This was adult life, and he was not ready to accept it.

He had started to drink heavily, usually at Toby's after work, and had grown confused and angry. And he quickly lost his connection to that lovely young thing, the fragile humorous affection for the world that he had nurtured and kept alive all through adolescence, and he grew increasingly angry at the loss and began to blame Lillian for it. The more he blamed her, the further he flew from it, until, indeed, he *was* like the men who surrounded him, and one night he lashed out at her with his fists and afterwards wept in her lap, begging forgiveness, promising to be different, new, clean, loving, gentle, funny.

But within weeks, he found himself breaking his promise, horrifying himself, and he began to blame the context of his madness, his life with Lillian, confusing it with the cause of his madness, and so he left her. He drove to Littleton and enlisted in the army and went to Fort Dix, New Jersey, for basic training, and wrote Lillian a long letter from there, asking her to divorce him, saying she could use any grounds she wanted, physical cruelty, even, and they could both start over again.

They tried, both of them, to do just that. Wade got shipped out to Korea—two Whitehouse brothers in Vietnam was evidently as much as the army was willing to risk that early in the war—and Lillian went to secretarial school in Littleton and worked nights as a waitress at Toby's Inn. They slept with other people—for Wade, there was the young woman in Seoul, Kim Chul Hee, and no one else; for Lillian, there were several men during the two years she and Wade were apart.

Two of the men she told Wade about; one she did not. I was only eleven years old then, but I knew that Lillian, briefly, was meeting Gordon LaRiviere, who was married and was thin then and attractive, and who from time to time stopped by Lillian's apartment in town, the apartment over Golden's store, where she had lived with Wade. LaRiviere usually came to visit her very early in the morning, and on several of these occasions I myself saw him arrive before six and leave by seven-thirty, for I had my first job that summer, working at

Golden's General Store as a stockboy, and pedaled my bike all the way into town to sweep out the store and clean the counters before it opened at seven. I was shocked by what I saw, and felt betrayed, as if I and not my brother Wade were off defending our country against the Asian Communists, and I suspect that I have not even today forgiven Lillian for her affair with Gordon LaRiviere, although she was of course quite entitled to it: LaRiviere was the married one, not she.

The other two men Lillian went out with and slept with during those years that she and Wade were divorced the first time, the men she told Wade about, were Lugene Brooks, then the sixth-grade teacher at the school, single and fresh out of Plymouth State, still single twenty years later but now the middle-aged principal of the school, and Nick Wickham, who made it a point in those days to bed all the unmarried and most of the married women in town at least once. Now the compulsion seems to have weakened, and although he still goes through the motions, it is mostly for effect. Twenty years ago, however, Nick had good looks and a brilliant smile and a sense of humor that was superior to that of most of the men in town, in that his was flirtatious and affectionate, and theirs was misogynous and violent.

Within a week of Wade's return to Lawford, he and Lillian were sleeping together in the bedroom of the apartment over Golden's store again and were talking about remarrying, so she confessed her affairs with Lugene Brooks and Nick Wickham. Wade accepted the news mildly, because she insisted that neither man had been able to please her the way Wade could, a comparison that may well have eroticized her for him.

As it happens, what Lillian told Wade about sleeping with Lugene Brooks and Nick Wickham was essentially true: compared to sex with him, it was boring and even a little embarrassing. He did not press her for further details, although he admitted to himself that he was curious—not about her but about the men.

When he confessed to her that he had indulged in a three-month love affair with the woman in Seoul, he lied: he said that she had meant nothing to him, except occasional mechanical sex. "She wasn't a hooker or anything, a prostitute," he assured her. "Just a woman who was there." In fact, however, she had meant a great deal to him, for she had renewed that sense of himself as a child that he had obtained with Lillian when they were first together. She spoke almost no English and he no Korean, and she tried with diligence and imagination, when he was with her, which was nearly every weekend and day off he could take, to be exactly what he wanted her to be—protective but dependent, bossy but unthreatening, sexually provocative and skilled yet innocent as a child and as personal as a sister. Impossible needs for any mere mortal to meet; she failed him, eventually. He contracted a mild case of gonorrhea, and when he went for treatment, Wade learned from the doctor—a young wise guy recently graduated from Harvard Medical School who insisted that Wade provide him with the name of the woman or women he had been sleeping with: his sexual contacts, was the phrase—that she was sleeping with at least three other GI's, two of them guys in his outfit, and was supporting her parents, younger sisters and several children of her own with the money he and the other GI's gave her. Wade never saw her again. But he felt guilty for that: he remembered her laughter, her black hair, her sad small beautiful breasts—her very tangibility; and he knew that he had not been wrong when, during those three months, he had believed that she was as real as he and as frightened. He spoke of her only casually and with disrespect after that, however—with the guys in his outfit and, when he got home, at work and around the bar at Toby's and at first, late at night, with Lillian.

And although Lillian felt a slight chill go down her back when Wade talked that way about his one sexual liaison during their two years apart, the only other woman he had dealt with intimately, she was nonetheless relieved: the Korean woman was different from her in a way that made the woman less than she. Just as Wade believed that Lugene Brooks and Nick Wickham were different from him in ways that made them less than he. Their bargain struck, Wade and Lillian had resumed sleeping together, and a month later, they were remarried and Wade was working for Gordon LaRiviere again and arranging to buy from him a three-acre plot of land out on Lebanon Road to build a house on. Lillian quit waitressing at Toby's, used her new secretarial skills as a part-time assistant clerk at the town hall, and stopped taking birth control pills. They tried for a long time to get Lillian pregnant, but it was not until after several miscarriages and the passage of eight years that Jill was born, to Wade's great relief, for he had long believed that his capacity to father a child had been damaged by his having briefly loved a Korean woman. And after Jill was born, Wade almost never thought of the woman again and was sure that he could not even remember her name. Kim Chul Hee.

"Wade Whitehouse. You look like shit. What happened to your mouth—somebody clip you?" Asa Brown smiled, as if amused. He swung his feet up onto his desk and lolled back in his chair and studied Wade for a moment, as if the disheveled man with the shifting eyes and swollen jaw were an odd museum exhibit, then waved with one hand to the chair beside the desk and said, "Sit. Take a load off."

The room was brightly lit by a bank of overhead fluorescent lights. There were several other desks, but Brown and Wade were alone in the office, which eased Wade somewhat, for he preferred to say what he had to say to Brown alone and not have to endure Brown's tendency to play Wade against an audience.

"I've got some information. I've got something you ought to know." Wade took his hat off and sat down and placed it in his lap. He felt like a schoolboy going to the principal's office for questioning. He was hot inside the office with his coat still on, and he began to sweat. He fumbled with the zipper of his coat but it jammed, and he finally gave it up and twirled his trooper cap on his finger, trying to look at ease and comfortable here in Asa Brown's territory, trying not to look the way he felt—trapped, hot, guilty, angry. This was Rolfe's idea, he probably thought. That goddamned smartass little brother of mine who believes that all you have to do when somebody does something wrong is tell it to the cops.

"The fuck happened to your mouth, Wade? Tell me that. What's the other guy look like? Not as bad as you, I hope. Somebody did that to me, I'd want him to look a hell of a lot worse than me." Brown straightened one crease on his trousers with his thumb and forefinger, yanked it taut and performed the same act on the other, then gazed at both creases with admiration.

Wade shifted uncomfortably in his chair and pulled a cigarette from a crumpled pack and with trembling hands lit it. Brown shoved an ashtray across the desk to him and smiled, waiting. Months later, on a bright spring morning, when I sat in the same chair as Wade, and Captain Asa Brown sat across from me with his feet up on his desk, he told me that Wade had looked like a man about to break down and confess a crime. Wade's shoulders were slumped, his feet drawn up under the chair, knees together, his hands fidgeting with the cigarette and lighter, while he looked off slightly to the right of Brown, refusing eye contact—like a guilt-driven man who had found the burden too great to bear and had finally decided to reveal the nature of his crime and accept his punishment. Not a man come to accuse others.

Wade suddenly sat up straight in his chair, looked at Brown and said, "What I was wondering is about taking the state trooper's test, maybe. I was wondering if I was too old for that. You know, to join the state police."

Brown said, "You kidding me, Wade? You want to be a trooper?"

"Well, yeah. I mean, I was thinking about it. I was just wondering about the test, if I was too old or something."

Brown looked at him thoughtfully, as if considering how Wade, in his present state, would look in a trooper's uniform. Like a man impersonating a cop, he thought, a man in costume, a drunk masquerading in a stolen uniform. "Well, Wade, I'd have to look into that for you. I think there is an age limit, but I'd have to check. What're you, forty-something?"

"Forty-one." Wade stood up and jammed his cap back on and put out his cigarette. "I was only wondering."

"Well, I'll check on that, okay? You give me a call in a day or two, Wade, and I'll let you know."

Wade mumbled thanks and backed toward the door. "Yeah, I'll call you," he said, and he turned and went out, walked quickly down the long hallway to the exit and was gone, leaving Brown at his desk, smiling and shaking his head. What an asshole, that guy. Drunk, probably, and pissed off at somebody he got in a fight with. And now he's got it into his head that he can be a state trooper so he can bust the guy who whacked him on the jaw. He used to be a decent town cop, Brown thought, but it looks like the booze has got to him. Young for that. Too bad.

Some time later, Wade pulled off the road in front of Golden's store. He put gas into the truck from the pump out front, went into the store and paid Buddy Golden at the register. Buddy, a thin sallow-faced man with a permanently soured expression on his face, said, "Wade," and handed him his change.

Wade said nothing, turned and left the store.

"Friendly," Buddy said. "Real friendly." He stood by the register and watched Wade out the window and saw him walk around to the side of the store and heard him clump up the wooden stairs there to the landing that led to the pair of small apartments upstairs. Buddy heard Wade knock on one of the doors and heard it open, which meant that it was Hettie Rodgers's apartment, since the other was rented by Frankie LaCoy, who Buddy knew was up in Littleton, probably buying more marijuana to sell here in town. He did not care how the goddamned LaCoy kid made his living, so long as he paid his rent on time and did not trash the apartment.

Buddy finished closing the store, flicked off the lights, locked up and went out, passing the old red truck as he walked around back toward his own car. As he strolled under the landing, he looked up and saw that, yep, he was right: no lights on in Frankie LaCoy's apartment and several lights burning in Hettie's. That goddamned Wade Whitehouse, he better be careful, coming around to visit Jack Hewitt's girlfriend. If Jack catches him, Wade will have some serious explaining to do.

None of my business, he thought, just so long as they don't trash the apartment. I've got to stop renting these places to kids, he decided, walking on. It was nothing but trouble. Of course, there was no one else in town to rent to, except single kids who could not afford a trailer or a house of their own and did not want to live with their parents anymore because they needed to screw each other and drink and smoke marijuana and God knows what else, and newlyweds, who never stayed long.

Hettie was surprised to see Wade. She invited him in and waited for him to tell her why he had come knocking on her door. He peered slowly around the small crowded room and tiny kitchen by the door and said nothing.

She fluffed her new short haircut at the nape of her neck and said, "What do you think, Wade? You like it short?" She spun around to show him all sides. She was wearing an aqua V-neck tee shirt and tight jeans with zippers at the ankles and rubber thongs on her feet. Just home from work, she explained, and out of that uniform they made her wear at Ken's

Kutters in Littleton. "It's like a damned nurse's uniform or something they make you wear," she said. "Ridiculous. They want, like, to call you a beautician, right? So I guess they figure you have to look like you work in a hospital. It's nice, though." She sighed. "The job, I mean." She chattered on nervously, feigning good cheer, while Wade prowled in silence through the apartment, looking out the window in the living room to the road below, where Pop's truck was parked beside the gas pump.

"You all right, Wade?" Hettie asked, suddenly serious. "What happened to your face there? It's all swollen."

He sat down heavily on the tattered old couch, still wearing his hat and coat, and drummed his fingers on the armrest. "You know, I lived in this apartment. Twice."

"No kidding. Twice. You want a beer, Wade?" Hettie moved toward the refrigerator. "I was just going to get myself a beer. It's what I like to do when I first get home, change out of that nurse's uniform they make me wear and have a beer before I start supper." She smiled eagerly at the refrigerator door, her face a question mark. "Beer?"

"When I first got married I lived here. And then I lived here alone a few years ago. When I got divorced." He pulled his hat off and flipped it to the end of the couch and smoothly unzipped his coat and wriggled out of it, tossing it on top of the hat.

"I know," she said. "About after the divorce, I mean. But not about when you were married. Before my time," she said, opening the refrigerator.

Wade agreed, it was before her time, and said maybe he would take that beer. He stood up again, moving from the living room toward the single bedroom in back, where he halted at the door for a moment and peered in. She had left the light on, and her white uniform lay rumpled on the unmade double bed. There was a three-legged dresser with a pair of bricks for the fourth leg, and several blue plastic boxes under the window were filled with record albums, and female clothing was everywhere, spilling from the dresser drawers, in piles on the floor, drooping off the ironing board in the corner. On the wall she had tacked up a poster of David Bowie in concert.

"Don't mind the mess," she said, handing him a bottle of Michelob. "It's Friday, like TGIF, and I do housecleaning on

Saturday. Cheers," she said, and clinked his bottle with her own.

Wade walked back toward the kitchen at the far side of the living room, looked into it and took a long pull from the bottle. "Looks like the same furniture that was here when I lived here," he said in a metallic voice. He looked strange, Hettie told me, when I asked her about that night, and he was acting and talking oddly, she said, right from the start, when he first came in, and she was a little afraid of him, even though they were old friends and Wade had always behaved decently toward her.

"I used to like baby-sit Jill, you know," she explained, "so I was used to Wade and his moods, and I had seen him get pretty ugly when he was drinking. But this was different. He wasn't ugly or anything, just strange. Like, he was all caught up remembering when he once lived in the same apartment, back when he and Lillian were first married and then later, when they got divorced. Like, it must have been hard on him, having to come back to the same apartment years later, where the marriage had first started out. I guess I told him that, about how hard it must have been for him, being his age and all, to live in a furnished little dump like this, and he must have been glad to get out of it and get his own trailer out there by the lake."

"I'm living in my father's house now," he said. "Up on Parker Mountain."

"Yeah, right. I guess I knew that. I heard Margie—your Margie, Margie Fogg—I heard she moved in with you. Nice?" Hettie dropped into a director's chair opposite the couch, crossed her legs and swung one ankle back and forth in a circular motion, stirring the air. She was nervous, a little frightened of Wade, not trying to be provocative—although, thinking back on it, she told me, she could see how Wade might have thought differently. The truth is, she wanted him to leave and wished that she had not let him in and offered him a beer. He was looking at her as if he did not know who she was, as if he thought she was Lillian, maybe, and they were newlyweds living in this apartment together. Or he may not have known who he himself was: it was as if he thought he was Jack—he was acting the way Jack did sometimes when he was drunk, especially lately: morose, inward, cryptic. These were not exactly Hettie Rodgers's words, of course, but they are her perceptions, essentially, as she remembered them six months later.

He moved closer to her, and she stopped twirling her leg in the air and looked up at him. Reaching out with one hand, he brushed her chin with his fingertips, then lowered himself down next to her and laid his head on her lap, facing away from her toward the shabby couch and across the cluttered room to the darkened window beyond. The room looked to him exactly as it had when he had lived here with Lillian twenty years before, and he had knelt beside her and had placed his head in her lap, and looking away from her, so that she could not see the tears in his eyes, he had begged her to forgive him. Hettie stroked his head, as if he were a troubled child, and he set the bottle of beer on the floor and reached around her legs with his arms and held her tightly.

"Wade," she said. "No."

"When we lived here," he said in a low voice, "it was mostly good. There were some bad times, but it was mostly good. Wasn't it?"

"Wade, that was a long time ago. Like, things change, Wade."

"No. Some things stay the same your whole life. The best things that happened to you, and the worst, they stay with you your whole life. When we lived here, when we were kids just starting out, that was the best thing. I know that. I can still feel that, in spite of everything else that has happened to us."

"Wade," Hettie said, her voice almost a whisper. "Why did you come over here tonight?"

He was silent for a few seconds, and then he said, "Will you let me make love to you?" He released her and sat back on his heels and looked up at her face, which was filled with confusion and fear, although he did not see that. He said, "Just this one time, here, in this place. In the dark, with the lights out, and you can be Lillian, and I'll be whoever you want. I'll be Jack, if you want. Just this one time."

"I can't, Wade. I'm scared. No kidding, really. I'm scared of this. You should go."

"In the dark I can call you Lillian, and you can call me Jack. And it will only happen this one time. I need to do that. Lillian."

"Please. Please don't call me Lillian." Her eyes welled up, and tears broke across her cheeks. "You're scaring me."

Wade reached up and touched her hair at the bottom of her long slender neck. "You look nice with your hair cut short like that," he said, and he reached beyond her to the light switch on the wall and doused the overhead light, a bulb hidden in a Chinese paper shade, dropping the room into darkness, with only the lamp in the bedroom showing now, casting a long plank of light into the room, so that they could see the shape of each other's bodies but could not make out the face. And he did look like Jack to her at that moment, kneeling next to her, one hand on her thigh, the other on her shoulder, his fingertips brushing her throat. He said, "I wonder what your hair smells like now. If it smells the same as it used to when I kissed you and we made love."

She was shaking; her heart was pounding and the blood roared in her ears.

"Lillian," he said. "Say my name. Say it."

"This scares me. Don't."

"I want you to say my name. Jack. Say it."

"I'm afraid. I really am."

"Lillian."

She whispered his name. "Jack."

He touched her lips with the tips of his fingers. "Say it again."

"Jack."

He took her hand and placed her fingers across his lips, and he said, "Lillian."

He stood slowly and said, "Wait here," and he walked into the bedroom, crossed to the bedside table and put out the light. Then he quickly returned through the darkness to stand behind her.

She said, "This scares me a whole lot. We shouldn't do this."

"It's all right. We're not who we are. I'm Jack, and you're Lillian." He reached down and placed his hands on her shoulders. He let his hands slide to her breasts and gently hold them, and she laid her head back against him, her breath coming rapidly now, as he moved his hands over her breasts, her nipples hardening, her hands on his, pressing them against her. Then he was kissing her neck, her ears, her cheeks and her lips, and she was kissing him back, and they were standing in the room holding tightly to one another, and in seconds they were moving through the darkness to the bedroom.

She said to me, "I knew it was wrong, but it isn't like I was married to Jack or anything. And things had been pretty bad between him and me lately anyway, Jack and me, since that hunting accident he was involved with. I guess I was mad at him. And I liked Wade, you know, he was like an old friend, ever since I was a kid, and he had always been real sweet to me, and he seemed so sad and all. I really felt sorry for him. And it was like just this one time. I had never been what you'd call attracted to Wade, but this one night, it was different. And making me call him Jack like that, and him calling me Lillian, it was strange, like being real high, and it kind of took me over, you know?"

Wade undressed her in the darkness, and then he took off his own clothes and moved onto her, gently kissing her with his damaged mouth, drawing her warm breath into him, gulping it down. He lifted himself up on his arms, and she opened to him like a flower, and he entered her, easily, with excruciating slowness, until he was all the way in, and he felt huge to himself, as if he had gone all the way up into her chest and were touching Lillian's heart.

Down in front of the store, a burgundy pickup pulled off the road and parked next to Pop's truck. The road was empty and dark. The store windows reflected the flash of the headlights, while Jack sat in his truck and peered up through the windshield and saw that there were no lights on in Hettie's apartment. Shit, he thought, and he looked at his watch in the green glow of the dashboard.

Then, wondering what the hell Wade's father's truck was doing parked in front of the store by the gas pump, he got out and looked inside, thinking that maybe the old bastard had passed out and was lying on the seat. Gone. Strange. The sonofabitch's probably three sheets to the wind down at Toby's, wondering where the hell he left his truck, Jack thought.

He moved around to the front of his own truck, and pulled a small notepad and pencil from his shirt pocket, and, in the reflected splash from the headlights off the store windows, scribbled a note and tore it from the pad. He walked heavily up the stairs to the landing and stopped in front of Hettie's door. He studied the door for a second, and thought, What the hell, maybe she came home already and fell asleep, and he turned the doorknob. The door swung open, and Jack stepped inside.

"Hettie?" he called into the darkness. "Hey, babes, you here?" Silence.

"By then, when Jack came," Hettie explained to me, "we were just lying there in the darkness, you know? Not saying anything, just thinking, I guess, about what we'd done. This terrible thing we'd done, Wade and me. I was really scared when I heard Jack outside, and then, when he actually came into the apartment, I jumped, and I was so scared I almost screamed. But I didn't. Wade, he didn't even seem to react. I mean, like he just lay there the same way, without even his breathing changing, his hands behind his head, like he was going to lie there on his back naked in bed and let Jack walk right into the room. It was weird.

"But then I heard Jack bump against something in the living room, and he swore and tried to find the light switch on the wall, you know, right by the door. But he couldn't find it, so he backed outside to the landing again, thank God, and a few seconds later, I heard him go back down the stairs, and finally I heard his truck drive off."

Slowly, Wade sat up and swung his legs off the bed, as if he were an old sick man. He stood and in the darkness began to dress. He and Hettie said nothing to each other, and when he was dressed, he walked from the bedroom to the couch, where he had tossed his hat and coat. He picked them up and put them on and went out onto the landing—closing the door behind him with care, as if he did not want anyone to hear him.

Jack's note fluttered from the door to the landing. Wade leaned down and picked it up and read it: *Meet me at Toby's. I got some good news today. Love, Jack.* Wade inserted the note between the door and the jamb just above the doorknob, where Jack had placed it, then went down the stairs. He started up Pop's truck and left, heading north on Route 29, out of town, toward home.

22

THIS TIME, FOR HIS MEETING with J. Battle Hand, Wade dressed up, or at least he did not appear in his work clothes: he wore the dark-blue gabardine sports jacket and brown trousers he had worn to Ma's funeral, with a white shirt and a green-and-silver diagonally striped tie—clothing he had purchased over the last couple of years at J. C. Penney's in Littleton, so that he could go to weddings or funerals or out with Margie for a movie and Chinese food, say, and not look like a hick, a woodchuck, a goddamned shitkicker from the hills of Cow Hampshire.

Lillian had always scolded Wade about his taste in clothing: he did not have bad taste, she told him, he had no taste, which was worse. He simply did not care how his clothing looked, she explained; he cared only that it functioned adequately to cover his nakedness and protect him from the elements. Early on, Lillian had actually found this quality endearing, but as she grew older and a bit more sophisticated herself, Wade's apparent inability to care how he looked began to embarrass and irritate her. Then, three years before, when he had gone to court for his divorce wearing what he wore every

314

day in those days—dark-blue twill trousers and shirt, with *Wade* on the left shirt pocket and *LaRiviere Co.* on the right—Lillian had been unable, even on so formal and momentous an occasion, to restrain her embarrassment and deep irritation with his clothing, and her words had cut him deeply enough to let him, for the first time in his life, see himself in his clothes as he thought others saw him, and he never wore LaRiviere's uniform again, even to work. They had come out of the courtroom, during the judge's lunch break, still waiting for their case to be heard, and were standing in the hallway outside, and, while talking strategy with their respective lawyers, had inadvertently backed into each other. When they turned to apologize for the bump, they both expected to see a stranger, but instead husband and wife suddenly found themselves standing face to face.

Wade looked into her eyes and gazed at the beautiful person he had loved since childhood, eyes as familiar to him as his own hands: in a series of transparent overlays he saw the child, the girl and the woman and mother she had become, and in a thin voice he said, "I wish we weren't doing this, Lillian, honest to God, I really do."

She took a step back and viewed him from his black high-topped work shoes to the V of his tee shirt at his open collar, and she pronounced, "You look just like you are, Wade."

Then she turned away and resumed talking with her lawyer, the tall handsome Jackson Cotter, of Cotter, Wilcox and Browne, a man with gray flecks in his charcoal-colored hair and wearing a three-piece navy-blue pin-striped suit. Clothes make the man, Wade thought. Clothes make the man, and the lawyer makes the client. He saw himself in his clothes the way a stranger would, and he saw a stupid unimaginative man, and he noticed that his lawyer, Robert Emile Chagnon, wore an ill-fitting kelly-green corduroy suit with a yellow knit shirt and no tie and had on a pair of old blue canvas deck shoes with white soles and laces. The man Wade had hired to represent him looked ridiculous and incompetent and dishonest. No doubt just as Wade himself looked.

Well, this time, by God, things would be different. This time his lawyer would be a man who cut the figure of a distinguished genius, a man wearing a three-piece suit, yes, but entering the courtroom in a wheelchair—a man so obviously skilled that he needed only his brain and his dark melodious voice to obtain justice for his client. This time that sexy tall lawyer of Lillian's would find that his good looks and clothes worked against him. Wade resisted an impulse to smile and rub his hands together with relish, as he followed Hand's secretary from the outer office to the familiar paneled room in back, with all the books on the shelves and the leather-covered chairs and sofa. This time, by God, Wade Whitehouse was going to have his day in court.

"I've taken a look at your divorce decree," Hand said. "And frankly, Mr. Whitehouse, if you want the custody terms changed, I think you're going to run into a few problems."

"What do you mean, 'if'? What the hell do you think this is all about? Of *course* I want the custody terms changed!" Wade pulled out his cigarettes and lit up, inhaling furiously. The lawyer pressed the reverse button on the control panel with his left hand, and his chair zipped away from Wade to the middle of the room, where he watched Wade like a guard dog.

"I'm afraid you don't understand," Hand said. "In this state, a judge is going to be very reluctant to change the terms of custody, unless conditions in the life of the child now are radically different from what they were when the divorce was granted—"

"*You* don't understand!" Wade interrupted him. "I thought we were going to nail her on the lawyer thing."

Hand continued quite as if Wade had said nothing. ". . . and unless they have changed in such a way as to be deleterious to the child's health or emotional well-being. Except, of course, when the original terms of custody appear to have been clearly and unjustly onerous—which frankly is not the case here—or when it can be shown that the judgment depended on information that was based on perjured testimony. Something like that, sometimes, can convince a judge to reconsider. But they hate to do it. They hate reconsidering divorce terms."

"I thought—what I thought was we were going after this guy."

"Who?"

"Cotter. Her lawyer. Her boyfriend. Remember?"

"Yes, I remember."

"And what about her smoking marijuana? What about that? In her lawyer's company, even. What about that?"

Hand sighed. "Mr. Whitehouse, let me ask you a few questions that you yourself would be asked in court if you tried to push this."

"Shoot." Wade exhaled a cloud of smoke and coughed.

"Have you yourself ever smoked marijuana?" He paused. "You're under oath, remember. Or will be."

Wade hesitated, as if trying to remember. "Well, I mean, yeah, I guess so. Who hasn't?"

"And you are a police officer, right?"

"Yeah, yeah. I get the drift." Wade waved him off with his hand.

"Let me go on. How much do you drink, Mr. Whitehouse? How much a day do you drink?"

"What the hell's that got to do with anything?" Wade bristled.

"Never mind that. Just answer the question, please."

"I don't *know* how much I drink. I don't keep count."

"Too many to count?"

"Jesus Christ! What the hell are you trying to prove? *I* haven't done anything wrong! Whose lawyer are you, anyhow?" Wade rubbed his cigarette out in the ashtray next to him. "Look, I'm just trying to make it so I can see my own child when I want to. That's all. I don't want to have to get permission from my ex-wife to see my own daughter!"

"You don't. The divorce decree says that you can have your daughter one weekend a month, except for Christmas and Thanksgiving, and for one week in the summer."

"Yeah, I get Halloween, she gets Thanksgiving and Christmas. It's wrong, you know that! Wrong. The whole thing is wrong."

"It's unusually restrictive, I admit. But there are reasons."

"Such as?"

"Apparently, you were physically violent with your wife on several occasions?"

"That's in there? That's not in there."

"No. But the divorce was granted on the grounds of physical and mental cruelty. And I did speak with her attorney about the case. Jackson Cotter."

"You did *what?* I thought you were on my side in this! I thought you were working for me!"

"Mr. Whitehouse, it's not unusual to communicate intentions like yours to the attorney of the other party."

"You mention his hanky-panky with Lillian? You mention that?"

"I didn't think it appropriate to threaten him," the lawyer said.

"You didn't think it appropriate."

"No."

Wade slumped in his chair and looked at his shoes. "You're telling me to drop this thing, aren't you? Forget about it."

"Yes."

"You're telling me I'm dreaming."

"Not exactly. But yes."

"I'm going to get married, you know. Soon. To a very nice woman, very motherly and all. And I have a house now, a regular house, the house I grew up in. That makes a difference. Doesn't that make a difference?"

"Not really." Hand stole a glance at his watch.

In a weak small voice, Wade said, "I've changed since then. Since the divorce, I mean. I really have."

"I'm sure you have."

"Did you explain that, to her lawyer, I mean, when you talked to him?"

"As a matter of fact, I did. And he offered an arrangement that should interest you."

Wade quickly looked up from his shoes and watched the man with suspicion. He thought, Lawyers—the sonsofbitches are all in cahoots, making deals behind your back, swapping favors, trading off one case now to win another later. "Tell me."

Hand wheeled in closer to Wade and smiled sympathetically. He did mention to Cotter—just in passing, he said, not as a threat—his knowledge of Mrs. Horner's relationship with her attorney, which relationship, while not illegal, was potentially embarrassing, to say the least, and he did explain to Jackson Cotter that Wade recently had changed his way of living to a considerable degree. The combination of the two, he said, convinced Cotter, after consulting with his client, of course, to agree that if Wade would abandon his suit, Mrs. Horner would allow him to have Jill stay with him on two weekends a month and on alternating Thanksgiving and Christmas holidays and for two weeks in the summer instead

318

of one. The arrangement, he added, need not be formalized in court.

Wade nodded solemnly. "I get it. You got Cotter to put the arm on Lillian, and now you're putting the arm on me. You guys cut a deal so that Lillian gives up something, and I give up something, and you two go away with our money in your pockets."

Hand backed his wheelchair to the middle of the room, where he slid his yellow pad into the carrier and his pen into his inside pocket. "This arrangement, if you accept it, keeps you out of court, Mr. Whitehouse, in a case you would surely lose. Which saves you ten times the money you have spent, not to mention the emotional damage these things inflict on all the principals, especially the child, whether you win or lose. And I have gotten your visitation rights doubled. What more do you want?"

"Nothing on paper. Right?"

"Mr. Whitehouse, you hired me for my legal advice. Do you want it?"

"Yes, goddammit."

"This is the best deal you will get in this state. And you only got it because Jackson Cotter made the mistake of becoming involved with your ex-wife and does not want to ask your ex-wife to perjure herself by denying it, which, of course, she would do, and then it would be your word against hers, that's all. And frankly, no one would believe you. Not even Mrs. Horner's husband or Jackson Cotter's wife. Consider yourself lucky," he said, and he wheeled toward the door and swung it open for Wade. "Or hire another attorney."

Wade slowly rose from the chair. "Lucky," he said. "Lucky, lucky, lucky." He walked across the room, and as he left he looked down at the man in the wheelchair and said, "Okay, so when's the next time I can see my daughter?"

"Your ex-wife expects you to pick her up today."

"You arranged that with Cotter."

"I did."

"Thanks," Wade said. He walked through the door and down the hall, past the secretary, who did not look up from her typing, and out to the street.

It was a bright sunny day, the air cool and crisp against his freshly shaved face. Wade stood on the steps of the building and looked down at Pa's red truck parked in front. The vehicle looked ridiculous and made him ashamed in the usual way. He rubbed his cheek and realized freshly that his jaw no longer hurt him. Touching his tongue gingerly against the place where the afflicting tooth had been, he felt only a swollen mass of tissue, numb and stupid, it seemed to him. He had tried, Lord, how he had tried to break through the pain and confusion of his life to something like clarity and control, and it had come to this—this dumb helplessness, this woeful thickened shameful inadequacy. At bottom, he knew, there was love in his heart—love for Jill that was as coherent and pure as algebra, and maybe even love for Margie too, and love for Ma, poor Ma, who was dead now and gone from him forever, and love for Lillian, in spite of everything: love for *women*—but try as he might, he could not arrange his life so that he could act on that love. There were all these other dark hateful feelings that kept getting in the way, his rage and his fear and his feelings of pure distress. If somehow, with one wild bearish swing of his arm, he could sweep all that away, then at last, he was sure, he would be free to love his daughter. At last he could be a good father, husband, son and brother. He could become a good man. That was all he wanted, for God's sake. To be a good man. He imagined goodness as a state that gave a man power and clarity in every conscious moment of his daily life. Slowly, he descended the steps and got into the truck and started the motor. He backed it out and drove west on Clinton Street, to pick up his daughter.

On the ground between the yellowed grass and the leafless forsythia bushes by the sidewalk, slubs of porous snow shrank slowly below the late morning sun. Wade parked the truck next to the curb, got out and walked up the front path to the door of the house, a charcoal-gray split-level with pink shutters, and rang the bell. He heard the chimes inside, the first four notes of "Frère Jacques," and the clicks of Lillian's high heels on hardwood as she approached the door.

She drew the door in and stood behind the glass storm door and gazed at him, expressionless and still, as if posing on the other side of the glass for her portrait, as if she were her portrait: tall and slender, wearing a pale-gray wool dress, silver-and-lapis bracelet and necklace, her chocolate-brown hair tied up behind her head, off her neck—and she looked intelligent as hell, Wade thought, like a schoolteacher, filled with information and judgments and opinions that he could never have.

How did she get this way? How did she get so damned smart, this Lillian Pittman of Lawford, New Hampshire? How did she end up in this nice house in Concord's west end, with shrubs and a neat lawn and a garage with an almost new Audi in it? That she had married Bob Horner, who sold insurance, did not explain it—that only explained the money, and lots of people Wade knew had as much money as Bob Horner, even people in Lawford. Bob Horner was not rich, and even if he were, it would not have made Lillian smart.

No, it was something else, something that had always been there, in her eyes, even when she was a girl and Wade had first fallen in love with her—and suddenly he realized that it was *why* he had fallen in love with her in the first place and why he had been so obsessed with her all those years: he had looked into her eyes way back then, when they were both high school kids, and he had seen her intelligence, the wonderful complexity of her awareness, and he had seen his own smart eyes looking back at him, and for a while he had felt intelligent too. Then, after a few years, because he no longer saw his own eyes looking back at him from hers, he had lost that belief in his own intelligence, and from then on, all he felt when he looked at her was stupid.

So it was not really a question of what had happened to her; it was a question of what had happened to him. How had *he* come to this? How was it that he, Wade Whitehouse of Lawford, New Hampshire, a man who had once been as intelligent and complexly aware as she and possibly even gifted, was standing like this on the stoop of his ex-wife's house, hat in hand, come begging for a visit with his child, a man wearing cheap mismatched clothes and driving a borrowed battered old stake-body truck, a man without a proper home to call his own, without a job, without any respect in the community, without a wife and with no one to care for but a drunken father who hated him and whom he hated—how had this sorry man come to be the adult version of the bright boy he had seen twenty-five years ago in Lillian Pittman's eyes?

Lillian's voice through the glass was muffled somewhat, but Wade heard her words well enough: "Wait there. She'll be right out." Then she closed the inner door, and Wade was looking at his reflection. It was Pop he saw looking back, twenty or thirty years ago, haunted and angry, kept outside the family of man, compelled to stand in the rain and cold and darkness alone, while the others sat around a fire inside; and because he was not there with them, they were unafraid and slung their arms over each other's shoulders and sang songs or whispered sweet secrets to one another, men and women and children full of good intentions and competence, people who were able to love one another cleanly. He, like his father before him, and like that man's father too, Wade's and my grandfather and our unknown great-grandfather as well, stood outside, hands buried in pockets, scowling furiously at the frozen ground, while everyone else stayed warm and loved one another.

All those solitary dumb angry men, Wade and Pop and his father and grandfather, had once been boys with intelligent eyes and brightly innocent mouths, unafraid and loving creatures eager to please and be pleased. What had turned them so quickly into the embittered brutes they had become? Were they all beaten by their fathers; was it really that simple?

There is no way of knowing about any of them but Wade. Pop was orphaned when he was ten and sent to live with an elderly aunt and uncle in Nova Scotia, and when he was fourteen he had run away, following the reapers west across Canada, chasing the harvest all the way from the Maritimes to British Columbia. When the crews had returned east, he had come back with them and had crossed down into New Hampshire to work in a paper mill in Berlin, and when he was twenty he married a Lawford girl, because he had got her pregnant. He took a job in the Littleton Coats mill, so she could stay near her family, he said, but also because she had a house, Uncle Elbourne's house, where they could live. Later, when we were children and Pop now and then spoke of his father, it was as if he were speaking of a distant relative who had died before he was born, and when he spoke of his mother it was as if she were a figure in an almost forgotten dream, an emblematic stand-in for someone who might once have been important to him. So it was as if he had no parents, no past, no childhood, even. His father had not even a name—Pop's father's and mother's graves were in Sydney, Nova Scotia, we were told: they had been killed one winter night when a kerosene stove exploded and their house burned down. That was the whole story.

As for Pop's grandfather and grandmother, there was nothing: they were as lost in history as if they had lived and died ten thousand years ago. Pop had sisters and brothers, we knew, although we did not know how many, and they, too, had been farmed out with Canadian relatives and friends, but he had never seen them again after the fire, for reasons he never explained. And we never thought to ask, did we? The children of a man like him and a woman whose only life was her secret unspoken life, we thought it was normal to be alone in the world, normal to have sisters and brothers and dead parents and grandparents that one never spoke of. And by the time we were old enough to understand that such a life was not normal at all, we were too angry and hurt to ask. It was unimaginable to us that we ask our father, "Why did you separate yourself forever from your family?"

The door swung open, and Wade looked up: Lillian held back the glass storm door and waved for Jill, who stood in the hall a short ways behind her, to come along. The child's face was sober, a little sad or possibly frightened, as if she were being sent away to summer camp. Lillian said to Wade, coldly, clipping her words, "Is there snow on the ground up there?"

"Yeah, lots."

"See," Lillian said to Jill, and she pointed down at the rubber boots on the child's feet. "Keep them on whenever you go out."

"Hi, honey," Wade said, and he extended one hand toward Jill. She was carrying a small overnight bag and wore mittens and a bright-blue down parka with the hood up.

"Hi," she said, and she passed Wade her suitcase and walked by him to the sidewalk, where she paused for a second at the rear of the truck, as if looking for his car, then stood beside the door on the passenger's side, waiting for him.

In a trembling voice, Lillian said to Wade, "Have her back here tomorrow by six. We have something to do at six."

"No problem. Look, I . . . ," he began, not sure what he wanted to say, only that he was sorry somehow, for something he could not name. What had he done? Why did he feel so guilty all of a sudden? An hour before, he was angry at her; now he wanted her forgiveness: he could not, for the life of him, connect the two emotions, rage and shame.

"You make me sick," she spat at him. Though her gaze was flinty, she seemed ready to burst into tears. "I can't believe you've sunk so low," she told him.

"As what? Low as what? I mean, what the hell have I done, Lillian? It's *bad* to want to see Jill? It's bad to want to see your own daughter?"

"You know what I'm talking about," she said. She suddenly pasted a smile onto her face and waved at Jill and called, "'Bye, honey! Call me tonight if you want!" Then her face filled with anger again, and her chin crinkled the way it used to when she was about to cry, and she said, "If I could have you killed, Wade Whitehouse, believe me, I would."

"For . . . for what? What did I do?"

"You know damned well for what. For what you've done to me, and what you're doing to that child you say you love so much. Love," she sneered. "You've never loved anyone in your life, Wade. Not even yourself. Whatever you once had, you've ruined it," she said, and she yanked the glass door closed, stepped back and slammed the inner door.

Slowly, Wade turned and walked down the path to the truck.

"Are we going in this?" Jill asked.

"Yeah. My car, it's in the shop. This'll be fine," he said.

"It's okay. It's pretty old."

"It belongs to Pop."

"Pop?"

"Grandpa. My father. It's his."

"Oh," she said, and she opened the door and climbed up onto the seat. Wade slung the suitcase in beside her and closed the door, walked around the front of the truck and got in and started the motor. Reaching in front of Jill, he switched on the heater, and the fan began to chirp loudly.

"You eat lunch yet?" he asked.

"No." She sat up straight and stared out the windshield.

"How about a Big Mac?" he said, winking.

"Mommy won't let me eat fast food. You know that," she said without looking at him. "It's bad for you."

"C'mon, we always sneak a Big Mac. And a cherry turnover. Your favorite. C'mon, what do you say?"

"No."

Wade sighed. "What do you want, then?"

"Nothing."

"Nothing. You can't have nothing, Jill. We need lunch. Mr. Pizza? Want to stop at Mr. Pizza's?"

"Same thing, Daddy. No fast food," she said emphatically. "Mommy says—"

"I *know* what Mommy says. I'm in charge today, though."

"*Okay.* So we'll get what you want. What do you want?" she said, continuing to look straight ahead.

Wade released the hand brake and pulled away from the curb. At the intersection at the end of the street, he stopped the truck and said, "Nothing, I guess. I guess I can wait till we get home, if you can. Maybe we'll stop by Wickham's for a hamburger when we get to Lawford. That suit you? You always like Wickham's."

"Okay," she said.

"Fine." He turned right and headed north on Pleasant Street, toward the interstate. They remained silent, as the old truck stuttered along the winding road. Then, after a few moments, Wade looked over at Jill and realized that she was crying. "Oh, Jesus, Jill, I'm sorry. What's the matter, honey?"

She turned her face away from him. Her shoulders heaved, and she held her head down. Her hands were clenched in fists shoved hard against her legs.

"I'm sorry," Wade repeated. "Please don't cry. Please, honey, don't cry."

"What are you sorry for?" she asked. She had gained control of herself, had managed to stop crying, and she wiped her cheeks with her sleeve and looked grimly ahead.

"I don't know. For the food business, I guess. I just thought, you know, we'd sneak a Big Mac on Mommy, like we used to."

"I don't like doing that anymore," she said.

"Okay. So we won't." He tried to sound cheerful. "Whatever Jillie wants," he said, using her baby name, "Jillie gets."

She was silent for a few seconds, and then she said, "I want to go home."

"You can't," Wade snapped back. His face stiffened, and he clenched the wheel with both hands, as they came to the Hopkinton interchange and drove up onto the turnpike. Soon he had the truck up to its top speed of fifty miles per hour, shaking and shuddering in protest. The wind blew in under the floorboards and fought the puffs of heat from the heater, chilling the air inside the truck. Jill curled up on the seat as far from her father as she could get and dropped into sleep, waking only when they stopped in West Lebanon for gas and for Wade to pee, and at the Catamount exit, where Wade picked up a six-pack of beer and a Coke at a roadside grocery. Jill declined the Coke with a shake of her head and watched while Wade, heading back up the ramp onto the interstate, cracked open a can of beer and took a long slug from it and stuck the can between his legs.

"That's illegal, you know," Jill said quietly.

"I know." Wade glanced over at her, saw that she was looking out the side window at the snow-covered fields and woods, and took a second pull from the beer.

"You're a policeman," she said without turning.

"Nope. Not anymore. I'm not nothing anymore."

"Oh," she said.

By the time they reached the Lawford exit, Wade had finished two cans of beer and was halfway through a third. The empties rolled back and forth on the floor, banging lightly against one another as the truck followed the curving ramp down to Route 29, turned left and chugged alongside the river into Lawford.

23

"WADE COME IN HERE LOOKING STRANGE, sort of like he always does—you know, with that kind of distracted nervous face he wears all the time, only worse this time, like he was a little drunk, maybe. Which was not unusual, even though it was only a little after lunchtime. The place was still pretty busy, it being the next to last day of deer season and all these Massachusetts assholes who hadn't got their deer yet up for one last crack at shooting a goddamned cow or a paperboy on a bike and hoping it was a deer—that happened, you know: couple years ago, some individual shot a kid on a bike delivering papers over near Catamount. Astounding.

"Anyhow, Wade was looking peculiar, you might say, like he hadn't gotten any sleep for a few nights, big humongous circles under his eyes; only he was all dressed up, like he was going to a funeral, coat and tie and all; and he had his kid with him, this nice little kid, I seen her lots of times, what's-her-name, Jillie: he goes, 'Jillie, you want a cheese grilled sandwich? You want a cheese grilled sandwich?' he says. He always says it that way, 'cheese grilled sandwich,' and normally I just leave the guy alone—what the hell, everybody talks funny sometimes. Only this time I have to correct him, I guess as a kind of joke. 'It's grilled cheese sandwich, you dub,' I tell him, because I was pissed he made such a big deal out of my sign a few weeks before just when I was putting the damned thing up. The sonofabitch cost me a hundred and fifty bucks and it come out wrong and Wade seen it and pointed it out to me in what you might say was an aggressive way.

"So I go, 'It's grilled cheese sandwich, you dub,' friendly, sort of, but like I said, pissed a little—probably mostly because we were busy as hell right then and Margie, as you know, had taken the day off at my suggestion for very good reasons, which you can use my story to illustrate the wisdom of my recommendation, because the sonofabitch reaches across the counter and grabs me by the shirtfront. He's sitting there on a stool, you know, right where you are, or a few stools down—I don't recall that exactly; and his kid is sitting next to him, looking bored like kids do—until this happens, of course, which is when all hell breaks loose. Wade looks up at me with his face suddenly gone red, and he just grabs my shirt, like this."

And here Nick Wickham reached across the counter and grasped my shirtfront and yanked, hard. Slowly, he let go and went on. I sat back, my legs suddenly watery.

"Everybody in the place goes silent. What the hell, this is unusual, right? This is really un-usual. And the little kid—I mean, she's just a kid, you know, a goddamned urchin, and she's naturally terrified. Her face goes all white, and she starts to cry, so Wade lets go of me—and listen, I was plenty scared myself, not to mention ticked off. I figure, the place is full of guys, so Wade can't do too much damage, but just the same, I'm a goddamned marshmallow; I don't need that kind of stuff, especially not in my restaurant. Guys come in drunk and start trouble, I sweet-talk them right out the door: let them settle it in the parking lot. Wade, though, there was no sweet-talking that guy that day. It's like he had this glaze over his eyes, like he couldn't see out right, and you couldn't see in at all; when the kid starts to cry, he looks over at her, surprised and puz-zled, like he's this gorilla, some kind of King Kong who hears a strange musical sound off to his side just as he's about to bite off the head of some guy; he lets go of me, acts like he was only hanging up his coat or something instead of physically attack-ing a fellow human being. Very strange. Very strange and weird. Of course I knew already about LaRiviere firing him, and I knew about Jack replacing him as town cop and all—everybody knew about it by then—but just the same, it was very strange, the way he was acting.

"He makes like he's comforting his kid: wipes her nose with a napkin, that sort of thing—like a regular loving father and nothing's happened; and she says she wants to go home. He got up, stiff—like she slapped him and he's holding back his impulse to slap her back because she's a kid—and he goes, 'Okay, let's go home, then.' Now this worries me more than a little, because I happen to know that Margie's out there at the house this very minute packing up and moving the hell out, like I told her to do. I mean, I know the individuals we're talking about here are your father and your brother, but—no offense—I was plenty worried about Margie living up there on the hill with those two acting the way they were. You can understand that. You would have done the same thing, probably: told her to move the hell out, I mean.

"So I say to him, 'Wade, I got a message for you.' He goes, 'A message.' Like it's in a foreign language. I say, 'Jack Hewitt, he's looking for you. Wants you to clear your stuff out of his office down to the town hall.' I do this real careful, standing back there, way the hell over by the coffee machine, so he can't reach me. Like I say, I'm a real marshmallow, and this guy is a hand grenade with the goddamned pin pulled; but I figure Jack can handle him all right, and most importantly, I don't want Wade to catch Margie moving out on him. She's a hell of a sweet woman, as you no doubt know by now. Heart as big as a house. So I tell Wade about Jack wanting him to clear his stuff out—which happened to be true. Jack was in that morning early. He had his license back, and there was only one more day for him to get his deer, so he was heading out; and Jack, he says to me, 'If you see Wade, tell him to get his shit out of my office,' was how he put it. I put it to Wade somewhat more politely, let us say. Although I did make the mistake of calling it 'his' office. Jack's.

"Wade picked right up on that. My mistake. I didn't realize—or I might not have said it—but at that particular time he had not yet been informed about Jack being the new town cop: which of course was Gordon LaRiviere's doing, him and Chub Merritt, the selectmen. Wade says to me, '*His* office. You mean my old office?' And what can I say? I tell him what he surely does not want to hear. He looks at me for a second like his stack is going to blow, and then he grabs his kid's hand and heads out the door—and I'm thinking, 'Oh boy, more trouble.' I didn't have any idea how much more, of course. But that was the last time I saw Wade Whitehouse. Ever. And I can't say I've missed him. No offense, him being your brother and all, but I expect you don't particularly miss the individual, either."

It was a question more than a statement, and I did not intend to answer it. Actually, I did not know how to answer it, without lying to the man. I switched off the tape recorder and reached for my check, which Nick had placed next to my coffee cup.

"Actually, yes, I did see him that day. Not to talk to. But I saw him from my driveway, as he passed by the house. I was filling the bird feeders in my front yard, and I looked up as he drove by, because of all the noise that old truck of his father's made. He had my grandniece in the truck with him—Jill—so naturally I noticed. And I always thought well of Wade, in spite of everything. He suffered. He had a terrible time growing up. And I never thought that Lillian was particularly good for him, although I loved Lillian and still do. She's my niece, after all. But that Saturday, when Wade and Jill drove past, there was nothing unusual—really, nothing worth commenting on."

"Well, sure, I was scared of him. Of *course* I was scared of him. Who wouldn't be? But it was like a long time ago, and I don't remember a lot. I remember Daddy took me out of the restaurant there, and we went down to his office. Big deal. Well, I know, it *was* a big deal—that's where he got the gun; he took his guns from his office. It *used* to be his office, I mean—which made him really mad. I didn't say anything anymore—once we left the restaurant, I mean. I guess I was too scared.

"He seemed sort of okay; I mean, I guess he was acting the way he usually did. Except when he got so mad at the guy in the restaurant that I thought there would be a fight. I mean, usually when I came up to stay with him, he was sort of nervous and wicked grouchy one minute and really nice the next, and that's how he was acting that day when we drove up in that really old truck. It was his father's truck. Sorry, I guess you know that. Then at the restaurant he lost his temper, and I *really* got scared. But then he calmed down a little, I guess because I started crying and all, and probably because everyone was looking at us; and then the restaurant guy told him about having to clean out his office or something like that; and then he lost his temper again; but this time he didn't do anything to the restaurant guy. He just grabbed me by the arm and we left, and then we went to his office. And that's it. Nothing happened."

"Nothing happened?" I asked. I looked across the room to her mother, and she frowned at me. We were sitting in her living room, Jill and I next to one another on the sofa, Lillian on an easy chair and Bob Horner standing behind her. After numerous pleas and lengthy negotiations, they had agreed to let me talk to Jill, but there were rules, Lillian told me. "The child has been through enough. Her doctor says that it's important for her to talk about these things, about her father, but only at her own rate, in her own way." I was free to ask her what she remembered of that day, but when she no longer wished to talk about it, I was to back off.

"Well, nothing *important* happened. I mean, he just put some stuff from his desk into a box and took his guns down from the thing on the wall—the gunrack; and we left. In fact, he was pretty calmed down by then. He wasn't smiling or anything: he was probably pretty bummed out by getting fired and all; but he was calm. Not like back in the restaurant. And later."

"Later?" I said. "You mean, at the house, with Margie?"

Jill looked over at her mother and said, "I *really* don't feel like talking about this stuff, Mom." She was almost twelve at this time, tall for her age, but thin and awkward-looking. She sat calmly, almost placidly, wearing jeans and a bulky white cable-knit sweater, with her hands clasped together in her lap. It was clear that she would soon be a very attractive young woman, attractive in the same way her mother must have been and in fact still was—swift-moving, graceful, in control.

Horner cleared his throat pointedly, and when I looked at him, he shook his head a fraction of an inch. I stood up. "Well, Jill, I surely do thank you for being willing to see me and talk to me as much as you have. I know that it is not easy . . . ," I said, and I heard Horner clear his throat again. I put out my hand, and Jill took it in hers and shook it lightly. I did not know what else to say, so I said nothing. I believe that I wanted to hug her, to hold the girl tightly, like an uncle, but I knew that

I could not do that. Wade had made it impossible for me to be his daughter's uncle. So I turned and nodded to her mother and stepfather. "I'll let myself out," I said, and walked to the door alone.

"I seen the cocksucker just once that day, when he come into the garage looking to pick up his car; only, Chub told me not to give it to him without him paying the bill first—which was close to three hundred bucks. He was pissed, tossed a shit fit right there in the garage, so I just muckled onto a fucking Stillson wrench and showed the sucker to him. I put the sonofabitch right up in his face like that, and he backed the fuck off. I don't take that shit from nobody. Nobody. He give me a bunch of shit about how we used to be asshole buddies and all—which has not got a fucking grain of truth in it. Wade Whitehouse never liked me, and I never liked him, the cocksucker. Piss on him. Ever since I was a fucking kid, he's had it in for me, always trying to put my ass in a sling—which he could do a little bit easier when he was the fucking town cop; but now that he was just another John Q. Citizen, I was ready for the fucker. He caught me a few years ago, when he first got appointed town cop; he grabbed me swiping pumpkins one Halloween from Alma Pittman's; I was maybe sixteen, seventeen, and he hit on me hard and told everybody I was a fucking Peeping Tom—that kind of creepy shit, which was ridiculous, fucking ridiculous. I can get laid anytime I fucking want to— which is not something Wade Whitehouse could ever say for himself—so why the hell would I go around peeping into some old broad's window for? You ask me, *he* was the one doing the peeping, and that's probably how he caught me swiping her pumpkins—which is just something kids around here do, you understand. On Halloween, I mean. What the hell, you grew up here: you understand. Anyhow, when he seen the fucking Stillson waving in his face, he backed off a ways and lit out down the road, toward Golden's, as I recall, where I saw him pull in—he was driving his old man's truck, I remember, and he had his kid with him. She stayed in the truck the whole time. That was the only time I dealt with the fucker that day. I should've split his fucking skull when I had the chance. I don't give a shit he is your brother—you know I'm right. I don't even give a shit you got it on tape: I didn't do anything illegal."

"Wade pulled up in front of the store in that shitbox of his father's, and I thought, Well, well, well, here comes today's problem. I thought it because he headed straight up the stairs to Hettie's apartment. Sent his kid, the little girl, into the store ahead of him with a dollar bill in her hand.

"She poked around in the cooler, looking for a bottle of tonic. Said she wanted one of those all-natural drinks—and who the hell carries that kind of shit up here? So she got a carton of milk and was standing there by the cookies, studying the goddamned labels. Checking out the ingredients, like a Goody Two-shoes. And though I feel sorry for the kid—what the hell, who wouldn't?—she still struck me as a whole lot like her mother. Who, if you ask me, is not the most likable person I've ever met.

"Meanwhile, Wade must've found out that Hettie wasn't home. Which he could have found out by asking me, of course. But he wouldn't do that. Although he sure was not making any particular secret out of his checking for her at her apartment upstairs. What with his daughter right there and me knowing who comes and goes up those stairs. Something I'd sometimes just as soon not know, frankly. This being one of those times.

"Then, like he was covering for himself, he came down the stairs and into the store and asked me did I know if Jack Hewitt had got his deer yet. And I said no, Jack Hewitt did not get his deer yet. Which I happened to know was true, since I have to tag every deer shot in this township, my store being the only official tagging station, and Jack would've had to bring his deer in for tagging. So, 'No,' I said, 'Jack did not get his deer yet.'

"Then Wade asked me did I happen to know where Jack Hewitt was hunting. Like I was supposed to believe he had stopped off at Hettie's to find out where Jack was. Sure, you believe that and I'll tell you another one, I thought to myself.

"So I told him. Not that I knew exactly. But Jack had stopped by early and picked up a box of shells, and we had exchanged a few words. Mostly about his being the new town cop and getting his license back and all. Which frankly I thought was good for the town, knowing what I knew then about Wade Whitehouse and what I know now. Anyhow, Jack had mentioned he was going up to Parker Mountain, where he had spotted a huge buck that we both knew had not been shot yet. Since the biggest buck that had come in so far was only a hundred-and-fifty-pound ten-pointer. Not your monster buck.

"So that's more or less what I told Wade. 'Jack's up on Parker Mountain somewhere,' I told him. That and nothing more exact than that, because I didn't know anything more exact than that. And I only told him as much as I did because he asked, and I figured he asked only because he was trying to make it look like he had legitimate business with Hettie. When he did not have legitimate business with Hettie. Actually, it figured that the one person in town Wade would want to avoid would be Jack Hewitt. So I didn't see anything wrong in telling him where Jack was. Anyhow, he said thanks, and the kid paid me for the milk and left without finding any cookies that met her standards. Not that I particularly gave a damn."

"I hurried—oh, Lord, I was frantic hurrying trying to get out of there before he came back. I was just tossing my clothes and things every which way into suitcases and plastic bags and boxes and stuffing them into my car trunk and the back seat; I felt guilty—leaving like that, without telling him or explaining anything; of course I felt guilty; but I figured I could explain later, and I also thought that maybe once it was done, once I was gone from the house, he wouldn't mind so much. It was the actual leaving, doing it in his face, that I figured would bother him the most; I was sure it would make him crazy—crazier, actually, because he was already pretty crazy, you know that; that was why I was leaving in the first place. I don't think he wanted me around, but I was afraid that he would literally come apart if he thought I was abandoning him, and that's why I was trying to get out of there before he came back with Jill, which I had learned from Nick, who had called me out at the house as soon as Wade left the restaurant. Well, it's more complicated than that. But you understand. It had to do with Pop too, I have to admit—or, more accurately, it had to do with the combination of Wade and Pop in that house: they were both getting worse, and so far as I could see, it was because of each other. Pop mostly sat in front of the TV set in the living room watching wrestling; once in a while he opened up a new bottle of booze, which he drank from until he got drunk enough to start talking cracked; and about then Wade usually showed up, or for the first time would start to act like Pop was in the room—having ignored the man up till that point: and then the two of them would go at it hammer and tong. That was no place for a woman. Not with Wade chasing people through the woods and cracking up his boss's truck like that, it wasn't. His obsession with that stupid hunting accident of Jack's: it was like he thought it explained *everything*, but in order to do so, it had to practically be invented all over from the beginning—by him! And the *wildness* he was displaying, like the way he pulled his own tooth out with pliers, which practically made me sick when he told me that's what he had done, although I had already figured it out for myself, thank you, when I found the bloody tooth and pliers on the bathroom sink. Well, you know how he was acting: you were in touch with him then. But you didn't *see* it. Except for the day of Ma's funeral, you were never here to see it and deal with him and Pop up close on a day-to-day basis. I guess I'm saying this because I feel guilty, guilty for leaving him right then, abandoning him, actually, when he had been fired from his job and fired from being the town cop, which was a very important position to him, never mind how he himself described the position; I feel guilty for leaving him alone up there in the house when he was so upset, so beaten down by his life, which he blamed mostly on his father, as you know; I feel guilty because I left him when he was feeling so frustrated by that stupid court case, that custody suit he was trying to bring against Lillian—although I did not at that time know what you told me about that: about how his lawyer had advised him to drop the case, so he still felt dependent on Lillian in order to see his own child—not that I thought he was an especially fit father at that time, believe me.

"So there I was, with most of my stuff packed and my car almost filled to the gills, when Wade drives up with Jill. Too late to hide, I figured, so I just stood there, with the trunk and the car doors wide open, and he drove past, looking out the window at the car full of my stuff, not making any sign of recognition, and drove the truck into the barn and parked it. Then he and Jill came walking back along the driveway from the barn to the front where I was—Jill lagging behind and lugging her little suitcase, looking forlorn—and I thought, Oh, Lord, what that child's been through; and I forgot all about getting out of there right then and leaving that child alone with those two men, one of them drunk and crazy and the other probably on his way to drunk and crazy—although I did not at that moment think either of them was particularly dangerous, which is why I decided that I should stay at the house for another night and day, or at least as long as Jill was there. So when Wade came up to me and looked over the items I had packed into the car, boxes and suitcases and plastic bags full of my things, and said, 'Going somewhere, Margie?' I tried to lie. Not only because I was leaving him right then, but also because I had changed my mind, due to seeing Jill. It was a stupid thing to do, I know: it was obvious what I was up to; but I was suddenly divided in my emotions between wanting to leave and wanting to stay, and I had not anticipated feeling that way, which is really probably the stupid part. But you get caught in these things: you make one small decision, and pretty soon you're stuck with a bunch of other decisions that you're not so sure of, and then you act stupid. So I lied to Wade and tried to tell him that I was taking a bunch of things to the church rummage sale and a bunch more to the cleaners and laundromat in Catamount, it being Saturday. And of course it didn't work; he saw right through me. He said, 'Don't lie to me. You're leaving me, I can see that.' I tried to change the subject and said for him not to be silly, or something light like that, and said hi to Jill, who smiled—or tried to smile—looking pathetic and miserable in spite of it—or because of it.

"I have no particular talent for deception, and that's why I'm easily fooled—unless I'm just not very smart, since most people who are smart are good at deceiving people and are hard to fool. Gordon LaRiviere, for example. But Wade—no. He was more like me than like Gordon LaRiviere, say, or Nick Wickham, who is sweet but full of it—which is why I think I was first attracted to Wade, back when he was still married to Lillian: I know you know all about it; Wade told me that he once confessed about it to you, our little extramarital fling (or whatever you want to call it—it didn't last very long, at any rate, and we both felt plenty guilty for it). But he was a man I never tried to lie to, and I don't think he ever tried to lie to me; he kept some things to himself, naturally, and I did too, but that was different, wasn't it? What am I trying to say? I guess I'm trying to say how sad I was that afternoon when Wade drove up with Jill and I tried to lie to him about moving out of the house; it suddenly hit me that what we once had was gone and could never return; I had finally learned how to be afraid of Wade, and the only way I could think of protecting myself was to lie to him. And because I was so bad at it, so inept, I only made things worse; I stirred up the situation and found myself having to protect myself against him even more than before I had lied; and I wasn't even able to make myself believable enough to protect anyone else from him. Meaning Jill. I realized that it was a lost cause, me and Wade, and that probably I would never again be with a man I did not have to lie to, as I had once been with Wade. And so I started to cry. Standing there beside my car in front of that old farmhouse, with the sun glaring off the snow, and Wade in front of me and his daughter watching—I started to cry. Like a baby. I actually bawled. I can hardly believe it now, but it's the truth: I started to bawl.

"Things got somewhat confused then—or I should say my memory of things gets somewhat confused: I know Wade tried to stop me from crying by putting his arms around me; he reached forward and drew me to him and patted my back; it was a gentle gesture meant to comfort me, although I remember the expression on his face as he came toward me—like a terrible sadness had come over him, a sadness greater even than my own: so that he must have been trying to join me in sadness but was unable to cry himself because he was a man, which resulted in his placing his arms around me and patting my back, as if I were a child. And that made me feel even lonelier than before he had tried to hold me. And so I pushed him away. I told him to leave me *alone*—I said it like that, with terrific emphasis, like he was doing something unpleasant to me: 'Leave me *alone!*' Then Jill must have gotten frightened, because she started to hit Wade on the back and arms, yelling at him to leave me alone: 'Leave her alone! Leave her alone!' I was weeping and shoving him away, and Jill was screaming at him and hitting him with her fists, and he moved like a bear then, covering his face with his arms and backing away in the snow. Jill kept after him; she was hysterical; she had him stumbling backwards into the snow. I went after them, and as I reached out to hold Jill off, Wade swung his arms wide and hit her, and she went flying backwards into me. Her nose was bleeding; he had caught her across the mouth and nose; she stood behind me and wailed. We did not say a word, Wade and I. I slowly backed away, facing him, but with my arms held behind me touching Jill, guiding her toward the car. He looked at me stunned, like someone had hit him on the head with a rock. I've never seen anyone with that painful and bewildered a look on his face: his mouth hung open, his eyes were wild, his arms draped down at his sides. I watched him like he was a beast about to attack us, and I half turned and managed to move my avocado plant off the front seat to the floor and got Jill inside the car and closed the door—with the lock down: I remember that, locking the door as I closed it. Then I edged my way around the back of the car and slammed the trunk lid down and got in on the driver's side. And still, no one said a word. I locked my door. I started the car and backed it out of the driveway, and Jill and I drove away, without once looking back. No, that's not right. When I had the car on the road and aimed toward town, I looked over at the house: Wade stood there in the same spot in the snow beside the driveway, staring down at the snow, probably at the spots of blood from Jill's nose, although I don't really know that, but he stood staring down at the snow like he could not believe what he saw there, his fingers in his mouth, like a little boy, and up on the porch, I saw that Pop had come out—maybe he had been there all along and had seen everything—and he stood there looking at Wade with a smile on his face, like a devil. It was horrible to see that, and I wish I hadn't looked, and I hope that Jill did not see that. When I glanced over at her, she had her eyes closed, and she said in a calm voice that surprised me, 'I want to go home. Will you take me home?' I said yes, I would, and I did. And I guess you know the rest."

24

"YOU KNOW THE REST," she said. But did I? I suppose that if there were anyone on this planet, other than Wade himself, who knew the rest, knew what happened in the remaining few hours of that cold bright Saturday afternoon in November, it would be me. Especially now, after these several years of meditating, investigating, remembering, imagining and dreaming the subject.

The historical facts, of course, are known by everyone—all of Lawford, all of New Hampshire, even most of Massachusetts: anyone who knew any of the principals or happened to read the Sunday papers or watch the news on television knew the facts. But facts do not make history; facts do not even make events. Without meaning attached, and without understanding of causes and connections, a fact is an isolate particle of experience, is reflected light without a source, planet with no sun, star without constellation, constellation beyond galaxy, galaxy outside the universe—fact is nothing.

Nonetheless, the facts of a life, even one as lonely and alienated as Wade's, surely have meaning. But only if that life is portrayed, only if it can be viewed, in terms of its connections to other lives: only if one regards it as having a soul, as the body has a soul—remembering that without a soul, the human body, too, is a mere fact, a pile of minerals, a bag of waters: body is nothing. So that, in turn, if one regards the soul of the body as a blood-red membrane, let us say, a curling helix of anxiously fragile tissue that connects all the disparate name-able parts of the body to one another, a scarlet firmament between the firmaments, touching and defining both, one might view the soul of Wade's or any other life as that part of it which is connected to other lives. And one might grow angry and be struck with grief at the sight of those connections being severed, of that membrane being torn, shredded, rent to rags that a child grows into adulthood clinging to—little bloody flags waved vainly across vast chasms.

Oh, I know that in telling Wade's story here I am telling my own as well, and that this telling is my own bloody flag, the shred of my own soul waving in the wintry dusk, and it might sound self-centered, peculiar, eccentric for that; but our sto-ries, Wade's and mine, describe the lives of boys and men for thousands of years, boys who were beaten by their fathers, whose capacity for love and trust was crippled almost at birth and whose best hope for a connection to other human beings lay in elaborating for themselves an elegiac mode of related-ness, as if everyone's life were already over. It is how we keep from destroying in our turn our own children and terrorizing the women who have the misfortune to love us; it is how we absent ourselves from the tradition of male violence; it is how we decline the seductive role of avenging angel: we grimly accept the restraints of nothingness—of disconnection, isola-tion and exile—and cast them in a cruel and elegiac evening light, a Teutonic village in the mountains surrounded by deep dark forests where hairy beasts wait for stragglers and deer thrash wild-eyed through the deep snow and hunters build small fires to warm their hands so as to handle their weapons gracefully in the cold.

Wade's life, then, and mine, too, is a paradigm, ancient and ongoing, and thus, yes, I do know the rest, as Margie said, and I will tell it to you.

Against the sound of the wind cutting through the pines, Wade heard laughter, a harsh cackle that at first he thought came from the crows, *Haw, haw, haw!* but then he realized that it was human, and when he looked up from the blood-spattered snow, he saw Pop standing on the porch—shirt loose and unbuttoned, trousers drooping, suspenders looped to his knees; he was unshaven, hair tousled, eyes ablaze and face bright red and, although grinning, held tight as a fist: as in triumph—a triumphant athlete, warrior, thief, a man who had come through harrowing adversity and risk with his bitterness not only intact but confirmed, for it was the bitterness that had got him through, and the grin and the crackled laughter was for the confirmation, a defiant thanksgiving gloat. The son finally had turned out to be a man just like the father. Ah, what a delicious moment for the lonely long-suffering father! Gunfire rattled the air in the distance. He waved the whiskey bottle at Wade, then turned it and held the bottle by the base with both hands and pointed it at him—a primitive masculine act, this affectionate mockery of aiming a weapon at a beloved son, this bitter tease: as if to say, *You! By God, you finally made it! And you did it the way I taught you! I love you, you mean sonofabitch!*

With a swipe, Wade waved the image away, turned and trudged from the trampled snow onto the driveway, and moved, head down, hands in his jacket pockets, toward the barn. He heard Pop hollering behind him, words mixed in the wind, loud broken demands: *Where the hell are you going now? You leave my truck where it is! I need . . . Give me the goddamned keys! I need to go to town!* Wade pushed on, and the voice thinned and diminished. *Nothing in the stinking house to drink . . . my house, my money, my truck . . . stolen!* The words evaporated in the darkness of the barn; a pair of crows lifted from a crossbeam at the back and fluttered clumsily out the open roof to the sky; the truck motor ticked quietly as a clock, still cooling from the long drive north. Wade placed his chilled hands on the hood and warmed them against the flaked metal. He leaned forward as if to pray and placed his right cheek between his hands and felt the last wave of heat from the motor pass through the metal and enter his face. After a few moments, the metal went cold and began to draw heat back from his cheek, and Wade sighed and straightened and moved to the truckbed, where he lifted out two cardboard boxes, the contents of his desk and office closet, and set them on the ground next to the rear tire. Moving slowly and with scrupulous care, like an old man on ice, he opened the door on the driver's side and reached for the three guns that he had carried back from town side by side, the butts on the floor of the cab, the blue-black barrels leaning against the seat between him and Jill: a 12-gauge shotgun, a .30/30 rifle and an old Belgian 28-gauge that had once belonged to brother Elbourne. He lined them up and gathered them together like oars, with the stocks slung under his arm, and backed out of the cab, when he felt a sharp blow in the center of his back, a stunning blow that shook him through to his chest and arms and sent the guns clattering to the ground and threw Wade against the open door of the truck.

He crumpled and fell to his knees and turned. His father stood over him, a chunk of rusted iron pipe the length and thickness of a man's arm in his hands: the man was huge, an enraged giant from a fairy tale with legs like tree trunks, and above his enormous chest and shoulders filled and made solid with calibrated rage his head nearly touching the rafters of the barn was so far in the distance that though Wade could barely make out the expression on the face he saw that there was no expression other than one of mild disgust in the mouth and eyes of a man compelled to perform a not especially pleasant task, the decision to do it having been made long ago in forgotten time by a forgotten master, the piece of iron pipe in his meaty hands a mighty war club, a basher, an avenging jawbone of an ass, a cudgel, bludgeon, armor-breaking mace, tomahawk, pike, maul, lifted slowly, raised like a guillotine blade, sledgehammer, wooden mallet to pound a circus tent stake into the ground, to slam the gong that tests a man's strength, to split the log for a house, to drive the spike into the tie with one stroke, to stun the ox, to break the lump of stone, to smash the serpent's head, to destroy the abomination in the face of the Lord.

Wade crouched and twisted away from the colossal figure of his father; he turned like a heretic prepared for stoning; he saw and in one motion grabbed and clutched the rifle barrel with both hands and with the weight and force of his entire body uncoiling behind it swung the thing—the heavy wooden stock sweeping in a quick powerful arc from the frozen ground into the air—and smashed it against the side of his father's head, whacked and broke it from jaw to temple: the crack of bone, a puff of air and a groan, *Oh!* and the old man fell in pieces and died at once, eyes wide open—a leathered corpse unearthed from a bog.

Wade looked down at the body of his father: it was small, curled in on itself, the size and shape of the body of a sleeping child. There was no chunk of old pipe, no cudgel—only an empty whiskey bottle dropped to the hard ground and rolled against the wall. Wade lifted the rifle slowly and slipped the butt against his right shoulder; he aimed down the barrel at the exact center of his father's forehead. *I love you, you mean sonofabitch. I have always loved you.* He shoved the bolt forward and back and with his thumb flipped the safety, and he squeezed the trigger and heard the dry click when the hammer fell. He smiled. A wintry smile, ice cracking. Then he lowered the rifle, leaned down and touched the man's crinkled throat with his fingertips; he caressed the lips and grizzled chin and cheeks, touched the small hooked beak of the nose; he traced the bony ridge above the eyes and smoothed back the stiff gray hair. The body was an accumulation of separated parts. Its soul was dead, murdered, gone to absolute elsewhere. He had never touched his father this way, had not once in his entire life identified his father with his hands, named the man's face gently, lovingly, and taken it into him, made it his own face. Made the dead face his.

He stood and leaned the rifle against the fender of the truck. For a few seconds he peered around the barn as if bewildered to find himself there; then abruptly he reached down and slipped his hands under his father's body and with grace and ease lifted it; he carried it to the back of the dark enclosed space and laid the corpse out on the workbench. He crossed the hands on the chest. Returning to the truck, he went directly to one of the cardboard cartons and pulled out a small green box and removed a handful of rifle shells from it and dropped them into his jacket pocket. He grabbed up the rifle, got into the truck; he started the motor and backed the vehicle out of the barn into the blinding sunlight. Then, leaving the motor running, he got out of the truck and returned to the barn.

Groping in the darkness beneath the workbench, he retrieved the kerosene lantern. He stood over his father's body like a priest blessing the host, unscrewed the cap on the base of the lamp and poured the kerosene over the body, from the shoes up along the torso and over the hands and face and hair, until the lamp was emptied. He moved to the end of the bench and looked up along the body from the feet. He had his cigarette lighter in his hand: he ignited it and extended it forward slowly, holding it before him like a votive candle, and instantly the body was wrapped in a shroud of yellow flames. Wade stumbled backward a few steps and watched the clothing catch fire and the hair and skin glow like gold inside the blue-and-yellow flames: the fire snaked across the oil-stained bench and leapt to the old boards behind it, growling and snapping, and the air darkened with the smoke and filled with the dry sour smell of burning flesh. The back wall of the barn was now burning, with the bench and the body on it a pyre, the flames fed by the wind blowing from behind him—the heat surging in huge noisy waves against his face, forcing him back step by step, closer and closer to the door. And then suddenly Wade was outside the barn, standing in the light, surrounded by fields of glistening snow and the black trees beyond, and above him, endless miles of blue sky, and the sun—a flattened disk, cold and white as infinity.

Wade drove the truck south on Parker Mountain Road, uphill and away from town, out of the valley and away from the darkened old house and the burning barn, drove not fast but at a deliberate speed—to all appearances a man on a civilized mission, wearing a rumpled sport coat and shirt and loosened tie, his face calm, thoughtful, kindly looking, as if he were remembering and humming to himself an old favorite tune.

Wade came over the rise, passed the frozen snow-covered muskeg and pulled in and parked behind Jack Hewitt's Ford pickup on the left. Up the slope to the right, at the edge of the woods, was LaRiviere's cabin. Wade got out of the truck and reached in behind him and brought the .30/30 out and slipped the six shells from his pocket into the clip. He chambered the first bullet and checked the safety. There were no tracks leading from the road to the cabin and no smoke from the chimney. Jack's footprints in the snow went directly from his truck to the old lumber trail, then headed downhill through low scrub and brush in a northeasterly direction.

The deer had long since moved into the deepest woods, far from the roads and houses, beyond the sound of the cars and pickups that still prowled the backwoods lanes and trails and the growl of ten-wheelers changing gears on the long slow rise of the interstate north of Catamount. Alone and in occasional pairs, the animals lay hidden, wide-eyed, ears tensed, motionless in dense stands of mountain ash and tangled knots of hawthorn and alder tucked into cirques and gullies, nearly invisible hollows located below scrabbled cliffs and scree, places too difficult to reach from the road in half a day. The deer lay in alerted peace from dawn to dusk, alarmed and quivering in fear only now and then, when the crack of a rifle shot and its echo drifted uphill on the wind, all the way from the more accessible valleys and overgrown fields below, where a few cold end-of-season hunters walking back from the woods toward their cars in the last remaining hour before sunset grumpily, almost randomly, fired their guns at hallucinated stragglers—an unexpected shadow in a birch grove and a mossy boulder browned in a patch of late afternoon sunlight and a sudden powdery spill of snow tipped from the branch of a pine by an errant breeze.

Though it was cold enough for Wade's breath to stream from his mouth in a visible cloud, he did not seem to notice the freezing air up here on the mountain, in spite of his light clothing. His jacket was unbuttoned and flapped in the breeze, his tie was unknotted and lay back across his shoulder, and he held his rifle with bare exposed hands loosely in front of him, as if his body were generating ample heat from inside and he were on his way out to sentry duty. Every few steps, as he walked in from the road, he slipped on the rough snow-covered ground, but he seemed not to slow or hesitate a bit because of it and crossed recklessly along the crumpled edge of the frozen muskeg, moved through a spiky grove of silver birches and made his way clumsily in hard slick-soled shoes downhill to the dry riverbed below, a path of boulders and flat rocks that ran away from the road and LaRiviere's cabin toward a row of spruce trees that blocked his view of the long north slope of the mountain beyond. It was as if his body were being drawn by a powerful external force, like gravity or suction, and to keep from falling he moved in a loose deflected way, ricocheting and careening off rocks and stumps and trash wood, keeping his balance like a broken-field runner by letting his body bounce off the barriers that arose one after the other to stop it.

Way behind him, halfway between the mountaintop and

the town, the house remained dark, empty and closed up, and the barn went on burning. The fire had quickly spread up along the back wall to the timbers and into the lofts, igniting the ancient hay and then the remains of the roof. Great clouds of dark smoke billowed against the sky. There was a loud raucous music to the fire, a crackling erratic drumbeat against the steady howl of the wind from the cold air sucked off the snowy overgrown fields and yard surrounding the structure and hurled into the hot dark center. Flames licked across the timbers overhead, racing and leaping from dry roof boards and shakes that one by one let go and fell in scarlet-and-gold chunks to the dirt floor, where they shattered and splashed like coins. And in the roaring center of the inferno, as if carved from anthracite, lay the body of our father, his face a rictus yanked back in a fixed gaping grin. His terrible triumph.

At the line of spruce trees, Wade hesitated a moment, examining the ground. The snow below the trees was thinner than on the old riverbed, and patches of bare ground showed through; he had followed Jack's footprints this far with ease and now had to search among the rust-colored spruce needles and rocks for the trail. A layer of ash-gray cirrus clouds had moved in quickly from the north, and a sharp breeze had come up, riffling the spruces overhead as he walked slowly, carefully, along the edge of the grove.

And then he saw what he was looking for, a break between the trees, a low broken dead branch and a cigarette butt rubbed out with a boot, and he passed under the trees and came out on the other side, where there was the remains of an overgrown switchbacking lumber road. There was more snow here, and he spotted the footprints at once, leading downhill to the right. It was easy walking, and he moved quickly now, gradually descending for several hundred yards to where the long-unused road bent back on itself and crossed in the opposite direction.

He stopped at the bend and looked down along the slope, over the tops of the trees below—all the way to Lake Minuit in the far distance, white and flat in the dark surrounding forest like a frozen wafer, where he could make out, at the farther shore, a cluster of pastel-colored boxes that was the trailer park. Mountain View Trailer Park—when he lived there he had been able to peer out his kitchen window and see the very spot where he stood now: a pale opening below a dark streak made by the spruce trees, and beyond that the lumpy summit of the mountain itself.

The clouds had spread and nearly covered the entire sky, a taut gray blanket stretched from the northern horizon to the dip of Saddleback in the west; there was a long shrinking ribbon of blue sky behind him, but even the rounded top of the mountain was in shade now. Specks of snow flew in Wade's face and struck his hands and melted at once. He shifted the rifle, slipped the stock under his right arm and moved on.

Below, along Route 29 and the side roads off it and outside of town, the last hunters were emerging from the woods, giving up for another year their need to shoot and kill a deer. There may have been a lucky two or three hunters who managed in these waning hours of the season to sight a straggler, a confused or inexplicably careless buck that had managed to survive the hunt almost to the very end and then hungry and restless had stepped too soon from its hiding place in the last light, only to hear the explosion and feel the gut heat and swiftly die. But this late in the season these killings were rare. Most of the hunters now were out-of-state, inexperienced or inept and often merely lazy, so had counted on luck, coincidence, amusing ironies, to get their deer. They hurried to their cars and quickly got the heaters blowing and their stiff hands and feet warmed and drove straight into town to Wickham's or on to Toby's Inn for a whiskey or two before driving home.

Wade walked more slowly now, casting his gaze to his right, downhill, into the dense hardwoods—oak and maple trees, thick yellow birches and alder—that had replaced the spruce and hemlock above. He had to squint to see through the billowing snow: it came at him like lace curtains tossed by the wind and clung to his hair and clothing, wrapping him in a thin white caul. Occasionally, he stumbled on a rock in the old road or a fallen tree branch or slipped on the wet new snow, then lurched on, unperturbed, as if it had not happened and the road were smooth and dry.

Several hundred yards beyond the first switchback in the road, he came to the second bend, and the ground beyond the road fell away precipitously and for a great distance: an old mud slide had torn open a long slash of scree, dumping uprooted trees and glacial till into the deep gully below. Wade stopped abruptly and stood at the top and looked out over the rock-strewn gash and piles of brush and tangled tree trunks that filled the gully, downhill and across the tops of the hardwood trees beyond to the north, where the land dropped away for miles. The wind had momentum up here, where the road was exposed to nothing but sky, and was cold and drove the snow at him almost horizontally.

A mile and a half away and well out of sight behind the long narrow ridge that leaned against the mountain like a low buttress, the barn continued to burn, and a dark cloud of ashy smoke rose from the woods and blew away to the south— while, unheard and unseen from the mountainside, sirens howled and a pair of fire trucks and a dozen volunteer firemen in their own trucks and cars raced out along Parker Mountain Road from town. Where he stood, looking north, Wade could see—through the dip between Saddleback and the mountain—all the way into the valley to town, and although he could not see the town itself, he could easily make out the spire of the Congregational church and the roof of the town hall and the break in the trees, a dark meandering line, where the river ran through.

He examined his rifle, wiped the snow off it and sighted down the barrel into the gully, lifted it and aimed it toward the town for a few seconds. Then he smiled—an almost beatific smile, golden and warm and filled with understanding, as if a beam of celestial wisdom had entered his brain. He lowered the rifle, slipped the stock under his arm and walked down along the road a few yards to a grove of low pines, where he stepped out of the wind, leaned the gun against a tree, buttoned his jacket and pulled the collar up and put his hands into his pockets, as if for the first time he had felt the cold.

On his left, a precipice dropped off to piles of brush and tangled knots of roots and old dead trees cast there by the mud slide; in front of him the overgrown road descended smoothly to a birch grove in the distance; there it switched back a third time, running toward Wade again, but way below him, below the cliff and the gully and brush, and nonetheless visible to him: so that a man walking uphill, laboring in the cold wind and snow and the vague late afternoon light, especially a man wearing scarlet or bright-orange hunting clothes, would be visible for a long time before he was able to see the other man, who stood waiting for him among the pine trees.

Wade drew his cigarettes from his shirt pocket, looked at the pack for a second and, as if reconsidering, slipped it back.

348

He checked the safety on his rifle, brushed a few flecks of snow from the barrel and hefted it in his hands in a measured appraising way, then turned slightly and leaned his left shoulder and hip against the trunk of a pine tree. When Jack came into sight below—a red flash of cloth moving through the breaks between thigh-thick white birches—Wade lifted the rifle and sighted down the barrel at the bend in the road ahead of him, where Jack would have to turn and face him.

Jack had shot his deer, a huge buck, and he was dragging it out of the woods. He had tied the large gutted body of the animal onto a travois made from a pair of saplings lashed together and extending in a V over and beyond his shoulders. He hauled the deer slowly uphill, leaning forward in the blowing snow and sweating from the effort. His rifle—Evan Twombley's Winchester—was slung across his chest, and as he trudged up the snow-covered lumber trail the gun slapped rhythmically against him, and he stared steadily down at the slippery rough ground in front of him, as if lost in thought. Behind him, the travois bumped along, causing the deer's carcass to lurch back and forth; its head, overweighted by the large rack of horns, lolled back against the ground, bloody mouth agape, black tongue extruded, wide-open eyes opaque as onyx, and a thin broken trail of blood dribbled over the trampled snow behind.

When he rounded the bend in the trail, Jack looked up to see how far he still had to go, and he saw the man with the rifle and saw that he was aiming the rifle at the center of his chest; the man was no more than ten yards away and slightly uphill; Jack recognized him at once.

Epilogue

ALL THAT I HAVE DESCRIBED is supported by physical evidence: Wade's footprints in the snow leading from the road down into the woods, ending thirty feet from where Jack's body was found, then returning straightway to the road again; Pop's truck parked there by the road and Jack's truck gone but turning up three days later in a shopping mall parking lot in Toronto; and, of course, the utter disappearance of Wade himself. His very absence is evidence.

Was he headed for Alaska, where his friend the plumber Bob Grant had gone, run out of money for gas and food in Toronto, abandoned the truck and merged with the migrant population of the city? We do not know; we speculate in solitude; we do not speak of his disappearance to one another.

Maybe we want to believe that Wade died, died that same November, froze to death in his thin sport coat under newspapers on a bench in Harbour Front Park—unknown, unclaimed. But he could just as well have hitched a ride on a train or a truck headed west: Toronto is where the Canadian West begins, where it is very easy to become a nameless wanderer. Maybe tonight, years later, he huddles under a Trans-Canada

Highway overpass in a suburb of Winnipeg.

Of course, he could have turned himself into another person altogether, a potter living under an assumed name in a commune in Vancouver. Or, more likely, somewhere along the line he drifted south at a rural border crossing into Minnesota or North Dakota and found a job pumping gas at an all-night truck stop, one of those men with long hair going gray, face masked by a full beard, gaze deflected whenever someone looks hard at them.

But all that is speculation now. We do know that he shot Jack Hewitt—as surely as we know that Jack Hewitt did not shoot Evan Twombley. And we also know that Wade killed his own father—*our* father. *My* father. That snowy afternoon, after the fire in the barn was put out, a child-sized pile of char was discovered in the blackened rubble, and a forensic specialist from Hanover easily identified it as the remains of a Caucasian male, aged 65–70, five feet nine, 135–145 pounds. Who else but my father?

It had been assumed at first that the old man's death was accidental: he was a drunk and probably set the fire himself, smoking, maybe, while fooling with a kerosene lantern. But then came scientific evidence that my father's death was caused not by fire but by a skull-crushing blow to the head, which must have been inflicted by the last person seen with the old man—seen, less than an hour before the fire started, by Margie Fogg, Wade's fiancée (for she was still that), and by his daughter, who was also the victim's granddaughter. And again, there was the incriminating fact that the last person seen with the old man had fled. The evidence, all of it, was incontrovertible. What was not scientific was logical; and what was not logical was scientific.

Just as the evidence that Jack Hewitt did not shoot Evan Twombley, not even by accident, is now seen by everyone as incontrovertible. Even by me. There was no motive, and Jack left no secret bank account, no stash of hundred-dollar bills: the links between Jack and Twombley, LaRiviere and Mel Gordon, existed only in Wade's wild imaginings—and briefly, I admit, in mine as well.

LaRiviere and Mel Gordon were indeed in business, buying up as much high-country real estate as they could, but there was nothing illegal about it, although it probably was not proper for Mel Gordon to finance the operation with union funds when he was a director and major shareholder in the company receiving the funds. It was a legitimate investment, however, one that has paid off handsomely—for the union membership, for Mel Gordon and Gordon LaRiviere, and for almost everyone else in town too. The Northcountry Development Corporation has brought enormous changes to the region: Parker Mountain Ski Resort is advertised all over the northeast, full-page ads in the Sunday travel section of the *New York Times,* the *Boston Globe,* the *Washington Post,* and so on. Fifteen lifts, seventeen miles of trails from beginners' to advanced, with several fancy lodges, over a hundred chalet-like condominiums installed along the old Parker Mountain Road in a development called Saddleback Ridge, a half-dozen après-ski lounges, restaurants and bars, including Toby's Inn, now called the Skimeister's Hearthside Lodge. The Whitehouse place out on Parker Mountain Road is still in Wade's name, along with mine and Lena's, and I keep paying the taxes on it, which keeps it out of LaRiviere's hands. The house remains empty and looks the way the barn did before the fire. Now and then I drive out and sit in my car and look at the wreck of a house and wonder why not let it go, why not let LaRiviere buy it and tear down the house and build the condominiums he wants there?

For it sometimes seems that there is no one in Lawford, except for me, whose life, seen from a certain angle, has not been changed more by the Northcountry Development Corporation than by Wade's awful crimes. Hettie Rodgers, called a hostess, is a salesperson for time-share units in a huge pool-and-pavilion complex under construction on the south slope. Jimmy Dame, tossed out of work for a while when LaRiviere closed down the well-drilling operation to devote all his energies to Northcountry Development, tends bar nights at the main lodge on Lake Minuit, where the trailer park used to be, and he seems content. Nick Wickham has sold his restaurant to Burger King—they wanted the in-town lot—and Nick is talking about opening a video game arcade at Northcountry's minimall at the new Route 29 cloverleaf. Frankie LaCoy started dealing cocaine and got nabbed in a sting operation in Nashua. Chub Merritt has opened a snowmobile and recreational vehicle dealership. Alma Pittman has announced that, because she does not want to move her office into the new brick municipal building going up on the site of the old town hall, she will not run for town clerk again; the truth is that she has no chance of beating the woman running against her, a bright young CPA, until recently a Dartmouth development officer, married to a geology professor and pregnant with her first child. The community, as such, no longer exists; Lawford is a thriving economic zone between Littleton and Catamount.

The lives of those who were closest to Wade have been altered in different ways, and I believe that, unlike the others, they are still stunned, perhaps permanently so, by the events of those few weeks and thus, having told their stories to me, wish now to remain essentially silent on the subject. I have not seen or talked to my sister Lena in recent months, not since she and her husband and children left Massachusetts for a religious community in West Virginia; when I did talk with her, she was unwilling to speak of our brother or of the death of our father. She would not speak even of the death of our mother. It was as if all three lives were inextricably wound together and, like a disease to which she was immune, excluded her. I let her alone and gathered my information for this account from other sources. Lillian and Jill and Bob Horner moved to Seattle, where Bob has a new position with Allstate Insurance, Lillian is studying for her real estate license and Jill, who has been legally adopted by her stepfather, is about to enter high school. Margie Fogg moved to Littleton, to be nearer her mother and tend to her dying father. She works at the women's health center there, and when I last saw her, she seemed more interested in talking about her plans to adopt a baby from Central America than about Wade, so our meeting was brief.

Which leaves me. I carefully unfold and read again the tattered news clipping from the *Boston Globe*, and begin anew, knowing that you have read the same kind of story numerous times in your own newspaper: a man in a small town evidently went berserk and murdered a few people thought to be close to him, murdered them apparently without motive or warning.

TWO SLAIN IN NH
Local Man Sought for Questioning

Lawford, N.H., Nov. 15. In a related series of events over the weekend, two men were killed in this peaceful upstate town of

750. The body of Glenn Whitehouse, 67, a retired millworker, was pulled from the ashes of his barn, which burned to the ground Saturday in a fire of suspicious origin. Whitehouse had been killed by a blow to the head, authorities said.

The body of the second man, John Hewitt, 22, the town police officer, was found by State Police Captain Asa Brown in the woods of nearby Parker Mountain, where Hewitt was deer hunting. According to police, he was shot once by a high-powered rifle. Hewitt was the hunting companion of Massachusetts union leader Evan Twombley, whose accidental death here was widely reported two weeks ago.

Police are searching for Wade Whitehouse, 41, the son of the first victim. Hewitt had recently replaced the younger Whitehouse as town police officer. Brown said, "We have plenty of evidence. The man didn't even try to hide his tracks."

Townspeople are shocked by the twin killing, the first murder in Clinton County in more than a decade. The suspect is believed to have left the state in a burgundy Ford pickup owned by Hewitt. A nationwide manhunt, with Canadian authorities cooperating, is under way.

You read the account and move quickly on to news about the Middle East or a flash flood and train wreck north of Mexico City or a huge drug bust in Miami, and unless you are from the town of Lawford or in some other way knew one of the victims or the man suspected of killing them, you forget all about it. You forget it, because you do not understand it: you cannot understand how a man, a *normal* man, a man like you and me, could do such a terrible thing. He must not be like you and me. It is easier by far to understand diplomatic maneuvers in Jordan, natural calamities in the third world and the economics of addictive drugs than an isolated explosion of homicidal rage in a small American town.

And unless the police in some other small American town happen to arrest a vagrant who turns out to be Wade Whitehouse—or maybe he won't be a vagrant; maybe he will have turned himself into one of those faceless fellows we see working behind the counter at our local video rental store, or the gray-faced man who shoves circles of frozen dough into an oven at the Mr. Pizza at the mall and lives in a town-house apartment at the edge of town until his mailman recognizes him from the picture at the post office—unless that happens, and Wade Whitehouse finally receives justice, there will be no more mention in the newspapers of him and his friend Jack Hewitt and our father. No more mention of them anywhere. The story will be over. Except that I continue.

ALSO BY RUSSELL BANKS:

CLOUDSPLITTER
0-06-093086-1/$15.00

Russell Banks's great American novel, a bestselling portrait of the mercurial
John Brown, is "a furious, sprawling drama that commands attention like thunder
heard from just over the horizon" (*Time*).

RULE OF THE BONE
0-06-092724-0/$13.00

Banks's novel of a homeless youth living
on the edge of society was acclaimed
by *New York* magazine as "a work of
can-do genius."

THE SWEET HEREAFTER
0-06-092324-5/$13.00

This compelling tale set in a small
Adirondack town was the basis for Atom
Egoyan's Cannes Award-winning film which
was nominated for two Academy Awards
including Best Screenplay Adaptation for
Banks and Egoyan.

CONTINENTAL DRIFT
0-06-092574-4/$13.50

Hailed by James Atlas in *Atlantic Monthly*
as "the most convincing portrait I know
of contemporary America...a great
American novel," this bestseller alternates
between two young protagonists—a
repairman from New Hampshire and an
illiterate Haitian mother—both seeking
new beginnings.

AFFLICTION
0-06-092007-6/$13.00

This spellbinding story of blue-collar workers
in a New England mill town, was hailed
by the *New York Times Book Review* as
"magnificently convincing...beautifully
sustained, suspenseful," is now a major motion
picture, directed and adapted by Paul Schrader
and starring Nick Nolte, Sissy Spacek,
James Coburn and Willem Dafoe.

Also Available from HarperPerennial by Russell Banks:

The Relation of My Imprisonment
0-06-097680-2/$10.00

Trailerpark
0-06-097706-X/$13.00

Hamilton Stark
0-06-097705-1/$13.00

The Book of Jamaica
0-06-097707-8/$13.00

Success Stories
0-06-092719-4/$12.00

Family Life
0-06-097704-3/$12.00

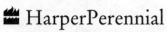 HarperPerennial

A Division of HarperCollins*Publishers*
www.harpercollins.com

**Available at your local bookstore
or by calling 1-800-242-7737.**